A BOUNTY OF LOVE
AND BETRAYAL

Billionaire Spies - Book Seven

AMARYLLIS LANZA

Published by Blushing Books
An Imprint of
ABCD Graphics and Design, Inc.
A Virginia Corporation
977 Seminole Trail #233
Charlottesville, VA 22901

Amaryllis Lanza
A Bounty of Blood and Betrayal

Print ISBN: 978-1-63954-174-4
v1

Cover Art by ABCD Graphics & Design

Scattered Seeds

Mariana enjoyed the little things: getting her babies' room ready, enjoying a light lunch while chatting with Morgan in the kitchen, teatime with Quincy and Pam. It wasn't so bad, having to stay home for a while. Mariana had traveled so much over the past ten years that a brief grounding before the big wedding was welcomed.

Her stomach was settling into pregnancy as the twins decided what they liked and didn't. An odd whiff of something in the air could still send her head spinning and rushing to vomit, but those incidents were rarer now and the crazy cravings had begun.

Mariana was trying to decide whether to stop by the Hot Plate on her way back from visiting Tracey and Jonathan at the Phoenix Lodge. She'd originally planned to go with William, but he wasn't back yet and these meetings were too important to miss. It had been a good meeting, though Tracey still felt heartbroken over her disconnect with the digital realm. Mariana decided to call Oliver about it after she got home, hoping he could get her a job in his organization, eventually. It seemed like a shame to lose someone who was so gifted in code. She didn't tell Tracey because she didn't want to get the young woman's hopes up. Oliver had once considered Tracey like a sister, but during the years that Tracey was presumed dead, she'd been working for the enemy as a hacker. It might be hard for Oliver to rebuild trust, Mariana worried.

On the way back, the twins demanded a banana shake. No good reason for it. She'd had a healthy breakfast. But they were clawing at her stomach walls, refusing to accept any substitutes. They wanted a banana shake. Now.

"Roger," she asked their driver. "Could you please stop by Fairfarm before we go back to Manhattan?"

"The lake house is out of bounds, right now," he said.

"*What*?" Mariana asked. "Why?"

"I don't have the details," he said. "I'm sorry."

Mariana couldn't help being a bit put out by this news, even if she hadn't planned to go to Will's cabin in the woods. Again, her husband had forgotten to mention something that might be important. She really *was* going to have to straighten him out soon.

"Is the Hot Plate also out of bounds?" Mariana asked.

"The what?"

"It's the little coffee shop and diner, right next to Fare Farm Feed and Sundry," Mariana explained. "It's in the small shopping center on Main Street, across from the library and next to the old cemetery."

"That should be fine," Roger said.

"Good, I just need to have a shake, pretty much this minute. I'm sure Joe and Joe will make one for me."

"Yes, madam," Roger said. "I'll head there now."

Mariana asked Roger not to park in front of the diner. She felt odd being seen getting out of a fancy black sedan. Will maintained his humble Smith persona in town. While she could make any excuse for having a driver bringing her around, she wanted to avoid lying to the two old friends who ran the diner. Roger parked in the old church lot instead, just a short walk past the cemetery to the Hot Plate.

As Mariana passed Fare Farm Feed and Sundry, she caught a whiff of something unpleasant, a heavy perfume, sweet, flowery, and nauseating. Before she could help it, Mariana had to turn towards an empty parking spot to vomit.

"He's done it to you too, huh?" the woman wearing the heavy scent asked. Mariana wished the woman would just walk away and take that cloying, funereal smell with her.

"Excuse me?" Mariana asked, her eyes still blurry from being sick.

"He hasn't even *told* you, has he?"

"Do I know you?"

"You've seen me. I was thinner, then."

She stared at the woman's face, trying to place it. Only a pickle came to mind. God, she wanted pickles, the good kind from the deli—dill, crunchy, refreshing. She had to have some right away.

"I'm sorry, you must have me confused with someone else," Mariana said, reaching for a tissue and a mint in her purse.

"You're William's wife, aren't you?"

"Smith? Yes."

"Tell him he will not get away with it," the woman threatened, straightening her back which stuck her prominent belly out further. She towered over Mariana, and her baby bump was more like a small house.

"Get away with what?" Mariana asked.

"Tell William that Sandra and the baby say hello."

With that, Sandra Price, Will's first love, his rival Robert Whitby's ex-wife, and now the bane of Mariana's existence, walked away, leaving a scented trail of rotting blooms in her wake.

Mariana vomited again, abandoned the idea of having a shake or any pickles, and ran back to Roger in the car.

"Is everything all right, Mrs. Wilson?" he asked, concerned, as he held the door open for her.

"No, Roger," she said. "Everything is far from okay. Everything is seventy shades of fucked. Take me home, please." She felt bad about using profanity in front of Roger, but the situation seemed to warrant it. "Damn him!" Mariana punched the back of the seat once she was inside. "Damn him! Damn him! Damn him!" Mariana had no cell phone to call Will. He never carried one. She needed answers, and only one other person might have them. "Roger, scratch that," she said. "Stop by Smith's first."

"Are you sure that's wise?" Roger asked.

"No," Mariana said, "but it's necessary."

"I can call for backup if something is wrong," Roger said. "You just have to tell me what happened."

"William happened, Roger," Mariana said. "What back up do you call for that?"

"I'll try to get him on the car line," Roger said.

"Good luck with that," Mariana scoffed.

Roger was busy making calls as Mariana stepped out of the car again, walking into the tiny offices of Smith's Arboriculture where Mrs. Jenkins sat alone on the phone, lording over her domain. Her mother-of-pearl cat's eye spectacles sat atop her graying hair like a funky retro diadem.

"Mariana?" Mrs. Jenkins put the phone down the minute she saw Mariana's face. "What in heavens is wrong?"

"I need Will, now!" Mariana's rage was getting the better of her, but she knew it wasn't fair taking it out people who were only trying to help. She took a deep breath to calm herself.

"Is it the babies?" Mrs. Jenkins asked. "Sit down. Are you all right?"

"Please, get Will, please," she begged. "I need to speak with him."

Mrs. Jenkins got on the short-radio and tried to get Will to pick up. Mariana wasn't sure how that worked, but after Mrs. Jenkins called out "code 10 and suspected code 10-91e" a few times, Will actually answered.

"What's happening?" He sounded breathless and angry. "I'm in transit."

"Are you in transit here now?"

"I'm four clicks out," he said.

"Well, good," Mrs. Jenkins said. "You can deal with this yourself. I'll give your wife a tea while she's waiting. She looks ready to faint."

"What is she doing in the office?" Will asked.

"You can ask her all about it in fifteen minutes."

Mrs. Jenkins offered Mariana coffee or tea while she waited, but she didn't have any chamomile, which was the only thing that seemed to settle Mariana's stomach when it roiled up like this. Instead, Mariana accepted some spring water from the large jug on the water cooler. She sipped on the pixie glass, small sips, while she stewed and raged.

"What were those codes all about Mrs. Jenkins?" Mariana asked.

"It just saves time," Mrs. Jenkins said. "And keeps snooping types out of our conversations. I just told Will that a bomb went off and I suspect there's an animal bite too. I'm guessing that somehow you bumped into Sandra Price while you were in town."

"So you *know*?" Mariana practically screeched.

"I know what Sandra's been saying," Mrs. Jenkins said. "I don't know that there's any truth to it at all, and I doubt there is."

Will ran in through the front door, pale as she must have been. He got paler when he saw her eyes.

"What happened, Mariana? What's wrong with the babies?"

"They are sick," she said, "because of the other one."

Will went completely ashen, silent as the grave, his eyes hard, his brown etched with pain.

"Let's get you home," he said, extending his hand to her.

"Where's home?" Mariana asked, digging the knife deeper.

"For me, it's wherever you are." Will took her hand gently and led her back to the car where Roger sat waiting.

They didn't argue in the car. Mariana knew Will valued his privacy, and she didn't want to have this argument where anyone could hear them. She was too tired anyway, from all the voices in her head, and the dizziness and the nausea. At some point, she fell asleep in his arms.

When they were back at the townhouse in Manhattan, Will woke her up and led her upstairs to their suite of rooms on the fifth floor. She followed quietly. As soon as they were in their sitting room, she sat on his lap and cried against his chest. He didn't let her go, comforting her, stroking her hair, rubbing her back. Then she felt the anger return, and she beat her fists against him. He let her do that too.

"How long have you known?" Mariana asked, finally.

"A few weeks, nearly three months now, I guess."

"Why didn't you *tell* me?"

"It wasn't the right time," Will said. "There were other, more important things to manage, if you remember."

"You're so sure of yourself! Of knowing what is important and what isn't! We've been here together for days now. You could have told me at any point!"

"I was lost in us, Mariana," Will said, putting his hand on her womb. "You're the only ones that matter."

"Jesus, Will! This is a disaster!"

"It may not be true."

"But you *fucked* her! You know you did! You told me so yourself!"

"That doesn't mean it's my child," Will said. "It was only once, as I told you. To me, the dates don't add up."

"She *insists* that it's yours!"

"She's only being vicious, but that is what paternity tests are for."

"Does she know everything about you, William?"

"No, she can't," Will said. "You remember what she said at our wedding. She has some bit of information based on what Robert Whitby would have told her. But even Robert is only scratching the surface of my organization. I'm sure of that."

"Why are you so confident?" Mariana asked. "She has to know something. Why push, otherwise? I mean, it's not like there's a lot to grab onto with William Smith."

"It's still more than she has," Will said. "Besides, there's her ego, her pride, and whatever is wrong with her mind."

"I need something to drink."

Will stroked her back. "Tell me what you want and I'll have Quincy bring it up. Anything."

"I want proof that it's not your baby! I want to know what you'll do if it is. I want Sandra Price out of our lives! I want a whiskey."

Will hugged her tight and kissed the top of her head.

"You can't have a whiskey."

"Fine! I want a banana shake."

Will grinned, though it didn't quite reach his eyes. "We'll get you a banana shake right this minute."

"And pickles. Dill."

"Okay. Dill pickles and a banana shake, then we'll sit calmly and talk about the rest of it."

It took Quincy no time at all to bring up Mariana's shake and pickles along with a platter of finger sandwiches, just in case, and a bottle of sparkling water. Will served himself a whiskey from the bar in the sitting room. Privilege of being a father.

Mariana sucked the thick shake through a straw, enjoying the rich, earthy flavor of bananas, and felt restored. The kids were happy, anyway.

"You are the most important person in this universe to me, Mariana," Will said, sitting next to her again on the couch. "The babies are second most important. Everyone else is a far third."

"Which babies?" she asked, reaching for a cucumber sandwich. She wasn't sure whether she had the stomach for it right now, but it gave her an excuse not to meet Will's eyes.

"Mariana, please," Will said, stroking her back. "I know you're upset, but don't be cruel."

"This woman is trouble, Will." Mariana put the finger sandwich back on the plate and turned to face him.

"Yes." Will's face was a dark blend of pain and anger. "I'm afraid she is."

"No, Will, you didn't see her eyes, her little smirk as she walked away," Mariana said. "She is one vindictive, nasty piece of work. She will not make this easy."

"I know." Will sighed. He looked tired, right down to his marrow. She had to remind herself that she was angry with him. Still, she couldn't stop herself from putting her hand on his thigh to soothe him.

"Why didn't you warn me, Will? So she couldn't take me by surprise?"

"It was a mistake. I had the foresight, before we married. I told you then about what happened between us," Will said. "But when I found out about her pregnancy, when she confronted me with it, it was while everything else was happening." Will shook his head. "Then, you were pregnant, and I got shot, and we both had too much to cope with. I put my lawyers on it and waited for them to advise me. These past few days, you're right, I should have said something. We've just been so happy, so perfectly happy, I got lost in it. I forgot myself."

"I don't want our babies hurt by this, Will."

"Neither do I. I won't let it happen."

"You let it happen in the first place!"

"Mariana, be fair," Will pleaded. "We've both had weak moments with lovers before we had each other. It's all in the past now. It has long been in the past."

"Yes, I suppose you're right, but the damage isn't. The damage will be here with us in the future," Mariana said.

An uncomfortable silence fell between them as the truth of Mariana's words sank in. "You won't be able to deny her, if it is your baby," Mariana said. "I know you. And her child will be first born. Her child will be your heir. Have you considered what that means?"

"Mariana, I've considered that more times than I'd like to say," Will said. "I've had my lawyers look into it. I'm trying to force a paternity test now—it's possible through blood-work or amniotic fluid—but she's fighting both. If it turned out to be mine… I couldn't leave any child of mine to be raised by her. She's unwell."

"So what? You'd fight for custody? You'd have *me* help raise *her* child?" Mariana asked.

"Only if it *is* my child," Will said. "I realize that's a lot to ask, but I would have to ask for your support, Mariana. It would in no way affect the legacy of the twins. They are my true heirs, the offspring of my wife—no matter who is born first—but I couldn't leave the baby to be raised by a spiteful madwoman."

"God help us," Mariana said. "She's not just going to give her child up, even if she's only using it to have a hold over you, not when she can gain more from holding on. You're up against a massive legal battle that will draw a lot of attention to what you do."

"Yes," Will said. "I know, Mariana, but I am going to make it right."

"Easier said than done."

Mariana couldn't help feeling bitter, though she knew Will had slept with Sandra before they got together. It bothered her, particularly because Will had known about Sandra's pregnancy back when they both thought Mariana couldn't conceive. A petty part of her thought Will hadn't told her about Sandra's pregnancy because it gave him a back-up plan for succession. But she knew he'd never get Sandra involved in his business. He had just been careless and let a moment of passion get the better of him. Mariana knew she had been careless too, with Martin Harper. Will had left her past in the past and she had to do the same for him.

"All right, darling," Mariana said, taking his hand in both of hers. "We'll get through this together. It's the only thing we can do. It's either a trap or a challenge, but either way, we fight on the same side."

Will cupped her face and kissed her gently, intensifying his kiss as she responded to him, until they were exchanging hot pants instead of breaths and casting their clothes on the carpet. Soon Mariana found herself pulled under Will on the couch, his knees between hers, his skin barely an inch away from hers, exchanging static which raised the hairs on her body. She was desperate with longing, eager for him to fill her, but he stopped, his forehead resting against hers.

"I never meant to hurt you," he whispered.

"I know, Will," Mariana said. "But could you hurt me a little now? I need you to claim me like you mean it. I need to work off some of this anger. Please."

"Oh, Mariana," he said, raising her legs over his shoulders. "You don't need to beg, though it sure sounds beautiful coming from your lips."

He stroked her with the tip of his erection before plunging himself into her depths, one hard thrust followed by another as he pinched and twisted her sensitive nipples. Mariana stretched her arms up over her head, and he grasped her wrists, binding them together in one hand as he continued to slam her core. "*Mi zorra arrecha. Hermosa. Divina. Toda mía.*"

She loved when he called her a horny vixen, the edge taken off any insult by the way he said it.

"*Pégame, Papi, que me he portado muy mal,*" she begged, needing to feel his hard hand on her, to help push her over the edge.

"You've been very good, baby," he said, his lips brushing hers.

"You can't read my mind, Will," she said. "Slap my ass hard, please."

He grinned. "As you wish." He alternated between smacking her rump hard enough to leave a palm print and ramming her with his cock hard enough to bruise her cervix. Mariana delighted in the pain, erupting in a deep guttural moan as her body creamed for him and Will built up momentum, quickening his thrusts as his face grimaced with his own violent completion.

He collapsed over her on the couch, lowering her legs,

which were pricking with tiny electric charges running through them. "You sure the peas are all right?" he asked, stroking damp hair away from her face and giving her a gentle kiss.

"Their mama is happy, so they should be happy too," Mariana said.

"Good," Will said. "Let's keep it that way."

A knock on the door reminded them both that they were not alone in the house, and whatever happiness they found could be short-lived.

2

Expecting

Two weeks earlier

Mariana Wilson Smith shot up from the mattress like a bullet and landed like a duck, her feet bare on the plush carpet in the master bedroom suite of the Wilson-family townhouse near Central Park. She waddled over to the bathroom down the hall as quickly as her swollen ankles would carry her and rushed to pee. William Wilson Smith was right behind her in case anything went awry for the short distance.

"I'm fine, Will," Mariana said and shook her hand at him to go back to bed. "I've got this."

"I know. You're a pro," Will said. "You've been peeing for thirty years. You don't need me around to do it. I still want to help you get back to bed."

"Don't be sore, hon," she pleaded. "I appreciate you are so caring and watchful, but I'm perfectly fine. You don't have to worry so much."

"Mariana, the thumb is still right here." He brushed his thumb lovingly over her lips and then pressed it between them for her to suck on, which would have been sexy if she wasn't sitting on the toilet.

Will had told her she was 'under his thumb' since they first saw the pregnancy test results at his grandmother's villa in the south of France. That was after all the hullabaloo of her kidnapping, her first – supervised – foray into espionage fieldwork under Will's watchful eye. Catastrophe followed. Mariana spent a night vomiting her guts out in a French jail cell, then had a dreary stint as a heart-broken widow in the North Pole, under the gentle care of Santa's son. After learning she wasn't a widow after all, just unable to see her husband who was fighting for his life, she spent a couple of days as a special care guest in the Phoenix Lodge in Connecticut recovering from all the trauma. Will recovered from his wound in one of the organization's secret medical facilities.

In short, Mariana had been through a hell of a lot on her own, while pregnant, including making her way to the bathroom, and back to bed, without an escort many times.

Since they'd returned home, though, Will insisted on circling her like one of his satellites in orbit, watching, recording, and sometimes just plain old interfering.

This was a sore point between them. Will, back from the dead by a hair—the bullet which struck his chest just missing its mark—wanted to ensure his wife and their twins would always be safe and comfortable. He'd become the ultimate alpha male. Much more so than usual. An alpha to the nth degree. A Six Sigma, details-matter, eliminate all deviations, type of Alpha. Times ten.

In France, Will had threatened to chain Mariana in a room in a tower somewhere in Romania if she couldn't follow his commands, and said he had a specific place in mind, but she figured he was joking. Probably.

He'd settled for keeping her grounded in their comfortable Manhattan townhouse where she had their cook, Morgan, their maid, Pam, and their butler, Quincy, to cater to all her needs.

Confinement in Manhattan was nicer than confinement in Transylvania, Mariana imagined, but it had become nearly as oppressive.

Will had been working from home in Manhattan since they'd got back, driving into Connecticut only to check with his top Smith Arboriculture clients and meet with Mrs. Jenkins, who ran the Smith Arboriculture business for him with impeccable aplomb. He'd made time, with everything else going on, to read up on pregnancy and was constantly dispensing advice and random facts.

He was always ready to reprimand Mariana for working too long, or ask her another awkward question about her changing body that she either couldn't or would rather not discuss. Yes, she was constipated, thanks for asking, but there ought to be a little mystery left between them, right? And he was so much bossier—eat this, don't eat that, drink this, don't drink that. Take a nap. Don't walk to the stores, have the driver take you there, have things delivered. Get a personal shopper to come to the house. Her name was Gail. The shopper. She was nice enough, but very judgmental on style and also probably a spy. All of Will's people seemed to be.

Of course, Mariana would not follow *all* of Will's commands without pushing back if she thought they were unreasonable. It just wasn't in Mariana's nature to obey him blindly. She wanted to make him happy, but she needed to understand the whys and wherefores of things.

Mariana had practically raised herself after her mother committed suicide. She'd put herself through university and got herself out of a terrible marriage. She could handle deciding what to have for breakfast without being told. Will knew that as well as she did. He was just concerned. He really cared. That was a pleasant change for Mariana, compared to life before Will, so she let him get away with a lot.

Some days it felt like he was Ricky Ricardo, and she was Lucille Ball. *Lucy, you got some 'splaining to do.* Except she was the fiery Cuban in the relationship, and they didn't sleep in twin beds. Thank God.

"You want to fool around a bit, since you're awake, anyway?" Mariana asked as she headed back to bed with Will right behind her.

"Are you sure it's all right?" he asked. "Don't you need sleep?"

This was another thing. Chronically horny Will had not been pouncing on her the way she usually enjoyed. Mariana missed the old days where she could count on Will taking her any way he pleased, any chance he got with little urging on her part. She absolutely loved that about him—the way he dominated her body, stretched her limits, and gave her the sort of workout that left her sweaty, dirty, sore and utterly blissful.

While they still fooled around, Will was holding back, concerned over hurting the peas, as they liked to call the twins. Her 'bump' wasn't much more than a swollen belly yet, but Mariana was definitely rounding out all over the place. She'd put on some weight, since she'd stopped vomiting everything she ate. That wasn't unexpected, and it kept Gail gainfully employed.

"I'm horny as hell again," Mariana shrugged. "Sorry. It's the hormones. Plus, your thumb was all suggestive. And that bare chest of yours is taunting me to bite it. And you're being all mega bossy all the time now, which still turns me on as much as it annoys me. I wish you'd spank me, Will, if you really are mad at me."

"I'm not mad at you, Mariana," Will said. "Only

concerned that you are not taking proper care of yourself. I can always go downstairs and whittle a ginger root for you, if you keep trying to press my buttons, though."

Mariana made a face, though he couldn't see it. There was no appeal to the peeled ginger root *at all*. It was a proper punishment. Not at all pleasant, especially now that she was hyper-sensitive down there.

"No. Don't go through the trouble," she said, getting back under the sheets.

Will stood at her side of the bed, staring at her, glowing in the dim light which came through the French doors that led onto to their private patio overlooking Central Park. *God, why did Will have to look so utterly fuckable when he was brooding?*

"What's the matter?" she asked, adjusting herself in the fortress of feather pillows Will ensured she had around her on their oversized four-poster.

Will didn't answer. Instead, he pulled back the sheets, pulled a pillow out of the side of her fortress, lifted her bottom and placed the pillow under it. Then Will climbed on the bed at her feet, and bent to hover over her like an angry Greek God set on revenge.

Will gripped the low neckline of her cotton nighty in both enormous hands and tore the bodice open, sending little pearlescent buttons flying. One button clinked on the Waterford crystal lamp on her nightstand, then was lost to history. Perhaps Pam the housekeeper would find the others, or vacuum them up. Mariana tried not to giggle. It would spoil the moment, and she didn't want to anger her Adonis.

Will brought his mouth to one of her swollen breasts, ignoring her hiss as he bit on the sensitive nipple. He was pretending not to care if she suffered a minor discomfort for his pleasure. *Good boy.*

He gave the other breast equal treatment before trailing his tongue through her cleavage and rising again to tear the rest of the flimsy nightgown apart. It had become a favorite because it was so soft and her skin was now hyper-sensitive. Still, she could always have Gail buy her another.

"I'm going to make you come until you are sorry you ever asked for it," he growled.

"Oh, I doubt that," Mariana sighed.

"Never doubt my resolve, wife," Will said, parting her legs and kissing the curve of her belly down to her folds, teasing her clit with the tip of his tongue.

"Oh, Daddy," she sighed.

"Can you not call me that just now?" Will asked, his breath hot on her sex and his deep voice reverberating through her. "I usually like it when you do, but it reminds me that the peas are in there all warm and cozy while I'm about to pervert their sweet, saintly mother."

"Yes, Master," Mariana said, biting her cheek to keep from laughing. She got over the giggles fast enough, though. Will got busy with some serious late-night dining on his wife, his tongue and fingers working in unison to bring her to the edge of oblivion. She gripped her pillow fortress hard enough to feel the tiny pricks of down feathers on her palms.

"Oh, God!" Mariana moaned as she fell, the orgasm enhanced by a soft pull in her womb. She guessed the twins were pleased too, though their mother was still hungry for more. "I need to feel you now, Will. Please, come inside me."

He kissed her inner thigh before rising to kiss her lips, working his fingers gently into her warm cavern. He stroked her sweet spot expertly and tossed her back on the wave. "Don't be in such a rush, beautiful," Will whispered against her lips. "We have all night."

"Please don't tease." Mariana wrapped one arm around Will's neck and kissed him with a desperate urgency, making her hunger clear. "I really want you inside me now, please."

"I am inside you," he said, scissoring his fingers to stretch her and prove his point.

"I need your *cock* inside of me, Will," she said, just to ensure there was no misunderstanding.

Will had moved his lips to her neck, where he was working to leave his mark as his fingers brought her back to climax.

"You will, my lusty pet," he said, biting her earlobe. "Just come for me again. One more time. You know you want to."

Of course she wanted to. Who wouldn't? Besides, she couldn't stop herself from coming even if he commanded her not to come at this point. She was drenched and aching for him, just as he intended. "Come, wife," he whispered in her ear. She moaned for him again as her body convulsed with a powerful orgasm. "Good girl," he said, kissing her ferociously, his own arousal, undeniable, pressed against her thigh. "Now, I need you to get on your knees, with that plump butt high in the air. Do you think you're up to it?"

"Yes, Master," she said, rushing to comply. Nothing felt better than Will's cock ramming her cervix. "*Plump?*" she asked, looking back at him, the word sinking in. Well, maybe she was. She'd go back to her previous weight in time. Hopefully.

"Delightfully plump and round, like a watermelon," Will said, biting her butt. "You are so very fucking sexy with my seed growing inside of you, Mariana. If you only knew."

"There's only one way to show me, Will," Mariana wiggled her ass. "So, please get on with it."

"You're so wrong, Mariana," he said, rubbing the tip of his erection along her lower lips before sliding inside of her gently. He bent over her back to kiss her nape. "I have many ways to show you. I just love the view of your delicious round ass. I would enjoy turning it a rich bright red. So keep testing my patience, please."

His threat was not entirely hollow. She knew that. Will's favorite paddle was still hanging in the closet. After their last big fight over his new rules, Will had dispensed a few good swats. But he wasn't inclined to spank her tonight. Instead, he took his good time savoring her, penetrating her slowly, even as she urged him to go deeper and harder. He made her come again by reaching around to pinch her clit, making her ride another wave. When he finally unleashed himself, he pounded her hard enough that she felt him in her stomach. She cried out his name over and over as he kept hammering into her. His fingers dug into the soft flesh on her hips, pulling her towards him with every punishing thrust. This was what she needed. Her old Will was back, claiming her without mercy.

When he was spent, he dropped on the bed, taking her down with him and wrapping her in his body.

"I hope I didn't shock the peas, by pounding on their door like that," he said. "But at least they know their father's name. Even squirrels in Central Park know my name now."

"I think they will have no trouble recognizing their papa."

"I guess I have to be careful what we say around them now," Will said. "We don't want them to come out of the womb cursing a blue streak."

"Don't be silly," she kissed his chest. "Can I ride you for a while?"

"Seriously, woman?" Will said in awe. "You need to give me a minute."

"A whole minute?" Mariana teased. "Can I have a word with Major Tom?" Will had once told her Tom was the name he'd given his penis, when she admitted she called her dildo John. Come to think of it, her dildo had been missing for weeks now, and Mariana hadn't bothered to ask Will whether he knew what had happened to it. "Maybe Tom just needs a good tongue lashing to get him back in line." Mariana reached for Tom, who was wet, sticky and not entirely flaccid.

"Mariana, what has gotten into you?"

"You, obviously," she said. "You got into me and now I can't get you out. I smell you every second of the day. You're in my pores. Your DNA has joined with my DNA and is now growing strong and overpowering me from the inside out. I have been invaded and conquered. So forgive me if I'm a bit more aroused than usual."

Will kissed her gently, "There's nothing to forgive. I'm delighted. I'm overwhelmed with joy. I feel like the cock of the walk."

"You're always the cock of the walk," Mariana said, rising to straddle his legs so she could take him in her mouth. "You only pretend to be a partridge."

"I never pretend to be a partridge, Mariana," he said. "If I'm ever a fowl, I'm a falcon."

"An eagle," Mariana said, caressing Major Tom with her tongue, who seemed more than eager to have a conversation.

"Yes, that's true, I am an eagle," Will said, sounding suddenly very far away. He stopped her before she wrapped her lips around his cock. "Mariana, I need to have a serious talk with you about that."

"About you being an eagle or about me giving you fellatio?"

"Both," he said. "I know you're super horny and I really want to please you, but we need to have a serious discussion in the morning."

"Something has happened, right? Things are falling out of orbit." Mariana sat up. "And you're leaving again."

"Only for a couple of days," he said. "You'll be well looked after here at home."

"Okay." Mariana bent over him to kiss the fading scar

from the bullet wound on his chest. His secret organization had some really advanced medical tech. Their healing patches had helped rebuild his tissue, but there was still a red mark where the bullet pierced his flesh that would probably never go away. "I've got lots to keep me busy, anyway," Mariana continued. "Just come back to me whole, or I'll give you hell. You still have a wedding to attend in Wales, mister. No backing down."

William's maternal grandmother considered their first wedding in Connecticut tantamount to eloping. It *had* been a rush-shot wedding which none of his family attended, though his friends in Fairfarm, Connecticut had all been there. Mariana had only invited Sandy Fine, her friend, once assistant and now business partner. Her own family, the ones she knew, had been dead for years.

Anyway, Anne, aka Lady Greystone, aka la Comtesse de Coquille, plus some other title in Scotland that Mariana couldn't recall, had insisted that Will and Mariana have a 'proper' wedding at the family's castle in Wales in July. Fortunately, her grandmother-in-law was taking care of all the arrangements. Mariana couldn't imagine having to deal with that at this point.

"I wouldn't miss our second wedding for the world," Will said, rising to kiss her. "Still want to ride your pony?"

"Yeah," she said. "Especially if he's going gallivanting on me."

"Well, giddy-up, little lady," he said, almost sounding like John Wayne.

He didn't have to tell her twice.

3

Homesick

Mariana had left most of the townhouse exactly as her late mother-in-law, whom she'd sadly never meet, had last decorated it. Elizabeth "Bess" Wilson Smith Greystone's choices appealed to Mariana Wilson Smith Perez's classic taste. But Mariana was still making her mark on the house in important ways.

She planned to convert the downstairs den into a pleasant home office from which she could keep in touch with the West Coast headquarters of her PR firm. Her business in Los Angeles was flourishing, despite her absence, thanks to her savvy partner Sandy Fine and their new assistant Laurel Leigh—another one of Will's agents.

Mariana still kept in touch directly with her VVIP clientele, particularly Mac, the author Arthur McClintock, and his partner Ernest, who lived on Long Island. The two were also helping her build a new contact list of influential people in Manhattan. They knew just about everyone.

Staying in Manhattan full-time was a compromise. Her husband had 'laid down the law' since her surprise pregnancy, forbidding Mariana from traveling from coast to coast, chasing one client crisis or another. But she was not about to abandon her first baby: the business she'd built up from scratch. After a few fiery arguments, with expletives exchanged in multiple languages, and a sound paddling delivered for back talk, Will had finally bowed to his own words.

Mariana had reminded Will he had said when they married he would never ask her to give up her career entirely. It was the truth. In his mind, her unexpected pregnancy with twins changed everything, but Mariana said it didn't.

Mariana knew if she gave in now to his demands that she live the leisurely life of a wealthy socialite, she would never get back to business. Worse, she'd lose herself.

Mariana liked the idea of being a socialite about as much as William Smith, the humble tree whisperer whom she'd first fallen in love within Orlando, enjoyed being William Wilson the magnate. That is not much at all. This argument won out, and Mariana laid claim to his father's old den.

Arthur Wilson Smith's beautiful oak desk remained a centerpiece of the room. The bookshelves loaded with rare finds and prized first editions stayed in place. Mariana had a computer installed, insisting that Will's technical team extend their secure network to the ground floor. This caused many complications—and required special biometric security access to be added to the door. Will had a similar, far more advanced secure office set-up on the fourth floor of the townhouse and in their other homes: at the cabin in the woods by a lake in Connecticut, which Mariana and Will both really missed; and at their mansion in Malibu, California, which Will had bought for Mariana as a birthday present. Now, he wouldn't let her go there.

That was another sore-spot for Mariana. Will had first thought to sell the Malibu house after someone had kidnapped Mariana from the cove below. That kidnapping led to the chain of adventures and tragedies which took her to the North Pole and back again. Mariana asked Will not to sell the house because she'd grown to like it. It seemed like a waste of money after Will had outfitted the house to meet their needs. And Mariana planned to go back to California on business after the babies were born. Besides, as she pointed out, it seemed unlikely that anyone would kidnap her from that house twice in one lifetime.

The disturbed woman behind that kidnapping, Tracey Whitby, was still in recovery at the Phoenix Lodge in Connecticut, along with her lover, Jonathan Castle, a former agent of Will's organization. Once thought dead, then found broken but very much alive, the two were better, though miles away from whole. Mariana had kept track of their progress.

She and Will had visited the couple at the special care facility in the Phoenix Lodge. They could carry on a mostly coherent conversation now, only occasionally falling through the rabbit hole to speak in coded similes, metaphors and snippets of poetry. Tracey was eating regularly and regaining her strength with Jonathan's support. Helping Tracey get better also helped Jonathan, who in his heart was a good, kind and strong man. Recovering from torture and prolonged imprisonment wouldn't be a quick process, but they had all the resources and expert care they needed. They could stay at the Lodge for however long it took.

Sometimes, Will went to Connecticut alone during the week, to check-in with Mrs. Jenkins, the savvy woman who helped him run Smith Arboriculture. That business wasn't just an effective cover for his espionage, it was Will's genuine passion. The tree whisperer needed his trees. But he always came home.

Still, they were only pretending to settle into life in Manhattan. There was no proper way for them to settle.

Mariana knew things were about to get messy again, before Will said anything. Will had spent the last three days locked in his command center on the fourth floor of the townhouse. Trouble rumbled. She didn't need him to tell her. There were still a few loose ends from their previous misadventures in Europe, taking down the anarchist terrorist group Nótt. There was also the ever-present threat to Will's business empire. No matter Will's effort to live a simple life, they could never really have that.

They could only play the part.

Will and Mariana had breakfast out on the patio of their private suite of rooms on the fifth floor of the townhouse, surrounded by plants, looking out as the morning sun played with the leaves of the trees in Central Park. It was mid-June, and pleasantly warm. Mariana enjoyed every chance she got to feel the breeze on her skin and get a little sunshine. Staying mostly at home and being driven around everywhere really grated on her nerves. Mariana was used to walking to clear her head. Going up and down the stairs of the townhouse wasn't quite enough.

"Mariana, I need you to promise me you will behave while I am gone, and take good care of yourself and the peas," Will warned.

"I *am* taking care of myself, Will," Mariana said, "*and* the peas. Just because I'm busy doing other things doesn't mean I'm not. You take care of *you*. That's what I'm concerned about. You have explained nothing about what's happening, which isn't fair. You're keeping secrets from me again, and I don't like it. Is it Nótt? Or is there trouble with Robert

Whitby? Or does it have something to do with you auctioning me off to the highest bidder in repayment of a debt? Which you have never *really* explained, by the way. What's going on?"

The auction in the South of France had been a sham—a play Will had put on to trap Nótt and save the technology for the self-aware AI, Zephyr, which helped run Will's secret operations. It fell apart when two people got shot—a young Nótt operative and Will—and French police invaded the villa. The boy died instantly. Will only survived by sheer luck and the quick reflexes of his agents embedded in the crowd.

"Seriously, Mariana? You want to have this conversation out here? Now?"

Will was cross. Maybe there were spying messenger pigeons carrying little recording devices around their necks on the roofs nearby. She suspected it was just Will reverting to type, preferring to keep everything to himself until it was fixed. This nasty habit of Will's irritated her, but maybe pregnancy had made her soft. She wasn't really willing to argue with him just then.

Instead, she coated a triangle of crispy white toast with a bit of marmalade and took a bite, then sipped her orange juice. Will wouldn't let her drink coffee anymore, which felt like some kind of torture and put her in a sour mood.

"Okay, we'll talk about something else," she said. "When are you going to invite Sandy into our circle? It's beyond ridiculous, especially with Laurel being one of yours. I don't want to keep treading on ice when I talk to my own business partner."

"It's up to Charlie," he said. "I've already told you."

"And I've told *you* you're wrong," Mariana said, pointing her triangle of toast at her husband like a weapon. "Charlie has said it's up to you, and I think neither of you will do it—for whatever reason. It should be *my* decision. She's an asset,

Will, in every way imaginable. Sandy is smart, loyal, resourceful and can keep very sensitive secrets—believe me on that."

"I know she keeps secrets," Will said. "I know it better than you do. It is Charlie's decision to make."

"What is that supposed to mean, you know better?" Mariana asked.

"I know something about Sandy that I'm not supposed to know," Will said, sounding sorry he'd even mentioned it. "I can't tell you what it is without breaching a confidence. Even Charlie doesn't know that I know it. Okay?"

"You two are a mess," Mariana snapped. "I love you both, but you are a couple of assholes. Whatever it is you know about Sandy, that you won't tell me, is it something that would disqualify her from joining your organization?"

"I don't know, honestly, Mariana," Will said. "I haven't decided. There are extenuating circumstances, but I just honestly cannot tell you more."

"And Charlie knows about it?" she asked.

"Yes," Will said.

"And he is still seeing her, right?"

"As I understand it, yes," Will said.

"So whatever it is, it must be something Charlie is okay with."

Will took a long drink from his cup of coffee before answering.

"That's harder to answer, but I assume he's made his peace with it."

"You haven't asked him?"

"I told you, I'm not supposed to know about it in the first place, Mariana," he said. "So no, I can't discuss it with Charlie."

"Whatever it is, I still trust Sandy more than anyone I've ever worked with," Mariana said. "And you trust her too.

You threatened to put her in charge of the business and buy me out, remember?"

Will had backed out of his threat to put Sandy in charge of her PR firm completely, so Mariana could live the pampered life of a Manhattan socialite. She still felt like he was poised for a hostile takeover any day.

"You wouldn't have suggested that, if you didn't know you'd need her," Mariana continued. "You know Sandy's damned good at what she does. But you still haven't brought Sandy in your circle. That just doesn't seem right."

"Mariana, it is up to Charlie," Will said.

"Fine, I'll call him."

"Okay, you do that," Will said. "I've got to finish getting ready and head out. I'll be off grid, but I will stay in touch and check with you every night. Just behave. Honestly, I don't think you can take more added to your list."

"My list should be tiny," Mariana said. "I've been an absolute angel. I've let you bully me into submission."

Will laughed. "Just don't make it worse."

"Grump," Mariana leaned over to kiss him. "Bully." He tasted like coffee. Delicious. She missed coffee. "Meanie." His lips were incredibly soft for such a hard man. "Sneak."

"Sneak?" Will said, pulling her head closer and assaulting her mouth. "You wound me, woman."

"You are sneaky, and you know it," Mariana said, as soon as he let her breathe again. "Sneaking around everywhere, not telling your wife things she *ought* to know. One of these days, I'm going to give *you* a spanking to remember me by."

"That," he said and kissed her again, just a peck, "is never." He nipped on her lip. "Going to happen." He savored her mouth, re-awakening the desire which always floated near the surface, until she was ready to burst. "Do you need a ginger root whittled before I go?" And that ruined it.

"No, I'm all set, thanks," Mariana grimaced. "We'll continue this discussion when you get back. And, if you don't stay in touch—every night—I'm going to call your grandfather to check that you're okay."

"Do not, under any circumstances, even in jest, get my grandfather involved in my business, Mariana. Ever." Now Will looked and sounded properly angry. Mariana regretted teasing him about something as sensitive as the tense relationship Will had with the hard-edged Lord Greystone.

"Sorry," Mariana said. "I'll call Howard."

She had only had a brief encounter with Howard Fleming and his wife Catherine, both in costume, but she knew he was Will's right hand in the organization and a friend of Will's late father, Arthur.

"You don't need to call him either," Will said. "If anything ever happened to me, Howard would call *you* right away. No news is good news."

"I hate that expression." Mariana wrinkled her nose. "It can be taken two ways."

"Yes, that's why I like it," Will said.

An hour later, Will stopped by Mariana's den, dressed in his usual Smith Arboriculture get-up, blue shirt with jeans and a green windbreaker with the logo. He walked up to where she stood looking over wallpaper samples for her other extensive project, re-decorating Will's former nursery for the twins.

"I'm heading out," he said, wrapping his arms around her. "Do you want to make up before I go?"

"I'm not mad at you," Mariana said, kissing his chin. "Are you mad at me?"

"No, darling." He tucked a loose curl behind her ear. After cutting her hair in a radical bob, which Will had very much disapproved of, Mariana was letting her hair grow out again and keeping it in its natural state of wild waves. It often went rogue, but Will said he preferred her with a bedhead. "I'm just worried about you," he continued. "Be a good girl, please?"

"You behave too," Mariana smiled. "What's with the uniform? Are you stopping by Fairfarm before going wherever?"

"Yes."

"Okay, say hi to Mrs. Jenkins from me, and stay away from the flower beds." William often looked after the gardens of the finer ladies of Connecticut. Mariana was painfully aware of the effect her husband had on these women. She didn't really worry that Will would stray, but Mariana was every bit as possessive as he was. She did not enjoy sharing her husband, even the sight of him. "And come back in time for the wedding," she added. "I'm *not* going to Wales alone."

"I'll be back in plenty of time."

"Or you'll answer to La Comtesse."

Will grinned. "We're already married, Mariana, but I'm very much looking forward to this wedding. I wouldn't miss it for the world. And, yes, grandmother would be furious with me, but that's not why. Do you want to know why?"

"Why?"

"Because I want all the Greystone family and all of their aristocratic friends to meet you and to see you are mine." Will caressed her belly.

"I'm going to look like a puffy ivory duck walking down the aisle."

"You'll look more beautiful than ever," Will said, "a gorgeous dove with a delicious full bottom."

"Stop making me horny," she said.

He claimed her mouth like he might never kiss her again, like this was his last chance to taste her. One large hand threaded in her wayward curls and the other gripped her bottom. She rose on tip-toes to respond, wrapping her arms around his neck, trusting him to keep her steady. Mariana felt anything but steady, though. Suddenly, she was afraid.

"Don't cry," he said, after tasting her tears between their lips. "Mariana, I'll be back soon. I promise."

"If you ever make a widow of me again, I'll kill you," she said.

"Yes, ma'am," he said, kissing a damp cheek. "Though you look very sexy in black."

"Go, William Wilson Smith, before I wring your neck and have to send Gail to buy a black maternity dress."

"I like the yellow wallpaper," he said, grinning, "the one with the little ducks. Get that one."

"*Sí, Papi.*"

4

Roots and Shoots

William Wilson Smith was betraying his wife. He knew it. He felt lousy for it, but he couldn't do anything about it. Some secrets were too big, even for him to manage on his own. He had heeded the advice of his right-hand man and his father's best friend, Howard Fleming, who had recommended he not give Mariana anything more to worry about. After all, the bomb ticking away in the dark corner of his mind might never go off. It might be a dud, just a dumb clock, with no charge attached to it. Still, the ticking made him uneasy as he drove to his unassuming headquarters in Fairfarm, Connecticut.

Fortunately, the implacable Mrs. Jenkins wouldn't tolerate any nonsense from him this morning, or any day.

"Everything is under control with the properties. You know that," she said. "I can only assume you've stopped by to find out whether your little trouble is spreading here in town. Unless you've suddenly decided I can't handle simple dispatch."

"Never," Will said. "You know the right Smith to send out every time, for every tree in every storm, Mrs. Jenkins."

"Good, so you're here for gossip," Mrs. Jenkins removed her cats-eye spectacles and placed them over her graying hair, like a diadem. "Bottom line, your good name is intact. Nobody in town thinks you'd be capable of what that hussy claims. She gets around so much that everyone is placing bets on a host of guilty parties. My money's on Robert Whitby. That man still has a pull on her, even if she denies it."

"Has the Board kicked Robert off his perch at the Country Club yet?"

Mrs. Jenkins sighed. "You know the meeting isn't until the end of the month, William. It doesn't matter. Things are going lousy with the people he brought in, from what I hear. He's facing a no-confidence vote, according to the vines. They will probably put Carter in charge. You know Carter is loyal to us. We'll have that contract back. Though, it wouldn't hurt if you wanted to spend some time schmoozing a few of the others."

"I don't schmooze. I have never schmoozed. I do not intend to start schmoozing," Will said. "We've got Patricia for that. If they want to keep enjoying the facilities of the Phoenix Lodge, then they should vote according to their conscience. If they delay, their own reputations risk being tainted by the stain of association with Whitby. They are with me, or against me. Being with Whitby is most definitely being against me."

"Don't be so irritable, William," Mrs. Jenkins said. "You will need to develop patience if you're going to be a father. Go look after those trees in foreign parts and leave these stumps to me."

Will nodded. "Please keep an eye on her for me," Will said.

"Poison ivy?" She meant Sandra Price, the bane of Will's existence. Now, more than ever.

"No, my mint," Will said. Mrs. Jenkins knew enough of

the language of flowers to understand he meant Mariana. Mint represented virtue, and it was vital for mojitos.

"She's no sage," Mrs. Jenkins warned, "you shouldn't expect her to sit home pining for you. Her head is in the field. Let her feel the breeze."

Mrs. Jenkins was not mocking Mariana for being unwise. She was using the language of flowers to warn Will that Mariana's virtues were not domestic. He knew that better than anyone. She'd never just settle at home. If things were different, if she wasn't pregnant and he hadn't been shot last time he got her involved in a play, it might even tempt him to bring her along. Mariana was resourceful and clever. She was a wonderful partner in crime. But right now, the breeze was more like a strong nor'easter. He just couldn't risk that she'd be blown away.

Once again, the source of Will's trouble was unknown. All he had to go on was that some shipments of one of the advanced materials plants that were part of his defense systems group had gone missing.

Will kept clear of projects in the weapons and armaments industry—which had been responsible for his parents' death—but he was still active in aerospace. His advanced laboratories had developed a newly optimized titanium, silicone and molybdenum alloy which was as strong as steel and as lightweight as aluminum.

His companies intended to use the material for various aerospace parts, including new long-distance, self-powered, intelligent drones which could deliver supplies to remote areas in times of crisis. But the material was also useful for weapons and missiles.

Will feared the worst. If a rival was stealing their supply, they might easily use it for those purposes. Of course, they might reverse-engineer the alloy in time. Will knew that. But he had an ace up his sleeve by controlling the raw materials supply chain too.

Will had recently gained a very productive mine from an attractive and troubled young Alaskan heiress, who had been living in hiding as an escort in Los Angeles because her life was a mess. Thanks to the savvy of one of Charlie's Hawks, and the quick thinking of one of Will's agents, they had found the troubled heiress before someone killed her or she went to pieces. The young woman was now training for a career in intelligence, for which she had shown high aptitude, despite her demonstrably disastrous decision-making in life.

Because of this buy-out, anyone who wanted to make the proprietary alloy—one of his labs had developed—would need to buy the materials in large quantities from mines which were both Will's now, even if very few people knew it. Will had set limits and heavy controls on who bought what ores and for what purpose. It would be much easier for a private rival to steal the alloy than copy it.

Unless the government itself was playing dirty tricks—which wasn't impossible. He had to make sure that wasn't the case.

Will flew to Maryland to meet with Howard Fleming. He could call Howard to ask about almost anything anytime, but not this. He needed to read the man's face carefully. Will trusted Howard, just about as much as he trusted his grandfather, Lord Greystone.

Will had realized while meeting with the two men to plan the disastrous play in France that almost killed him, that Fleming and Greystone were more alike than he once thought. They both kept close ties to their governments. They welcomed the efficiency of killing their enemies who got in the way. Lord Greystone was just more direct about it. Both supported Will's core missions—tackling the growing wealth gap, conserving the environment, and preserving the democracies which had helped both the U.K. and the U.S. advance. But Howard Fleming and Richard Greystone had lost their idealism with the years, and with that they had lost their hope. They saw the struggle in much darker terms than Will did, and they made pragmatic decisions in cold blood.

This made both men valuable advisors to Will, but also very dangerous ones.

Will had to assume they wouldn't tell him about everything happening in the undercurrents of government if they thought he was better off not knowing.

He'd had enough of that.

This situation with the missing shipments of alloy was too similar to the exploit of his organization's capabilities by a rival defense firm which had led to the death of his father and mother when Will was still a child. His father, Arthur, tried to stop a British firm from stealing their intellectual property and using the technology for armaments. He'd gone to Richard for help in a play in the UK. Richard had warned Arthur that the rival involved had government connections he could not control. Arthur had insisted and, with help from Richard's own private espionage firm, he had sabotaged the rival company. That success, however, came at a terrible price when the firm put out a contract on Will's father.

Will had grown up thinking his parents had died in a car crash, a white lie forged by his paternal grandmother who raised him in the family's cabin in the woods of Connecticut. He grew up in blissful ignorance, protected by their humble Smith identities, unaware of his legacy of wealth. While his grandmother had taught William to value life, to avoid killing except in the most dire circumstances, he had learned from Greystone and Fleming that his Nana Smith took revenge on the group who had killed her only son. To protect the memory of his late grandmother, Howard had said the kill orders were his idea, but Richard said otherwise. Will knew in his heart that Richard was telling the truth.

The Greystones resented Nana Smith for a very simple reason, in the end: she had William. They had effectively lost their only daughter and their grandson at the same time.

William did not really regret for a minute growing up in Connecticut, thinking of his other grandparents only as strangers who lived too far away to get to know better. He had forged wonderful friendships in Fairfarm and got to live without pretense or the pressures of wealth.

Despite being the head of an organization worth trillions, Nana Smith left the business in the hands of her advisers. She trusted Howard Fleming to run the show in terms of intelligence operations, and she raised Will as though they only had enough income to live on if they used it wisely. The ruse wouldn't have worked if Will had flown to his maternal grandparents' castle in Wales every summer. Yes, it had been cruel, and Will regretted the pain caused to his maternal grandmother, Anne Greystone, especially. But he would have probably done the same if he had been in Nana's shoes.

Children should grow up free to roam in the trees and forests. This train of thought irked him. Could he offer his children the same thing? Didn't they deserve it? Would Mariana agree?

***?

Will put troubling thoughts aside as his helicopter approached the landing pad at the Fleming compound on Chesapeake Bay, with its seven houses of various sizes. A colonial plantation-style two-story mansion, which was the family home, stood on the center of the property, along with five smaller ranch-style and cottage-style homes for special guests. There was a tiny house used for company best kept at bay, literally by the bay.

The place only made sense when you knew the Flemings had an enormous family—seven children of their own plus cousins and close acquaintances treated like family. They also did a bit of recovery and field training on the grounds when the situation called for it. The seven houses were rarely empty for long.

Will had become one of the family, after learning about his legacy. He'd spent some time with the Flemings here in the compound during his training and spent summers at Catherine Fleming's—Catalina's—home near Salamanca in Spain.

One of his favorite Flemings greeted him at the door of the big house—the iconoclast Cathy. She was the Flemings' youngest daughter and going through a phase questioning everything about her family, her identity, and even the nature of reality. She was easy to love. Cathy wore torn jeans and an oversized gray T-shirt, with two pencils stuck in a messy hair knot at the top of her head. She still looked adorable.

"Will!" Cathy squeaked, as she reached up to hug him tight. "I'm so glad you didn't die!"

"Me too!" Will laughed as he returned her hug. "Dying would have been terribly inconvenient."

"Where's your wife? I've been dying to meet her. Mom says she's *picante*, though I don't know whether she means that she's very attractive or problematic, or maybe both?"

"Still unfiltered, huh, Cathy?" Will smiled.

"What's the point of filters?" Cathy shrugged.

"Filters put your opponent at ease so you can set the trap

which ultimately forces them to reveal the truth," Will explained.

"Nah," Cathy said. "People lie, even when they are telling the truth. It's all subjective, and people believe many lies. Some even make people question objective facts. We're taming shrews or shrews being tamed, or whatever. You know, is that the moon or the sun shining in the sky?"

Will knew exactly what Cathy meant, and he got the reference to Shakespeare's play, *The Taming of the Shrew*, which never got the credit it deserved for exposing the practice of gaslighting.

"Maybe we can discuss this indoors?"

"Yeah, sorry, come in," Cathy giggled. "Dad's in the den. Mama went out shopping with Miranda for some things she'll need in Los Angeles. You know she's going to work with Angel and Charlie, right?"

"Yeah, I heard about that," Will said. "I thought she'd already started."

"Well, that was the plan, but then *somebody* got kidnapped and all hell broke loose and *somebody* went to the North Pole, and put on a play in France which nearly got Angel arrested, and Dad needed all hands on deck here so Miranda came home. Now she's going back to Los Angeles to stay, at least until she tires of 'Hawking around', as Dad says."

Will agreed with Howard that it was a shame to lose Miranda to the "dark side" of Charlie's business, but the Flemings thrived in twilight. It didn't hurt to have another Fleming in Charlie's organization who was also loyal to Will.

Will's best friend, Charlie Green, ran his special operations firm independently and was far more comfortable diving into dark tasks than Will could allow within the charter of his own organization. It was an uneasy compromise of principles, but that seemed to be true of everything these days. The slide to brutality seemed inevitable as the stakes went higher. Will tried to keep his hands clean as much as the situation would allow.

"When are you going to take my test, Cathy?" Will said. "I could really use someone like you in the gardens."

"Are you serious?" Cathy said. "I haven't even finished college."

"So?" Will dismissed the concern.

"Mom and Dad insist I go back, but I don't see the point," she said. "It's all just so theoretical. Half of my professors had never set foot in the real world. Philosophy is all good, but only if it's put into practice. You know?"

"Take the test, Cathy," Will said. "I'll give you a good job tomorrow."

"Really?"

"Cathy, have you ever known me to say things and not mean them?"

"No, but I have known you to mean things and not say them."

Will laughed. "You have the game system here in the house?"

"No, it's in the little house," Cathy said.

"Good. Go there and play with HARPO and leave me to meet with your Dad."

"Is it like a puzzle?" Cathy asked. "I mean, I've heard about it, but I've never actually seen anyone play it."

"I suppose you could call it a puzzle," Will said. "Though it's more dynamic. The world of the game is elaborate and subtle."

"Good, I love those."

"Go!" Will shooed her out. The girl ran happily to the little house on the property, eager to try her hand at the game. Will could almost predict how she would test. He wouldn't be surprised if Cathy exceeded the recent stellar performance of the wayward cat whom his agent Duncan

McEwan had recently rescued. In fact, he was counting on it.

As an added advantage, Cathy would be somewhere else, where she couldn't overhear 'accidentally on purpose' while Will carried on a hard conversation with her father.

5

Lies of Allies

Howard Fleming sat at his oak desk in the den, looking through the pages of an incoming fax on the credenza behind him.

"You still use faxes, Howard?" Will joked.

"It's still secure, mostly," he said.

"Not really, Howard," Will said. "Anyone can listen in to the pings and whistles on the phone line."

"Not this line," Howard said. "Nobody has it. Not even the President. Plus, I still like to have a paper in my hands. I know all of you prefer working on ether, but I still like to jot my thoughts in the margins."

"I can respect that," Will said, taking a seat on one of the Burgundy leather-covered chairs opposite the desk.

"You seem to have recovered well, son," Howard said.

"I still get a twinge in my chest from time to time, if I make a wrong move," Will said. "I'm doing exercises the doctors prescribed and the patches perform remarkably well. We should start distributing those soon in the open market."

"I wouldn't, Will," Howard said. "The military contract

you just signed is fine, but you don't want to get the pharmaceuticals all riled up."

"Yes," Will spat, "heaven help them if they couldn't get people hooked on painkillers."

"I don't think you're here about the drug wars," Howard said. "At least, I hope not. We've agreed to table those until we're stronger again."

"I wonder whether we'll ever be strong enough for that," Will said. "And, no, you're right. I've come about something else."

"Trouble at home?" Howard asked. "I don't see your orange blossom settling easily into domestic life."

"Howard, it's one thing when Charlie calls Mariana that, and another when you do," Will smirked. "You make it sound too official."

"That's her handle, though," Howard said. "Officially."

"Yes, but please just call her Mariana," Will said. "And no, she's about as happy being Mrs. Wilson as I am being Mr. Wilson. She's taking care of herself and the babies, though, which is all I can ask for, really. Mariana has a powerful mind of her own. She's bound to find it difficult to just join the ladies who lunch."

"Take it from a man with considerable experience handling difficult Spanish women," Howard said. "Just accept that she will have her own agenda, keep a very close eye on her, and dole out the discipline where it's needed. She'll expect it anyway, and she's probably happy to exchange a bit of pain for power. And don't think you can keep secrets from her for too long."

"If you are referring to my trouble in Connecticut, *you* insisted I keep that quiet," Will said. "I hate keeping that to myself. It feels like a double betrayal."

"Our attorneys are handling it, Will," Howard said. "They are pushing for the paternity test in utero. Don't make it a problem until you *know* it's a problem. I was referring to something else. You still haven't told her the full function of her necklace, which seems foolish."

"She might take it off," Will said.

"Or she might accept it is what it is for a reason. Regardless, she should know," Howard said. "But, it's up to you. You already had to replace the first one because of a potential breach, which turned out to be no breach at all. That doesn't mean the system is untouchable."

"Oliver believes it is," Will said. "The only one who could have hacked into it chose not to and used other material instead."

Will's cousin Oliver Greystone headed Aidos, the cyber-security branch of Will's organization. They had all recently learned that the suspected threats to their systems came from another former member of his organization, someone they thought was dead: Tracey Whitby, a computer science genius captured by his enemies who had turned to hacking for the enemy in her captivity.

"How are Tracey and Jonathan, by the way? Will you reactivate her at some point? A mind like hers comes once in a generation."

"Her mind is still in tatters, but it's mending, and what she can do working with a broken mind is remarkable," Will said. "Jonathan is better, now that he has her safe. I believe he will have an opinion on whether Tracey should ever go back in the field. I'm hoping Tracey will join Oliver's team in Monterey."

"We could use her, too, if they want to stay on the East Coast," Howard said.

"Only for our business," Will said.

"If you insist," Howard said.

"Let's leave it up to Tracey and Jonathan as soon as their therapists deem them competent to decide," Will said. "I'd love to have Jonathan back on board too, but he may never want to return."

"Or he could just become a Hawk," Howard said. "It would help him work off some of his anger."

Will shook his head. "Jonathan is an Eagle to the core."

"So what is your business, Will?" Howard said, tiring of the dance sooner than Will had expected.

"What do you know about the missing shipments from Hephaestus?"

"That's what this fax is about," Howard said, giving Will the papers to review. Obviously, the man knew exactly what was coming when Will announced he was flying down. "It may just be poor tracking or duplicated production records. They just installed a new ERP system so there may be some confusion."

"That makes me even less comfortable," Will said. "Those kinds of mistakes are usually a sign of somebody playing with the books. Materials like this don't just go missing."

"According to the head of production, they never really made those lots," Howard insisted. "The new ERP system erroneously updated them as finished goods, and documented the shipment, but the tracking numbers correspond to previous shipments on previous work orders. These work orders are still in production."

"Has anyone accounted for the raw material consumption?"

"Yes, that report is on page three," Howard said. "It's a bit more difficult to reconcile because they use various ores and ingredients for different alloys. There is also loss in each lot, but the raw material volumes consumed correspond to the orders, excluding the missing shipments. They have used no excess materials. The missing orders just didn't happen.

They notified customers that the shipping notices were an error."

"Let's work on the assumption that this is wrong," Will said. "Just as an intellectual exercise. Who would need these alloys, outside of our own programs?"

"You know the answer to that already, Will," Howard said.

"I know the major players among the weapons makers," Will said. "Are there any special projects for our friends that I'm unaware of, which I might want to support if I knew about them?"

Howard kept Will's gaze for a while, then reached into his drawer to pull out a large pack of Big Red gum, offering Will a stick.

"No thanks," Will said.

Will knew Howard would rather smoke a cigarette, but the cinnamon gum was all he got. Catherine had put her foot down over three decades ago. Still, the impulse was there. It wasn't nerves. It was anger. Will knew that too.

"I have heard of projects which might benefit from this material. If anyone knew it exists, then they might claim a share," Howard said. "I can't give you any of the details. They are all classified. They have not approached me with a requisition if that's what you are thinking."

"No, Howard, I think you would tell me if they had approached you," Will said. "But where there is a demand for anything, hook or crook will satisfy it. If it serves the greater good for me to lose some lots from time to time, I don't care. I'd rather know about them. My concern is that our technologies don't fall into the wrong hands. I'm also worried because the bidding for Mariana went tits up—sorry for the expression, but it fits."

"You knew that was a crazy play anyway," Howard said. "Has she forgiven you, by the way?"

"She has not forgotten, though she has set it aside," Will smiled. "Apparently, she was just happy to find me alive. She's put off killing me for a while. With her hormones working overtime, she might kill me soon enough."

"There are worse ways to die," Howard said. "Will the Brits honor their bid for her safety?"

"Well, after they heard the reserve, they felt they underbid," Will shrugged. "I understand from Lord Greystone that they have accepted the contract for her protection as Lady Stevenson, without revising their figure. What about *our* cousins?"

"The whole idea offended them, about as much as Mariana," Howard said.

"What you are really telling me is that no one at *any* of the agencies will promise she wouldn't be used as a pawn in a play, for any amount of money," Will said.

"All is fair in war," Howard said. "Don't get into a war, William. Heed your advisors."

"So I have to accept some losses, not ask too many questions, be a good boy, bend to the whims of politicians bought by my enemies, and only *then* do I get to keep my wife and my children alive. Is that it?" Will was fighting to keep the rage out of his tone. He should have accepted a stick of gum. Now he just wanted a stick of dynamite. "I am fighting for my country, Howard. Is this how my country protects me?"

"William, you're not," Howard said. "Don't delude yourself. You are fighting for *your* vision of your country. And it's a splendid vision. I agree with it. We dedicate my entire family to ensuring you succeed. But there are others with other visions. Others who also have money, power and influence. You know that. This is an open market. We're capitalists. Loyalties are as fluid as the money they flow to. Values are cheap."

"We're overrun by cowards," Will said. "We're being led

by mayflies who don't care what comes after their day is done."

"Get into politics and change it," Howard said.

"I don't do politics, Howard," Will said. "I'd never survive it. You have your lobbyists. Do what you can. Perhaps this is all just a wave that will wash over. The people are still the same good people, but they are being manipulated."

"William, if push comes to shove, you may need to take Mariana to the castle and keep her there for a while. You know that, right?"

"How imminent is this threat?"

"I can't say." Howard took a second stick of gum, while still chewing the first. This time, Will accepted the foil-wrapped stick. It helped clear the taste of bile from his mouth. "It's not that I don't want to say or that I am bound to secrecy. I really do not know. It could be tomorrow. It could never happen. But leaving this matter of the missing shipments at rest would be a wise move."

"Fuck it," Will said. "The only way to win is not to play."

"I heard about that too, William," Howard said, understanding Will's reference to the instructions Will's AI, Zephyr, had given to her digital twin, Brian, in the South Pole. The advice came from the movie *War Games*, which Zephyr had made her digital twin Brian 'watch'. "I am not the *only* one who has heard the words." There was a warning in Howard's tone that Will did not like.

"I meant what I said when we met in France," Will told the man. "I intend to make the Zephyr's technology open source."

"Now is not the time." Howard tried to sound cool, but there was a worrying undercurrent of desperation in his voice. He was warring with himself not to say too much or too little. "Right now, the only thing you should do is add to the guest list at your wedding. That's it. I know it's only a few weeks away, but your grandparents will understand and approve. Gather a Convocation of Eagles. You have the perfect excuse. Bring all your allies together in one place for something which won't raise alarms. Invite enough random players to confuse our purpose. Let's forge a stronger alliance over the Atlantic. You will need it. At least you know the Greystones are with you, even if things here are muddy."

"I never thought I'd hear you recommend Grandfather," Will said. "The situation must be dire."

"These are fucked up times, Will," Howard said. "I never imagined the rot would reach so far and so deep."

"I'm taking Cathy," Will said.

"As a hostage?" Howard was only half-joking, and he was half-right.

"No, I'm giving her a job," Will said. "Something she'll love, I think. Mariana needs an office here on the East Coast, or wherever she goes. She needs another Sandy. I believe Cathy is perfect for the job."

"Very well," Howard said. "You'll have to talk to Catherine about it. She will not be pleased."

"Cathy is going stir crazy here at home," Will said. "Am I right?"

Howard sighed and nodded. "She needs a purpose, that's true. Unfortunately, I don't see her going back to college."

"She graduated a long time ago," Will said. "A university could never keep up with her brain."

"Speaking of Sandy," Howard said, taking a step back in the conversation which avoided the uncomfortable notion of Will taking their youngest daughter away. "Is Sandy really as sharp-eared as Angel claims?"

"From what I understand from Charlie, yes," Will said. "She hears all the code. Apparently, she has from the beginning."

"And she hasn't slipped up with Mariana at any point?"

"No, which is remarkable," Will said. "I don't really know why. I know she's loyal to Mariana, but she seems to be loyal to us too. Laurel tells me she plays the fool professionally."

"And Sandy is not a plant?"

"Charlie is positive that she is clear," Will said.

"Then he must really have her on a tight leash." Howard smirked. "She didn't slip up at Angel's wedding reception either. Catherine thought she might admit to her relationship with Charlie being more serious than they claim, but she wouldn't take the bait. Has Charlie said anything to you?"

"All I know is he's off the market, and I know they see each other when he's in Los Angeles," Will said. "He hasn't talked about leaving Connecticut, or discussed her much with me at all. Mariana wants Sandy officially in our group. I think she's right, but I want Charlie to tell me he's okay with it. I don't want to have a situation turn sour there, if he moves on."

"That's no reason to keep Sandy out," Howard said. "They're both adults. Charlie has fucked enough of our agents to make his peace with someone being in the group whom he had a fling with at some point or other."

"Yes, but this is different," Will said. "I think Charlie has a lot more invested in Sandy than he will admit. If she decides he's too dangerous to her, in the long term, things could turn ugly."

Howard had nothing to say to that.

Will considered telling Howard about what he'd learned from one of his agents, Duncan McEwan, who had been in Los Angeles—that Sandy had killed two monsters single-handed and Charlie cleaned up the evidence. Maybe Angel knew about it also, and had told his father, but Angel had said nothing to Will. Will had promised Duncan to keep his confidence, even if Charlie finally told him what happened.

The background was murky—somehow Sandy had a history with the men she killed. So did the young heiress, whom Duncan was now engaged to marry. There were so many tangles involving Charlie's Hawks it made Will's head spin, and his own side of things was messy too.

Will longed for the sort of simple life his Nana Smith had worked so hard to give him. He might never achieve it again unless he let everything go. He wouldn't. Will couldn't afford to, especially now that the rot had set in, as Howard put it. When you're surrounded by rot, it finds its way into your roots in time. That was all he could think about now.

"I suppose it's a good thing that Charlie is getting Miranda too," Will said. "We're going to need more soldiers on his side."

"Yes, Catherine is absolutely thrilled," Howard said, clearly meaning the opposite. "Empty nest for us, at long last."

"Not for long," Will grinned. "You'll have grandchildren wearing down the floorboards soon."

"I suppose we will," Howard said, smiling. "So where are you off to next?"

"Well, given what you've told me, I'd waste a trip going to the foundry," Will said, though he was still considering it. He had no qualms about lying to Howard, just as Howard had no qualms about lying to him when the circumstances called for it. "I'm going to check on Oliver and then I'll go back home."

"Stay for lunch, at least," Howard said. "Catherine and Miranda will be sorry they missed you. If you're taking Cathy away from home, you may as well tell her mother yourself."

"Sure," Will said, rising from the chair. "Speaking of which, I'll go check on Cathy."

"Will," Howard said, "it's time to rest for a while and

gather your forces. The battle is coming, but don't give the game away until you have all your pieces in place."

Will thought about Howard's words through the rest of the afternoon, while he enjoyed a lively lunch with the three Fleming women in residence. Catherine was every bit as excited about the prospect of Cathy moving to live with them in Manhattan as Howard had predicted.

"She doesn't know the first thing about communications or PR," Catherine scoffed. "And if you think she's going to be a babysitter, you have another think coming."

"It'll be fun, Mom," Cathy said. "I'll be in New York, at least! I can learn what I need to know from Mariana."

"You're assuming she *wants* to teach you," Catherine said. "I bet Will hasn't even asked her. He just decided. *Machista empedernido.*"

Will didn't think of himself as sexist, though perhaps he was, as Catherine claimed. But if wanting to protect his wife made him sexist, he could live with that.

"I'll discuss it with Mariana tonight. I'm sure she'll be happy to have help," Will said. "We will need more sharp brains on media. I know she's determined to do that, and she'll need someone who is a quick thinker. Cathy is perfect for the job."

"Maybe Cathy will do a better job watching Mariana than Angel has done," Miranda joked, though Will struggled to find the humor.

"I'm not a bodyguard," Cathy grumbled.

"You can say that again," Howard said. "You are the opposite of a bodyguard. Will, honestly, you may think you're solving something, but you're only doubling your trouble if you put Cathy and Mariana together."

"Dad, I'm not a complete idiot!" Cathy pouted. "I know to keep out of trouble. And I've had the same training as you guys, Miranda. I can handle a gun and I can handle myself."

"Nobody thinks you couldn't handle the job, if you set your mind to it," Catherine said. "It's just that Mariana is a trouble magnet and you are a whirling dervish."

"Will obviously feels differently, don't you, Will?"

"I think you're perfect," Will said, giving Cathy a smile and a wink.

"*Bueno*," Catherine raised her palms up to heaven, pleading with whatever angels watched over her offspring. "*Que será, será.*"

6

Return of the White Wolf

A fter meeting with Howard, Will flew out again by helicopter to the private airport to board a jet headed for California. He made a call from the jet, just working on a hunch.

"Hey, man, are you in Los Angeles right now?" Will asked Charlie as soon as Charlie picked up.

"As it happens, yes," Charlie said.

Will smiled. It was definitely time to have the talk with Charlie about bringing Sandy onboard. "Good, I'm headed there. I need to meet with all of you at the house today. Could you arrange it? I'm flying out now and should be there this evening around five. I'd like to have an hour alone with you first. Could you invite everyone for dinner at my place?"

"Who is everyone?" Charlie asked.

"Adams and yourself, and Oliver—I'm going to ask him to fly down now," Will said.

"And Angel?"

Will hesitated a moment. Could he trust Angel not to share details of the operation with his father?

"Yes, of course," Will said. "Angel too, and Alfred—I'll have Adams reach out to him. Who do you trust implicitly on your team?"

"Everyone, Will," Charlie said. "Either I trust them implicitly or they are out. How big a play are you planning?"

"The biggest so far, and you will not like it," Will said.

"Any chance I'll be the one getting shot this time?"

"I'd say the odds are good," Will said.

"Outstanding," Charlie said. "It's been a while."

Oliver Greystone had to make up excuses for leaving San Francisco in a rush, but he agreed to be there for Will's meeting. Will's younger cousin—under cover as a hipster conservationist—was wooing Caroline Boots, assistant to the tech billionaire Martin Harper, Will's rival and Mariana's former lover. They were making a play for Martin's company, Play-Tech, which was almost complete. A far more dangerous rival, Robert Whitby, had hooked Caroline and was using her to make his own moves on PlayTech. Oliver's mission was to unhook her, and he was apparently very good at it. Will had learned from his agent, Penny Pink, who now worked in Robert Whitby's head office in Manhattan, that Caroline and Robert had parted ways.

"How bad is it?" Oliver asked when Will told him about the meeting.

"Mariana is in play on home base," Will told Oliver. Saying it aloud made it a thousand times worse than just thinking about it.

"No, she fucking isn't," Oliver said. "Not as long as we have breath and superior technology."

"Thank you, Oliver," Will said. "I know she loves you too."

He called Mariana next, after checking the security stream from her necklace and noticing she hadn't taken an afternoon nap yet.

"How's my naughty girl doing?" Will asked when she picked up.

"I'm being very good," she replied and smiled. He could see it because she was in the closet near the mirror, changing out of her dress and her necklace streamed her reflection.

"Did you take your afternoon nap?"

"I was about to when you called," she said, putting down the phone to slip on one of her cotton nightgowns. He got a quick glimpse of her full breasts before she slipped the garment over her body. His dick twinged with anticipation. He would prefer to be home right now, deep inside of her, but he had to make sure she would be safe.

Mariana picked up the phone again. "I got delayed with a couple of things this morning and had a late lunch, but I'm going to go to bed now for an hour or two. How are you doing?"

"Good," Will lied. "Just in transit. Listen, I need you to do me a favor."

"Sure, hon, anything." He knew Mariana meant it. She was so generous that it was dangerous.

"Do you remember Howard and Catherine Fleming?"

"I remember Catherine, and I think Howard was one of the Dread Pirate Roberts by her side, right?"

"Yes, the first one," Will said.

"Their youngest daughter, Cathy, is very intelligent and very lost. I hoped you would take her on as an apprentice. She doesn't have a college degree, but I swear she's really gifted. I think you'll like her when you meet her. I want to offer her a room in the house. She would have time to live in New York and find herself. If you could keep her busy, it would be so good for her."

"This would be Angel's sister?"

"Yes, the youngest of all the kids," Will said. "He has three sisters, but the other two are older. Cathy is nineteen, and she just dropped out of Georgetown."

"Why?" Mariana asked.

"Boredom, mainly," he said. "I can get you a profile on her. She took the HARPO test. I think that living in New York could inspire her, and I know she would learn a lot from you. She'd be happy to do anything you ask, and she'd do it well."

"Okay," Mariana said. "I have a lot going on, so I don't know if I'm really up to training someone. Still, if she's as sharp as you say, then it shouldn't be too much effort. I feel like I owe Angel, anyway."

"You don't owe Angel anything," Will said. "This is for your benefit."

"Well, I got him clobbered by Lady Divine, and I cursed him out in France, though I wasn't really cursing *him*."

Will winced. He had handled the bid for her protection so clumsily and broke her heart. Sometimes, trying to be too smart makes you dumb. "Yes, let's put all that behind us now," he said.

"Not *all* of it," Mariana said. "I'm being patient, but eventually you *will* explain the debt for which I am payment in kind."

No, he wouldn't, if he could help it.

"Go to sleep now, sweetheart," Will said. "I'll call you later tonight. Okay?"

"Chicken," she teased. "*Bok, bok, bok, bok, bok.*"

"Mariana, I can still spank you properly, you know, risking no harm to the kids," Will said. "I'll show you when I get home."

"Looking forward to it." She hung up.

Will watched her stream a little longer until she was all

tucked in. She was so beautiful, so kind and caring. Mariana was going to be a wonderful mother. His arms ached to hold her. Will wanted to be lost with her again, in his cabin in the woods, forgetting that his other life existed, watching his children play freely in the trees and swim in the lake. Will wanted more things that money can't buy, things that money makes impossible to keep. His ancestors were right about their gift. The Midas touch was a curse.

Will tried to be a good man, but he wasn't, really. He could be just as violent and deadly as the next desperate man. Nobody was going to use his wife as a pawn in a power play. No one. He would keep her safe, even if it meant salting the soil in every forest he'd planted and poisoning every well.

Charlie looked chipper, which was not unusual given an opportunity to go to war. He had long ago urged Will to be more forceful, but Will still had his ancestors' charter to contend with. It wasn't just that the rules of his ancestors required he make every reasonable effort to preserve life. Will believed that starting a war among the one percent of the one percent would ultimately claim the lives of the helpless and vulnerable. There were too many among the few who had no scruples to guide them, and no qualms with passing on the pain. Some even got a kick out of it.

"You don't look half dead anymore," Charlie said when Will greeted him at the door of the mansion at the northernmost end of Malibu, which he'd bought expressly for Mariana. It was on a large, secluded property with access to a cove below which had seemed secure until they took his wife from the shore. Will half-liked and half-hated the place, but it was convenient for meetings like the one tonight.

"I'm mostly back to myself," Will told Charlie. "I'd like to stay that way, if possible."

"Well, that depends on what you're willing to let me do," Charlie said. "I've invited a couple of people you haven't met yet on my LA team. You didn't really give me enough time to fly people from my other bases, but you already know most of those guys and they're ready for whatever we decide."

"Thanks, Charlie," Will said, leading him indoors to the living room, which had a view of the sea through sliding walls of glass that led to an outside patio. "What do you want to drink?"

"Whiskey, neat, if you're having some," Charlie said.

"I just discovered Darkness, and I've grown to like it," Will said.

"Is that a metaphor?" Charlie asked.

"No, it's a single malt, from Speyside," Will grinned, walking over to the bar cart to get the bottle and two crystal whiskey glasses. He placed the bottle and glasses on the coffee table, opened the bottle and poured out a finger full for each of them. "It's an eight-year-old, sherried, very pleasant."

"Okay," Charlie said, taking the glass. "Wild Turkey works for me just fine, though."

"Now, *that*'s a metaphor," Will said, taking a sip from his glass.

"Yeah, it's good," Charlie said after tasting the drink. "So what are you setting me up for with all this pleasant Darkness?"

"I wanted to talk to you about Sandy," Will said.

"What about her?" Charlie's voice deepened by two octaves.

"Mariana wants me to bring her onboard, and I don't want to do it unless you say it's okay," Will said.

"Why?"

"Well, if you decide she's not someone you want around," Will said. "I don't want there to be any awkwardness."

"That's not an issue." Charlie shook his head.

"Are you sure?"

"I'm positive," Charlie said.

"Good, then I'm going to offer her a formal role in comms."

"That you can't do," Charlie said.

"What do you mean? I thought you said it was okay for me to bring her onboard."

"She's a Hawk, Will," Charlie said. "A crossover like Angel. You should bring her into your circle, make her aware of your identity and your plans, give her full security clearance—she can handle it, believe me—but she's mine."

"When did that happen?"

"She's my *wife*, Will," Charlie said. "She has been for months, pretty much since you sent me down to set up this pretty place for you. You remember when I called you about that threat to Mariana at the office? I knew about it because of her. Sandy already wore my collar. After we dealt with that, I took her to Vegas."

"How *did* you deal with that?" Will asked, knowing the answer but wanting to hear it from Charlie directly. "You never really said. You told me the threat was neutralized, and you didn't need the bounty for the hired hand."

"Both the culprit and the hired hand I had considered using were killed in an unfortunate sideshow," Charlie said, without mentioning his wife's role in it. Will was sorry Charlie wouldn't tell him what he already knew. Would he tell Charlie if Mariana had killed two men? Yes, he would. Nobody else, but he would tell Charlie. He'd have to ask for Charlie's help in the cleanup. That was the dark chasm between the two friends. "They are both dead, as are their associates," Charlie continued. "There's no trace of their evil left on the planet." And that was why Will still considered Charlie—Cailean, the killer—the best man he knew. Charlie hunted monsters. Somebody had to.

"Well, man, I have to say I wish you had at least mentioned you got married. I feel like a fool," Will said, "and I owe you a wedding present."

Charlie waved off the notion of a present with a sweep of one of his giant hands and made a face that was a cross between mirth and embarrassment.

"You've been busy almost being dead and all," Charlie said. "Besides, I didn't want to give you the satisfaction of wearing that knowing grin you have on your face. I also wanted you to decide to bring Sandy onboard because of who she is, not because she's my wife. Very few people know, Will. I want to keep it that way, especially if we're going to war now."

"If you're married, someone will find the records," Will said.

"I married her under my name," Charlie said. "Though I admit they won't have to stretch their imagination too far to figure out it's still me. It's not like I used an alias last name. Sandy has kept Fine, at least officially, so it's not too obvious. Sandy can defend herself, but I don't want her to have to; especially not now."

"What do you mean?"

"She's pregnant," Charlie said, grinning from ear to ear. "The damned girl only told me recently because she didn't want to distract me."

"Well, hell, let's toast to that," Will said, pouring them each another whiskey.

"Will, I know you know," Charlie said, after a long sip. "If you're going to pass judgment, let's talk about it."

"What do you mean?"

"Trying to bait me into telling you." Charlie shook his head. "Fine. She had no choice. They would have butchered her. They had been hunting her for a long time, but she had been expecting it. I'm fucking proud of what Sandy did, Will. I only wish I'd been there in time so she didn't need to do it, but I'm very glad she slit their throats and claimed their scalps for me. You don't get that shit, and I don't need you to get it. Just accept it. She's my property and my soul. Nobody will harm Sandy. No one will harm Mariana either. The Hawks will make damn fucking sure of it. You've got your rules you have to live by. I get that. But it's time to kill. They are gunning for you."

"Have you heard rumblings?" Will asked.

"You have heard them too." Charlie shrugged. "I've been waiting for you to call this meeting for days. They're trying to bait you by going after your assets first, to see what triggers you into a stupid move. They'll keep pulling strings until you twang. They want you to give them a justification, to paint you as the bad guy."

"I can't fight the government," Will said.

"You're not," Charlie said. "The government isn't behind it. It's not an official operation, or declared war. Anyone they have involved in this at the agencies is someone they can and will burn in an instant. They'll deny all knowledge. That works to our advantage. We just have to find and burn them first. Let the players know you're not playing. Shatter the board. It's time to kill, Will."

"Howard wants me to use the wedding as a Convocation of Eagles, to gather our forces and plan a viable defense," Will said. "It's only a few weeks away, but I just don't know if we have that long."

"Howard wouldn't lie to you, but he also wouldn't tell you the whole truth," Charlie said. "You know that, right?"

"Do you think Angel would?" Will asked.

"Yes, Angel picked sides a long time ago," Charlie said. "So did Jason, Percy, and Miranda. Tree—I don't know. He has his roots planted on both sides of the fence. Iris is... Iris. I can't make her out."

Angel, a former Navy SEAL, had signed-up for a contract with Charlie, finding the no-killing rules of Will's organization too restrictive. Jason, the youngest Fleming son, a Marine, had followed suit, joining Charlie's forces on the East Coast.

Percy, the second eldest Fleming son, had stuck to the family business—intelligence gathering. But after a falling out with the powers that be, he'd joined Will's organization. He headed up Will's West Coast 'gardening' branches from Seattle.

Miranda, the second eldest Fleming daughter, was also former Navy. After trying to work in analysis with her father, she had recently signed on to Charlie's West Coast team as a right hand to her brother Angel.

Tree was the Fleming's first-born son. He was Howard Fleming the Third. The family called him Three, but one of his smaller siblings couldn't pronounce it properly. Tree was such a silent man that the new nickname stuck. He worked directly with his father in the mostly private Fleming intelligence agency, which did some outsourced contract work for agencies with letters and agencies without.

Iris, the Fleming's eldest daughter, born only a year after Tree, was a silent mystery too. Ostensibly, she had no job. She was a floating socialite who hobnobbed with the upper crust and traveled often. Most likely, Iris had followed in her mother's footsteps, becoming a charming, beautiful, deadly assassin. Whenever Iris came up in conversation with Catherine, the woman always said, "Iris is being a rainbow." So it must always rain like hell wherever she was.

"I'm bringing Cathy home to New York," Will told Charlie.

"Claiming a hostage as safety," Charlie grinned. "Man, when you get old-fashioned, you *really* get old-fashioned."

"It's best for the girl, and Mariana could use some help at home," Will said.

"Bullshit," Charlie said. "I mean, it's a good excuse, but I'm sure Howard knows exactly what you're doing and why you're doing it. I'm positive that Catherine knows. What did she say, by the way?"

"She put her hands up to the angels and said, '*Que será, será*'."

"I don't think that's good," Charlie said. "You'll want to ask Angel what she might mean by that. You know she'll be the first to poison your coffee if any harm comes to her children. That being said, I don't think she's too happy about what's going on in the background. Catherine has a sweet spot for you. She'll *still* kill you, but she likes you very much. She might shed a tear."

"That's comforting, I guess." Will laughed.

Just then, Adams, their household agent, who served ostensibly as a butler, just as Quincy did in New York, came over from the staff house on the property. He wore the same black slacks and black shirt he always wore, though as a sign of the casual nature of this meeting, his top two shirt buttons were open. Adams was twenty years Will's senior, and had worked in the organization previously as a forester, developing sources and plants. He'd handled all his missions well, with minimal losses, and had a reputation for handling crises without being rattled. Only the recent kidnapping of Mariana from the shore below the Malibu house had finally unsettled the man, Will had learned from Angel. Adams was furious with the on-site security team for being duped. Of course, it hadn't been their fault. Tracey Whitby had set off alarms, which sent everyone running to the gates of the house just as the team on the shore grabbed Mariana from the boulders. Charlie had warned Will something like this might happen, when he first checked the house for defenses. But Mariana had mentioned she loved the idea of a house by the sea. He wanted to give her what she loved.

"Hello Mr. Wilson, Mr. Green," Adams said standing by the couch. "Sorry if I'm late. I made a few calls, as you instructed. I've got the vine on alert."

"You're just in time, Adams, and call me Will, please," Will said. "We're past formalities at this point."

"I think dinner will be here soon," Adams said. "I could have prepared something."

"Not tonight. You're part of the meeting so I don't want you distracted," Will said. "Besides, Charlie loves Chinese food, don't you, Charlie?"

"We could have just had In-N-Out for all I care," Charlie said.

Will gave Charlie a curious look.

"He means burgers and fries," Adams explained. "It's a chain here. It's good."

"Well, I see you've gone full California native," Will said. "Are you going to sell the old house in Connecticut?"

"I haven't decided yet," Charlie said. "A lot depends on what happens in the coming months."

"Join us, Adams," Will said, waving for the man to take a seat. "Whiskey?"

"Sure." Adams smiled. He went over to the bar cart to grab a glass before sitting opposite both men on the long, L-shaped couch.

"So what was the consensus among the foresters?" Will asked the senior agent.

"There was a certain level of anger," Adams said. "I'm sure Alfred will share more details on his thoughts when he arrives tonight. Some of them have worked on the home team before joining us, as you know. They can't believe some of the changes which have taken place, but we are not without allies. I think it's all temporary, anyway, but even a temporary threat has to be taken seriously."

"It was a stupid move, Will, letting them know you would give up so much to keep her safe," Charlie said. "The only thing that auction accomplished was making Mariana angry."

"It was sloppy, in retrospect," Will said. "I couldn't think of a better way to negotiate her immediate protection. I was putting the Zephyr technology on offer, at least that was the ploy. Howard said there might be some immediate push-back as soon as they knew Zephyr was self-aware. Grandfather worried about the same thing, and he'd just told me the truth about how my parents died. I didn't have time to have a sit down with everyone. It was only an offer of good faith to continue discussions. At least the Brits came through, but as you know everything went to shit when the Nótt hitman struck."

"I understand why you did it," Charlie said, "but look at it from their perspective: you have things they want, technologies they can't get their hands on, which would cost them too much and take them too long to develop. All they have to do is take them from you. Now, you've told them what to do to force your hand. They will not get *one* thing out of you. They are going to get *everything* out of you. The only advantage you have is that you hold those technologies now, and they don't. Protect what you own. Go after anyone trying to take your toys. Break them. They have to feel pain. They will try to make a move on Mariana, but we will keep her safe."

"Howard suggested I turn a blind eye to the missing inventories at the foundry, for now," Will said. "He advised against starting a war until we've had the Convocation of Eagles in Wales."

"So, two for the price of one? A wedding and a war meeting. Nice," Charlie poured out a second whiskey for all three men.

"It would allow some time to plan," Adams said.

"Time we may not have," Will argued.

"We'll discuss it with the others," Charlie said. "I have an ace up my sleeve—more than one—but there's one man I invited to join us tonight who could be really handy. He's a cold thinker, meticulous, and a persistent hunter. He won't leave a trace back to you, and he is very productive. We could set him on cutting off heads now, leaving the limbs disoriented, which will buy us time."

"I can't just sign off on this," Will said.

"You've never signed off on a single fucking thing I've done, William," Charlie barked. "I'm not asking. I'm telling you *my* options. What's the point of this meeting if you don't want to know? Just give us the information we need, go home to your wife, and let us loose. Or rewrite the damned rule-book, once and for all. Your precious ancestors never took it seriously, anyway."

"Hold up, Charlie," Will said. "When I say I can't just sign off, I mean I can't leave this with you and keep my hands clean. I have to get my hands dirty. I can't allow anyone to target Mariana to get to me. You and I work this one together, Charlie. I'll be claiming more than a pound of flesh."

"Well, it will be fun to have the White Wolf back in my pack," Charlie said. "I missed you, brother."

7

Salting the Soil

C harlie introduced Quinn as the newest member of his team, referred to the Hawks by Rick Curtis, who was also present.

Adams and Alfred briefed everyone on what the foresters knew about key threats at strategic companies within Will's group. They shared a list of known operatives and agencies, both public and private, who might spearhead the thefts of Will's intellectual property and assets, including the missing shipments of alloys.

Quinn listened intently, Will noticed, his face unreadable. When the two men finished their briefings, Quinn finally spoke up.

"How willing are you to be wrong?" he asked Will. His English was nearly perfect, but there was a slight rhythm to it which sounded Nordic to Will's ear.

"What do you mean?" Will asked.

"Do you only want to cut off the heads of organizations you know to be involved, or do you want to eliminate everyone on the suspects list?" Quinn replied. "There are advantages and disadvantages to both. Obviously, being sure is more just, but it also paints a nice trail back to you. If you want it to be known by those who would know, that's fine. Taking out suspects is quicker, no need to verify. It creates confusion as it's less certain who is behind it or why. It's less just, because you will take out some innocents, but nobody on this list is really innocent. Everyone on this list is guilty of something. They knew what they were getting into when they chose these careers."

There was a chilly detachment in the way Quinn weighed the options, which Will found strangely reassuring. This man did not dance in gray. He was black and white and saw things with clarity.

Will knew this was a war. There would be casualties. He just wanted to keep the numbers down on both sides.

"I would like to be more right than wrong, and I would like to keep more of us alive than them," Will replied. "I trust this team to use their judgement and find a balance."

Charlie had also been listening and watching, reading everyone at the table with his intense and deadly focus disguised behind a wry smile and occasional mocking jabs. Now, he shifted in his chair and put on the bright smile which usually made people feel very good, unless they knew him well.

"Right now, we need pandemonium," Charlie said. "We're trying to unsettle. We're trying to confuse the issue, to buy ourselves time. There will be time to get fancy after the Convocation. Our resources will quadruple and we will be more aware of any overseas actors. I say we just blitz the fuck out of anyone who might spearhead these thefts. Let's not start with the foundry. That's too obvious. Howard gave you a cover story for the missing shipments, he wants you to accept. So, accept it, for now. But there are some actors listed here in Adams and Alfred's list more than once, as likely suspects for different incursions. Which of these losses do you give less of a shit about?"

Will knew what Charlie had in mind, and it made sense. Make minor thefts too expensive to carry out, and you discourage larger thefts. Salt the soil so nothing grows.

"The medical units are harmless," Will said. "I don't know of many ways in which they could use those for nefarious purposes, except if they are reverse engineered by the majors and priced high. We could always undermine those sales, but the bastards have charged us with patent violations before for products they stole from us. I'd start with them."

"Big Pharma has deep pockets," Charlie pointed out.

"True, but they also have a lot of rival firms acting for them, and some of those are on our suspects list for other thefts," Will said. "We'd be taking out various threats with each kill."

"What if I could make it look as though it's an internal war between those players?" Quinn asked. "Do you want a signature that sends a message from you or not?"

"Could you set it up so they're too busy fighting each other to mess with us? I need to buy a month, or a month and a half at most. Then we can declare war outright," Will asked. "And by war I mean making anyone regret targeting any company even remotely connected to our group."

Quinn grinned a disquieting sort of twisted smile which revealed prominent canines and dead eyes. Will knew this man was, as advertised, a cold, meticulous and calculating killer. "A few of these names are familiar. Right, Rick?"

Rick Curtis, the colossal bear of a man whom Charlie had also invited to join their meeting, was deceptively easy going and chill. Will understood from Charlie that Rick had referred Quinn to the Hawks, and that they both had a history on joint special forces operations going back to Afghanistan.

"Yeah," Rick said. "We know which strings to pull. If you want it to look like they're at each other's throats. We could do that. Be careful with Crowe, though. Don't mess with that bitch, at least not for now. She'll send the devil to skin your entire family."

"Rick is talking from experience, Will," Charlie warned. "He was on Crowe's team before he came to us, back when I had that disagreement with the Chimera. Do you remember?"

"What you told me of it, yes," Will said.

Calling it a disagreement was a typical Charlie Green understatement. The Chimera tried a hostile takeover of Charlie's operation, and the two private armies were at war with each other for a while. Charlie won, and came out stronger for it, but it was a hard-fought battle.

Will knew little about Cynthia Crowe and her private espionage firm, other than they danced between darkness and light. Crowe did enough legitimate business that people didn't notice her picking on carcasses.

"Rick helped us out by sharing a list of Chimera operatives he'd taken from his time working for Crowe," Charlie explained. "The list saved a lot of lives, but Crowe didn't take that betrayal well."

"She had my mother, sister and grandmother slaughtered by a monster who is now resting in pieces," Rick explained. "Whenever you are ready to take Crowe off the map, I'm the one who will do it."

"Not alone, Rick," Charlie said. "You'll have us all to back you. But you're right. Now is not the time to mess with the mad witch. Let's leave her for dessert. I hear she's sweet, anyway."

"Like ambrosia, laced with arsenic," Quinn said.

"Okay, so while you are taking out these side-players and causing a war among the filth, what do I do?" Will asked.

"You take care of your wife, asshole," Charlie said. "Plan your fucking second-wedding slash Convocation and leave us to do our jobs."

"No, Charlie, I've already told you. I am going to be by your side on this," Will said. "You have as much to lose as I do, if this goes wrong."

"It won't," Quinn said, "not if you follow our lead. Let me and Rick plan this tidy. The rest of you keep us informed of any changes, give us your support and backup. It would be best if you keep clear, at least initially. The two of us have nothing to lose. You three have families to watch over."

Quinn included Angel in the three which was a surprise.

"Angel, you too?" Will asked.

"Yep, Marisol is pregnant." Angel smiled. "But she's got the whole Fleming clan and my mother's reputation keeping her safe. I can afford to get my hands dirty."

"Do you see any trouble for the Flemings, in any of what we've discussed?" Will was really only asking about one Fleming, Howard senior, possibly two, with Tree. Will was sure the others would understand why he couldn't just sit on his hands.

"If you steer clear of Crowe, and turn a blind eye to the foundry, for now, you're golden with the rest of this list," Angel said. "You won't be able to keep up the pretense for long. Someone will put together that they all share activities in your various companies and put us all on a list if this goes too far."

"But we'd know before we make the list, right?" Will said.

"That depends," Angel said. "Tree would warn me right away if there was any buzz. Father wouldn't. But neither of them are hearing as much buzz as they once did. There are factions growing that don't like the old guard."

"Tree is new guard," Will said.

"Not really. He has principles." Angel shrugged. "Things

are getting very muddy on home base, but father says it's just a passing storm. Tree is less confident."

"I want to have a long talk with Tree in Wales," Will said.

"Good luck with that," Angel said. "Unless you mean you would like to talk for a long time and have Tree listen."

"I've got Tree to talk before, Angel," Will said. "I think I can squeeze a few words from him again."

"You'll have to explain how you do that." Angel smiled. "Some day."

"Tree and I have a lot more in common than you think," Will replied.

"That's true," Charlie laughed. "Neither one of them can get their wives to behave. My, my, my, my Sharona."

"It's Xirona," Angel corrected.

"What did Xirona do this time?" Will asked, ignoring Charlie's knock for his own handling of Mariana.

"Nothing," Angel said. "She went to Naples for the season, to debut her fashion new line, and crossed the path of some unsavory types at a party. Tree couldn't go with her on this trip, so Charlie had sent some Hawks to watch her back. There was a bit of a scuffle and she ran away from her guards in all the confusion. It took a while to find her again because she lost her necklace, but she called Tree for help after the dust settled. They brought her home safely."

"This was unrelated to any Nótt aftermath?" Will asked Charlie.

"Yes, it was just local Naples crap," Charlie said. "She just gravitates to trouble. Nótt is not active anymore, as far as we know. Greystone says they're just digging in the dirt waiting, but we're waiting too. I don't think they made a link to Tree, anyway, though he was at your little party. Xirona wasn't there so they wouldn't have identified her."

"Are we done here?" Quinn asked, bringing everyone

back to the agenda of the meeting. "Can Rick and I count on your support for our play?"

"You have a green light and all the funding you need," Will said. "Charlie is in charge of the operation, of course. Alfred will be your contact, on our end. He'll keep you and Rick up to date on our intelligence in the field, in case of any changes."

Will noticed Alfred wince at the suggestion. He was missing something.

"What's wrong?" Will asked Alfred. "You've both been fairly quiet. Do you object to the plan?"

"I'm happy with the plan," Adams said. "It's about time we shook the leaves a bit."

"Alfred?" Will insisted. The man remained silent, his firm jaw clamped.

"Alfred hates my guts," Rick said, smiling.

"For any good reason I should know about?" Will asked.

"I have no objection," Alfred said, finally.

"We will not have a problem, right?" Charlie asked.

"No problem on my end," Rick said.

"No," Alfred said, curtly.

"What the fuck is it?" Will asked, exasperated. The last thing he needed was for everything to go to pot because of a petty squabble between the Hawk and the Gardener he didn't know about. "You need to be of one mind in this. You need to trust each other. This isn't a game."

"William, I know what I need to do," Alfred seethed. "I will do it."

"Somebody better tell me what is wrong," Will growled. "I'm not at ease."

Rick looked to Alfred, and Alfred stared him down for a moment, then Alfred turned to Will.

"It is a petty personal matter," Alfred said. "It won't affect my ability to do my job."

Charlie laughed, "Do you still have a hard-on for Rick because of that little misunderstanding at The Unkindness? That was more than a year ago, man."

Alfred turned his full intensity on Charlie, his voice steaming. "If Rick had had a similar little misunderstanding with Sandy, what would be your statute of limitation on a grudge?"

Charlie had no ready answer, but his amiable smile vanished.

"Is this all about a girl?" Will asked.

"Look, we may as well get this out of the way." Rick sighed. "I was wrong, Alfred. I should never have spoken to, or looked at your sweet, sweet Susana. I was clumsy and maybe a little too horny, and I broke the code. She's beautiful, admit that. If you don't want her to be approached at gatherings, then keep the chain around her neck tied to your cock."

Alfred turned a deep shade of red, nearly purple.

"This is all too much information for me," Will said. "I do not know what you get up to at these events, and I don't care. If they interfere with work, then that's no good."

"Will is right," Charlie said. "I put together the gatherings to help you all work off some steam, not to blow up the works. You're right, Alfred. I would never let Rick within a hundred feet of Sandy again in his life if he had done the same to her. However, Rick is also right. I keep Sandy's chain short for a reason. Now, you two shake hands, and let's never speak of Susana again."

"Speaking of Susana," Angel said, as if Charlie hadn't just insisted that they drop the subject. "Are you just going to keep playing house with my little cousin or what?"

"Oh, she's your cousin!" Rick smiled. "I figured something like that, or an ex-girlfriend."

"Can we *not* discuss this right now?" Alfred asked Angel.

"You should take some tips from Jenkins," Rick said. "He knows how to claim his property. Took a frisky kitten right out from under me."

"Oh, for fuck's sake!" Will had had enough. "Men, there are lives and livelihoods on the line here. I need to know that whatever is going on in your colorful sex lives will not cause us grief."

"Yes, because *your* colorful sex life hasn't caused us any care in the slightest." Charlie smirked.

"Charlie." William gave his friend a dark look.

"William," Charlie replied, unfazed. "Life is messy. Sex is messier. Killing is messiest. We know how to clean up. Okay? We've got this. Let it go."

After everyone else left, Will and Oliver sat out on the patio by the fire pit, and caught up on everything that had happened since their time together in Finland.

Oliver had let his beard grow bushy and his hair grow long, held back with a green elastic in a tiny ponytail which poked out from under his gray beanie—all to win over Caroline Boots, assistant to Martin Harper the CEO of PlayTech and Mariana's former lover.

Will found it difficult to understand how a woman who had an affair with Robert Whitby and worked with Martin Harper might fall for the hipster activist that Oliver played. He'd trusted the HARPO profile, when it suggested this disguise would appeal to a suppressed desire, luring her away from Whitby. They hadn't been wrong. The real question was what would happen when Oliver eventually had to go back to being Oliver.

"You're going to give Grandmother a fright," Will said.

Oliver chuckled. "She loves me as I am. Besides, I'm

getting really comfortable in this persona. I might get a tattoo."

"No tattoos and no piercings," Will said, reminding him of the rules. "Nothing permanent. You can be identified too easily."

"Hawks get to have tattoos. And piercings. And guns," Oliver grumbled. He was mostly joking, though the young man had a running fantasy about being a killer instead of a hacker. No doubt he could do both, but they needed his brain far more than his brawn.

"Is she on the hook for good, then?" Will asked.

"Yes, she was angry about my missing dinner tonight," Oliver said. "Caroline's a really sweet girl, you know. With the right guidance, she'll be fine to help us manage the transition at PlayTech."

"Are you going to be around for that?"

"I'm not sure. How soon is it happening?"

"Any day now," Will said. "Of course, with all this going on... But Tom feels it's on track, so I trust it will be."

"Who will head up the company?"

"I was hoping you would," Will said, "Do you think Caroline can cope with you revealing your true identity, or would it cause a mess? The whole point was keeping her with us. Simmons says PlayTech is much more your cup of tea than his. He's got other things to manage at X-Sci-Gens."

"I'm going to put Janet Breuil in charge at Aidos. She's more than ready, but we'll need someone sharp to manage some threats we reviewed tonight. There's a lot we could do with cyber to even out the odds, you know. We could really fuck with some people if we went on the offensive. It might be time. As for Caroline, I'll enjoy seeing the look on her face when she walks into the office to find me transformed." Oliver smiled. "I'm sick of the beard and hate playing her for a fool. She isn't. She's a very smart woman. Mariana was right. It's not good to play with the heart."

"So it's become serious, then?"

Oliver nodded. "Do you think Tracey might come back to us? I could use the Reaper on our team."

"Howard wants her too," Will said

"No, absolutely not," Oliver said. "If she's ready to go back, she works for me and no one else."

"Jonathan might have something to say about it," Will said.

"Look, I know you have her tucked away at the Phoenix Lodge because she was really in an awful state—so were both of them—but I don't see her getting better unless she's swimming in the depths of the dark sea. She needs to be in the cyberworld. It's where she can truly breathe. Besides, Zephyr misses her, I think."

"Seriously, now?" Will asked. He'd accepted that the AI Oliver's father had developed had become self-aware, but it was still difficult to attribute any emotions to her.

"She queries an old address frequently," Oliver nodded. "Like she's hoping for the Reaper to send a message."

"Okay, I'll have a talk with the specialists looking after Tracey and Jonathan," Will said.

"We could find a home for both of them near us, in San Francisco," Oliver said. "That way, if anything goes wrong, they won't be without a support network."

"We?"

"Caroline and I." Oliver smiled.

"Next, you'll be asking if she can come to the wedding," Will said.

"Actually…" Oliver started.

"Let's see how the last play on PlayTech goes first," Will said. "You may no longer be together by the time we gather in Wales."

"I doubt that," Oliver said.

"And if you're wrong?"

"I'm not," Oliver said.

"Ah, the magical Greystone charm," Will joked.

"Yes, Grandfather just oozes charm," Oliver said.

"Grandmother seems fond of him, for all his asperity," Will said.

"Perhaps because of it," Oliver suggested.

They both laughed.

"All right," Will said. "Just get everything ready and have Zephyr on alert. We'll talk more about your cyber attack strategy in the morning before you go. I'm exhausted, and maybe even a little drunk."

―――――

Will called Mariana before going to sleep. It felt odd lying alone on the bed which he had only ever shared with her, which had been hers when she was alone. This entire house felt strange without her. Everything felt hollow when Mariana wasn't there.

"*Hola Papi.*" She sounded hoarse. He had woken her up, and he felt like a heel.

"I'm sorry it took me so long to finish," Will said. "How are you feeling?"

"Lonely, though less lonely," Mariana said. "I've got the peas sleeping with me now."

"I should be there," Will said.

"Yes, you should." Mariana yawned. "Where are you?"

"I'm in your bed," Will said.

"Is that you imagining yourself here?"

"Yes," Will said. It was quicker than explaining the truth. He could tell she was still very sleepy.

"I'm going to put the phone by the bump. You want to say goodnight?"

"Don't do that," Will said. "I don't like you putting the phone by your womb."

"I'm sure it's safe, Will," Mariana said. "It's by my head all the time, and that doesn't bother you."

"Who says it doesn't bother me? I don't carry a phone. You know I hate gadgets. You only have one because you insist on it."

"Stop fussing," Mariana said. "You're upset over something else. What is it?"

"I'll tell you when I'm home," Will said.

"And when will that be?"

"Soon, I promise," Will said. "Go back to sleep, darling. I love you all."

"Is it really bad, Will? Would you tell me if it was?"

"Yes," Will said. "Go to sleep, though, you have angels watching over you."

"How *is* Angel?" She was baiting him. Too smart for her own good.

"Go to sleep."

8

In the Nettles

Two weeks later

Mariana awoke in the middle of the night to find the bed empty, only a dent in the pillow where her husband's head should be. She'd spent most of the afternoon and evening alone, while Will was up in his bat cave on the fourth floor, dealing with whatever had Quincy clearly antsy.

She had at least enjoyed having him in bed at night. Now that peace had been shattered again, and Mariana knew there was more to it than the Sandra problem.

She made her way from the bedroom to the sitting room down the hall to check on him, but as she passed the bathroom nature called, and it took another few minutes before she finally made it. Will stood by the desk, in his pajama pants and bare chest, talking in hushed tones on the telephone.

"If anything goes wrong..."

"What goes wrong, honey?" Mariana asked, coming up behind him. "What are you doing here so late? Who are you talking to, Will?"

"It's nothing, baby," he said. "Go to bed. I'll be right there with you." Whoever Will was talking to obviously wrapped up the conversation, because Will just said, "Goodnight," and hung-up.

"Who was that, Will?"

"One of my team," Will said, without elaborating. "It was just an update on an operation."

"Is it dangerous?"

"They always are, darling," he said and kissed her head, "you know that."

"Is it why the lake house is out of bounds?"

"Let's not talk about it now," Will said. "You need your sleep. Come on."

He nudged her out of the sitting room and they both walked back to the bedroom in their suite, getting back under the covers. Will was trying to act cool, but it did not persuade Mariana. Even in the low light, she could see how tightly he clenched his jaw.

"Come here," Will said, pulling Mariana closer as they lay in bed.

"No," Mariana said. "I'm mad at you."

"Puppy."

"Don't call me puppy."

"Kitten."

"Will, for the love of turnips! Leave me alone."

"No."

"*What?*"

"No. I won't leave you alone," Will said. "My job is not to leave you alone. I will do my job, even when you don't like it."

"So why won't you tell me more about this operation? The dangerous one which you are obviously so concerned about."

"I'm not concerned about *it*, I'm concerned about you. Now come here. Don't pout."

"I'm not pouting, Will," Mariana snapped, "and don't patronize me."

"You are pouting," Will said. "Just a little, but you are. See, right here, your lip is poking out a little, right there. Here, I'll kiss it, maybe it won't swell so much."

"Will, I'm more than just a nice round ass and a firm pair of tits, you know," Mariana said.

"I know that, Mariana."

"Stop smiling like that! I'm being serious!"

"I know, sweetheart." Will took her hand in his and kissed her palm. "I take you seriously. You know that."

"Not right now you don't."

"Well, right now I'm distracted," Will said, bringing her hand down to feel his erection. "That's my fault, not yours. You could help me, you know, so I can focus."

"No," Mariana said.

"Very well, I'll have to suffer then."

"Unbelievable." Mariana sat up on the bed, crossing her arms.

"No, really, see for yourself," Will brought her hand back under his pajamas.

She pulled her hand away, *"Déjame en paz."*

"No te puedo dejar en paz, hasta que tu no me dejes a mi en paz," Will said, knowing damn well the effect his Castilian accent had on her. *"Con esto no duermo, ya tu lo sabes."*

"Why can't you just tell me what is dangerous, Will?"

"I used the wrong term." He sighed. "I didn't mean dangerous to you or to the babies. I only meant tricky. It's a tricky proposal, Mariana, what my agent suggested. I'm not sure I like it."

"What is it?"

Will sighed. "Just tangling with a firm that has some

murky connections. It's not part of the plan I agreed on with Charlie. I don't like murky waters. I like clear springs."

"What does any of that mean?"

"Nothing. It's only code." Will rose to put his arm around his wife. "But no code cracking, please, Mariana." He kissed her shoulder. "It's the middle of the night, and you're grumpy. Let's get you not-grumpy again, please?"

"Will, you promised not to leave me in the dark!"

"I'm not leaving you in the dark," Will said. "I'm trying to join with you in the dark. Besides, I also told you I decide what you need to know."

"Are you *ever* going to tell me everything?"

"How do you mean?"

"You know what I mean."

"Here's everything," Will said and kissed her neck. "I adore you. I want to always ensure you are happy." He stroked her back. "I want to always ensure the children are well. I am always going to keep you and the children safe." He kissed her gently. Then he smiled and continued, "However, I am very aroused right now, and I need your help to do something about it, or else I will have to handle it myself."

"*¡Dios mío, este hombre!*"

"Mariana." He bit her earlobe. "I know a secret."

"Keep it to yourself, along with the others."

"Now you're just being mean and denying yourself to spite me." Will reached down under her nightgown, caressing her thighs gently as he worked his way up to slip his fingers under the gusset of her panties.

"Will."

"Mariana."

"Why don't you trust me?"

"I do trust you, Mariana, with my life, or you wouldn't be my wife. Believe me."

"So why do you keep so many secrets from me?"

"Because *Silence is Golden*, Mariana." Will repeated his family motto, his voice deepening into a reprimand. "I've explained it to you many times before."

"Do you know how many of my clients trust me with their deepest, darkest secrets, Will? I've never betrayed any."

"I know that, Mariana. You're a very honorable woman. That's why I love you."

"You don't respect me." She smacked his arm.

"What a ridiculous thing to say. You know I do."

"No, you don't. If you did, you would just speak plainly and tell me what is going on."

He leaned in closer to her then, right up to her ear, and whispered, "There are always termites in the wood."

"What?"

"It is safer this way," Will said. "Trust my wisdom, it comes from experience. I don't question your wisdom in your business. Don't question mine on this."

"Are you saying..."

Will silenced her with a gentle probing kiss, which she fought at first, then yielded. After, she leaned into his ear and whispered, "Aren't we safe in our own home, anymore?"

He whispered back, "Absolutely, but we must maintain good practices at all times, especially now."

"But..."

"No buts, Mariana," Will said. "The question is whether *you* trust *me*." He grabbed her chin and brought his nose up to hers. "I am Will, your husband, look me in the eye and tell me—do you trust me?"

She hesitated, but not for long. She always saw truth in his eyes. "Yes. I do."

"Good. I trust you too, Mariana. Believe me. I trust you with my life."

Mariana turned on the bed to straddle him, pushed him back against the mattress and kissed him, teasing his tongue until their joint breath turned to fire as a raw, urgent hunger overcame them.

She caressed his muscular chest, and kissed the shadow of his bullet wound, planting more kisses on his prominent abs. She pulled down on the waistband of his pajamas, exposing the hard V of his lower abdomen, until his erection sprang free. "Let's ensure you get a decent night's rest," Mariana said, licking the pre-cum then taking his cock deep in her mouth.

He pulled her head back. "I love your mouth, but I need your pussy," he said, his voice raspy and demanding.

She made quick work of removing her panties and lowered herself onto Will's shaft.

"*Ay, Mariana*," he sighed. "*Tienes un coño de seda.*"

"*Llamame, Mami,*" Mariana said, bringing his hands around her ass as she rode him slowly.

"*Mamita linda, hermosa,*" Will said. "*Mi gata. Coqueta. Mi nena majadera.*" He slipped in a little reprimand, slapping her butt gently, calling her his naughty girl.

"*Ay, Papi, no me regañes cuando te estoy follando tan tiernamente,*" she protested. "I am trying to be good. *You* make me bad."

"I'll make you better," he said, thrusting up to reach her depths. "Take off your nightgown, Mariana. I want to see all of you."

Mariana slipped off the silk chemise, pulling it over her head and exposing her growing breasts and swelling belly. She tossed the garment over the side of the bed and arched her back to grab his thighs behind her, steadying herself as she rocked on his hips and set herself loose. They built up rhythm in a heated dance of abandon, her warm sheath swallowing his hot steel. She impaled herself upon him over and over until she was right on the edge of falling. Will's fingers slipped between them to press her button, and her thighs tightened around him. She raised her arms and dug her fingers into her wild mane as the shudder of completion rocked her body.

"Fuck," Will cried out, reaching his climax. "Fucking hell."

"What's wrong?" Mariana asked, bending over him to brush her lips against his.

"I'm going to wind up burning down the world for you, Mariana," he said.

"Don't," she said and kissed his chest wound. "We need somewhere for the peas to grow up."

"I'm going to deserve you someday, wife." Will wrapped his arms around her tight.

"Don't be silly," she said, kissing his neck. "Just don't leave me. I'm afraid I might char the world myself if I lost you."

"You won't," Will said, kissing her head. "If I am ever really gone, do what Nana Smith did. Put the whole thing on auto-pilot with the Executive Committee, accept some losses, the assets will always grow back and you'll never go hungry. Move somewhere quiet, somewhere where the children can grow free and healthy. Look after yourself and have a good life. Trust Charlie to protect you from your enemies. If he's gone, trust Sandy and Angel. Trust no one else entirely."

"Except Marsha, you mean," Mariana said, referring to Will's cousin and Mariana's college friend, who lived with her husband, Tom Waters, in Palo Alto. "She's been my friend longer than I've known you."

"Marsha is a wonderful woman, and she has many talents, but she thrives in the gray and is comfortable with compromise," Will said. "If I'm dead, you'll need people behind you who won't equivocate, who act in black and white. The only truly safe place for all of you would be with Lord and Lady Greystone, in Castle Gwaed. Promise me you'd go to them while the children are small, if things became too dangerous here."

Mariana gripped him tight. "Will, you're scaring me. How bad are things getting, really?"

"It's no worse than we might expect, Mariana," Will said, stroking her back. "It's not about that."

"What is it, then?" She kissed his chest wound again, suspecting it had something to do with Will's sudden dark mood.

"When I was sure I was dying, back in Nice, I was furious with myself," Will said.

"You're kidding, right?" Mariana faced him. "You found time to make a joke before passing out on me. I was the one who was angry, Will. I am *still* angry when I think about it."

"I was only trying to stop your crying because I couldn't bear it," Will said. "That was a worse pain than the bullet in my chest. But all I could think about was that I had let you down. I had fucked up. We never talked about what you should do when I'm gone. I didn't think I'd need to have that conversation. Now, I'm making sure you know. That way, if things go wrong again, I can die in peace."

"I hate this whole thing, Will." Mariana sat up. "I'm here, sitting on you, we're both naked, you're still inside of me, even if just barely, and you're talking about dying in peace. Don't you dare die, William Wilson Smith!" She slapped his face hard enough for the sound to shock them both.

"Did you just *slap* me?" Will said, smacking her rump. "*Again?* I can still get a ruler, you know. I'll have you standing by the desk in a minute if you don't apologize immediately."

The last time Mariana had slapped Will hard was in The Pierre, back when she thought he was having an affair with one of his agents. He definitely wasn't, and it turned out the agent was Penelope Pink, Quincy and Pam's daughter, who was really a very sweet girl. Will had spanked her with the ruler as punishment. The sting had been intense; she remembered. She wasn't really eager to feel that searing pain again.

But she was also sick of Will's shit, taking risks and only sharing information when he thought he should. He'd put her through hell in Nice, and in the days that followed, when she thought he was dead. Will had never really apologized for *that*.

"I will *not* apologize," Mariana said, crossing her arms over her swollen breasts. "You *earned* it, Will. You're being an *ass*. Do you think I need to be told how to protect my children? I will do *anything* to keep them safe. And I have news for you, mister. If anyone kills you, they will soon learn that they should never have fucked with us. I will definitely have someone hunt down every motherfucker remotely responsible until there is no one left who will touch the Wilson Smiths, or whatever we're calling ourselves. Anywhere. Ever. Do you understand?"

"*Fiera salerosa*," he growled. "*Te voy a pelar el culo.*"

His outrage was belied by him calling her a "*charming wild beast*" and the fact that his dick had gone hard inside her again. The threat to skin her bottom might be genuine.

"I don't think that's what you want, Will," she teased, shifting her hips to take him in deeper.

"That's where you're mistaken." Will grabbed her hips tight to stop her grinding. "Tom only perked up at the memory of you bent over the arm of the couch, getting your bare ass striped hot pink by my ruler. I have a better one at this desk, slimmer, more flexible, like a whip. It will stripe that watermelon of yours a lovely shade of magenta. You should never forget that I enjoy disciplining you, Mariana, as much as you enjoy being disciplined. I will not allow you to slap me, without paying a price. It doesn't matter whether you believe I earned it."

"*Está bien*," Mariana said, dismounting him and getting off the bed, recovering her nightie from the floor and putting it back on. "If it makes you happy. Stripe my ass red if you please. But I will *still* kill anyone who gets in our way, and I'll chase you to Hell or Heaven, or wherever you're hiding, and I will slap your ghost."

"Time for a hiding, I guess," Will said. He followed her out of bed, his erection tenting the pajama pants he put on until he tucked the head under the waistband. "I think you need this."

"I think *you* do," Mariana said, walking ahead of him to the desk in the sitting room.

Mariana opened the drawer to search through the orderly stationery supplies stored there—monogram letter-head, a fancy black pen set, a box of pencils and a small blue notepad, other bits, and a 24-inch wood ruler with, as Will said, a very slim profile. Maybe it would break before she did.

"Here you go, Daddy," she said, sticking her tongue out as she handed him the ruler. Then she immediately bent over, with her palms pressed on the edge of the desk, waiting for him.

"What the fuck," Will sighed, standing behind her, lifting the bottom of her nightgown up and over her waist, exposing her bare ass. "I know you've gone out of your way to earn this, Mariana, but I just don't understand why."

"You don't?" Mariana asked. "Well, what does it matter."

"Is it because you're scared?" he asked, stroking her butt gently with his palm.

"*¡Pégame en el culo, joder!*" Mariana snapped, refusing to answer his question.

"Fine," Will said, bringing the ruler to the fullness of her ass, then flicking it quickly and soundly. The hissing of a sharp intake of breath followed the snap of the thin wood against her flesh. The stinging sensation seared her nerves and spread through her body, raising the fine hairs on her arms. Mariana refused to cry out as each strike fell. She would not make this easy for Will. While the wood was light, Will's strong wrist put a lot of power behind it. He was right, it felt like a whip. Her skin burned. The world blurred around her as tears filled her eyes. She waited for him to strike again, but she saw a blurry shadow of her husband moving to the other side of the desk, to put the ruler away.

Will bent over the desk facing her, his hands next to hers, his pinkie caressing her. He kissed her tear-drenched nose. "*Majadera*," he chided. "*Te amo*." He kissed her damp lips. "We're even now. You hurt me. I hurt you. We hurt each other. Okay?"

"I want to hate you so badly." Mariana's voice cracked on the words.

"No, you don't," Will whispered.

"No, I don't," she conceded, whimpering.

"Can I have my sweet wife back, please?" Will asked. "I need her desperately. Do you know where she might be hiding?"

"Will, please," Mariana cried.

Will rushed over to her side of the desk, picked her up, and sat on the couch with her on his lap. He wrapped her in his arms, and she cried against his chest. "Don't be afraid, baby," he said. "I'm going to make it right."

"We're never going to have Vermont, are we?" Mariana asked.

When she'd first gotten together with Will in Connecticut, during the whirlwind week that they married, he had taken her to a hill where he planned to build a house just for them, overlooking an abandoned town in Vermont which he said he aimed to transform into a self-sustaining community, for people who needed a fresh start. It was a project he wanted to work on with her, reviving ghost towns by bringing back employers. It seemed like a crazy ambition because Mariana only knew about Will Smith, the arborist. Somehow now, knowing William Wilson Smith, the spy, it seemed even crazier. How could he hope to gain support for any of that if he was in the middle of a war for control over the empire he held, if those who toyed with power wanted him dead and gone?

"I have not forgotten about Vermont," Will said. "It seems more important than ever now, with the babies on the way. I'd rather be a nobody, lost with you and the children in our house on that hill than be a magnate or a spy anywhere. I just have to clear the terrain. We need to be on steadier footing."

"Make it right, *Papi*," she begged him. "Make it all right and let's just disappear in the woods."

"You don't mean that." Will kissed her head. "What about your business? And you like it here in Manhattan. I know you do."

"I like the lake house in Connecticut too, and now we can't even *go* there," Mariana said. "Just make it right, so we can be whoever we want, wherever we like, whenever we please. Otherwise, what's the point of all your money?"

"It's not my money," Will put his hand on her belly. "It's their money, and that's the point of it. I *will* make it *all* right. I promise."

"I'll hold you to that, Will," Mariana said.

"Can we go back to bed now?" Will kissed her. "And be nice to each other again?"

"Only if you plan to fuck me unconscious." Mariana kissed him back.

"Oh, absolutely, darling," Will said, rising to carry his wife back to bed.

9

Under Pressure

M onday's check-in with the doctor showed the babies were developing well, which made both Will and Mariana happy, but Mariana's physical hinted at some trouble.

"I'd like you to watch your pressure a bit," Dr. Austin warned. "It's high. There's a risk of pre-eclampsia later in the pregnancy. You need to be monitoring that regularly and your swelling ankles. I'm worried you may be prone to edema—retaining water."

"Is it still okay for her to travel by air?" Will asked. "If Mariana is in any danger by traveling, we'll cancel the wedding."

"No need to cancel your plans," the doctor said. "It should be fine. I'm only making you aware of a slight risk. For now, it's only something to be mindful of. You need to relax as much as possible, Mariana. That's all."

"Okay," Mariana said, not wanting to go into why she couldn't 'just relax' with the doctor. Will knew. She could see it on his face.

When they were back home, Will followed her to her office for a serious sit-down.

"You need to get help with your work, Mariana. You can't keep pushing yourself."

"It's fine, Will," Mariana said. "You heard what Dr. Austin said. It's only a warning. I'll be mindful of it, but I've already left enough up to Sandy and Laurel. I can't let go completely."

"I'm only suggesting that you let Laurel carry more of the weight," Will said. "She is extremely clever and resourceful. You don't have to worry about secrets with her because she's already part of my organization. If you clue her in on what you need, she can take it from there and report back to you."

"Maybe she'll clue me in on all the blanks you leave me with," Mariana said, unable to keep a bit of spite out of her tone.

"No, she can't," Will said. "She doesn't know the blanks and don't set her on filling them. It won't help. Trust me. It will harm. I have to take care of some things upstairs before lunch, but please take it easy with work." He kissed her shoulder. "Everything will be fine if you do what I say."

Will seemed to be set on helping her get rid of stress that evening. They had a light meal then watched a couple of classic movies together, which was a new thing with Will. By the time the credits rolled on *Charade*, they were kissing on the sofa like two kids on a first date, getting hot and bothered. Will shut off the television, closing the mural which hid it, and led his wife upstairs by the hand. They were kissing in the hallway before they even reached their bedroom door. Will picked Mariana up and carried her all the way to bed like she didn't weigh an ounce more than she had when they first met. *Show off.* Mariana wasn't complaining. She hung her arms around his shoulders, smiling a flirty smile. "Cave man."

"Me Tarzan. You *Juana*," he said, uttering the guttural hard 'j' like a hungry growl.

"Yes, I *Juana* very much," she joked. "I *Juana* right now."

"Give me a minute," he said, laying her down gently on the mattress.

"Where are you going?" she complained. "I'm scorching and bothered and wet, you know."

"Start without me." Will grinned. "I'm just getting something I need and I'll be right back."

"Ooh, a mystery," Mariana purred, kicking off her shoes and unbuttoning her blouse seductively. Will forgot, for a moment, that he intended to go and just stood by the side of the bed enjoying the show.

"God, you have great tits," Will said. "I mean, they were always perfection but now they are…" He breathed deep. "A bounteous wonder of nature."

"You sure know how to sweet talk a girl, Tarzan," Mariana cooed with a Southern twang.

"Yes, about that," Will said, and left the room.

Mariana giggled and made quick work of turning down the bed and getting naked. Whatever Will was up to, Mariana was confident she would enjoy it.

He came back with a bottle of exotic oil, which he placed on the night table by his side of the bed before undressing. Now it was Mariana's turn to enjoy the show, and what a show it was.

Will's body was a perfect symphony of well-trained muscles, strong, broad pecs above a well-defined six-pack and that V, that magical, wondrous V leading the eyes to what, in her considerable experience, was definitely one of the best dicks nature had ever crafted. His arms flexed as he joined her on the bed, kneeling over her, one knee on either side of her hips and one fist down on either side of her head.

"*Juana* play?" he said.

Mariana giggled. "Please, Will, don't…" She didn't want to laugh she wanted to get that hard dick working its miracles inside her.

"I Tarzan. You dry."

"No, I soaked," she said. "Trust me. Tarzan check."

He savored her mouth, silencing her with a prolonged exploration of her tongue, which left her breathless and reeling.

"*Ay, por favor, Will…*"

"*Tarzán.*" He growled, with that Castilian 'z' she loved so much, his eyes fixed on hers.

"*Por favor, Tarzán, dame en la cola.*"

"Oil first," he said, with a wicked grin. Reaching for the bottle, he rose above her, his erect penis near enough for her to raise her head to lick the pre-cum from the tip. "Do I have to tie you down for this?" he asked, his growl intensifying. "I'd rather not. I'd rather *Juana* behaves."

"I can be good." Mariana put on an innocent face. "But Tom could be better."

"Tom's fine," Will said, unscrewing the gold top on the bottle.

"I know," Mariana replied. "Tom is very fine indeed. What is that?"

"It's coconut oil with Dilo," he said, dripping a long stream of the richly scented liquid right down her middle, from her clavicle to her belly button. "It will make your skin smooth and help you relax. I have a soothing cream too, for aftercare. The villagers sent it to me through a friend."

"What villagers?"

"The ones who live on our island in Fiji," Will said.

"You have an island in Fiji?" Mariana rose on her elbows.

"*We* have a home on an island in Fiji," Will said, pushing her back down and gently working the oil around her chest and breasts. "The island belongs to the villagers. They just let me buy land."

"Can we go?" Mariana asked.

"Well, it was a surprise for our honeymoon, but I guess I ruined it now," he said. "This oil will not only help your skin, but it will also relax you and soothe any aches you have."

"I have a terrible ache that I am sure the oil can't soothe," Mariana said, and the ache was only getting worse as Will continued to use his firm hands to work the oil over her shoulders and arms, then gently rubbed it around her baby bump.

"Our little peas like the scent," Mariana said. "Do you think Morgan could make coconut ice cream? With chocolate. Those two together are delicious. Like our wedding cake, remember?"

"Would you rather stop and have Morgan bring you wedding cake-flavored ice cream now? I think she might be in bed already."

"No," Mariana said. "I'm just saying the scent gave the babies a craving, but my craving for you is much, much stronger."

"Good," Will said. "I just want to help you relax, while making sure they have room to grow without hurting their mama."

"Would you still love me with stretch marks, Will?"

"Sweetheart," Will said. "I love you every which way. If I have my say, you're going to be knocked up again as soon as these two settle. Whatever it takes to keep these tits full and that gorgeous ass of yours nice and round. We'll have twenty kids."

"And I suppose I'll be barefoot in some kitchen some-where, Tarzan?"

"Honey, no one in their right mind would let you in a kitchen unsupervised," Will joked. "With or without shoes, though especially without. You're likely to drop a chef's knife on those delicate feet."

Mariana giggled. She really wasn't all that bad in the kitchen. She could make sandwiches, boil eggs, and occasion-ally flip an omelet. But she had nowhere near Will's chef's skills and preferred helping, then washing dishes with him in their little cabin in the woods. Where they couldn't go anymore because of all their troubles. The thought made her feel sad and anxious again, even though Will was doing his best to clear her mind of what bothered them both.

"You have to stick around to make twenty babies, even two at a time," Mariana said.

"I plan to be," Will said. He kissed her, then gently nudged her to flip over on a pillow. She rested her head on her folded arms and shivered when he dripped more oil along her spine. Will worked her muscles with his firm hands, releasing all her knots until she sighed. She felt untangled and light, focused only on the moment and the joy of having her husband home.

"Tarzan," Mariana said, as he worked more oil onto her buttocks. "This is lovely, but I really am going to need you to put your elephant trunk to work soon."

"Believe me," Will said, hovering over her to kiss her neck, "all this relaxation for you has been torture for me. I've been holding back, but I am more than ready to mount my Jane if she'll have me."

"Please, Tarzan," Mariana raised her ass to rub up against his erection. "Bring on the wild part of the evening."

"*Ay, Juana*," Will said, lifting her rear up and giving it a firm smack before thrusting himself deep into her warm, drenched channel with such ferocity that she thought she felt him strike her teeth.

"Fuck, Will!" Mariana cried out.

"Yes, ma'am," he said, sliding out then slamming into her core again.

She groaned and moaned for him as he built up a furious pace, taking her harder than he had in days. Her muscles clamped around him, but he kept thrusting as she orgasmed, forcing her to take more. He dug his fingers into her hips and pulled her hard onto his cock, keeping her pinned against him as he spilled his seed inside of her with a furious shudder and a roar. He left her wet and raw and unsure whether she could walk straight in the morning, which was just what she needed finally to relax. Then Will nestled his wife in his muscular arms, naked and slippery from the oil and sweat, and held her as she drifted off to sleep using his chest as her pillow.

The phone on the desk in their sitting room rang at two in the morning, and it kept ringing despite Mariana cursing at it.

"I'll get it," Will said, kissing her before pulling his arm out from under her shoulders. "Go back to sleep."

She followed his advice, and was back asleep almost immediately, though only for a short while. Soon Will nudged her shoulder to wake her up again.

"Mariana," he said. "It's Sandy. She says it's urgent."

"At this hour? What time is it?"

"Past midnight for her and three for us, but if she used the bedroom line, then I think you should take it," Will said. "She sounded pretty distressed and she wouldn't tell me what it was about."

"That's not like Sandy," Mariana said.

"I know," Will said. "That's why I'm waking you up."

"It's not about Charlie, do you think?"

"I don't think so," Will said. "I think she would have told me if something happened to him."

"Maybe not if something happened between them," Mariana said.

"Whatever it is, she's waiting for you on the phone."

Mariana got up and rushed to the desk to pick up the call, her stomach churning with dread.

"Hello, Sandy," Mariana said. "What's the matter?"

"I'm sorry to wake you up in the middle of the night," Sandy said. "I'm at Crystal's house. I think you need to come see her."

"What?" Mariana asked. They had heard little from the young performer Crystal since she met with Mariana at Marsha's party, hanging from Martin Harper's arm. Sandy had agreed that they should cancel their contract with her. Whatever trouble Crystal was in this time must be bad if Sandy was on site to handle it. "What happened?"

"Her mother is hysterical, so I went over myself, but Crystal doesn't want to talk to me," Sandy said. "Crystal says she will only talk to you. It's Martin, you see. He... Mariana he—he's a monster."

"What did he do to her?"

"There's a doctor with her," Sandy said. "We called someone from the team, someone discrete, and he's going to sedate her. Karen, though... She's threatening to sue you."

"Sue *me*? For what?"

"She's not making any sense," Sandy sighed. "Karen says you endangered Crystal by introducing them."

"I didn't introduce them!"

"I know that. She knows that, too, if she's being honest.

You know how she is," Sandy sighed. "She needs someone to blame and you're handy."

"I just don't know what I'm supposed to do about it," Mariana said. "The last time I saw her, Crystal made sure I knew she was thrilled with Martin. I didn't have time to warn her, but I don't think she would have listened to me, anyway. And we haven't heard from any of them all this time. You stopped billing her the retainer, right?"

"Only last month," Sandy said. "I know it feels like years have passed, but it hasn't been that long. She had already paid up through May. I just didn't bill her for June, but I came anyway because it sounded urgent when Karen called. It's pretty bad. He tore her back to shreds. She has some severe bruises all over her body, and a black eye."

"Jesus," Mariana gasped.

Will had come into the sitting room after her, and he was pacing in front of the desk, stitching together the conversation from what he could overhear. Mariana knew that stance of his. It was his silent storm brewing. Will was livid, and he was planning something.

"The medical team put some advanced healing patches on her back—do you know the ones I mean?"

"Yes," Mariana said. The mention of the medical team and the patches was the first time that Sandy had given her any clue that she knew something about Will's organization. It made her wonder just how much Charlie had told her about what he did. "They work really well," Mariana said.

The scar on Mariana's arm, from the cut Tracey Whitby made to insert a memory card chip, had vanished. Will's chest wound had healed. Mariana hoped they would be as effective at erasing the scars of whatever Martin had done to Crystal.

"Okay, I'm going to get dressed and arrange for a flight," Mariana said.

"Definitely not!" Will barked.

"Hush, Will." Mariana waved him away. "I have to go."

"Then we're *both* going," Will growled.

"Fine, whatever." Mariana shrugged. "Will's coming too," she informed Sandy.

"Don't bring him to Crystal's house," Sandy warned.

"I don't intend to," Mariana said. "I'll be there as soon as I can."

"Okay," Sandy said. "Again, I'm sorry, Mariana, though it will be good to see you again."

"Yes," Mariana said. "We have a lot of catching up to do."

"Definitely. We'll get all caught up."

Though Will had been reluctant to bring Sandy into the organization, obviously Charlie trusted her. There was no way she would go to Los Angeles now and continue the pretense with her friend and business partner that Will was just an arborist and Charlie was just a handyman. It was time to clear the air. Besides, she needed Sandy on her side, now more than ever.

Will had already disappeared into the closet where Mariana found him angrily packing a bag for each of them.

"You don't have to do that, honey," Mariana said. "I can pack, if you make the flight arrangements."

"Motherfucking asshole," Will growled. "I should have taken him down sooner."

"I'll take him down, Will," Mariana said. "You can bet on that."

"It's all going to come out," Will said. "We've kept the videos he took of the two of you off the net, but I'm sure Robert still has copies. If the news hits that Martin hurt Crystal, Robert will ensure your videos get out to the press. Be ready for what that will mean."

"You saw his videos, then?" Mariana said.

"Yes, I fucking saw them, Mariana!" Will howled. "Did you imagine for a minute I wouldn't?"

His anger took Mariana aback. Will was usually more reserved, but she couldn't really blame him. She suspected whatever he saw would have been hard for a man to take.

"You never mentioned them, so I wasn't sure," Mariana said, muttering. "I couldn't watch them. Were they terrible?"

"Mariana, please don't make me talk about that," Will said. "I know they were in the past, before we even met, but I can't believe you let someone do that to you. You should never have been with Martin Harper. Ever. It has taken all my strength to keep from wringing his neck, you know. He's only alive because my advisors have insisted he stay that way. At least, for now."

"I guess, we've both done stupid things that we're ashamed of," Mariana cried.

"No, darling," Will said, his demeanor changing in an instant from resentment to concern. He took her hand and kissed it. "You have nothing to be ashamed of. I didn't mean to make you feel shame. I'm just so angry with Martin and I don't need to give Roger something else to grab onto. He's pushing Sandra's claim about her baby to bring a stain to my reputation. Now this. You're smart enough to know how it might spin. First you, then one of your young clients. It's too good an opportunity for someone like Robert Whitby to ignore."

"He's always planned to use me as your weakness," Mariana said.

"Yes, I'm afraid that's true."

"No, I mean when I met him at Marsha's, do you know what he whispered in my ear?"

Will went stiff, like he was fighting not to say the wrong thing, or not to punch something random. Back when she was married to Bill Stein, she might have been afraid to be the random thing that got punched. She never worried like that around Will.

He avoided the question which had so clearly upset him, focusing back on business. "Robert will want to make his move on PlayTech now too as soon as the news gets out."

"I thought you had already gained enough shares for control of PlayTech," Mariana said.

"I have, but not merged," Will said. "We've had to keep them in separate groups, not to give the game away. I'll handle that part with Tom. I was thinking more that Robert might try to sabotage things, but I'm not really concerned about it. I'm just worried about you. Do you think you can get Crystal to keep quiet about it, if I sort out Martin?"

"Will, I can't ask her to do that," Mariana said. "She has a right to press charges against him for assault. She *should* press charges, or he'll do it again to someone else. Besides, her mother will get the information out. She's threatening to sue me for putting them together."

"And you're *still* going?" Will snapped.

"Sandy wouldn't ask if she didn't think it was important. And Crystal may be a royal pain in my ass, literally," Mariana said, thinking of the paddling she'd earned from Will for an unfortunate incident when she'd followed Crystal to a nightclub. "But she is *still* a young woman who has counted on me to help her for years. I will not let her down now."

Will hugged her. "I know, darling. I support you. I'm just furious with Martin Harper. Now, be a good girl, take a shower and get dressed. I'll take care of everything else."

"*Gracias, Papi.*" She gave him a kiss and scooted out to get ready.

By the time she was out, Will brought her a cup of coffee with a warning. "Just this one cup, okay? No getting back in the habit."

"Denying a Cuban coffee is some sort of human rights violation," Mariana said, enjoying the aroma. "Even this weak stuff you *gringos* drink. I've been drinking coffee since I was three, you know."

"Well, the doctor said you should avoid it," Will reminded her. "You will not be giving the twins coffee when they're toddlers either. And *never* call me a *gringo*." He slapped her butt like he meant it. "*Hablo Español mejor que tú.*"

"Ouch! That *really* hurt," she complained. She was only teasing Will. It wasn't really an offensive term to Latins, mostly playful ribbing, but Mariana made a mental note that Will really did *not* approve of the label.

"You deserve more, but I'm mindful that you'll be sitting on a plane for five hours." Will shook his head, then stepped into the shower. She was tempted to follow him back under the water, just to enjoy the view, but there wasn't time.

Instead, she enjoyed her special treat coffee. Whether he intended it as a boost or a peace offering after their brief argument made no difference. She felt better.

Her husband was going with her to tackle a special mission of her own. With Will by her side, she could handle anything.

10

Broken Crystal

Will and Mariana flew over to Los Angeles on a new Gulfstream jet Mariana hadn't seen before. From what she'd experienced of her husband's flight ops so far, it seemed they owned at least one of everything with wings or propellers. Mariana wondered whether that included fighter jets. It would be tempting to bomb Martin Harper's home, in San Francisco, if they could do it with enough precision to leave the rest of the neighborhood intact. Will didn't expressly say they *didn't* have fighter jets in their fleet, but did said Martin Harper wouldn't be worth the fuel burn.

While en route, over more coffee for Will and sadly no more coffee for Mariana, they discussed a more realistic strategy to deal with the man, while minimizing the fall-out to Mariana and Crystal. Mariana wasn't sure she was comfortable with one idea Will had floated. It involved getting someone else to press charges on Crystal's behalf, so the press wouldn't speculate about the girl's role in any of this. Will hoped that might also prevent Robert from involving Mariana in the mess, since there was no easy connection for the press to pick up on. Nothing was guaranteed, of course, but it was something to consider.

"A man with these tendencies has done this before, Mariana," Will said. "He has had someone satisfy his needs, a professional who could point a finger."

"So you're suggesting an escort could accuse him of this abuse," Mariana said. "I hate to say this, because it's just wrong, but why would the police take that seriously? It's hard for women to be believed, and even more so when they are sex workers."

"Yes, but with the proper documentation—medical reports and such—it's difficult for Martin to deny," Will said. "You could leak images to the press."

"I'm not connected to the escort scene in LA, Palo Alto, or San Francisco," Mariana said. "I don't run that kind of business."

"No, of course not, but there are people, professionals, who set up honeytraps for intelligence," Will explained. "They will have those materials safely tucked away."

"And you know these people?" Mariana wondered just how well Will knew the honeytrap business. It did not really thrill her he might have any connection to sex workers, but she wasn't naïve either. There were many ways to negotiate with enemies, and dirty pics were a popular choice for blackmail going back to the invention of cameras.

"I know people who know these people," Will said.

"You know too many people," Mariana said, taking a bitter sip of orange juice. "So you're saying you can get me dirt on Martin?"

"Yes, and you know who can spread the dirt, don't you?" Will's coffee seemed to be pretty bitter too.

"I guess I could call a few key contacts, and send them a video feed, or pictures," Mariana said. "Plus, I could call

Orlando. We could pay her to spread the videos online. I bet she'd be happy to do it."

Mariana had met a hacker by the name of Orlando in Los Angeles, previously, who had warned her when her own intimate videos with Martin went online. The two women had remained on friendly terms.

"I think we can get other harder evidence on Martin, which would be enough to do him in," Will said.

"Will, you can't mean paying an escort to go through that intentionally," Mariana said. "We can't put anyone in that position! Think of what you are saying!"

"The people I know already have the evidence you need, Mariana," Will said. "We've been tracking his behavior for a while. We just did not know he'd be stupid enough to try something like that with someone who was so high profile."

"You told me you'd watch over her," Mariana reminded Will. It was a lot to ask. Mariana knew better than most that Crystal gravitated to unpleasant situations, but she cared for the girl.

"We did, Mariana," Will said. "It was Charlie's people who got her out. They brought her home and have been looking after her. They just couldn't be in his bedroom round the clock, unfortunately."

"I'll go calm Crystal down," Mariana said. "You handle whoever has the dirt. We'll talk through all of this together with Sandy later tonight."

"She and Charlie will come to the house," Will said.

"Our house?"

"Yes."

"Sandy doesn't know about the Malibu house, Will," Mariana said. "I don't know what she'll make of it."

"Sandy knows about the house, Mariana," Will said. "She knows a lot more too. She and Charlie are married."

"*What*?" Mariana was shocked. "When did that happen? Why didn't she say?"

"Well, it happened months ago, long before you were kidnapped and we set off to the North Pole." Will grinned.

"I can't believe she kept that from me this whole time!"

Mariana had felt so guilty over keeping secrets from her business partner since she'd married Will, but at least Sandy knew she got married—she was there for the rush wedding, as Mariana's Maid of Honor. It was disappointing. She really thought of Sandy as a friend.

"Her relationship with Charlie differs from ours," Will explained, clearly understanding why Mariana might feel hurt. "Charlie is a full-control kind of guy. He collared her."

"What does that mean?"

"They have a strict Dom/sub relationship," Will said. "She is his property, and she does what he says. He wanted her to keep their marriage secret, for her own protection. She couldn't breach his confidence, not even for you."

"I'm not sure how I feel about that," Mariana said. It wasn't something she had even thought Sandy was into, or Charlie for that matter.

"You don't have to feel anything about it," Will said. "It's their private life, not ours. How they express love is none of our business. Charlie is taking substantial risks for us right now, Mariana. He needs to know people won't use Sandy as a vulnerability to get to him. Especially not now since she is pregnant."

"Sandy is pregnant too? Jesus! I know *nothing*!"

"Well, like I said, they've been married a few months," Will said.

"Why didn't you tell me sooner?"

"I did not know, Mariana," Will said. "I thought they were dating, casually, just as you did. I knew Charlie felt something stronger for Sandy than he had for any other woman for as long as I've known him, but he insisted it was just casual and I accepted that. He only told me the truth when I last saw him out in the field. I understand why he wanted to keep it secret. Don't be angry with Sandy, honey. She really is a good friend and an excellent business partner for you."

"So are you bringing her into your circle?"

"She's practically already there, through her connection with Charlie, but I'm going to do something special about it in Wales, during the wedding."

"Why there?"

"I'm having a Convocation of Eagles," Will said.

"What does that mean?"

"I'm gathering some very important people together for a meeting we haven't had in decades," Will said. "I'll ask for protection for Sandy, just as I'll ask for your protection. It will be my wedding gift to them, but don't mention it just yet. Okay? I don't know how Charlie will feel about it."

"Why would he mind?"

"Because he's not an Eagle. He's a Hawk. He has his own firm. I don't want him to think I lack confidence in his abilities to protect his own wife," Will explained. "It's something to leave aside for now. Let's just focus on this Crystal mess. Charlie will help a lot. His people are all over this now, and he has the closer connection with the woman who has the evidence to use against Martin."

"Why is that?" Mariana asked.

Will sighed. "It's not really my place to tell you, but Charlie and I have a working relationship with a woman who provides a safe-space for sex workers—several who enjoy different kinks. She offers them security, housing if they need it, and ensures they aren't cheated or abused. She maintains an exclusive list of clients, all of them pre-screened. Martin was one of her customers, for a while. We had asked that she put our special collars on the girls who went to see him. Recently, this woman had to take Martin off her client list because of what he did to one of her girls at his house. We have the video and sound, from her perspective. We also have the medical reports that followed, and some other things which could devastate Martin."

"And you know this madam, how?" Mariana asked.

"I don't really know her at all," Will said. "We've never met. She's an old friend of Patricia Cornwall's and she's become a friend of Charlie's."

"A friend of Charlie's? Does Sandy know?"

"I'm sure she does," Will said. "They're all part of The Unkindness."

"The what?"

"An unkindness of ravens—it's the collective noun for the bird which is their symbol," Will explained. "It's a BDSM 'gathering' of private members, by invitation only. Charlie and Morrígan put it together. I'm not really supposed to know about it, so you shouldn't either. Anyway, that's how they all know each other."

"Sounds like fun," Mariana teased.

"No, it doesn't," Will grumbled. "Orgies are a no-go for us, Mariana."

"If you insist." She smiled. "I'm not really in any kind of shape for an orgy, anyway."

"You're in perfect shape," Will said. "You look absolutely delectable, but I wouldn't allow any other man to enjoy you, even if it is just by looking."

"I don't like women looking at you either," Mariana said.

"Really?" Will grinned, with a meaningful nod at the flight attendant. "I hadn't noticed."

Mariana ignored his taunt.

"So this Morrígan—what an unusual name—she will

have the evidence to use against Martin, if we can persuade Crystal to let someone else take him down."

"More than enough evidence," Will said. "While you're with Crystal, I'll be with Tom in Palo Alto. We're going to make our move on PlayTech quickly, the minute you confirm she's onboard with the plan, and before Robert acts. Angel will take you to the house and we'll meet there tonight with Sandy and Charlie. We'll all get on the same page, for this and for everything else. Okay?"

"We should alert Oliver, don't you think? So he can take down anything that Robert tries to put up," Mariana said.

"I'll take care of that," Will said. "You focus on putting Crystal back together again and getting her mother to back off her threats to sue you."

"That's easy," Mariana said. "We can always influence Karen with enough money thrown her way."

"You can't settle with her," Will warned. "You can't even imply any wrongdoing on your part. A woman like that will use it against you in the future."

"I understand that, Will," Mariana said. "I just meant that if I can get her to see there is more money to be made with silence, then she'll keep her mouth shut. I have something in my safe on Karen too, if she ever really gets on my nerves."

"My clever little spy," Will grinned.

"I'm not so little now," Mariana said, adjusting her now tight-fitting ivory silk power blouse with the buttons straining to contain her growing bust.

"You're perfect." Will bent over the table to kiss her, just as the flight attendant came to clear their breakfast plates.

The inflight breakfast food didn't sit well with the twins, or maybe it was the situation. At Crystal's house, Mariana kept having to run to the bathroom to throw up.

"Are you going to do something besides vomit?" Crystal whined. She was lying face-down on her bed, covered in a blanket of the special healing patches Will's medical division had developed, which healed muscle and tissue quickly. "I'm the one with the marks and bruises all over my body! Do you know how much they hurt? Do you know how long this is going to take to heal? I have to go on tour soon!"

That was news. Apparently Karen had made another problematic management decision for her daughter.

"Who else knows about this, Crystal?" Mariana asked, gathering herself together again.

Focus! This poor girl needs you. The ghost of Rosa Castro de Perez, Mariana's mother, who always showed up when the situation was dire, suddenly popped into the room.

I'm here aren't I, Mom?

There, but for the grace of God...

I know.

"Well, my mom knows," Crystal said. "Consuelo and Magda, our maids, saw a little. Plus, the goons who got me out."

"The security team?"

"Yes," Crystal said. "Who the hell are they, anyway, and what were they doing there?"

"You don't have to worry about them," Mariana said. "I suspect they were people tracking Martin and they just intervened."

"Not in time!"

Mariana had no simple answer for that. She was sure Charlie's men had acted as soon as they thought it was prudent. It would have been better if Crystal hadn't been at Martin's house in Malibu at all.

"I think you should put off your tour, Crystal," Mariana said. "Just until you recover."

"You should become my agent," Crystal said.

"I've told you before, I'm not really qualified, Crystal. It's not what I do."

"Well, think about it."

"Let's not talk about that right now," Mariana said. "Let's focus on how we're going to handle this. Do you want to press charges against Martin?"

"I should! That fucker. I should destroy his career. Except…"

"Except then people would know," Mariana finished what Crystal didn't want to say.

"Yes." Crystal started crying. Mariana wanted to soothe the girl, but in her current state the best she could do was to sit beside her on the bed and take Crystal's hand.

"There are other ways to get back at him," Mariana said. "Leave it to me."

"Are you going to get him for me?"

"I'm going to get him good." Mariana squeezed Crystal's hand to reassure her.

"It's been getting worse each weekend," Crystal wept. "I should have stopped going there. I'm so stupid. Everyone is going to laugh at me."

"No one is going to laugh at you," Mariana said. "I won't let them."

"What about you?" Crystal asked the question Mariana had dreaded. "Won't they laugh at you when they find out? I mean, it may not have been this bad, but he did things to you too, didn't he?"

"Yes, he did," Mariana said.

"Will you tell me?"

"You don't need to hear it. You know already. He probably always starts out the same way."

"Tell me something, so I don't feel so alone."

Mariana never wanted to say a word, not even to herself. Some things were best kept silent, but Crystal needed to hear it. Mariana could see that, even understand it.

"The sex was fine at first, nothing earth-shattering. You know how he is, just routine. It's the humiliation that turns him on, though, and it's knowing that he's causing genuine pain. He liked to slap me around and he liked to make me hurt. He took it further than I would normally have allowed. Finally, he ignored the safe word I had given him for edge play. I just cut him off, after that. He was bitter, but by then I was married and my husband made it clear he should stay away."

"And he took it out on me!" Crystal wailed.

Mariana didn't appreciate Crystal implying somehow she was to blame for Martin's abuse, but maybe that was just more of Karen's negative influence. Mariana let it go.

"He has done it to other women," Mariana said. "I'm sure of that."

"Why didn't you warn me?"

Mariana sighed. She had expected this. "Crystal, when I last saw you, you were glued to his side and rubbing my nose in it," Mariana said. "I wanted to warn you, believe me, but I couldn't figure out how. Would you have listened to me if I had? Or would you have thought I was just being jealous?"

"Honestly, I don't know," Crystal admitted. "It doesn't matter. It happened. So what are you going to do about it?"

"I'm going to work with some contacts," Mariana said. "They could make sure Martin's career is over without harming ours. You and I will have nothing to do with it. We keep what happened to ourselves. You tell no one anything, even when they come asking, and they will. Your mother would have to agree to do the same."

"You're not saying I should pretend like nothing happened!"

"Listen, Crystal, your career is more important than he is, and so is mine," Mariana said. "The most important thing is for him to be exposed. How it happens—how you get justice—doesn't matter. He shouldn't take you or me down with him."

"But once he's exposed, people are still going to ask us whether... You know..." Crystal choked on a sob. "And even if we deny it, some people will still think it."

"Yes," Mariana said. "That's why it would be better if nothing came out, but if it has to, then we won't deny it. We'll say he had a dark side that few people knew about. That's accurate enough, isn't it? We'll pretend to be on the fringe, but that's our privilege. It's no lie. I'll give you the lines to say. I'll coach you on every detail, but this is about you rising above Martin, not letting him bring you down."

"These scars—do you think they'll heal?"

"The injuries on your body will need treatment, but the patches the medical team gave you work wonders," Mariana said. "It's the other ones I'm most concerned with—the ones on the inside. You'll need counseling. Crystal. If I help you get the right care, get whole and healthy again, you will need to follow my advice to the letter, every single bit of it, in terms of your public image."

"So the scars will heal?"

"Eventually, Crystal, they'll get so you can barely notice them," Mariana said. "I wouldn't be surprised if those scars vanish."

"I guess I can use make-up, if there are any shadows."

"We'll get you back on track. I swear it, Crystal."

"Whatever you say, Mariana, I trust you," Crystal said. "You're like the sister I never had."

"You have an older sister, don't you?"

"Yes, but you're the one I never had."

After her meeting with Crystal, Mariana had a predictably uncomfortable confrontation with her mother, Karen Langford. It was as infuriating as it was tragic. The woman was trying to profit off her daughter's pain. Mariana was in no mood for it. When Karen threatened legal action, she passed her a card Will had given her for the organization's attorney's firm in Los Angeles and invited her to call them to discuss it.

"I'm sure you'd also be happy to have a Q&A with the press about how you missed the danger signs in your daughter's relationship, considering that you live in the same house. There may be stories about a pattern of abuse and neglect on your part over the years," Mariana added. "You'll want to hire your own PR firm to handle the fall-out from that. I represent Crystal. She would like to handle this quietly, with minimal impact to her career. You know, the one which keeps you living the good life. I suggest you discuss this with her. I can promise that if you bring the press to her door, I'll make sure they focus all their lenses on you."

It was no idle threat, Karen knew that. Mariana didn't want to do it, but she would not be railroaded by Karen Langford either.

Angel was waiting for Mariana outside of Crystal's mansion in Holmby Hills, to drive Mariana to her own home in Malibu. She was delighted to see him again, out of his pirate's costume, and not trying to force her to sit still while being auctioned off to the highest bidder. Okay, she was still sore about that. But it wasn't Angel's idea. Besides, she owed Angel a pass for the time he got clobbered by the gigantic burlesque performer Lady Divine because of her.

"I'm glad you're home safe," he said as he let her in the

car. "We're going to keep you that way this time, Mrs. Wilson. I promise."

Once he settled in the driver's seat of the bullet-proof Mercedes, which was part of their fleet of cars, Mariana asked Angel whether he was ever going to call her by her first name.

"And just call me '*tu*' not '*usted*'," she added. "It makes me feel like your grandmother."

"Not while I'm on duty, no," Angel said, plainly. "Getting too familiar with the principal leads to lowering your guard. Lowering your guard leads to a dead principal."

"You sure know how to cheer a girl up, Angel," Mariana joked.

"I'm sorry we couldn't intervene with Crystal sooner, Mrs. Wilson," Angel said, ignoring her quip. "We couldn't expose our agents on-site. We got her out as soon as we could."

"Will is going to take care of it," Mariana said. "Martin is going to regret what he's done."

"I'm sure he will," Angel said.

Back at the house, Adams, their butler and agent in charge, seemed thrilled to see Mariana again. The somewhat formal man handled it pretty well when Mariana gave him a big hug.

"We've set up a shore detail, now," he told her, "in case you want to go for a walk on the beach. No one will take you out to sea again, Mrs. Wilson, unless you choose to go."

"I'm frankly too tired right now to walk down to the cove, but thanks for thinking of it," Mariana said. "Has Will said what time he'll be back from Palo Alto?"

"Mr. Wilson will be here by seven, and Mr. Green will be

here too, along with Ms. Fine," he said. "I'm making a pork loin roast for dinner, with herb-crusted new potatoes and a grilled vegetable medley. I've made coconut and chocolate ice cream for dessert, at Mr. Wilson's request. Morgan shared her recipe with me, and I really enjoy using the ice cream machine."

"Thanks, Adams," Mariana said. "That sounds perfect. I think I'm going to take a nap."

"Not until you have your lunch," Adams said. "Sorry, but those are my orders."

"I guess Will's thumb reaches here too," Mariana shrugged. "Bossy, bossy, bossy."

Adams chuckled.

11

Revenge Goes Cold

William

Will spoke softly. He didn't want to raise his voice because he knew if he gave way to the rage bubbling underneath the surface, he wouldn't be able to contain it. The meeting with Tom and his advisers wasn't going as well as he'd hoped. They'd made their move on Martin Harper, taken control and demanded his immediate resignation as CEO of the company he'd founded. That part was straightforward, in the end. They'd positioned themselves for a rapid hostile takeover for months. The minute Oliver presented Martin with the evidence they'd gathered against him, the man buckled and folded like the coward he was. But Will wanted more. He wanted Martin to suffer.

"Come on, William, the man is broken." Tom Waters spoke up. They were on the speakerphone with Aaron Silverman, his advisor in Manhattan, who handled the markets.

"Hardly," Will said. "I'd like to break him."

"We got him off and away," Aaron said. "That was the plan. Maybe we acted sooner than we'd planned and didn't buy at a low-point because of scandal, but we still took his assets at a heavy discount. Now we have Oliver in there and nobody can touch PlayTech."

"What more do you want, Will?" Tom asked.

"It's not enough," Will spat, "not this time."

"William, you know we have rules," Tom said.

Tom was being patient, reserved. He was allowing for Will's personal stake in this mess. Will knew that.

"We don't make it personal, remember?" Aaron said. "We have met our mandates, ensuring a sound development of worthwhile technology instead of pointless crap. It's time to focus on phase two of that plan and leave phase one as it is."

"William, we leave justice to God, remember?" Tom insisted. "Those are your words, not mine."

"Sometimes God needs a hand," Will said.

That was wrong. Will knew it the minute he said it. His anger kept surprising him.

"What do you want us to do, William?" Aaron asked. "Think carefully before you answer. Remember, we base our confidence in you on your excellent track record: your detachment, your fairness, and your values. If you break your own code now, because you make this personal, you put far more at risk than you think."

"Don't patronize me, Aaron, and don't threaten me either," Will growled. He'd been holding back, but it was getting harder.

"No one is threatening you, William," Tom jumped in. "Everyone respects you. We have confidence in your good judgement. We're only saying, take your time to decide. Enjoy your wife, take care of those babies in the oven. You're a very fortunate man, William, don't let spite ruin that. If something happens to Martin, it will be all over the news. We won't be able to prevent that. And Mariana will know, Will.

No matter what you say to her, she'll know you were behind it. What will that do to her? To both of you? Ask yourself that."

Will wondered what Mariana might say. For all he knew, his now ferocious wife would delight in the news that someone had killed Martin. No, that wasn't really true. She had surprised him by insisting that she wanted to learn how to kill, but she only wanted to do that in self-defense, or to protect her family. She wouldn't want Martin dead any more than the others did. No, Will was sure that blood lust belonged to him alone.

"Fuck, Tom, you always get your way," Will said, finally.

"Just looking out for you, buddy." Tom smiled.

"Yeah, well, thank you. And thank you, too, Aaron," Will said. "Sorry, both of you, I'm going to have to cut this short. I've got to get back to Malibu to meet with Mariana. Congratulate your teams on pulling this off on such short notice."

"Well, we just need to find out what the fall-out will be for Oliver," Tom said. "Caroline Boots may seem meek, but she has plenty of fire in her. I don't think she appreciates finding a surprise visitor waiting for her in the office this morning."

Will chuckled. It was true. Oliver's cover was blown, and he was now in trouble with his girl. But Will was pretty confident his cousin could handle the heat. He was a Greystone, after all.

Mariana

Will arrived at the house just moments before Charlie and Sandy. The minute Mariana saw the couple together, she realized she'd had blinders on. No one who saw them would think they were just dating casually. They moved in-sync, like dancers. Mariana recognized it as the choreography of two lovers who could communicate without words. Charlie's demeanor differed from the jovial man she'd first met at the Hot Plate in Fairfarm, back in January. She'd seen another side of him since then, the warrior who only wore a mask of a clown to put people at ease. But tonight she saw yet another side of Charlie, the dominant protector who clearly cherished the woman who had pledged her life to him, giving him total control over her. What surprised Mariana most was that Sandy seemed far from meek around him. Instead, she seemed more confident, more secure of herself, and more beautiful than Mariana had ever known her to be. Sandy was walking sunshine.

Mariana hugged them both tight as they came in. "It's so good to see you," she said to Sandy. "Despite the circumstances."

"It's good to see you too, Mariana." Sandy returned her hug with equal fervor. "I can't believe this house of yours! It's amazing!"

They walked over to the living room and sat together on the L-shaped couch, the two couples facing each other. Will put his arm around Mariana's shoulders, and Charlie hid his hand behind Sandy's lower back.

"It's a bit much, isn't it?" Mariana asked, referring to the oversized mansion.

"Well, you could host some brilliant parties for our clients here," Sandy said.

"They'll just figure our fees are much too high!" Mariana was only half-joking.

"You don't have to tell them it's your house," Will suggested. "You could always say it belongs to a friend. I think it might be good for you to set up networking events here, like Marsha does in Palo Alto."

Yes, so you can spy on more of my contacts, Mariana thought, smiling at her husband.

"That might be fun," Sandy said.

"We can talk about all of that when the weather turns more social," Charlie said, gruffly.

"Yes, Daddy," Sandy said, and the topic was officially closed. It made Mariana do a double-take. Sandy didn't seem to realize she'd said 'Daddy', but Charlie noticed Mariana's reaction to the word and grinned. Will gave her shoulder a gentle squeeze. Well, bossy, bossy bosses all around.

After Adams served refreshments—whiskey for Will and Charlie, and ginger ale for Sandy and Mariana—Will filled them all in on what had happened with the PlayTech takeover.

"So, wait, nothing will come out about Martin at all?" Mariana asked Will. "He just gets to make money from selling his company and retire? How is that fair?"

"It isn't fair," Will said. "It's what I had to agree to with the Executive Committee because we can't touch him. We had planned to expose his behavior. It would have even benefited us, by lowering the stock value before we took the last shares for 100% control. We changed those plans because we don't want to risk you and Crystal getting tangled in the scandal."

"Still," Sandy spoke up, "what he did is unforgivable, and you're giving him a pass. This is what he does, and he'll do it again. You know that. You're endangering the next woman who is unlucky enough to cross his path."

Will and Charlie exchanged looks. Sandy shifted in her seat and Mariana wondered what Charlie had done with his hidden hand.

"You two need to have more faith in karma," Will said.

"I'm not sure whether Crystal will wait for karma," Mariana said.

"Do you want him dead, baby girl?" Charlie asked Sandy, as if he were asking her whether she'd like to have a refill on her Canada Dry.

Mariana wasn't sure what to make of the dynamic between Charlie and Sandy, nor of Will's cool reaction to it. There was a silent conversation happening between the two men. Mariana felt like they were testing their wives.

"I think he's evil, but he's not my scalp to claim, Daddy," Sandy said. "Only Mariana or Crystal could ask for that."

"Can't ask Crystal," Charlie said. "She's not a level-headed girl. She'd go blabbering about it. So would her mother. That leaves you, Mariana. Do you want me to bring you Martin Harper's scalp?"

Mariana wasn't sure whether Charlie and Sandy were using a figure of speech, but she had the feeling they were dead serious. Will was still and steady, not even offering her a light tap with his thumb to reveal his thoughts. She went through various scenarios in her head, and several of them were bloody, but she couldn't find a scenario in which Martin died suddenly that wouldn't make headlines.

"Killing him will bring us more grief than joy," Mariana said, finally. "It would draw unwanted scrutiny to the Play-Tech takeover. I don't even think it would make Crystal happy to know he was dead. And you're right, Charlie. She's not level-headed. There's nothing to be gained and something to be lost from killing him. We need to hold Martin accountable, but we have to find some other way to do it."

"Instant Karma wins," Will said, squeezing her tight and planting a gentle kiss on her lips.

Charlie laughed and then kissed Sandy like he was ready to fuck her on the couch right in front of them. "Don't worry, baby girl," he said. "We can always castrate the fucker."

"So what does that entail?" Mariana asked. "Instant Karma, I mean, not castration."

"Well, wife, I'm sure you'll find out soon enough," Will answered, cryptically.

After dinner, Will and Charlie went downstairs to Will's command-center to deal with secret business stuff, leaving Mariana and Sandy alone to catch up. It was a lovely evening, not too hot for mid-June. The two women sat out on the patio, looking out over the ocean with the stars twinkling above them.

"It's so peaceful here," Sandy said. "I know you love Manhattan, but this house is heavenly."

"Yes," Mariana agreed. "Will wanted to sell it after they took me from the shore below, but I'm glad he hasn't." Mariana looked for any reaction from Sandy, since the official cover story was that they'd been in a car accident. The woman didn't blink. Mariana was sure Sandy knew the truth from Charlie, of everything that followed, but she would never say it. "I hope we get more time to be here at some point," Mariana continued, "though right now I don't see how."

Sandy nodded and was quiet for a long time. Mariana sensed her friend was putting her words in the right order.

"I'm sorry if this night has been awkward," Sandy said. "I wanted to tell you about me and Charlie, Mariana. I really did, but Charlie insisted we should keep our marriage secret and I understand why. I hope you do too."

"Well, we've both kept secrets from each other, so I don't

feel like I have a right to judge you," Mariana said. "But are you happy with him?"

"Very happy," Sandy beamed. "He really gets me, in a way nobody has ever gotten me before. Daddy can be a bit of a jerk sometimes—a lot of times—but he's also a very loving man."

"What's with the Daddy thing, though?"

Sandy laughed. "He's my Dom, Mariana. I'm a little and he's my Daddy. I also call him Master, when we're playing on the darker side, alone, or at a gathering."

"Well, I get that," Mariana said. "I call Will Daddy, and *Papi* and Master too, depending on how we play, but not full time."

"You mean not in front of other people." Sandy smiled.

Mariana nodded.

"We are full into the lifestyle," Sandy continued. "It's a round-the-clock thing for us, not just playtime. Sometimes we drop our roles, with strangers, and it's very uncomfortable for both of us. There's a certain power in submitting to him as my owner that I miss when we have to pretend to be strangers, or even just pretend to be an ordinary couple on a date. But you and Will are family, so we're at ease with both of you knowing the truth."

"I'm so glad you feel that way, Sandy," Mariana said. "I can't tell you just how glad I am. I feel that way too, and I know Will does."

"Will feels that way about Charlie," Sandy said. "He hasn't decided about me yet, which is why Charlie didn't tell Will about our marriage. He wanted Will to grow to respect me on his own. I think I scare Will."

"Don't be ridiculous." Mariana dismissed the notion with a grin and a wave of her hand.

"I'm serious. He worries I may rub off on you, which is what that whole thing was about earlier," Sandy said. "To see whether you'd agree to have Martin killed, just to get him out of the way. Will needed to know you hadn't lost your center."

"What do you mean?"

"Well, you asked Charlie to train you to kill," Sandy said. Boy, Mariana marveled, Charlie *told* Sandy everything. "Will was pretty pissed about that. He told Charlie not to interfere with his woman, in no uncertain terms."

Mariana laughed.

"Mariana, listen, the situation right now is pretty grim," Sandy said. "Will is in the middle of something—I don't really know all the details, but it's bad. It's got Daddy really busy and very hard, which means it's dangerous. I know Will's on edge, too, just from overhearing their arguments. Daddy will probably spank me raw for telling you, but I think you need to know. Will worries you'll try to help, like you've done before, and make more risky moves when you go off fixing things. I know you're independent and have always had to deal with things on your own in life, but don't do that right now, Mariana. Do whatever Will tells you. Let him take charge."

Mariana thought about this for a long while. "Doesn't it bother you? Just obeying Charlie, without questioning him?"

"Not really," Sandy said. "That's not how it works, anyway. I do what I need to do, if I feel strongly enough about it. I just pay the price when Daddy disagrees with my choices. The point is, I know he values me and he keeps me safe. I know he truly loves and respects me. We're both broken people, but our shards fit with each other just right. Together, we make a whole being." Sandy stroked her belly.

"Congratulations," Mariana said.

"You too!" Sandy said. "I can't believe we're both going to be moms. Fortunately, Laurel is really competent and part of the organization, so she can handle things when the time comes. I won't take a long maternity leave, though. Don't worry."

"You take as much time as you need," Mariana said. "And I did not know you knew about Laurel. Did she tell you?"

"Mariana, I figured out a lot about what Charlie and Will were up to on the night we all first met. I have an ear for the way they talk," Sandy said.

"I wish you had warned me," Mariana said.

"Well, I couldn't tell you everything, really," Sandy said. "But I tried to clue you in. Remember, I'm the one who told you to go home to your husband when those videos came out."

"Fucking Martin," Mariana shook her head. "How did I ever fall for him? Even briefly? What does that say about me?"

"It says you're human," Sandy said. "There's nothing wrong with you, Mariana. He's just a fucked-up son-of-a-bitch."

Mariana wrapped her arms around herself. Even in summer, there could be a nip in the air in California in the evenings, especially with the breeze rising from the sea below. Mariana's arms were full of goose pimples.

"Did I do the right thing?" Mariana asked her friend. "Should I have asked Charlie to kill him?"

Sandy smiled and reached across their deck chairs to put her hand on Mariana's.

"Do you love Will more than you hate Martin?"

"Yes, definitely," Mariana said. "A thousand times more."

"Then you did the right thing, Mariana," Sandy said. "If you'd claimed Martin's scalp, you would have broken Will's heart."

Will and Charlie came out on the patio not long after that. Mariana knew, just by looking at her husband, that the men didn't bring good news. He came up to where she sat and knelt by the deck chair to give her a kiss.

"Mariana, I'm sorry." Will pressed his forehead to hers. "I know you're tired, but we have to go."

"Go where?"

"We have to leave the country," Will said. "Right now."

"What? *Why*?"

"I'll explain on the plane."

Mariana would have argued, given Will a hard time, but she was mindful of what Sandy had said. It was time to let Will take over. She just wished she knew what that really meant.

12

Flying Revelations

C harlie and Sandy drove them to the airport to board Will's safe-house—used for situations when they were under a high level of threat. It was a custom Boeing 777 jet, equipped for anything they might need during an emergency; even when they'd have to keep flying around the world, only making quick stops for refueling.

It was a flying mansion with a large living/entertainment room and dining/board room, several bathrooms, private sleeping cabins, a fully equipped galley kitchen, and a large master bedroom with an ensuite and shower. There were also advanced defense systems, and satellite telecommunications connected to Will's satellites in orbit and his systems on the ground. Mariana had just flown on it for the first time, only weeks earlier, when they set off to Finland to check on Zephyr, the AI which served the organization.

Mariana noticed that Cordelia, an overly flirty flight attendant who had really irritated Mariana on that last flight, was not working today. The other flight attendant, Connie, who Will said had been flying with him before, was. Connie was okay, though, maintaining a professional distance. A new redhead flight attendant, Susana, had joined them as the second cabin crew. Susana was extremely solicitous of Mariana and avoided Will. In fact, Mariana noted, Susana didn't even dare meet Will's eyes.

It seemed Will had made some wise staff changes. That was good because Mariana was in no mood to deal with any more bullshit tonight. She felt confused, exhausted and anxious. At least, Will was with her, but she couldn't help wondering what the hell was going on. Mariana was trying to take Sandy's advice to heart. It just didn't come as naturally to her to let Will take over completely.

Still, she waited patiently for whenever Will thought the time was right to explain, all the while thinking he'd better hurry and make the time. He waited until they were at a cruising altitude before exchanging anything more than pleasantries.

When they were alone in the living room, Will finally brought her up-to-date.

"I know you're busting for answers, Mariana," Will said, warming her hands in his. "I don't have very many because I don't know them all. Charlie told me there was a credible threat, and we had to go. That's all I can say, for now. Except, I want to give you a little background which might make it easier to understand."

"Okay," Mariana said, weary. Will's face was calm, but his eyes were on fire. Whatever had happened, Will was livid.

Will took a deep breath and kissed her gently before starting. "First thing, and you *have* to know this. It's really important. I love you more, much more than myself—much more than my organization. There is nothing I wouldn't do to keep you and the children safe. But, sometimes, what I do makes things worse." Mariana opened her mouth to say something comforting. He seemed so frustrated and angry, but all she got out was a sigh before Will cut her off. "Can you just listen for a bit and hear me out without interrupting?" He said it gently, but the words still stung.

"I feel like you're setting me up for some terrible news," Mariana said.

"I am."

"Okay, whatever it is, I can take it." Mariana sat up straight.

Will smiled, kissed her cheek, and took a deep breath.

"All right, let's start with the auction in France," he said. "I think that's the first thing."

"I've *definitely* been waiting on an explanation for that." Mariana had repeatedly asked Will to share what made him put that crazy scheme together, but Will had always avoided a detailed answer, which was annoying as heck.

"You remember what Grandfather said about my parents being killed because my father went up against the wrong people, trying to protect assets which were being misused by rivals?" Will asked her.

"Yes, of course I remember," Mariana said. "I'll never forget the pain on your face."

"You remember I asked Grandfather to leave the table and meet me in the library. When we were there, I called Howard Fleming, and we talked through our plans," Will continued. "I couldn't really keep Zephyr secret anymore, at that point, but I still had to protect the technology. You remember Brian, her digital twin in the South Pole, is also self-aware. Brian had been functioning as a defense system back up for certain British allies of my grandfather's; some are with unofficial government agencies. I have not offered Zephyr out as a resource to any agencies, public or private. It would give those agencies far too much power. Now that she's self-aware, the risks of that are less. Zephyr won't serve agendas I wouldn't approve of, and she's clearly more than capable of self-defense. But she's more desirable, her offspring are, anyway—you know what I mean, the algae soup that makes up her neurons."

"Yes, I know all of that," Mariana said. "But what does it have to do with auctioning me off as an asset to the highest bidder?"

"Well, darling, first, I'm always the highest bidder, that's a given." Will smiled. "You belong to me, no matter what. I was negotiating contracts to keep you out of play. If any agency or private party wanted to come after me, for whatever reason, their bids were a ransom for you to be left out of it; also, to offer you aid if you were ever under attack from any agency and we couldn't handle it. Santa rescued you from that French jail, remember? When I was unconscious and fighting for my life and everything was a mess. That's what the bids were for, at least the ones from players who knew why you were really on the program. Other bids, from some hostiles I invited, we disregarded. They didn't know they were bidding for anything more than to get their hands on the capable spouse of the mysterious mercenary Bill Marlowe."

"*Kit* Marlowe," Mariana said, using the nickname Will's grandmother had insisted on because she refused to call her grandson Bill; a name he hated.

Will smiled. "That's right. Now, do you remember the Scottish woman who joined others objecting to the reserve?"

"The cat," Mariana said. That woman was seared into Mariana's memory. The cat was fortunate to have been wearing a mask to hide her face, or Mariana might scratch her eyes out if she ever bumped into the bitch on the street.

"Yes, well, she was sour because she had underbid on behalf of some important British allies of my grandfather's," Will said. "But they have accepted their contract at bid price on behalf of their joint agencies, which includes both private and government players. Grandfather would protect you, no matter what, but the threat is too great right now for anyone to take on all our enemies alone. The problem is that the US agencies which came to the party didn't even bother to bid. I kept raising the sum, remember, but they never attempted to top it. When I said they had not met the reserve, and you were still on the block, I meant I would take any figure they threw out. It also alerted them I *knew* you were in play. After that, it all fell apart. We have no guarantees in the US, unfortunately. Right now, it's open season on Mariana Wilson Smith."

"Why wouldn't they bid?" Mariana asked.

"It's complicated," Will said. "There's a shakeup going on at certain agencies. There are some big players who want to get their hands on all of our technology—not just Zephyr, but other resources we have. For example, I've recently bought a mine in Alaska which is very near Zephyr's new home base, giving her a much larger secure perimeter. That mine also helped us corner the market on ore that one of our companies is using to forge some very specialized materials. We use those materials for peaceful purposes, but they can also produce weapons of all kinds, rockets that won't show up on radar, and guns that won't show up on x-rays, that sort of thing. The materials are very light and very strong. With a few tweaks we can convert them to smart materials, enhancing digital capabilities. We intend to make smart drones which can travel long distances on solar power alone and deliver emergency supplies to cities that storms or wars have ravaged."

"That's amazing," Mariana said.

"It is only part of it, Mariana. We make so many things that people want but they can't buy." Will smiled. "These things we make, we use for our own operations. You understand? It makes us nimble and keeps us ahead of people with larger forces, but slower capabilities. But enough people know about these different technologies that it's dangerous. Those people will do anything to get them."

"Like killing or capturing me," Mariana said.

"That's right," Will said. "I won't allow it. Neither will Charlie. But we need to minimize the risk. Do you understand?"

"I do." Mariana sighed.

"I keep enough unique identities that very few people know how much of it belongs to me, remember," Will continued. "But the rot has spread to people who know far more than they should. It's brought me to a hard decision. I'm working with Charlie to take out key hostiles before they can strike."

"You're killing them?"

Will nodded gravely. "The Hawks are hunting and I've rejoined them," Will said. "I always told you I would kill to protect you."

"But what about your rules against killing?"

"These aren't people whom I've targeted for their business assets, for take-overs," Will said. "The business side of the organization will continue to abide by the laws of my ancestors. We won't take a life for money or to gain power. But these are exigent circumstances. We're trying to avoid an outright war by winning strategic battles and taking out key players. When I'm gone, that's what I'm doing. I'm going hunting with Charlie, but I'll be back. Act like you understand we're fighting for our lives, though. You need to take these threats seriously, Mariana, and follow my instructions to the letter."

"That's what Sandy said to me tonight," Mariana said.

"Good, you listen to her."

"So they know about Smith's, then?" Mariana said. "Is that why there's a target on the lake house?"

"It's a likely target, yes, and the lake house is harder to

defend. Nana Smith had the protection of people who are no longer around. She had the sort of contract I can't get for you. In exchange, she also allowed greater access to our organizational assets than I will allow. Times have changed and we must change with them."

"I agree," Mariana said.

"Good." Will kissed her gently. "There's more."

"More?"

———

Mariana couldn't imagine things being worse than what Will had already told her. It seemed impossible to believe that she wasn't safe in her own country. Still, she needed a break from all of this worrying. It must have shown because Will stopped for a while and called on the flight attendant to bring them some refreshment. Mariana wasn't hungry since they'd already eaten. She would have been sleepy, except her mind was racing and she couldn't imagine relaxing well enough to sleep. She took a break to stretch her legs a bit and to use the lavatory. When she came back, Will asked her to sit sideways on the sofa and put her feet up on his lap. Her ankles had swollen again, only slightly, but enough for Will to notice. He took off her shoes and started massaging her feet.

"Do you remember I mentioned a Convocation of Eagles?"

"Yes." Mariana sighed as he put pressure on her arch, pressing his thumb hard into her sole, while massaging her raised ankle up to her calf, then doing the same to her other leg.

"Howard Fleming suggested I hold it during our wedding in Wales," Will spoke as his fingers worked magic. "I want you to understand what that means. We are largely gardeners and foresters and gamekeepers—they work on corporate espionage, nurture sources, and recruit people with special skills. We find vulnerable technologies and keep them from falling into the wrong hands. We invest, we nurture, and we grow. It's a passive exercise, mostly. Again, we have the rules to abide by. For example, I can't kill Martin Harper, despite what he did to you before we married, and despite the absolute pleasure it would give me to make him suffer. I can't kill Roger Whitby just because he's evil and a royal pain in my ass. If we started killing every business rival who came our way, we'd become the mob. Besides, we operate at the highest levels of influence and wealth. You wouldn't have to kill too many people before someone would take notice. I know Roger is developing something that could hurt people, if used the wrong way. I've got Penny in there, gathering intelligence, and we've got other things happening in the background. But unless Whitby targeted you directly, he will keep breathing. This thing with Sandra is part of his scheming, to drive a wedge between us, but even that is not a reason to kill him. I have to take some responsibility for allowing it to happen. Do you accept that?"

Will swept his firm hands, again, from her ankles to her calves. Another deep sigh escaped her lips before she answered.

"Yes, Will, it makes sense," she said. "I wouldn't want to worry that you'd kill any man who ever did me harm in my life, nor would I want you killing people just to take their assets."

"I don't, Mariana, I swear it," Will said. "I recently had to stop someone from putting a contract out on someone who stood in the way of a major deal. The woman who owned the asset had an excellent reason to want this man dead. Instead, I exposed his criminal acts, and he went to jail. Instant karma."

Mariana smiled. "Is that what you'll do to Martin?"

"Yes, I'm going to make him regret being born," Will said. "He won't have a friend left in this world. But I won't be responsible for his death."

"Good."

"I'll go to extremes to avoid getting blood on my hands, Mariana," Will said, "but everyone has a limit. You are my limit."

"What do Eagles have to do with all of this?" Mariana asked.

"Well, Charlie has his Hawks—his killers, who are mostly former special forces, all military. We have our Eagles. They are all intelligence operatives with a license to kill. The Eagles watch over the gardeners and foresters. Grandfather is an Eagle. Catherine Fleming is an Eagle also, but she's a solo-actor, a very specialized assassin."

"Catherine is an assassin?" Mariana was shocked. The woman was intense, from what she recalled from meeting her in France, but she looked like a refined Spanish socialite, not a killer. "Is your grandmother an assassin too?"

"Catherine is a very lethal assassin. Her handle is Medusa because she floats invisibly through the waters and will kill you with one quick sting. You won't ever see it coming. She is mostly retired now, though," Will said. "Grandmother is an Eagle, but she's specialized in intelligence gathering. She's deadly, and she's killed to stay alive, but she didn't kill for a living. That's the difference between them."

"Okay, I'll try not to piss either of them off," Mariana said.

Will smiled. "They won't kill you. Well, Grandmother won't, for sure. Catherine might kill you if you ever get Angel in trouble again. He's her fourth favorite child."

"I'll keep that in mind," Mariana said. "Wait. Isn't he her fourth child?"

"Yes; Tree, Iris, Percy, Angel, Miranda, Jason and Cathy," Will listed the Fleming brood in order. Mariana wondered that Catherine would have time to raise seven children while working as an International assassin. "The legend is each being born nine months after a headline-grabbing assassination, but that's probably lore," Will said. "She tells each of them they are her favorite child, but everyone knows she dotes on Tree."

"You are friends with some colorful people," Mariana laughed. She knew Will was just trying to lighten the mood, to calm her down. Her heart was still beating a thousand beats a minute.

"So where are we going? To Wales?"

"Not right away," Will said, pulling her around to his side on the couch, her head now resting where her feet had been as Will worked his fingers gently through her hair. "People might expect us to do that, and we never do what people expect us to do. First, we're going to Scotland."

"Oh, do I get to be Lady Stevenson now?"

Will had mentioned that he had inherited a title, Baronet, from his father's Scottish side of the family.

"No," Will said. "You get to be Mariana Smith, the humble wife of a humble banker who works for a big finance guy by the name of Stevenson. Stevenson has given a place he owns in Scotland to my cousin and his family to live in for a while and offered him a job. My cousin is a black sheep. Do you remember what I told you about the branches of my family that fell away from the practices of my ancestors?"

"Like Marsha's family," Mariana said. "She told me you were rebuilding bridges to those black sheep cousins, though. Is that what you're trying to do here?"

"I have been trying, yes," Will said, "but I don't know that Fraser will be as wise as Marsha was."

"Okay, so where in Scotland are we headed?"

"Near Edinburgh," Will said. "We may even have some time to visit Stevenson's castle near Inverness while we're there, but I don't know."

Mariana rose, sat on his lap, and hugged her husband tight. He seemed to need it at this point. "I'm going to be a good girl, *Papi*, don't worry," she said. "We're all going to be fine."

"From your sweet lips to the Lord's patient ear," Will whispered against her nape.

"You want to join the mile high club again?" Mariana asked.

"Oh, yes, baby, very much."

13

On Lucifer's Wings

Will lifted her right off the couch and carried her down the aircraft cabin to their master bedroom at the back, laying her on the queen sized bed which one of the flight attendants had already turned down for them before disappearing to their respective stations. He went back to shut the door and walked towards Mariana slowly, undoing his tie and unbuttoning his shirt. Mariana licked her lips and started unbuttoning her blouse.

"Stop," Will commanded. "You sit still. Hands at your side, young lady."

"*Sí, Papi,*" Mariana said, placing her hands on the mattress, her arms extended, she sat up, with her knees together and her feet apart, giving him a view only of the shadow of her crotch under her skirt.

Will took off his shirt and let it drop on the carpet. He looked even better, bare chested in the slacks of his navy suit, half cave man, half CEO. He unbuckled his belt slowly, keeping his eyes on her as he inched closer, and pulled the belt out of its loops, winding it in his right hand.

"*¿Me vas a zurrar?*" She hadn't really earned a hiding, that she knew of, but Will just felt like playing rough. That was just fine by Mariana, she was wound up so tight she needed the release. She worried the flight attendants might hear her whimpering and crying out, but they were probably paid well to ignore whatever noises came out of the bedroom.

"*Sí, nena,*" Will confirmed.

Mariana couldn't help the fluttering in her belly and the instant tightening of her channel, any more than she could keep her panties from getting soaked by her desire. She breathed deep and bit her lip.

"*¿Porqué?*" she asked.

"Because I can," Will said, moving forward another step. "Because you love it. Because even when you're being a good girl, you're naughty."

"What about them?" Mariana nodded her head towards the door.

"I don't want to whip them. I want to whip *you*. Properly. Every night."

Mariana's breath hitched. There it was. Robert Whitby's threat. The words the Leviathan had whispered in her ear at Marsha's party. As she had long suspected, Will had definitely heard them. Just how didn't matter. He knew. He had always known. Yet, when Robert had said the same words on Marsha's patio in Palo Alto, Mariana had felt cold, like a mouse about to be swallowed whole by a snake, doomed to suffocate in the acid of the monster's digestive tract. When Will said it now, she felt hot. Still prey, but the prey of a soft-furred Artic wolf, with sharp teeth and a warm beating heart. She felt like the sub of a strict, angry, but loving Master.

"I'm sorry," she said.

They both knew she was apologizing for letting Martin use her so badly, and for failing to tell Will the whole of what happened between her and Robert Whitby. They both knew she had nothing really to apologize for. This wasn't about that. This was about them: the wolf and the lamb. They both needed this to work off their tension.

"You will be," Will said, taking one more step forward, then folding and snapping the belt.

"*Ay, Papi*," Mariana sighed.

"This is who you are now," Will said. "You are my slave. Wherever we go, you show you fear and respect me. You will not look another man in the eyes and speak only if I give you permission to speak. You will walk by my side and sit at my feet. You will prostrate yourself to me and beg for forgiveness for whatever fault I find in your behavior. Do you understand?"

"Is this the play now?" Mariana asked, seeing that this was more than a night of fun. Will had a plan.

"It is the only play," Will said. "Until I draw the curtains and shut off the stage lights. This is who you are. Who are you?"

"I am your slave," she said.

"What is your name?"

"Whatever you call me," Mariana said.

Will smiled, climbed up on his knees at the foot of the bed, and kissed her. "You're such a smart pussy," he said. "You just slide right into a new life as needed, don't you? I think I'll let you have some milk when I'm done."

Mariana felt good about the compliment on her acting skills. But then Will pulled her up by the arm and tossed her down again—every movement tempered to protect the peas —face down on the mattress, with her lower belly lying over a pillow. He gave her another pillow to bite down on before taking off her shoes, tearing the back slit on her skirt open right up to the waist, and landing a hard lash from his belt on her upper thighs.

Mariana wept and screamed into the pillow as the belt whistled and struck again, this time landing on her calves.

When she kicked back, another followed on the soles of her feet.

"Ow-ow!" Mariana cried out. "Not there, *Papi*, please!"

"You will settle and take your punishment, or you will regret it," Will said.

His voice reached her depths and sent a shiver running through her flesh. Her wayward pussy only got warmer and wetter. He surely saw the evidence of that when he pulled her panties down to mid-thigh. Mariana knew Will would see her glistening pussy. He stroked her drenched folds with two fingers and painted a cross on the fullness of each cheek with the moisture he'd gathered.

"X marks the spot," Will warned, then put one hand on her lower back and began crisscrossing her ass with the belt. Will had spanked, paddled, blistered and whipped Mariana soundly many times, but the strength he put into this whooping was like nothing else that had come before. Mariana was screaming against the pillow, blinded by tears, her ass aflame. Soon, she was sure, she wouldn't be able to sit for the landing, much less sit in a car for however long it took for them to get to Will's cousin's house. Will just kept going, and she couldn't take it. She didn't dare kick up, for fear that he would strike her soles again.

"Pippin!" she cried out. Will had told her to use his middle name as a safe word. She'd never had to use it before, but this was much too much. He stopped immediately, just as he had promised he would.

Except, Will had claimed being called Pippin would quell his passion entirely, because it was what his mother and his maternal grandmother called him. Having met Anne, his grandmother, Mariana understood that this name would have an immediate chilling effect on her husband. Yet, when she finally dared to turn around, she saw through her tears that Will was very hard. He had taken off all his clothes and stood naked by the side of the bed with the sort of erection which might traumatize a virgin and frighten a whore into taking a vow of chastity. His phallus was dark with blood, the head of his dick swollen and glistening.

Will bent to whisper in her ear. "Pippin is dead," he said. "If you seek mercy, beg Lucifer for it."

Mariana shuddered. That's what he was. She could see it in his fierce, hungry eyes, his dark hair damp with sweat, his perfect muscles tense. He was a gorgeous, terrifying, fallen angel. The brightest of all could become the darkest of all.

She was properly afraid, but not of Will. Mariana feared her sudden, desperate need to be claimed by the devil who now crouched over her on the bed, fucking her with his fingers. She wanted him more than she ever had, which couldn't be right. What was *wrong* with her? She was in pain —far from the worst pain she'd felt in her life—but real scalding pain. As her ass and thighs recovered their senses, she could feel the welts forming on her skin, but this only made her wetter. When Will shifted from having three fingers inside her to putting his entire hand in her channel and forcing her open, she moaned for him like a *Moura Encanta-dora*, the wanton mythical creature her mother had always warned her she'd become. She was transformed. She had been Will's woman from the beginning. Now, she was his succubus.

"Come, slave," he commanded. "Come for your Master. I'm going to break you open. Come."

Mariana squeezed the pillow with her fists until her knuckles were white. As Will's hand reached for the limit of her inner flesh, touching the borders of her cervix, she convulsed, her entire body shaking, and screamed for him again. "*¡Joder!*"

"On your knees," Will said, pulling his hand out of her, "and face me."

Mariana complied, coming head to head with his erection. She stuck out her tongue to gather some of the moisture dripping from the tip. Will grabbed her up by the hair and viciously ravaged her mouth.

"I give. You take," he growled. "You do not take what is not given."

"Yes, Master," she whimpered.

He let go of her hair and she dropped back onto the mattress, her cheek flat against the ivory Egyptian cotton sheets, her ass up in the air, her arms stretched to her sides, her hands flat on the mattress. She waited for his command.

"Do you want your Master to fuck your mouth?"

"Yes, please."

"You understand I will fuck your mouth hard and deep?"

"Yes."

"Will you swallow every drop of cum?"

Mariana nodded, her eyes pleading with him.

"If you behave, I will take your mouth tomorrow," Will said. "Right now, I'm going to break your bright red ass. Get up."

Mariana rose on her knees to face him. Will tore her silk blouse off and ripped what remained of her skirt apart, leaving her clothes in tatters on the floor. Mariana stood with breasts at attention, her nipples hard as two deep red pebbles pressing against the stretchy, sheer fabric of her ivory brassiere. Her panties had fallen down between her knees. Will flicked the front snap of her bra open and set her breasts free, then he took both nipples between his thumbs and forefingers and squeezed hard, turning them like dials on a radio. The only music he switched on was the sound of Mariana's tearful whimpers. He slapped her breasts for complaining.

"I'm tempted to whip these," he said.

"No, Will," Mariana pleaded. Her breasts were so sensitive she couldn't imagine the pain of having him strike them with the belt.

He grabbed her chin hard. "Did you say 'no' to me?"

Will didn't wait for an answer. He just invaded her mouth again, his tongue wrestling with hers as his hands kept her from pulling away. He left her utterly breathless and melting, the slickness of her desire dripping down her thighs.

"There is no 'no'," Will said. "There is only 'yes, Master' or 'Lucifer, please'. Nod if you understand."

Mariana nodded. She wondered about Will's mysterious cousin Fraser and what sort of man he might be if Will thought this Master/slave role play was a necessary part of their cover. Still, she trusted Will to know the script. Besides, the truth was she was so turned on by this new, demonic face of her husband that she didn't really care what the play was about. She might feel differently tomorrow, but tonight she needed more of her fallen angel.

Will pushed her back on the mattress, parted her legs and crawled between them, bringing his erection to the mouth of her channel while wrapping one hand around her throat. He entered her with a vicious thrust, but still ever mindful of the babes, and locked his free hand in hers as he stroked, filling her completely, nearly pulling out, and ramming her again. With each thrust he pushed her closer to collapse, until she could no longer think, she could only feel his absolute possession and the fire it ignited on her flesh.

"I own the best cunt in the world," Will said, as she melted under him. Her head reeling. He pulled out and kissed her deep again. Then looked down on her, his eyes alight. "And the best ass."

Will flipped Mariana over, and then he pulled her up by the hips and parted her cheeks, spreading the moisture from her folds to her rose, and entered her from behind. Mariana couldn't suppress a scream as he filled her, his balls slapping her lower lips with each deep thrust.

"Scream, baby," he growled, grabbing her by the hair as he slammed into her ass again. "Beg me to hurt you."

"Hurt me, please, Master," she wept. "Hurt me bad. Mark me, Will. Fuck me up."

He bent over her and bit her shoulder, while reaching around to pinch her swollen clit. His thrusts became wild. She cried out his name as they joined each other in the fall.

Will collapsed over her, laughing, his breath strained from a blend of mirth and exertion.

"Fuck me up," he chuckled. "Baby, your will is my command."

"You're my Will," she said, panting.

"Exactly."

They had slept peacefully for most of the flight over, Mariana snuggled in his arms like a plush toy. She awoke to gentle kisses on her neck. Mariana purred and whimpered as her body recovered its senses, a delicious ache coating her body.

"Are the peas okay?" he asked, spooned on her back.

"Yeah, they think their daddy is a freak, but they like it."

"I think you're projecting," Will chuckled. "Their mommy is a freak. Their daddy is the devil himself."

"Why, Will?"

"Many reasons," he said, squeezing her tighter against him. "First, I need you to act as I said last night. No looking at other men. Stick to me like glue, don't wander. Say nothing unless I allow you to speak."

"Is your cousin expecting you to have a slave for a wife?"

"No, my cousin is a trap. I don't want you tripping. Be a

dutiful wife and you'll make it out of Edinburgh unscathed. Otherwise, the Scots have this thing called a tawse. I don't recommend it." He rubbed her sore ass in case she needed reminding that she'd had enough. Mariana whimpered, but the pain was less than she had expected. Will knew how to handle his implements. He had never really explained how he gained these powerful skills, but he'd obviously practiced plenty before she came along.

"There are other reasons too," Will continued. "For one, I need the Eagles to see you like this at the Convocation— fully dominated and chastised, especially after your behavior during the auction in France. You have earned a reputation as a shrew. I want to prove that you are now fully tamed—an easy asset to protect."

Will reached his hand around her hip to her mons and reached through the part on her lower lips with his middle finger to stroke her clit. She felt his erection pressed against her ass and she wiggled to get closer.

"Besides, I love this role," he said and nibbled on her ear. "Remember, I've always warned you that your wolf has sharp teeth. I know you're wound tight, with good reason. I know you need to release pressure. As Charlie put it, you need more rough than you've been getting. Never let it be said I don't give my wife what she needs."

"You discussed this *with Charlie*?" Mariana's voice went up two pitches.

"It came up in a pertinent conversation," Will said. "Lord knows I don't seek him out for advice in bed. But Charlie already knows everything about you, and about me too."

"Oh, Jesus Christ! He saw the videos Martin took, didn't he?"

"Mariana, he's not judging. By his standards, we're pretty

mild, verging on vanilla," Will said. "He doesn't think any less of you for anything, believe me. He gets it."

"Oh, geez." Mariana covered her eyes with her palm. She'd never be able to face Charlie again without turning a dazzling pink.

Will turned Mariana on her back and kissed her gently. "Don't fuss, sweetheart," Will said. "Everybody has a dark side. Are you up to the play, lamb? Will you walk down the aisle with me again, as the bride of Satan in Castle Blood?"

"Is that what Castle Gwaed means?"

"Yes."

"So, not a scary place *at all* to have a wedding," Mariana joked.

"It's more life blood than flowing blood, and it is a beautiful castle," Will said. "You're going to love it."

"I love my gentle Will too, you know," Mariana said, kissing him. "Is Pippin dead for good?"

"Did you never see the musical?" Will gave her a funny look. Mariana couldn't remember ever seeing it, but she made a mental note to check it out. "Don't worry, Lucifer can be very gentle with a deserving little demon. Just play your role. There will be no room for error."

"Okay, *Papi*, however you think we should play this, we will," Mariana kissed him again, rubbing up against his erection.

"My luscious, lustful slut," he said, smiling and sliding his fingers deeper along her folds. She parted her legs for him. "Have you ever given head in the shower at 40,000 feet?"

"Has *anyone*?"

"I couldn't say. We're not the only ones with a shower installed on their aircraft."

"How about in *this* specific shower?"

"Don't be impertinent," he said, slapping her butt and

avoiding the question. "Follow me, minx. Let's get me clean and get you dirty."

"What about the water timer?"

"I'll come quick. Believe me." He bit her lower lip. "And you never come dry, my little WAP."

Mariana followed her Master out of bed, trying really, really hard not to giggle.

Before they landed at the airport, Will removed Mariana's diamond necklace. "This jewel is much too rich for your role," he said. He replaced it with a metal collar instead. It was a thick, solid circle of platinum with an oval of amber trapping an ancient dragonfly, and was closed with a gold lock at the back. Will kept the key. He put the diamond necklace in the bedroom's safe. "You'll get it back. I promise."

Will also picked out a dress for her to wear for the day. His staff had helpfully filled the closet with outfits in her size, assembled for the trip on short-notice. Again, Mariana wondered at her husband's ability to get things he needed practically at the drop of a hat, but he could afford to have shoppers on-call in every major city around the world and many of the larger towns.

His choice of costumes for his slave/sub wife on this trip was intriguing. They were basically repetitions on a theme, a form-fitting dress with a plunging neckline and easy access. All the dresses were jet black. The one he picked out had a gold zipper back. He had also ordered three sets of slipper mules with low kitten heels for her in matte black, patent leather, black and gold. No bras, panties or stockings. "You won't need them," Will said simply.

"Won't I need makeup either?" Mariana asked, searching

for the handy kit which had been in front of the mirror on the bathroom drawer on her last trip.

"Definitely no makeup," Will said. "This time I need all of your beautiful blushes on display. And you have perfect skin. You don't need it."

"Not even a little lipstick?"

"Mariana," Will said, standing right up behind her at the mirror, his hands caressing her body, his erection pressed against her ass. "You're glowing. Your lips are sinfully plump and rosy, above and below. You need nothing added to get me hard as steel. That should be your only concern. What others think of you shouldn't matter. My slave lives to please me and me alone."

Will kissed her neck.

"I feel fat," she admitted. "And this dress hides nothing."

"You are full of life, because of me," Will said and breathed against her ear. His breath warmed her neck, raising goosebumps on her arms. "Do you think for a moment I wouldn't want to put that on display?"

Mariana met her husband's eyes in the mirror and gave him a crooked smile.

"You're making me wet again," she complained, "and I'm going to stain the dress when I sit down."

Will raised the gold zipper on her dress, slowly working up from the slit at the back, exposing her rear.

"Spread your legs," he commanded. "Put your palms on the counter." Mariana complied. Only moments later, Will thrust his cock deep into her. "You're right." He grasped her breasts, spilling them over the low shelf of the collar of her dress. He thrust again, hard enough to make her whimper, her flesh still sensitive after his rough handling the night before. "You're drenched." He growled, pressing his thumb between her lips, against her tongue, pulling and bruising her mouth just as his cock bruised her pussy. "Let's get you wetter." He reached down between her lower lips, pounded into her again, and squeezed her bulb. "I want you staining all your dresses." She sighed. "I want you smelling of my cum. I want it dripping down your inner thighs." Her eyes closed as her head reeled again. "I want you ready to fuck in every way, anywhere, anytime." She was ready, so ready to fall on her knees for this demon husband and she might never rise again. "Open your eyes!" he commanded. "Look at me." She saw his reflection in the mirror, the dark, inverted twin of the man she knew. A man capable of anything. "I want you knowing this rod is ready to pierce you and break you any hour of the day." His thrusts intensified as he pushed her over the abyss. She moaned and struggled to stay upright. Will gripped her hips to hold her up as he continued to ram his cock against her cervix. "I want everyone to know, Mariana." His face contorted as his warm seed filled her. "Everyone." When Will finally pulled out, he slapped her bottom, reawakening the soreness from the hiding he'd given her the night before. "Straighten yourself out," he ordered, with a twisted grin, lowering the zipper of her dress again. "It's nearly showtime."

Will stepped out and headed for the main cabin of the plane for breakfast. Mariana was breathless and speechless. And still very turned on. Who was this unmasked, raw man who walked in her husband's body? She wanted him to stick around a while.

14

The Lost Cousin

They were near to Edinburgh, but in the countryside in East Lothian, within view of the sea. Mariana enjoyed the view of Scotland in the sunshine and the way her skin vibrated every time Will touched his pinkie to hers in the car. It was a sign of life, more than a sign of possession—a reassurance. He was still there, in the depths, the man she loved wearing the skin of the man she served.

They arrived at what looked like a small castle, a country house made entirely of stone with battlements on the roof. They filled gaps in the ancient structure with steel beams and glass walls. Fraser Andrews greeted them at the covered entrance in the driveway, standing in front of double oak doors reinforced by large iron nails. He was a tall man, with bright red hair, wide at the chest and narrow at the hips, dressed all in tweed, like he was going hunting in the moors. He had a bright white smile on his lips and worry in his eyes.

"William, man, it's so very good to see you!" Fraser's voice boomed.

"Fraser!" Will called out.

They exchanged hugs with lots of hard back-slapping.

"Meet my wife, Mariana."

Will's accent had changed immediately to Scottish, matching Fraser's. Mariana felt as though she were with a different man again.

"You poor woman, brought here to the middle of nowhere," Fraser said. "Your husband is a heartless bastard. She's as pretty as a rose, Will. You should take better care of her."

Mariana did not dare reply, she only nodded and gave him a shy smile. Will gripped her shoulders, pulling her close to his side. "She is a beauty, and she comes as I please," Will said.

Fraser laughed, a deep belly laugh that echoed far enough to reach the birds in the trees.

Mariana was always good at meeting new people, except Will's people. Well, not entirely. She liked the folks in Fairfarm, took to Charlie right away, and had been friends with Marsha even before Will came along. But his grandmother and grandfather had unnerved and irritated her when she met them in France. The Flemings were a puzzle. Fraser struck her as a bit of a jerk. Having to keep up with this alternative version of Will, also unsettled her. But Mariana intended to prove to him she could roll with any cover and deal with anything that came their way in the field. After all, this was a mission. One she didn't understand, but she could stitch it together soon enough. All she had to do was stick by Will's side. She could do that.

"Come inside," Fraser said. "Rhiannon is with the children somewhere, but we'll find her. Jonas, the butler, can take care of all your things and get them upstairs. Are you up for some coffee, and a pleasant chat, or are you too jet-lagged?"

"No, coffee would be good," Will said, "for me. Mariana will have chamomile or herbal tea, if you have it, or orange juice."

"I wouldn't know whether Rhiannon has chamomile, but we'll get it sorted. There's sure to be orange juice."

"That will be fine," Will said.

If Fraser thought there was anything odd in Will answering for her, he didn't show a hint. Mariana couldn't stop thinking about coffee since Fraser offered, but she'd drink whatever at this point. Her mouth was dry.

Inside, the mansion was an eclectic blend of ancient and modern, airy, thanks to large glass roof panels filling gaps where the ruins had collapsed, with strong, raw wood beams overhead in closed parts. Mariana admired the blend of cozy chic in the décor.

"You've made yourselves at home," Will noted as they walked past a sitting room littered with children's toys.

"It's not our home, as you know. We're just caretakers."

"Don't be silly, Fraser, you're living in the place," Will said. "It's your home, every bit as much as it is Stevenson's."

"Well, we'd be in some fix, if it weren't for you, cousin," Fraser said. "Things are hard nowadays, as you know."

"Yes," Will said, somber. "I came to see what I can do about that."

Fraser shrugged this off. "Let's get our coffee and chamomile and get your wife somewhere to sit down. She must be tired from the journey. Also, we'll find Rhiannon to join us. You'll love Rhiannon, Mariana. She's a mad, feisty Welsh woman, but I'm hopelessly in love with her."

"I'm sure they'll get along beautifully," Will said.

Mariana wasn't sure, not really. She didn't want to meet anyone else until Will had time to explain more about his cousin, but Will had promised her a full explanation tonight.

They finally settled around a wood table in a cozy nook in the kitchen. She sat quietly by Will's side, sipping a raspberry tea that Fraser had found in the cupboards, and listened as the men got down to their business. Mariana hoped that whatever she overheard would help her make sense of the tangle with Fraser. Will's words were still rolling around in her head. Why was Fraser a trap? Why would she trip?

"It's all down to the banks," Fraser said, "heartless, greedy bastards. They've taken their bail-outs and they're still casting people from their homes, as if the public money we gave them didn't more than pay for the bad debt. They're doubling their money, stuffing their pockets, and putting good people on the streets."

"We have the same problem in the States," Will said.

"The same shit everywhere," Fraser seemed furious, as though it were personal. "Meanwhile, the bonuses keep being paid out, on profits they made from outright theft."

"And this is what you said to the Board?"

"Yes, I wanted to restructure debt at lower interest for those who had defaulted because of loss of employment," Fraser said. "I said we could verify the claims, ensure there was a legitimate need. I told them we could justify the losses over time, just in people staying on their feet, you know, that the economy is replenished from the ground up, not from the top down."

"So, they fired you."

"They didn't just fire me, Will. I'm persona non grata," Fraser spat. "Everyone turned their backs on us—everyone. Even Rhiannon's so-called society friends, and Rhys was bullied terribly at school. It goes that far, man."

"Well, you're safe here," Will said.

"Yes, and we're grateful, but I can't live like this," Fraser said. "You know me, I need to do something useful with my life. I'm no good living on charity."

"It's not charity when family helps family," Will said. "It's a moral obligation."

"Yes, well, it feels like charity." Fraser stared at his coffee cup. "I'm sorry, William. I'm grateful to you, and to your boss, but I'm a man, dammit. I'm used to standing on my own two feet."

Will nodded and drank his coffee, letting silence settle for a while before asking his cousin a delicate question.

"What happened to your savings?"

"What savings?" Fraser scoffed. "I had some in the market, you know, but most of my investments were in my bank—more fool I. I relied on the promise of a Golden Parachute. Who knew they would make it of lead? Our house belonged to the bank, too, as part of my compensation package. They threw us out, like bad tenants. They used me as a scapegoat, Will. It was humiliating."

"Stevenson is interested in the micro-loans market," Will said. "He and his partners have a plan. I have approval to involve you, in a Directorate, here in Scotland. Would you consider joining our group?"

"Well, man, I can see they've treated you very well, but are you sure they would want me? I mean, what is it they say in America? My name is mud."

"People have very short memories, when money is involved," Will said. "If my employers back you, then you might find that you are golden once again, quickly."

Fraser shrugged. "My mind is open to the right offer."

"We'll arrange for you to meet some key people," Will said. "By the way, Stevenson told me there's a man coming on the property—an Arborist from America—who will check the forest. He should be here today. By coincidence, his name is also William Smith."

Mariana looked in Will's eyes, but Will didn't even blink.

"Could you see he's put up comfortably with Marshall,

the gamekeeper?" Will asked. "He should only be here a week, maybe two."

"Well, you can give the orders, as you are here now," Fraser said.

"No, Fraser, you're in charge here," Will said. "It's your home. I'm just the messenger."

"Sorry it took me so long!" Rhiannon hobbled in, breathless, a small boy attached to her right leg, like a little ginger koala-bear. He got his hair from his father. His mother's hair was jet black.

"Rhys, for the love of pudding, let go of my leg," Rhiannon said. "I'm sorry. He's in a mood."

Fraser got up immediately to pry his son from his wife's leg and flew him up in the air, like a jet plane, making engine noises. The little boy giggled until he was red in the face. "Come with me ye wee brownie," Fraser said. "Stop making trouble for yer poor mother."

Will was already standing up, and had motioned to Mariana to stay seated, but he went up to Rhiannon and gave her a warm hug.

"Rhiannon, you look like a million bucks!"

"I feel like a penny."

"We'll soon fix that. Please meet my wife, Mariana," Will said.

Rhiannon's blue eyes scanned Mariana carefully before deciding on a broad, toothy smile.

"You've got a good man," Rhiannon said, which was a curious thing to say upon meeting another woman, Mariana thought. She felt her jealousy rising, though she knew it would disappoint Will.

Will must have sensed it, because he lifted her up out of the chair and gave her a deep, intimate kiss. "She's an excellent woman."

"William's all right, when he's not being a heartless

bastard," Fraser joked, but Mariana got the sense there was some genuine bitterness there. She couldn't really understand why.

Mariana wasn't up to all the false levity, but she tried her best to hide it. Will's eyes told her to be patient and promised resolution to the millions of questions racing through her mind.

"Mariana," Rhiannon said, "you must be exhausted from the flight. I bet these two have been boring you with nonsense about finance. Why don't we get you to your room, so you can have a rest?"

"I'll go with Mariana, if it's all right with both of you," Will said. "She'll need some help to unpack. To be honest, I could use some rest myself."

"Go, both of you," Fraser said. "Rhiannon will show you the way. Should we expect you for dinner?"

"We're not having haggis, are we? I don't think Mariana's stomach is up to it."

Rhiannon laughed. "No, I'll be making salmon. I'm sure you'll both like it fine."

"Rhiannon is a chef," Fraser, explained to Mariana, "or she was until she sold her restaurant to a partner, and stopped to take care of the children for a while."

"I'm thinking of opening one again," Rhiannon said, "here in Edinburgh."

"As well you should," Will said, "if you're ready. You don't want to be locked up with three children all day."

"We only have two, Will," Fraser said.

"No, Fraser, Will is right," Rhiannon said, "and it's the oldest who gives me the most trouble."

"Hey, you!" Fraser said, with mock affront, kissing her on the cheek, even as he protested.

"Follow me, you lovebirds," Rhiannon said to Will and Mariana, "let's get you to your nest."

15

Too Many Smiths

Mariana

Their bedroom was on the far end of the house, a wing away from the one where Fraser and his wife and children lived. Like the rest of the mansion, the décor was eclectic, and the room well-lit and airy. The windows overlooked a wild garden with an old fountain in the center, going green with moss, and the forest beyond. Mariana could not really appreciate the beauty of it. She was much too angry.

"I know," Will said, coming up to her and hugging her from behind, since she insisted on turning her back on him, "it's a lot to take in."

"There's another William Smith coming here?"

"I've told you, I train apprentices."

"Will…"

"I have several William Smiths—all over the place," he said. "It helps to keep things straight."

"Does it? It just seems confusing to me."

"What is in a name? A rose by any other name…"

Mariana pulled away. "Shut up, Will. I'm in no mood."

"It works, Mariana." Will grabbed her hand and pulled her up against his hard chest, lifting her chin with his finger. "If you weren't angry, you'd realize how necessary it is."

"Don't you ever tire of having to keep all these false identities straight?"

"I know who the real Will Smith is, and so do you."

"Yes, the actor," Mariana said, bitterly.

"I admit I have to act and play a part, but darling, don't you? Isn't all of life a play?"

"Stop with the Shakespeare!"

"No, I like that William very much," Will said. "The point is, Mariana, that in this life we have to do what we have to do to get by. You know that. My family labors for the common good, and that is all that should matter. The books are open to you. If you can find a single firm we manage or a single transaction we make, motivated by greed, or operated with no ethical core, then tell me, because I'll break it down overnight."

"How big is your organization, Will? The whole of it?"

"It's global," Will said. "We have gardeners and foresters on every continent. Some places, we've only seeded and collaborate with allies. In other places, we have deep roots."

"What about Charlie's?"

"Charlie floats on the wind," he said. "The Hawks go wherever there's trouble and vanish when there's peace again."

"Is there *ever* peace?"

"Yes, Mariana," Will said, holding her close, his arms and chest emanating heat. "And there will be again."

"Do you think Fraser believes it's just a coincidence that Stevenson sent a man to check out his trees who has the same name as you?"

"It doesn't matter whether he bought it." Will kissed her gently. "It's not that uncommon a name, after all. Fraser thinks I'm a low-ranking finance man, working for Stevenson in New York. He knows nothing about my trees and forests. He probably never will."

"Why?"

"Because he lies too poorly," Will sighed. "You need to be a more persuasive liar to work in the field. His roots are rotten, and it seems the rot has set in."

"Wasn't anything he said true?"

"It was almost all true, but it wasn't true of *him*," Will said. "They fired Fraser for pushing risky high-interest loans on people who couldn't afford them and who would never get out from under the burden of that debt. Too many of his loans failed, so they sacked him. There were also accusations that he made up some of the loan applicants, and pocketed the funds, but the bank didn't charge him with fraud. I'd like to understand why that was. It makes me suspicious about the bank he worked for, and our organization has some dealings with them from time to time. Fraser reached out to me for a loan to get him through this crisis, and I gave him some money with no strings attached. When he asked for more, I offered to get Stevenson to help him instead. Let's see what he does with Stevenson's offer, but I have little hope for him. It's a shame because I like Rhiannon."

"She seems to like you too," Mariana said.

Will smacked her ass. "Jealous wench."

"Ouch!" Mariana protested. "I don't like other women ogling my man like that. You know that."

Will took her face in his hands and kissed her with a desperate hunger. "Say that again."

"I don't like other women ogling my man," Mariana whispered, breathless.

Will pressed her hand against his slacks so she could feel his erection. "Do you think this is for her?"

"No," Mariana answered, meekly.

"Who is the only woman who gets this cock?"

"*Me?*" Mariana's voice squeaked.

"Do you doubt it?" He put his hand on her throat.

"No," Mariana answered as his gaze burned her from the inside out.

Will stuck his hand under her skirt and caressed her naked pussy. "Whose cunt is this?"

"Yours," Mariana sighed as Will slid his fingers between her lips and thrust them inside.

"Do you think I could find a better cunt anywhere in this world? A wetter one? One that responded to its Master as this cunt does?"

"No." Mariana was on the edge of coming again, but Will took back his hand.

"Don't you dare," he said, speaking against her parted lips. "Don't you dare come, Mariana." He nudged her feet apart. "Keep those thighs open. No squeezing your legs together. No coming until I say you can come."

"Yes, Master." Mariana kissed him gently.

"Good girl," Will said. He turned her around, pulled the zipper open and took her dress off. "Now go stand in the corner and think about what you did. Don't move an inch until I get back. Don't touch yourself, or you'll regret it."

"Where are you going?"

"To fetch a tawse."

Will was gone for what seemed like a very long time. Despite her desire to obey him, to be a good sub and stay with her nose pressed in the corner, the babies had other plans. She was suddenly ravenous. She wished she had something better to put on than the silly dress that made her look and feel like a hooker, but the other alternatives in their luggage weren't much better.

In the end, she slipped the dress back on, checked herself in the mirror, and snuck out of the room to find the kitchen again.

She found Rhiannon there with her two kids. Rhys sat in the nook eating baby carrots, and a younger baby sat on a highchair spreading mush around as Rhiannon tried to feed her.

"Mariana," Rhiannon said, putting down the plastic spoon. "I thought you two were napping. Is there anything I can do for you?"

"Sorry," Mariana said. "I didn't mean to disturb your feeding time. I just wondered whether you might have a banana or something?"

"If you're hungry, I'm happy to make you a snack," Rhiannon said. "Would you like a sandwich?"

"No, it's…" Mariana sighed. "I'm just having a craving. I don't want you to go through any trouble."

"Are you pregnant, then?" Rhiannon looked her over again.

"Yes," Mariana smiled.

"Funny that Will didn't mention it. Silly man." She shrugged. "I don't have any bananas in the house right now, but I could have Jonas go to the shops."

"No, I don't want to trouble anyone," Mariana said. "I know you're busy. What's the little one's name?"

"Lucy," Rhiannon said, wiping the girl's face clean. "Fussy, messy, Lucy. I have some banana flavor baby food. Would you like a jar? I know it's not quite the same, but if you have a craving…"

"Yes, that would be good," Mariana said, answering for her stomach. "Thank you."

Rhiannon went to the cupboard. Mariana pinkie wrestled with Lucy, who giggled with a broad toothless grin. Lucy's hair was a chaotic fluff, dark like her mother's. Mariana picked up the spoon and tried to feed her a little of mush, and the girl swallowed it. Her eyes, two large blue orbs, fixed on Mariana. "*Que linda la nena*," Mariana whispered to Lucy. She offered the baby another small spoonful, and the girl swallowed.

"Oh, look at that," Rhiannon said, returning with the baby food jar and a spoon for Mariana. "Lucy's taken to you. I can't believe Will didn't tell us you were expecting. I guess that's why he said your stomach couldn't handle haggis."

Mariana gave Lucy one more spoonful before taking the banana mush jar her mother offered and digging into it like it was manna instead of mush.

"I'm fine to eat almost anything, now," Mariana said. "Though they surprise me, sometimes."

"They?"

"The twins," Mariana said, between spoonfuls. "They get many ideas about food and then they change their minds."

"Oh, you're expecting twins! I don't envy you that," Rhiannon said, struggling with Lucy again. "One at a time is bad enough."

"I'm sure you're right." Mariana smiled. "I'll just have to make it work somehow."

"Take my advice and get the epidural," Rhiannon said. "I wanted to be all natural with Rhys, and I quickly changed my mind with Lucy. There's nothing to be gained from the pain."

"I haven't thought that far out yet, which is silly, I know, but I've just," Mariana shrugged and stuffed her mouth again. She would not say her more immediate problems had distracted her, like being on someone's target list, but that was the truth. She hadn't even discussed giving birth with Will. They had both sort of taken it for granted that the kids would eventually come out. Mariana thought she might want a Caesarean section. She was definitely going to ask Dr. Austin about it during their next visit. Assuming they could go back to the US in time for their next visit. Or would she get stuck in Wales now? The uncertainty bothered her.

"Whatever you do, make it easy on yourself," Rhiannon advised. "And have some help around. I really miss our nanny."

"What happened?" Mariana asked, without thinking. Then she realized they'd probably had to give up the luxury of having any staff to deal with their current circumstances. The staff at this house worked for Stevenson and were probably not up to babysitting.

"Fraser has always had grand ambitions," Rhiannon said, answering a different question. "His family came from money, though most of it was lost. He wants to get it back, and sometimes he takes too many risks. I didn't just give up the restaurant because of the kids. That was part of it, but I also had an offer from my partner which got us out of a financial ditch, so I took it. The way things are now, I really need to figure out a way to make some income, but these two keep me really busy, as does Fraser."

"Have you thought about working from home?" Mariana asked. "You have such a lovely kitchen. I bet you'd build up an enormous fan base with short cooking shows recorded here."

"Pull a Nigella, you mean?" Rhiannon laughed. "I don't have those connections anymore, since all our bridges burnt in London."

"Well, you could start a cooking vlog or even short videos for social media," Mariana said. "Those are popular. You could grow from there and get sponsorships."

"Do you know a lot about that sort of thing?"

"Cooking shows are not my specialty," Mariana admitted. "I work in public relations and specialize in crisis management."

"Well, we could have used you six months ago, when the reporters were still hounding us," Rhiannon said, her tone as sour as Mariana's stomach suddenly was. The baby food was kicking back.

"It must have been hard on you," Mariana said.

"You can't imagine." Rhiannon wiped Lucy's face again. "We lost all our fair-weather friends and found we had none strong enough to weather a storm."

"I'm so sorry you went through that," Mariana said, not sure what else to say. She still did not know what exactly Fraser had done that was so controversial, but she didn't know enough about banking. If Rhiannon wanted to share more, she'd listen. Except not right this minute. "Oh, geez. Rhiannon, where is the nearest bathroom? I'm afraid the baby food wants to come right back out."

"Just down the hall there," Rhiannon pointed back the way Mariana had come. "First door on your left."

Mariana had to rush over to avoid vomiting on the polished stones of the hall, and just made it in time. As she washed out her mouth and splashed cool water on her face, she wondered where Will had gone. It wasn't like him to leave her alone in the corner waiting for a punishment and then forget all about her. She worried that something had gone wrong, but she couldn't imagine what.

She went back to the kitchen and Rhiannon offered to make her something that she might keep down. It was upsetting to be back to where her stomach rebelled at foods, but she racked it up to the other stress. Mariana was supposed to relax, according to Dr. Austin, but how could she do that? People actually wanted her dead. People she didn't know and would never meet. She had done nothing at all to deserve it, other than fall in love with an impossible man who was now hell bent on acting the role of a hard master. What a mess.

Worst of all, she desperately wanted Lucifer to come back with his tawse.

William

Will hadn't intended to leave his wife waiting. He recognized the vibration on his watch for what it was. An urgent request to call Charlie. He figured he'd only be gone long enough to make that phone call securely. Will snuck out to the forest before putting in his earpiece and returning Charlie's call through his watch.

"What's wrong?" Charlie wouldn't have buzzed him with good news. He knew that much.

"The story will break later today and I thought I should warn you," Charlie said.

"What story?"

"Harper's dead," Charlie said. "Someone made him into burger and dumped him in a prominent place—on the beach in Qatar."

"Are you *kidding*? He only just left!"

"From what I gather, the first thing Martin did when he landed was take out his anger on the wrong girl. There were permanent repercussions."

"But not from us." Will just needed to hear it.

"No, some friends of mine with an extensive client list over in that part of the world," Charlie said. "They gave me a courtesy call. They knew he was on my shit list."

"Karma's a bitch," Will said. "Though it wasn't what I had intended, I frankly don't care at this point."

"Well, just make sure the orange blossom doesn't mind,"

Charlie said, using the handle he had assigned to Mariana. "The result may confuse her, even if it is just a damned coincidence."

"It wasn't coincidence as much as fate," Will said. "He was always going to fuck with the wrong girl. I'm sure the orange blossom will see that."

"There's another thing," Charlie said, and then went quiet.

"Out with it, man, I've got her waiting."

"Shit, I don't know how to say this," Charlie sighed. "Call the Herald." Charlie meant Howard Fleming.

"Are you getting burned for something we did?"

"No, I'm not burned, but you are crisped, brother," Charlie said. "It's about Poison Ivy. Apparently, she has proof."

"Fucking hell!" Will said, understanding Charlie meant Sandra Price. "I'm a goddamned idiot!"

"I'd love to disagree with you, man, but you knew better," Charlie said. "She was always going to burn you."

"I'll never be able to get rid of the bitch now," Will said. "Fuck!"

"The Herald has a theory," Charlie said. "You'd better call him."

"Okay, thanks," Will said. "How's the situation in New York? Any point in us coming back before the wedding?"

"It's sticky all over here," Charlie said. "You've got less than two weeks, anyway. Everyone's gathering. We'll sort all the shit out. Spend the next few days enjoying the moors or whatever the fuck you want with your beautiful wife. How's the dark side working for you, by the way? Is it loosening her knots?"

"Shut up, Charlie," Will said.

"Just remember what you once told me, William. The trick to being Lucifer is not to get too attached to the wings.

Though I know they suit you. The Unkindness haven't gathered in Manhattan for a while, but we could arrange something when you get back. You'd both be welcome."

"No, Charlie," Will said. "Thanks for the offer, but I'm not into exhibitionism if I can help it—certainly not with the blossom."

"Suit yourself," Charlie said. "Just take good care of your bride. She needs you now more than ever."

"Speaking of which, I need to find a tawse," Will said.

"Yeah, man, I don't need to know all the details," Charlie said.

Will chuckled. "Goodbye, Charlie."

Will called Howard next, who confirmed that Sandra was expecting a son who, based on amnio testing, was Will's child. But Howard suggested that Will not take Sandra's test results too seriously.

"They were her lab, not ours. Remember The Leviathan's big project," Howard said, referring to Robert Whitby's troubling foray into genetic engineering. Howard wasn't wrong that Robert had everything to gain from seeing Will tied to Sandra through his child, but he doubted they'd need to use Robert's genetics division for something like that. It would be easy enough for them to fudge test results without needing those technologies.

Still, Howard's point was valid. Will needed to contest the tests and demand Sandra get new tests conducted by his own people. He asked Howard to put his lawyers on that right away and made his way back to the country house.

He didn't get far before bumping into himself in the forest. Will looked at the slightly younger version of William, now concerned that Fraser might see through the cover story, just as Mariana suggested. The man really could have been his brother. Then again, Will looked like many men.

"What do you think of the property? How will our forest

fare here?" Will asked the arborist who wasn't just there for the trees. He had come to ensure that Will was as free to roam around his properties in the UK in case he needed to stay longer than he'd originally planned.

"There are some termites in this house," he said, meaning someone, likely Fraser, had given access to the house to someone who had planted bugs. Jonas, the butler, had detected them. "Don't worry, boss, Jonas told me it was nowhere near the foundation." So they hadn't found his hidden office behind the wine cellar. That was fortunate. It had been one serious concern of allowing Fraser to use this home, though Will kept little in it that would be useful to his enemies.

"Is it something you and Marshall can address quickly?"

"Yes, he's having the men come in to fumigate tomorrow."

"Good. What about Inverness? I've been away too long. Is it safe for me to go there?"

"I came here first," the other William said.

"Okay, I need you to make sure all the root systems are sound again before you return home."

"Yes, I've already told Mrs. Jenkins that this assignment will take a few more weeks," the young man said. "She told me I'm an irresponsible bastard, keeping my wife on such a long trip, at a delicate point in her pregnancy."

Of course, that message was for Will, and the young man knew it.

"Mrs. Jenkins is a very straight shooter," Will said.

The other William chuckled.

"What about my shadows?" Will asked, referring to the threat alert that caused them to leave the country. "Do we know what's casting them?"

"We don't know yet with certainty," the younger William said. "The Hawks are chasing things down, as I'm sure you know. There are no shadows here. Only busy bodies. They may only try to get to know Stevenson better. Someone could have told them Stevenson was worth tapping for sap, Marshall feels."

"Tread with caution in reversing what they did, until we have all our facts," Will warned. "I don't want it to be obvious we knew. I don't want to call more attention to us. I won't allow anything to happen to my wife."

"Nothing will happen, we have you closely monitored and all the Eagles here are on alert."

"How do you feel about Jonas?"

"He told me to stick to trees, and he'd watch out for the good housekeeping."

"Well, he's a bit territorial."

"He and Marshall have an understanding, and Marshall is supportive. We'll all get on fine."

"You do excellent work, William, keep it up."

"Yes sir, for life."

"Are you married, William?"

"Still sowing oats."

"Well, that's fun too, but find yourself a good wife and don't make her fly when she's pregnant."

"Yes, sir."

As he crossed over to the gardens, Will ran into Fraser.

"William, what are you doing in the forest? I thought you were with your wife," Fraser said.

"I needed to walk off the flight. Mariana is sleeping. I was going to go check on her now."

Fraser nodded. "Well, sit with me a while so we can talk properly."

Will couldn't see how to get out of it, so he joined his

cousin on the bench by the fountain where Fraser apparently came out to smoke. He had taken one of the stone planters beside the bench as an ashtray. Fraser lit another cigarette as Will sat down.

"This boss of yours, Stevenson, he's a bit of a stiff, isn't he?" Frasier joked.

"How do you mean?"

"Well, I just get that impression, based on the staff here," Fraser said. "They all seem very formal and uptight."

"It's their job to maintain the house, I guess," Will said. "They're not really used to having a family with children."

"Why? Is Stevenson single?"

"Yes, I think so, anyway," Will said. "I don't really talk about much with him, beyond business. You were the exception. I asked Stevenson for a favor because I thought your experience might benefit the business."

"That wife of yours is a peach," Fraser said. "Why do you keep her on such a tight leash?"

"She needs it," Will said. "And I like it."

"Rhiannon wouldn't let me get away with treating her like that," Fraser said. "Even before the children, but much less now."

Will let it pass. It was really none of Fraser's business.

"You should stay awhile with us," Fraser said. "Rhiannon will enjoy having another woman around."

"I'm afraid Stevenson will need me back at headquarters soon."

"So tell him, no," Fraser said. "Learn to be your own man for a change, Will."

"You think?"

"Of course! You must have done well for yourself by now. Why not branch out? Go into business for yourself, instead of working for someone else."

"How do you mean?"

"You know this micro-loans thing, there's an excellent opportunity there we could capitalize on with offering lines of credit," Fraser said. "If you'd back me for a short while."

"What did you have in mind?"

"Well, I couldn't get back to business under my name, but yours is in good standing. I could support you. We could make the small loans, to businesses and individuals, offering them credit lines they can pull from as needed. We could give them small monthly payment plans, on longer terms, at a fair rate of interest to cover the risk."

"What rate of interest?"

"It depends on the market and the specific applicant," Fraser said. "I think we could maintain an average rate of twenty percent, monthly."

"That's usury, isn't it?"

"Don't be silly. It's not at the level of a pay-day loan. We'd have a captive market," Fraser said. "We'd be doing them a favor."

"Our firm has a ceiling at prime plus two," Will said. "We never give people debt they can't rise above."

"That's why they'll fail, Will. I mean, you're backing a losing horse. There's no way they'll make money on a venture like that."

"Well, they keep trim overheads," Will said. "The intent is to ensure return clients, who are stronger, less high risk, with each new loan."

"It still won't make you rich, man."

"No, I suppose it won't."

"You need to worry about keeping that beautiful wife of yours happy," Fraser said. "Whatever money you have won't make it very far, if you don't put it out to make more money."

"Is that the point, though, Fraser? For money *only* to

make more money? Isn't it supposed to grow things, employ people, and help build communities?"

Fraser laughed. "Oh cousin, you are starry-eyed—that's your problem," Fraser said. "You are an idealist, at heart. You're a dreamer, and, I'm sorry to say it, a bit of a fool."

"Fraser..."

"No, listen to me, cousin," Fraser interrupted. "The world isn't what you'd like it to be. It is what it is. Kill or be killed. Look at what happened to me. Don't let it happen to you. Strike first, if you have the strength for it. Don't wait for them to reach your jugular."

"Is there any truth to the claims that you made up loan applicants, Fraser?"

"None," Fraser said, and Will wished he could believe him. "They couldn't prove any of it. They only put that out there to discredit me because I made them look bad."

"So many bad loans, though," Will said. "You must have known at some point that the applicants didn't really qualify for that risk."

"It became a house of cards, after a while," Fraser admitted. "If it hadn't been for the crisis, the numbers would have evened out. We just ran into some bad luck. The interest from paying accounts wasn't high enough to bridge the gap on those who defaulted. I'd fix that on this new venture with you, if you have the mettle for it. Otherwise, I suppose I will take the position Stevenson is offering. It's a job, isn't it? I can do it for a while, anyway, until I get myself on my feet. But their salary offer is laughable."

"Isn't it a fair wage?"

"Not for someone of my caliber! I mean, they pay you more than that, don't they?"

Will was silent.

"Sorry, I'm not trying to pry, William, but you wouldn't work for so little, would you?"

"It's the same salary I get from the firm, Fraser."

"It can't be!" Fraser scoffed. "I mean, how do you even live?"

"I'm frugal, Fraser. I save what I have. I invest in growth. I spend only what I need."

"You pinch the pennies until they scream, don't you?" Fraser laughed.

"Fraser, I would never disparage you."

"I'm not disparaging you, Will," Fraser dragged on his cigarette. "Only trying to get you to wake up. Things can be different, you know, if you're clever."

"Yes, I suppose if I were clever, I'd realize that," Will said.

"So are you going to give it some thought, my proposal, I mean?" Fraser asked.

"I don't think I have the tolerance for the risk."

"Can't say I'm surprised." Fraser stuck the cigarette butt in the planter and reached in his jacket pocket for a new one. "It's a shame." Fraser lit the next cigarette. "We could have worked well together, you and I, Andrews and Smith, like in the old days. Like our great grandfathers. I suppose, those days are gone."

"Yes, I suppose they are."

"Don't worry, Will," Fraser slapped Will's thigh. "No hard feelings on my part. It was only an idea. I know you have to live your life your way, just as I have to live my life my way."

"I understand," Will said. "Whatever you decide, tell Stevenson by next Monday. He won't keep the offer on the table beyond that."

On the way back in, Will found his wife in the kitchen, chatting with Rhiannon and the children. He couldn't even be mad that she had left the bedroom. He had been gone much too long. The sight of Mariana bouncing Lucy on her lap as the little girl giggled, pulled on his heart. Mariana was clearly in her element as a mother, despite the sultry disguise he'd made her wear.

It reminded Will that Fraser's children would suffer if he acted as he knew he should. He ought to shun Fraser at this point. His ancestors would have. The man was corrupt beyond repair. But Will couldn't do that to Rhiannon. She only met Fraser because of William. Whatever else Fraser was, whatever foolish schemes he cooked up, he was a decent father and husband. Fraser's flaw was greed, but that greed could be managed with the right supervision. Will had the staff in place, here and at the Edinburg branch of his finance firm, to keep Fraser in check and out of trouble. He could try to keep Fraser employed, even if he had to double the salary offer.

"You heel!" Rhiannon said as soon as Will walked in. "You didn't tell us your wife is pregnant. The poor woman was starving."

Mariana looked at him to see whether he was angry that she'd shared this information, but he suspected she would have kept it a secret if she could have. Something must have gone wrong while he was away. He hadn't properly allowed for her needs. Will hated himself for being so careless.

"Well, we're not really making an announcement until well into the second trimester," Will said.

"I just got a craving," Mariana said, her eyes pleading with him for understanding. He felt like a monster. "It passed," she added.

"I thought you were with Mariana, what happened?" Rhiannon asked.

"Oh, I couldn't sleep. I had to go stretch my legs first," Will said. "Saw your husband in the garden."

"Smoking again, I imagine," Rhiannon made a face.

Will shrugged. It was none of his business, and he didn't want to get more entangled with these two than he needed to be.

"I got some quality time with little Lucy here," Mariana said.

"Mariana has a gift," Rhiannon said. "She got my fussy eater to finish all her porridge."

"Nearly all," Mariana joked, pointing at a stain on her dress. "A bit still landed on me."

"Let's get you changed," Will said, going to Mariana's side. He picked up little Lucy, who giggled merrily for him as he put her back in the highchair. "Will you be all right, Rhiannon? Or do you need some more help?"

"It might be good for you to get some practice, if you're going to be handling two at a time," Rhiannon said. "But, no, I'm all set. If Mariana needs some suitable clothes to change into, I could lend her something. This isn't New York."

Will shot Rhiannon a look, but she only glared at him. He didn't remember this vicious side of the woman. Mariana turned beet red. He was very wrong about Rhiannon and Fraser. They were both toxic people. Suddenly, the path forward was simple. Will closed the door on any thoughts of compromise. His ancestors were right. Chop off damaged branches, so they don't harm the tree.

"We'll be leaving now, Rhiannon," Will announced. "Mariana, come with me."

Mariana rose to his side without questioning. She was as obviously as eager to go as he was. *What a fucked up, wasted trip.*

16

Instant Karma

M ariana didn't really need Will to explain why he wanted to go. There had been something uncomfortable in the air since they had arrived at the house that morning. Despite Mariana's brief friendly exchange with Rhiannon, she had sensed some resentment emanating from the woman which went beyond the snide remark about her wardrobe. True, she hadn't dressed quite right for the place, or for any place, but it was none of Rhiannon's business how Mariana dressed.

The driver took them to Edinburgh, where they booked a suite at an exclusive hotel near Edinburgh Castle. Will had never liked the idea of them staying anywhere but one of their residences. It turned out Will owned the place, and the chain of hotels it was part of around the world, through his organization.

"I'm sorry about everything I put you through today, baby," Will said, stroking her hair. They were alone in the room, freshly showered and nestled comfortably on the sofa, wearing fluffy bathrobes, with a room service cart full of treats for Mariana and the television on. "I should never have even introduced you to Fraser. They're too much trouble you don't need."

"Can you explain to me what really happened?" Mariana said. "You went for a tawse and then, *poof*! Then we just split. Not that I mind. I like it much better here, just you and me."

"The house is compromised," Will said, "and a few other things came up. But let's just relax. Okay? You need it."

"So do you," Mariana said, running her hands along his leg.

"That's very true," Will admitted.

The pleasant, warm silence that followed was short-lived.

"Oh my God!" Mariana said, noticing the chyron on the news and reaching for the control to turn up the volume. "Martin's dead!"

Will took the control out of her hand and turned off the television. "That's why I don't like these things."

"You knew already?" Mariana turned to look at Will.

"It was why I left the room this morning," he said. "I had to get out of the house to talk. Charlie warned me when he heard about it from his sources. There wasn't really a good time for me to tell you, but I was going to. I promise. It wasn't us."

"How did Charlie reach you when we were alone in a room with no phone?"

"I was buzzed." Will showed her his wristwatch.

"You didn't tell me they could buzz you through your watch? You know how many times I needed to get to you and I didn't know how?"

"It's only an open channel between Charlie and me," Will said. "It works sort of like a walkie-talkie. I get a very gentle pulse, a haptic notification, that he needs to talk. I can also make outgoing calls through the watch, when I need to, but I can't take incoming calls. It would be too risky when I'm officially off grid."

"Wow, that's so fucked up." Mariana was furious. "Charlie has a better chance of reaching my husband in an emergency than I do."

"Yes, but you don't go hunting with me, Mariana, or with him," Will said. "You don't need a channel like this. I know when you need me. I get updates and always respond as soon as I can."

Mariana folded her arms.

"Don't be a brat," Will warned. "You know the logic of this, if you think about it for half a minute."

"Fine, whatever," Mariana spat.

"Don't pout, baby," Will warned. "This is neither the time nor the place for you to earn yourself another hiding."

"Wanting to reach my husband when I *really need him* shouldn't be a punishable offense, for heaven's sake! It should be a given! We should be able to walkie-talkie too."

"I get one line like that, and it's taken," Will said, his tone allowing no compromise. "The person who has it keeps me alive and he will keep *you* alive, even if I'm not. It benefits you. It doesn't harm you. I guess I shouldn't have told you about it. I thought you'd be more mature."

"Okay, Will, I know you and Charlie have your own thing," Mariana said, ignoring his snide remark, "which predates me by decades. Let's just leave it aside. How did Charlie know Martin was dead before the news broke?"

"Some sources warned him, like I told you," Will said. "They knew he was a person of interest to us."

"And these sources didn't act on his behalf or yours?"

"No, Mariana," Will said. "If I had wanted him dead, I wouldn't have carried it out in Qatar, even by proxy. It's too messy. Martin went there on his own, took his anger and viciousness out on the wrong woman and paid a just price. It was instant karma. I didn't have to do a thing for it to happen."

"I believe you, Will," Mariana said, "but won't it raise questions? I mean, he sells his company, suddenly, and then his body washes up on the beach in Qatar. That's pretty suspicious."

"I couldn't tell you what it means," Will said. "I don't know myself. We're just going to wait to see how it plays out. There's other bad news too. You may as well hear it."

Mariana knew just by looking at Will's expression of regret. "Sandra has done something else, hasn't she?"

Will nodded. "She presented some test results which seem to prove I'm the father of her child," he said. "Our people did not vet them. I'm asking for fresh tests run by labs I trust."

"Great!" Mariana put her arms up in a mock cheer with tight fists.

"You're right to be angry, but give my people time to sort it out," Will said, taking her hand in his and kissing the plumpness of her palm at the thumb. "I really wouldn't put it past Sandra to fake tests. It was too convenient. She refused to cooperate with my request for testing, and yet she ran her own tests. I didn't even volunteer a DNA sample, so I have that to use as a legal argument for running the tests again."

"How'd she get a sample to use?"

"I do not know, Mariana," Will said. "Maybe she kept something of mine over the years, a lock of my hair. I haven't seen the reports. I just heard about it and we're contesting the tests."

Mariana got up and started pacing around the hotel room as she catalogued a list of things she wanted to ask, though she had little confidence that Will would tell her. "What do you mean the house was compromised, by the way? Fraser's house."

"It's my house, as you already know," Will said. "My staff found bugs there. Maybe Fraser let someone in, though

Jonas, the butler should have seen it. It's more likely that Fraser got the bugs from someone and planted them himself."

"Why would Fraser do that?"

"He thinks the house belongs to my boss, Stevenson, who he only knows by reputation as a wealthy financier," Will explained. "I don't think Fraser plans to stay there very long. Only as long as he has to. I think he did plan to use whatever information he gathered on Stevenson to make a profit. Someone could just as easily have paid Fraser to put the bugs in for future use. He needs money, and he's not too worried about how he earns it."

"Rhiannon seemed okay for about five minutes, but she obviously didn't like me," Mariana said. "There was something between you two at some point. Wasn't there?"

"I've told you, jealousy doesn't suit you, Mariana," Will said, his stern tone returning. "I don't dwell on your other lovers."

"So she was a lover, at some point," Mariana said.

"No, in fact, she was never my lover," Will spat. "She was a girl I knew who was attracted to me. I wasn't looking to get tangled with her or with anyone, and she wasn't the type for a one-night stand."

"Like *me*, you mean," Mariana said, bitterly.

"Honey, that was a whole different time, and you were obviously much more than a one-night stand," Will said.

"Yes, but you thought I would only be a one-night stand, at first."

"You're projecting," Will said. "I always knew you'd be mine, from the moment I first set eyes on you. You thought I was just good for a quick fuck."

"You were very good, for a quick fuck," Mariana grinned, "and for a slow fuck too. And for a moderately paced and yet infinitely memorable fuck."

"I love you too, sweetheart," Will said, still sitting on the couch, letting her get it all out of her system. "Anyway, back then, I was into different things."

"Like what?"

"Let's just say that it was when Lucifer was really coming into his own." Will grinned.

"Ooh, I wish I'd been around for that," Mariana teased.

"You are, naughty minx." Will gave her a long look that made her want to leap back on his lap, but she resisted. "And you keep bringing me closer to him with each passing hour. I might get stuck in that mode, you know, and then where will you be?"

"I guess I'll be damned." Mariana shrugged.

"No, babe, I'll always redeem you." Will smiled.

"Okay, we're getting off topic." Mariana crossed her arms again and faced off with him. "And I'm still mad at you." It was really hard to stay mad, though, especially the way he looked at her, like he knew she was wet for him already. "Rhiannon," she reminded him, with a coaxing wave of her hand. "Explain."

"There's nothing to explain, Mariana," Will said. "She met Fraser through me. We went to a local pub together. Rhiannon was there. She stopped by to flirt with me, but ended up with him. That's all there is to it."

"So what happens with them now?" Mariana asked.

"Nothing," Will said. "Whatever Fraser does from now on will decide their fate. I'm done helping them. I won't kick them out, for the sake of the kids, if nothing else. It's not as though I need that house. But I'm done. They're shunned."

"You sound Amish," Mariana said.

"Hardly." Will smiled. "I just won't toss them any more lifelines and we will never see them again."

"Because Rhiannon said something mean about my dress?" Mariana asked.

"No, because of all of it, mainly his lies and his cheating. He's irredeemable," Will said. "And he represents a risk to us if he's willing to compromise Stevenson."

"Because you're Stevenson," Mariana said.

"Exactly," Will said. "See how much better it is to be relatively anonymous, even with people close to you?"

"So what do we do now?"

"Well, right now, I'd like you to sit back on my lap and apologize for being bratty," Will said. "Then I'd like to make love to you, if you're up to that. Then you'll get some sleep. You need it—you're grumpy. Tonight, we'll wake up, have a nice dinner, make love and sleep again. Tomorrow, I'll get a threat assessment. We'll go for a brief tour of Edinburgh. Then I think it's best we fly down to Castle Gwaed. Things are too messy right now. Grandmother and Grandfather will keep us safe, and it's the best place for us to be right now, really. You can make your arrangements for the wedding and I can prep for the Convocation."

"I can't go to your grandparents dressed like your sex slave." She stepped close enough for him to grab her legs, but she didn't sit down. "Your grandmother always makes me look inadequate, even when I'm trying. It's not her fault she's gorgeous, but…"

"You look devastatingly gorgeous dressed as my slave," Will said, untying the knot on her robe and running his hands up her thighs, wrapping them around her hips, nudging her one step closer, and kissing her belly. "That's what made Rhiannon bitter. I'll get more clothes delivered to the castle. Don't worry. Our costume department is the finest in the world. You can easily outshine Grandmother, if that's what you want."

"I doubt it," Mariana said. "Your grandmother oozes elegance. She was born into it. The best I can ever do is dress a part. I'm still that girl on a raft, you know. Except the sea is different now. Angrier, even."

"You are my wife, Mariana," Will said. "You will never drown. I won't allow it. Just let me navigate. All right?"

"Can we see *Pippin*?" Mariana asked, climbing on top of his lap, and wrapping her arms over his shoulders.

"Oh, yes," Will said, kissing her. "I'm sure we can arrange that. It's online. I'll have the front desk bring us a computer so we can play it on the television here tonight. I think you'll like it."

"Okay," she kissed him back. "Sounds like a plan, Damian."

"Say you're sorry." Will gripped her buttocks hard.

"For what?"

"For being bratty," Will said. "For giving me a hard time, when you know I always have your best interest in mind."

"I want to walkie-talkie you." Mariana pouted.

Will sighed. "No, what *you* want is for me to bend you over my knee and swat the brat right out of you. Now is not the time."

"When is the time, then?" Mariana asked, her lips brushing his lips.

"When we get to Castle Gwaed, I will make you regret misbehaving," Will said. "I will make you cry loud enough to wake the ghosts of the place."

"Tease." Mariana kissed Will deep, drinking him in, enjoying the sensation of his cock hardening against her naked pussy as she straddled him.

"Don't worry, chit," Will pinched her butt. "I *will* sort you out."

"Yeah, okay." Mariana smiled. "Fuck me first."

17

War is a Science

William

The plan had been to fly to Wales on the 777. It was a short flight for such a large aircraft, but they had the plane on standby and weren't going to just leave it behind. Will made sure Mariana was comfortably settled in the living room and went to one of the guest cabins, which doubled as an office onboard, to get caught up on the latest alerts. The captain, Sean Flynn, came by before Will read his daily briefing.

"William, we have a situation."

"What is it?"

"Come down into the cargo hold."

Will followed Sean down the tiny stairs hidden under the floor and to one of the half-moon metal cargo containers which they used to transport supplies between field offices. Sean opened it with a concerned look on his face.

"What am I looking at?"

"Just what you think."

"How did that get here?"

"It's not in the manifest. You know I always do a thorough check myself."

"Yes, Sean, thank you for that, but that means the ground crew..."

"I imagine," Sean said, "or someone at the freight company."

"We have to inform the authorities," Will said.

"What about you and your wife? They're not going to just let you go. They won't believe you did not know this was on your plane."

"But if we call it in, ourselves..."

"There will still be inquiries. Are you up to that? Is she?"

"So what do we do?"

"I think we need to have a conference call with the crisis team, now," Sean said.

"Yes," Will agreed.

They rushed back up to the conference room, passing a flight attendant who was all too familiar.

"Mr. Smith." She smiled. "Good to see you again."

"Not now, Priscilla," he snapped. "If my wife needs me, tell her I'm on a call to Headquarters. Make sure she's comfortable and taken care of, and that she has anything she needs."

"Are we all clear for take-off?"

"No, not yet," Sean said, "stand by for my further instructions."

"We'll need a story," Will said to Sean as soon as Priscilla walked away, "or the tower and airport authority will start asking why we aren't queuing up for take-off."

"Alec is already on that," the captain said, referring to his co-pilot. "He's notified the tower that we're checking a minor fault with the in-flight entertainment system and waiting for technicians."

"Good."

It took only a short while to get everyone online. Will took command right away. He trained for this, he just never liked it, and he never meant for it to come anywhere near Mariana.

He had to be careful with communications at this point. Everything was too sensitive, too critical for plain speaking, but none of the people he would speak to on this call needed things said to them in anything but code.

"Adam here, a reminder of the minutes," Will said, just confirming an emergency communications protocol.

"The minutes from the last meeting are in order. All attendees are present and accounted for." The voice was that of Howard Fleming.

"Before we get started, we have a technical fault on the plane. The captain is here to explain."

"Go ahead, we're listening," Charlie confirmed.

Sean was a pro. He could handle the lingo. "It's the IFE. We have a short in the system, I believe. I'm worried about sparks in flight."

"Can you get it to re-start?" Howard asked.

"No," Sean answered.

"Will the local tech team be able to fix it?" Charlie asked.

"No, it's beyond their capabilities," Sean said.

"Is the device hot?" Charlie asked.

"Very," Will answered.

"Battery issues?" Charlie asked.

"Risk of runaway fire," Will said.

"We want to ensure Mr. & Mrs. Smith a pleasant carefree journey to Wales. This might only be a minor inconvenience, but it's worth using the other hardware."

"There will be a two-hour flight delay, to get the right equipment to your location," the head of Flight-Ops interjected.

"I am sure Mr. Smith would approve. His wife is in no

condition to be inconvenienced. We should entertain her to her heart's desire."

"We will arrange it," Flight-Ops confirmed. "We'll make them comfortable in the private lounge of the FOB, for the duration, and take them to the new equipment when it's ready."

"Experienced technicians are en route," Charlie said.

"Thanks gentlemen, details matter," Will said.

Sean left the conference room, and the head of Flight Ops hung up, but Will stayed on the phone to finish his meeting. They had successfully communicated the critical issue of the findings in the cargo hold, but Will still needed to deal with the implications. For that, he needed to speak with Howard and Charlie, though still in code.

"I have my reports from Mr. Williams' meetings, and my own findings, to present to the committee, if we can proceed."

"Yes, go ahead." It wasn't Howard, it was Lord Greystone.

"Hello, Sir," Will said. "It's good to have you out of retirement."

"Good to be here," Greystone said. "So how's business?"

"Well, it's moving at a healthy pace," Will said. "I'll detail my findings to you now, with your permission."

"Yes, everyone is looking forward to hearing what you have to say," Greystone said, taking command. It was appropriate. They were on his turf and they'd need his help to get rid of the problematic weapons stored in the hold. "Well, there are some administrative issues, detailed in the reports we forwarded yesterday evening. We see a potential booming market for key products among our core product lines. We should concentrate on the Industrial Capitals, and centers of major manufacturing, in the outskirts. There are untapped resources, ready to be exploited. I've detailed our major infrastructure liabilities, and I'll await a personal meeting to inform of the competitive strategies. I believe the best description for the lay of the land in the region is bumpy. There may be agents of our competitors on the move within our territories. I believe that a general Executive Committee Meeting is in order, as I've already suggested. I think we should move the dates up. If we can gather everyone by Sunday, at least the key players, that would be ideal."

"I'd like to hear more from you personally on this, Adam," Lord Greystone said. Will had been expecting as much since he hadn't caught his grandfather up on what he'd learned in the States.

"I'll meet with you later today, sir," Will said.

"Bring your lovely lady friend," Lord Greystone said. "We hear she's entertaining."

"I'm sure she'll appreciate your hospitality."

"Adam," Howard said, "US Headquarters will want to be informed every step of the way. They'll join the Executive Committee meeting and will be at UK Headquarters in seventy-two hours. The others might be delayed."

"Thank you, sir," Will said.

"One more thing, Adam," Howard said.

"Yes, sir."

"Please let Mr. Williams know US Headquarters is aware of key trades in the futures markets. Expect some volatility." Howard was confirming what they already knew. Mariana was in play. That he'd repeated it made Will worry that there had been a new escalation, perhaps somebody too close to them. Coupled with the armaments hidden on his plane, Will felt the situation was getting out of control. Trouble shadowed them, much too close for comfort. He'd made a promise to protect his wife, and he intended to keep it.

"I will inform Mr. Williams," Will said, "but he has an investment plan in place for the futures market." In this way

Will notified Howard that he was already taking out enemies through Charlie. "I don't think he's keen to change that aspect of his portfolio. Headquarters will need to check with his chief investment advisor."

"I can speak on his behalf," Charlie said. "The trades are fixed and they are being carried out according to pre-set limits. There is no backing out on the buys."

"It is unfortunate that Mr. Williams did not consult with Headquarters before booking those trades," Howard said.

"Perhaps Mr. Williams has better foresight than you credit him with," Lord Greystone said. "We believe his futures trades will yield a profit."

Well, there was a surprise, or maybe not. Lord Greystone knew the White Wolf was back to work with the Hawks. The old man had won his argument on the expediency of killing. There was no simple way to put that genie back in the bottle.

At least, their little loading problem—contraband armaments in the cargo bay—was reported to the right people. A plan of action was underway.

Now, Will only had to deal with the tough part: telling Mariana of their change in plans, giving nothing away.

———

He found her sitting on her flight chair, looking through a fashion magazine in the curious way she had—starting with the back page and flipping forward. It was an adorable quirk of hers, one of many things that made him wonder just how her mind worked.

"We have a situation," he whispered in her ear after leaning in to give her a kiss.

"What does that mean?" Will hated this part, the look in her eyes accusing him of repeated betrayal. "What happened, Will? What is going on?"

"We need to go now."

"Go? Do you mean take-off or 'go' as in leave the plane?"

"Go as in leave the plane."

"What is happening?"

"There is a problem with the Inflight Entertainment," Will said. "It might be dangerous. There could be a spark during the flight. We can't risk it. I've booked another plane to take us to Wales."

"Inflight Entertainment? You mean the movies?"

"The movies, the internet, it ties in with communications and flight controls as well," Will said. "Get your bag, please, I'll explain later."

"No!"

"What?"

"No, Will," she said. "I'm not budging. There's something else happening, isn't there?"

He knew he should tell her. If he could speak without raising alarms, he would have, but Will couldn't allow this behavior.

"I realize you're irritable, with the pregnancy and all, but come along," he said, sternly. "You'll feel better once we leave the plane."

He pleaded with her, with his eyes, but she wasn't seeing the right expression on his face. She could be so stubborn, so closed off. He wished he could just throw her over his shoulder and carry her out, but that would cause a greater scene.

When she didn't budge, he whispered in her ear, as softly as he could.

"I am giving you an order," Will said. "Consider what that means."

Her eyes opened wide, and met his, tears pooled on her lashes. She said nothing. She let them well up and flow over onto her delicate cheeks, without giving them a voice. Then she got up out of the flight chair. She slapped his hand away when he tried to help her get up, and she walked off ahead of him.

He'd have to accept that for the time being. There was no other choice.

"It's going to be fine," he said, putting his arm around her shoulders when they were back at the FBO. "Only a slight flight delay. We'll relax quietly in the lounge while we wait for the other jet. Then, we'll be at Castle Gwaed where we can talk at length."

"Whatever you say, *Sir*," Mariana replied. She sounded like a little girl. It was only a squeak. Her voice was cracking, and she really did not want to cry.

Will felt her little squeaks, like three daggers in his belly.

18

Bloody Castle

William

Will lowered the privacy screen inside the Bentley which had collected them at Cardiff Airport.

Humphrey, the Greystone's head driver, had changed little since Will had last seen him. A little gray on the back of his head, but otherwise the same stoic face in the rear-view mirror, only a wrinkle or two more to mark the passing of the years.

"Are we clear now, Humphrey?"

"Yes, sir, completely clear."

"And grandfather knows our position?"

Mariana shot him that look again, but he was developing a thick skin for it, at least he told himself he was.

"Yes, sir, Lord Greystone knows."

Mariana only squeaked a little 'Ha!' and shrugged her shoulders, then went back to closing herself off from him. She hadn't said a word to him since they left Edinburgh.

"Thank you, Humphrey. How is your wife by the way?"

"Oh, fine, fine, sir, thank you. Our eldest, Fiona, is expecting a boy, her first."

"Congratulations, Humphrey, and our good wishes to Fiona and her husband."

"Thank you, sir."

Will raised the privacy screen again.

"Do you need to pout a while longer?" he asked Mariana.

She was a statue, just staring out the window, which was obscured by raindrops. All he could see was gray. He closed his eyes for a bit and waited for his wife to thaw.

"Sir, we've arrived."

Will hadn't expected to fall asleep, but it had made the two-hour drive on the M4, to Castle Gwaed, overlooking the coast of Cardigan Bay, quicker for him. Mariana remained frozen, deaf to all around her, and mute.

"Thank you, Humphrey," Will said.

He waited as Mariana took the driver's hand and stood just to the side of the car in the lower bailey, staring at the covered parapet walk above.

He couldn't let this scene breakdown in front of his grandfather and grandmother. He had to keep up appearances. As soon as the situation permitted, he'd have a good long argument with his wife in the relative privacy of their bedroom. He hated that Lord Greystone kept such a large staff, though it was inevitable given the size of the place. The walls had ears which would certainly turn as red as he intended to paint her ass.

"Welcome back to Castle Gwaed, sir," Tyler, the butler, greeted them at the door which led to the main hall.

"Thank you Tyler, this is my wife, Lady Stevenson," Will said.

"Welcome madam, we've been awaiting your arrival," Tyler said.

Mariana only nodded.

"Is Grandfather in the library, then?"

"No, he is in the India room, as is your grandmother, sir."

"Lovely, we'll make our way there, then. It's still in the same place I assume?"

Tyler grinned. He and Will always got on well. Tyler understood Will's wit. "Yes, sir, but wouldn't Lady Stevenson prefer some time to refresh herself from the journey first? It must be very tiring, such a long trip and under such circumstances."

"Lady Stevenson will certainly want to rest, but that is why I think we should go see Grandmother and Grandfather first, so we can go to our room."

"So you won't be at dinner tonight?"

"Not tonight," Will said. "Grandmother will understand, I believe. We'll just have some light supper in our room, if Cook can arrange it, perhaps some sandwiches, and soup."

"Very well, sir, if you think that's appropriate."

"I do."

"I'll let Cook know then."

"Thank you, Tyler."

Will walked to meet his grandparents, Mariana following quietly, taking a right at the Main Hall and following the hallway to the India room, on the ground floor of the Southeast tower.

"Oh Pippin!" Will's grandmother ran over, tears in her eyes, then kissed him on each cheek. "My lord, you look fully recovered, so strong, handsome, and smart!"

"Anne!" his grandfather protested, "Leave the poor man in peace. He's not a boy anymore."

"Hello, Lord Greystone," Will said, extending his hand to his grandfather.

His grandfather refused to accept it. It was an awkward moment. Nothing had changed. Will had started it, really, with the mess in France. He knew it.

"Good to see you again, Mariana!" his grandmother said, going over to Mariana who tried to be good about the woman getting her name wrong, again. Under the circumstances, Will was grateful his wife didn't lash out.

"It's Mariana, Grandmother," Will reminded her.

"Oh, yes, I'm sorry. I had forgotten," Anne lied so smoothly. "I've never been very good with Spanish names. You were in Madrid for a time, weren't you Richard?"

"Yes," Lord Greystone said curtly.

Will shot his grandmother a disapproving look. He knew his grandmother was having a dig at her husband, but he didn't like her using Mariana as the spade. Mariana was already upset enough.

"Richard will always get your name right," Anne said, looking at Will, "and I'll be sure to, in the future."

Mariana gave everyone a weak smile, her attempt at civility. Just as well.

"Mariana must be exhausted, Pippin!" Anne declared. "You should let her get to her room, not keep her here with us. We can always talk later, at dinner."

"We're going to miss dinner tonight," Will replied. "I've already informed Tyler."

"Nonsense," Richard said, "dinner is at six. We have already arranged proper dress. You'll find it in your rooms."

Will winced. Mariana would take that personally, though it wasn't what his grandfather had meant at all. They had got her some more comfortable clothes for the trip over. Though

Will loved seeing his wife in the slinky black dresses he'd picked for her cover in the UK—and a dark part of him would like to keep her dressed like that every day of the week —he knew the outfits might make the wrong impression on his grandparents. Yet, it seemed there was never a way to get the right outfit for Mariana around his grandmother. Maybe he should just let the woman pick his wife's clothing from here on. Then his grandfather's words sank in, and he had a different concern on his mind.

"Grandfather, you didn't place us in separate rooms, did you?"

"Naturally," Lord Greystone said. "Mariana doesn't want to be bothered with your goings-on, and you don't want to be bothered with her primping."

"I don't find her 'primping' bothersome," Will said, "and I don't keep my goings-on a secret from Mariana."

He expected her to react, to embarrass him but she was silent as the grave. For once, he was grateful for her silence. At least she was loyal, even when she was angry.

Lord Greystone furrowed his brow, his ice-blue eyes piercing when focused.

"The rooms are connecting, William. I am not a fool. I do not believe your wife is in the state she is in without your paths crossing, occasionally. I was merely looking out for your comfort. Both of yours. Mariana may need considerable bed rest over the next few weeks. And you, as you know, will work very late hours. I saw no point in you disturbing her sleep when you return late at night, or in the early morning."

"Your grandfather was only looking out for you, Pippin," his grandmother said, "and they are lovely rooms, both of them, with a view of the gardens. You'll be quite comfortable. Certainly it's none of our concern, what you decide to do with the arrangements. The rooms connect."

"Separate rooms will be fine," Mariana said. "May I go

to mine please? I'm tired. If I have to be ready by six for dinner, I will need to put my feet up now, and have some time to get dressed."

"Of course, dear, didn't I just say so?" Anne said. "Pippin is a very bad boy, putting you through all this nonsense. Let's get you settled. Tyler, can you please show Mariana the way?"

"I'll go with Mariana," Will said. "We'll talk later."

"No, William, I'm afraid we must talk now," his grandfather said. "Tyler will ensure that Meredith takes care of Mariana, directly. Won't you, Tyler?"

"Of course, my Lord."

Will clenched his fists and his jaw as he watched Mariana led away.

"We should go into the library," his grandfather said. "Anne, we will be awhile. Check in on the girl, will you?"

"She's not a girl, she's my wife!"

"I meant it as a term of endearment, you stubborn Yankee!"

"Boys, please!" Anne said. "This is not the way to start, especially when matters are so grim."

"Grim?" Will asked.

"Come to the library." Lord Greystone stormed past him. Will followed close, his heart beating wildly in his chest and between his temples.

"Why do you have to be so bloody stubborn!" Richard pounded his desk, not for the first time. It had no effect on Will. He was accustomed to his grandfather's gruff manner. When the Black Wolf was riled, delicate things broke.

"Being firm in one's convictions is not stubbornness, Lord Greystone," Will said. "It's character."

"Stop calling me by my title, dammit! You do it to irritate me, and I have no patience for your games. This situation today requires a cool head, and quick action."

"I won't approve what you propose, Richard," Will said. "We must do it without owing a debt to people with unclean hands."

"Everyone has unclean hands, Will! Everyone—including bloody you!"

"These people you're recommending I use are beyond dirty, Richard," Will said. "They are little more than thugs. Even Charlie has warned against using them. We cannot trust that any intelligence they gather will come to us or *stay* with us. We have to find other interrogators."

"We have to act quickly, William, and they are available on site," Richard said. "It will take Charlie's men too long to get here. We may lose an important advantage by waiting. I can't keep the people we captured this morning on ice indefinitely. We need to know for certain who set them up to do this."

"Fine," Will said. "I'll do it myself. Can you have them brought to the farm? If not, I'll fly back to fucking Edinburgh this minute. I won't delegate to those men."

"You can't be serious, son," Lord Greystone said. "Putting yourself in the thick of it right now will cause you more grief. Your wife is already angry enough. How do you think she'll take it if you suddenly vanish?"

"She won't be alone," Will said. "She'll have you to explain. I need answers and you're right. Charlie's men won't get here in time. I understand you can't touch this with your people. I can't ask my people to do it either. I'll do it myself. In fact, I'll enjoy it."

"Don't let the wolf overcome you, son," Richard warned. "You'll frighten your girl."

"My *girl* is a bloodthirsty *woman*," Will said. "If I gave her half the chance, she'd come with me to carry out the deed."

"Fine," Richard said. "I'll make excuses for you at dinner.

Just come back whole or I'll be trapped with two harpies to answer to. I'm not up to it, at my age."

"I'll be back before dawn," Will said. "If I don't return, she's your responsibility to protect. Don't let her out of your sight, Grandfather. You may need to lock her up so she won't fly away. I'm counting on you to do that."

"She'll be fine," Richard said. "Anne will take her under her wing."

"Fuck it to hell." Will shook his head. "I guess the Greystone line will out."

"There are worse things for your children to be than Greystones, William."

"I suppose you're right," Will said. "But they deserve to be Smiths. They should grow among the trees."

"Don't worry, son," Richard said, "just do your job and you can raise them in any forest you please."

19

Bad Tea

Mariana

Mariana was seething. Will had assured her the point of coming all the way to the UK was to escape the threats they faced in the US and that they would be safe here. Obviously, somebody had done something to the jet he used as a safe house. They really weren't safe anywhere, probably not even in this crazy castle for all its reinforced walls and lofty towers. And Will had never really explained anything about why they were under threat in the first place, though Mariana could guess. After all, he'd done a bunch of things when they were last in Europe that riled up enemies. Maybe Nótt had reorganized, or a splinter group was ready to strike, or perhaps other enemies had followed them over the Atlantic.

It didn't matter. What mattered was that they now forced her to hang out with people who clearly hated her, who thought she wasn't good enough for their grandson. Mainly Anne, Lady Greystone, La Comtesse de Coquille, the

Wicked Witch of Wales. Calling her Marina again. *You make that sort of mistake once, not twice in a lifetime. Bitch.*

"Mariana, dear, it's Anne. Is it all right to come in?"

Mariana tried to compose herself. She sniffled and checked herself in the mirror of the antique dressing table. She looked a mess: eyes red and swollen, face red, and lips dry. She tried her best to sort it out, put on a pleasant face, but the woman did not wait for her to reply, choosing to enter anyway, slowly, carefully, until she surprised her.

"Oh poor dear," she said, "come to mother."

Perhaps it was her tone, or how she extended her arms generously, but Mariana ran to Will's grandmother and cried herself out, as the woman hugged her tight. Mariana hated herself for needing this comfort, even from someone who so obviously disliked her.

"I'm sorry," Mariana said when she was done weeping. "I don't know what has come over me. My hormones..."

"Nonsense," Anne said. "I know what it is as much as you do. It's all too much being the wife of a powerful man, and entirely unfair."

Anne brought Mariana to the robin's-egg blue velvet covered armchairs by the fireplace and sat her down. They decorated the entire room in shades of antique white and cyan, with highlights in coral which capitalized on the light coming through the narrow windows and made the room feel much lighter and cozier than it must have been five-hundred years earlier.

"Would you like some tea, dear?" Anne asked before sitting with her.

"Yes," Mariana said. Will hadn't banned tea, and it had caffeine which would be welcome. She needed a boost and something warm.

"Good." Anne tugged on an embroidered bell pull on the wall. "We'll have some warm tea, and a pleasant chat, get you feeling better. Then I'll help you get ready for dinner tonight. You have nothing to worry about."

She sat down in the matching chair, across from Mariana, just as a maid, Meredith, came back in the room dressed conservatively, in a long gray wool skirt, buttoned up blouse and gray cardigan, all of which, along with her unusual height and thin frame, made her look imposingly prim and proper.

"Meredith, we'll need tea and perhaps some biscuits. You like biscuits, don't you, dear?"

"Yes, that's fine."

"I'll see to it," Meredith said, leaving the two women alone in the room.

"The situation is grim, Mariana," Anne said, though Mariana had her eyes focused on the blue and white vine pattern of the carpet. "You are right to be upset, but it can always be worse."

Mariana looked in the woman's clear green eyes, and saw a brief smile there, among the subtle crow's feet, though her face showed no other emotion.

"It's bad enough for me," Mariana said, "having to fly out of the US, suddenly. But something's flown over with us, am I right? Something dangerous? Or was it always here waiting for us?"

Anne's eyes darkened. "Ours is a very complicated life, dear, for all of Will's aims at simplicity. Danger will always follow you like a shadow. Make your peace with it, and prepare to fight, or you will go mad."

"I'm ready to fight, Anne, but Will won't let me!" Mariana protested. "He keeps treating me like a child and keeping me in the dark! Despite everything we went through in France, I still don't know the truth about what happened that night. You left me alone believing that Will was dead for days! You two scurried out and disappeared. The Flemings vanished. I had to go hide out in the North Pole, for fuck's sake! I didn't hear a word from any of you to show concern. And now we have this wedding and this meeting, and I don't know what else. I don't know a goddamned thing and I'm sick of not knowing!"

Meredith came in carrying a tray for tea and a plate of biscuits, and set it on the little side table, preparing tea for the two women.

"Would you like cream or sugar, Lady Stevenson?" Meredith asked.

"Please call me Mariana."

"Madam..."

"It's all right, Meredith," Anne said. "I think Mariana just needs to hear her name, to feel at home. All our formality is stifling the poor girl."

"Yes, my lady."

"Do you want cream or sugar, Mariana?" Anne asked.

"Just lemon, please."

"Yes, quite right. Better to have your vitamin C. I'll take mine as usual, Meredith."

"Yes, my lady."

Meredith did a quick job of serving the tea, observing all the proprieties, extending the biscuit tray to both ladies, but clearly wanting to be done quickly. Mariana did not take a biscuit, even for courtesy's sake. She was in no mood for sweets. As soon as Meredith left, Anne continued the conversation as if there had been no interruption.

"To be honest, I don't know all the details either," Anne said. "Neither do Richard nor Will. They are only now trying to put it together, but there was a trap in your aircraft. That, I know. There were automatic weapons, in your cargo hold, and bombs, grenades, some short-range missiles."

Mariana dropped her teacup onto her lap and the carpet.

"Shit!"

"Don't fret, dear," Anne came over and helped her pat down her dress, "did you burn yourself?"

"Only a little."

"Poor thing. There, is that better now? All mopped up."

"Thank you, I'm sorry... I..."

"You don't understand any of it, I know, but you will," Anne said. "I'll ring Meredith to bring another cup for you."

"No, don't bother," Mariana said. "I'm not in the mood for tea anymore."

"Suit yourself, dear," Anne said, sitting back down and picking up her own cup. "I'm sure Pippin will tell you all he can. The important thing, for now, is that you give him some time to get to the bottom of things. Pippin is under tremendous strain, more than you can imagine, and he worries about you. So does Richard. He misses our Bess. He always has, ever since she married Arthur, and left for the States. She was his heart, his little girl. Richard doted on her. Now, I imagine, you're taking her place."

Anne was a staggered tea drinker, pausing her discourse with a sip of tea, but in her cool green eyes, Mariana could tell she was raging. Mariana knew that this dainty socialite had also been an agent in the field and that she had seen some very hard things, but probably nothing so hard as the death of two of her children by enemy hands.

"I hate to say it, but Bess tore Richard's heart asunder," Anne continued. "The prospect of living to see his great-grandchildren well settled and happy..." She sipped again, and her eyes looked out the window behind Mariana to nowhere in particular, then focused back sharply on Mariana's. "It's something Richard would kill to ensure. Richard is not a proclaimed pacifist, like Will. He will actually kill to protect you both and the children, if he has to. He will kill as many as he has to, no matter who they may be. But he needs to avoid an international escalation. That could compromise the public side of his firm. He has to rely on allies for actions abroad."

Her eyes probed Mariana's eyes, and Mariana let her see she could handle more.

"What do you mean by 'no matter who they may be'? Who is Will at war with, at this point? Where is abroad?"

"Only Howard Fleming can truly answer that," Anne said.

The implications of what Anne had said blended with what little she'd gotten out of Will, and the extent of the danger sank in.

"I'm sick of only finding out things piecemeal." Mariana stood up to pace around the room. "What is it with this family? I married Will thinking I was marrying one man and then learned I had married quite another. I thought he was a humble gardener, then I had to find out he was a magnate, then a spy, and now it turns out I'm in the middle of an international espionage ring bent on outright war! He has deceived me, repeatedly, and I'm sick of it!"

Mariana's heart pounded. Her head ached. Anne rose to calm her, putting her hand on her shoulders.

"No, Mariana, I believe you misunderstand the situation. There is no deceit involved, only secrecy. Those are two very different things. You need to take your feelings out of it and try to put yourself in Pippin's shoes. He couldn't tell you all of it at once, don't you see? As far as his family history, you wouldn't have believed him even if he told you the truth when you first married. That's what this second wedding is for. It's an opportunity for you to enter a contract with each other in full knowledge of the implications, with the full support of everyone who will ensure your protection for life. I'm filling you in on what I know so far, because I know you need to hear some truth, and I am concerned about your well-being."

"That's very hard to believe, Anne. You have already shown me some of your false face," Mariana said, bitterly. "You clearly think little of me because of where I come from, playing games over not being able to pronounce my name. I heard your snide remark about my being Spanish. I may be tired and pregnant, but I am not deaf and dumb."

Anne laughed, and Mariana scowled, until she heard her speak.

"Oh, you are right, my dear," Anne said. "That is my fault and a grave flaw in my character. I am a very jealous woman, and I do not forgive easily. Sit, be calm, and it will all make sense to you."

"I stood. I will stand. If you have anything worthwhile to say, I will listen. But do not waste my time with nonsense," Mariana said. "I'll tell you one thing, I would not have treated you so rudely if you had been a guest in my house."

"No. I am sure that is true. I am sorry," Anne said. "It was Richard I meant to sting, you see. I used you as my pin cushion, when I had another pricking in mind. I have let myself down by treating you this way, you poor thing."

"Don't patronize me, Anne!"

"No, no, I'm sorry, Mariana..." Anne tried to stop laughing, though the giggles rose like bubbles from her mouth interrupting her speech. Was the woman crazy or just perverse? "Oh!" She grasped her aching sides and took a breath. "I was afraid that Pippin had found himself a Barbie doll to play with. I am so relieved to know he has a real woman in his bed."

"Anne, I'm sick of having you mock me, and I have not had my answers yet!" Mariana snapped. "You must have a cruel heart to treat me like this when I've done you no harm."

"Oh, poor dear," Anne said. "I promise I only want us to be friends, like mother and daughter. Forgive me for being petty and vindictive. Please, please sit."

Mariana sat. Her eyes slit against the older woman who seemed to have more ringlets in her head than in her hair. Anne sat down too and retook her teacup with a wink.

"Well, I shall tell you," Anne started. "You see my dear... No, I will ask you instead. Has a man ever betrayed you?"

"Are you *serious*?" Mariana asked.

Anne chortled.

"Yes, I see your point. Well, it was a Spanish woman in my case, quite a precious thing, a rose. Very blonde, soft, voluptuous, possibly larger in bust than you, though certainly it's hard to judge from your current size." Anne shrugged. "It happens, you know how it is. I wouldn't have cared so much, perhaps, if it hadn't been for my burden. I was not well."

"I'm sorry to hear it." Mariana didn't sound sorry. It was just something to say.

"Well, I know you're impatient with me. I can't blame you after your ordeal in France," Anne said. "I prize Pippin above all things. I guard him like a fierce mother bear. Unfortunately, I took you for goldilocks when I first met you."

"I am not with Will because of his money." Mariana was slow and deliberate as she said this—fuming. It was a threat, not an explanation.

"No, precious, I don't think you are," Anne said. "I did when I first met you, but not anymore. As to the thing with the Spanish, forgive me. Some scars heal slowly, you must know. I've already admitted that I've got a vicious, jealous nature. Richard really seems taken with you. He hasn't stopped talking about how well you handled yourself after we left. And we had to go, my dear. We didn't have a choice, but you were never alone."

Mariana softened, despite herself. Though she didn't like to admit it, she knew how the older woman felt.

"Yes, Anne, I understand," Mariana said. "But you and I will have to work together if this is going to be fixed. I can't worry that you hold a grudge against me for something a completely different woman did to you."

"I don't," Anne said. "I won't. I promise. I have been busy planning for your wedding. It will be a beautiful affair. Please accept that as my peace offering and forgive my slip this afternoon. My only excuse is stress over the news this morning and everything Richard and Will have set into motion. Have you heard that we are having a Convocation of Eagles? That has only added to my workload now since the dates are being moved up."

"Maybe I can help," Mariana said. "I've got nothing better to do, and work keeps me sane. Can you explain what it means, though? Why it's so important?"

Anne took a deep breath.

"It's a war meeting. We haven't had a Convocation in thirty years," Anne said. "The last time we gathered, it was to address the attack on Arthur and Bess, to protect Will and his grandmother. We made pacts in blood and we fulfilled those promises. It's a risky venture for everyone involved, gathering all the loyal Eagles in one place. In fact, this is one of the few places we can hold that sort of meeting. Castle Gwaed is more than adequately protected, both by nature and clever engineering, but it's still a delicate meeting inside the walls. There is a good reason why Eagles perch in relative solitude. People will be on edge. They bring their baggage with them, from the outside world. We have to keep some people away from others, show the right people the right deference. Fortunately, some of the wedding planning over-laps. I had invited many Eagles to your wedding already. All my living sons will be here, and several allies. Key allies of

Richard's will come too, as well as Fleming's, but that's where things get prickly."

"Is Richard at war with Howard after what happened in France?" Mariana asked.

"No, not really," Anne said. "Richard and Howard are both compromised in different ways, because of their ties to their governments. After France, there have been some complications that each of them has handled differently. Will has added to the problem. That idea of keeping clean hands, planted by his other grandmother, had persisted. Now, it seems, Will is ready to get his hands dirty again. It's all because of you, of course."

"I told you in France that I wouldn't plant ideas in his head and I meant that, Anne," Mariana said. "But after what happened... I asked Charlie to teach me to kill. Will apparently is angry about that, from what I've heard. Maybe he worries that I've become something he wouldn't approve of. I don't honestly know because he won't tell me straight."

"No, I don't think that's it at all," Anne said. "I think you reminded him of why the White Wolf needs to hunt. He has regrets over it, but probably fewer than he expected. He's unleashing a darkness, of course. I imagine that worries him. See, while Will may believe in the value of preserving life, there's a part of him that enjoys dispensing justice. Do you understand?"

"A blood thirst," Mariana said.

"Yes," Anne said. "And the current escalation of things will probably intensify his thirst. If he presents a threat to you, at any point, let me know."

"Why would you say that to me?" Mariana asked.

"I think you know why," Anne said, holding Mariana's eyes hostage. "I know how the White Wolf loves. He is my grandchild, after all. I know the Black Wolf too. I am his wife."

Mariana absolutely did not want to have this conversation with Anne. In fact, Anne was the last person on Earth she ever wanted to discuss her sex life with. But, it seemed best to get things clear between them.

"You would be wrong to think I do not know how to please my Master," Mariana said. "More deceived if you think I would want anything other than to please him. I'm not about to run out of my bedroom in shock and make a scene in front of your fancy guests, if that's what you're worried about."

"That is exactly what I was worried about," Anne said, smiling. "I know you have a passionate relationship—you made that clear on the dance floor—but I worried you couldn't handle a turn to dark."

"I love the dark as much as the light," Mariana said. "I love all of William—*all* of him. I just want him to treat me like a woman who can take it—not just the agony and ecstasy, but the blood and the bone, the secrets and the shadows, and the ghosts. I want him to treat me with the same respect he shows *you*. You are my superior in countless ways. You have an experience in the field I can never share, and you have a legacy to back you up, but I want to learn. I want to help him strengthen his empire."

"I noticed your necklace has changed to a collar, but people wear jewelry in keeping with fashion. The Eagles will be pleased to see this side of you, if we can get you polished in time," Anne said. "Are you willing to do exactly as I say?"

"For Will's sake, I'm willing to do anything," Mariana said. "You should take me at my word on that."

"Great," Anne said, grinning a toothy grin. "We will start your lessons immediately."

20

Love Bites

Dinner alone with Lord and Lady Greystone in the formal dining hall of Castle Gwaed was an awkward affair. Mariana wore the red dress that Meredith had brought for her, selected by Anne. It felt like she was stepping into a trap when she slipped it on. It was a crossover wrap dress with long sleeves and a plunging neckline, made of a fine silk that hugged her curves, with a long enough slit at the legs that she worried she'd be showing her panties to the world if she walked too fast. She might not have minded if Will had got to see her in the dress, but Anne said Will had "slipped out to make inquiries about the morning's events." Whatever that entailed. Anne wouldn't go into specifics. She only assured Mariana that Will was "a professional at handling this sort of thing."

The dining room would have been dark, at some point in its history, but they had painted it to feel like you were sitting in the forest on a sunny afternoon. The walls were hand painted with trees and birds and the arched ceiling with clouds, cherubs, and lithe angels in white gowns blowing horns.

Richard and Anne sat on opposite ends of the long oak table, with Mariana in the middle. She hadn't really expected much conversation. Perhaps that was what the Greystones intended. Still, the high ceiling of the place, and all the surrounding stones, made sound carry easily. It was like being in church. Even the light clinking of cutlery was loud. So when Richard finally spoke up, it sounded like he was shouting.

"Will tells me you're a bloodthirsty woman," Richard said. "Whose blood are you hoping to drink?"

Mariana nearly choked on her bite of roasted new potato. She coughed to clear her throat and her thoughts before answering.

"Anybody who threatens us," she said.

"Who is us?" Richard asked.

"Will, or the children," Mariana said.

"No one else?"

"If you're asking me whether I would kill to protect you and Anne, I don't have an answer for that," Mariana said. "I think we'd need to know each other better, and trust each other completely. I would kill to protect Oliver."

"But you trust your husband completely?" Richard asked.

"Yes," Mariana said. "I may not approve of everything he does, or how he does it, or even know or understand everything he does, but I know what kind of man he is. I trust him implicitly."

"Even when he betrays you?" Richard asked.

"Will has never betrayed me," Mariana said. "He simply wouldn't."

Silence fell again for a while, as they returned to the business of eating. But Richard's meal didn't seem to settle.

"What happened to your diamond necklace?" he asked. "The fancy fiery one?"

"Richard, don't tease Mariana," Anne warned.

Mariana didn't think Richard was teasing, nor testing her either. She thought something else was behind it, but she couldn't say just what.

"Will thought this necklace was more appropriate for this trip," Mariana said. "He will probably give me my other necklace back for the wedding, if you worry this one is inappropriate to wear with a wedding dress."

"A collar is probably the most appropriate thing to wear with a wedding dress," Richard quipped. "I doubt you'll see the diamond necklace again until you're back in the States."

"Richard…" Anne warned again. "I'm sure Mariana will have a lovely pearl choker to wear for her wedding. In fact, I intend to give her mine. You know, the one you brought back for me from… I don't recall where exactly… The one with the beautiful shell cameo at the center."

"Yes," Richard said, "good choice, Anne." He turned his focus back on his plate.

Mariana was almost grateful for the restoration of silence, except for the light sounds of eating. Dessert was an aromatic dish of small baked apples, stuffed with cinnamon, nuts and raisins paired with a rich vanilla ice cream and crispy fingers of puff pastry drizzled with sugar crystals. Richard started up again.

"You should ask Will about the necklace, next time you see him."

"Richard!" Anne protested. "Mariana has more important things on her mind than a flimsy bit of jewelry."

"You certainly crooned over it, when you first saw it," Richard said.

"Well, it was unique," Anne said.

"All of Will's jewelry is unique," Richard said. "Even that plain platinum collar, I expect."

"I'm sure it's just an innocuous collar," Anne said. "It looks very attractive on you, Mariana. It suits you."

"Okay, you two," Mariana said. She put down her dessert spoon, which was a shame because she was really enjoying the flavor of the apple compote inside what turned out to be a red candy apple shell. "What are you trying to tell me and *not* tell me about the necklaces?"

"Nothing, dear," Anne said. "Richard is only making conversation. He's not very good at talking to women. He thinks we're only interested in trinkets."

"Ask your husband when you see him tomorrow," Richard said.

"Richard, really!" Anne said. "Will has more important things to deal with, right now."

"They should clear the air, don't you think?" Richard asked. "Before the enormous commitment, I mean."

"What don't I know about my necklaces?" Mariana asked. "Are there bugs in them or something?"

"What would make you ask a thing like that?" Richard asked.

"Well, you're acting like there's something suspicious about them!"

"It's nothing at all suspicious," Richard said. "I think the word you're looking for is surreptitious."

"Richard, enough!" Anne said. "She's under enough stress. Stop needlessly upsetting Mariana."

"May I be excused now?" Mariana asked. She felt like a child asking to leave the dinner table, but she needed some fresh air. She felt like her skin was too tight, suddenly. Mariana worried she might pop like a tick and stain the elegant, embroidered tablecloth with her blood.

"Well done, Richard," Anne said, clearly furious with her husband. "Come, Mariana, we'll both go for a walk in the gardens. It's a pleasant night for it."

"Thank you, Anne," Mariana said. "But I'd like to be alone right now."

"Of course, my dear," Anne said. "If you need anything, just ask one of the staff or ring the bell in your bedroom."

The walled gardens of Castle Gwaed were beautiful, even under the moonlight. They were built on tiers, like a green wedding cake, leading down the hill on which the castle stood tall and imposing, overlooking the land and the ocean below. Each garden tier represented an added level to the castle proper, underground, with archways and French doors leading to sitting rooms and ballrooms and a grand library at the base. At the bottom was a broad rectangle lawn, split down the center by a pebbled path, lined with topiaries. It led to a fountain at the center, with a lawn chess set to the left. The lawn melted into the forests, which surrounded and protected the property better than any moat might do. They were wild and led to sharp drops downhill. Mariana sat on the edge of the fountain a while, looking up to get a better view of the castle, with its four enormous towers at the corners and the chapel where they would marry off to the right. She could see the window to her bedroom in their wing of the main house above, with a soft light emanating from the bedroom lamps which she had left on.

It was an odd sort of place, Castle Gwaed, though Will was right to say it was beautiful. The original castle was still intact, and the additions made over the centuries, above and below ground, to expand the size of the main house, showed the builders' care and respect of the original structure and the surrounding land. It all looked like it belonged here, and would not be possible to build anywhere else.

It also felt surreal to Mariana that she should be in this

place at all, and that the people who owned it were now somehow family.

¿Bueno, y qué más quieres? The ghost of her mother, Rosa Castro, who popped up at random, sat next to Mariana on the fountain, glowing blue in the moonlight.

"I didn't want any of this, Mother," Mariana said, speaking to the night air. "It's much too much. He tricked me, you know. He led me to believe he was a completely different man."

Did he, though, or did you just ignore all the hints along the way? Who owns an entire town and the surrounding mountains in Vermont? Certainly no ordinary gardener, Marianita. Besides, don't you love the man as he is? Didn't you say so to that uptight French bitch, his abuela?

"Every time I turn around there's another ugly revelation," Mariana sighed.

Kid yourself all you want, but don't lie to me. You long suspected the necklaces were bugged, and you still wore them.

"He's interrogating someone, isn't he?"

Obviously.

"He's going to kill them."

Probably.

"He's going to return broken."

You'll patch him up. This is your life now. You've chosen it. You speak big words. You say you are ready to handle more. So handle it. Stop whining each time it hurts. The bitch warned you. It will hurt more. It will get worse. Keep your head and fight for your place; here and everywhere. None of these people are better than you, Marianita. Their names aren't even as ancient as yours. When they still battled as tribes, our people were already a stronghold in the Roman Empire. We were also a jewel in the crown of Arabia. Your history predates theirs. Tú desciendes del Cid. Sé guerrera, y olvídate de Quijotadas.

"He won't forgive me, if I join him in the fight."

So don't join him. Give him what he needs, whether it's support or opposition. Keep yourself intact. You know who you are. Never let the man you love define you.

"Like you did, you mean," Mariana said.

Did I, though? How would you know? You were only a selfish child, tuned in to your own thoughts and feelings. You hardly knew me.

"You hardly gave me a chance."

Still complaining. I killed myself, but I live on in you. That's something, anyway.

"But what is the truth?"

The truth is nobody knows what goes on underneath another's skin. The truth is as changeable as the weather, and as murky as the fog coming in from the sea. The truth is you are chilly and need to get back inside before you catch cold. The truth is you love your husband. That's the only truth that matters right now.

"Wake up," Will said, nudging her shoulder under the thick covers of the canopy bed. "I'm sorry, but I need you awake."

"When did you get back?" Mariana asked, her voice hoarse from sleep. "What time is it?"

"It's around four in the morning," Will said. "I just got in. I need you."

"Sure, honey." She sat up to put her arms around his shoulders, where he sat at the edge of the bed. "Let me kiss it better." She reached for his lips, but he stopped her.

"No," Will said. "I need you crying."

"All right, Master," she said. "Do whatever you like."

"Don't hate me," he said, whispering, as he ran his fingers through her bed-tussled hair.

"I could never hate you, Master," Mariana said. "I will always love you."

He gave her a rough kiss, which hinted at the tension he barely suppressed.

"Never disobey me again, like you did this morning, Mariana," Will said when he let her breathe again. "When I tell you to go. You go. You don't refuse to budge and you don't make a scene."

"Yes, Sir," Mariana said.

"I cannot keep you safe if you don't heed my commands," he said. "We cannot survive together if you close yourself off to me each time I give you an order you don't understand. The only thing you need to understand is that I gave you the order. You do it. You don't question it."

"Yes, Sir, I promise," Mariana said.

"That's not good enough, I'm afraid," Will said.

"I know," Mariana said. "Where do you want me?"

"Are you strong enough for this?" Will asked. "Are the peas all right?"

"The peas are fine. Everyone is fine. We're much stronger than you think," Mariana said. "I've been a very naughty girl and I need my *Papi* to set me straight. Can you do that?"

"Yes, I can," Will said. "Strip and go stand by the fireplace."

Mariana obeyed, removing her ivory silk nightgown and leaving it on the bench at the foot of the canopy bed. Will had apparently re-started the fire because the flames burned intensely. Mariana wondered how long her husband had sat staring at the flames, fighting his urges, before finally deciding to wake her. She was grateful for the heat. Her body was covered in goosebumps, and her breath shook, but she knew Will needed to work off his demons. So did she. If her flesh could carry some of the burden, then so much the better.

"Turn around," he said, as he approached. Will held her shoulder tightly with one firm hand while swatting her ass with the other. "You need to listen to me, Mariana," he said. "There is no room for error. You do not get to be in charge unless I'm dead. Do you want me dead so you can take over?"

"No!" Mariana wept. He was making it worse with his words. If he would only spank her, she could easily take it.

"No matter what happens between us, you need to behave like everything is as it should be," Will said. "You cannot go around showing your disdain for me to strangers."

"I don't have…"

"Quiet!" Will slapped her ass even harder. "Don't argue with me! You know you were telegraphing your anger to the entire world. I don't give a shit what you think you should know. You'll accept what I tell you and trust me to tell you more when I can. And if I don't tell you anything, you'll accept that too."

"No, Will, I won't!" Mariana said, surprising even herself. "I won't accept it. You can spank me harder. Go on. Spank me as hard as you need to. Ravage my mouth. Fuck me in the ass. Do whatever you want to my body. But you tell me what I need to know when we're alone together. You tell me *everything* and trust me to take it. You think I can only take this pain? I can take anything you dish out. I can take all the ugliness."

"I can't always tell you everything you stubborn woman!" Will said, smacking her even harder. She was sure her ass was bright red, but she barely felt that pain because her heart ached much harder.

"Because we're never alone, right, Will?" Mariana said. "That's the problem. Isn't it? You've planted a spy in our bed. Didn't you?"

Will stopped.

"Take it off!" Mariana pulled at the collar on her neck. "Take them all off! Leave me without a tracker. Leave me truly naked, then do what you wish. Unleash yourself. Unburden yourself, dammit!"

Will let go of her shoulder, leaving a print of his fingers on her flesh. He walked over to the fireplace and just stared at the flame.

"How much did Grandfather tell you?"

"Nothing," Mariana said. "Everything that matters. He suggested you betrayed me. I can only imagine what that means. The necklaces aren't just trackers, right? And they're not just bugs. There's more that you're not telling me!"

"Not that one," Will said. "That one is just a GPS tracker. That's it."

"And the others?"

Will had given her a blue diamond necklace, originally, which he had taken from her when he thought a rival had compromised their systems. He'd replaced it with the necklace of diamond flames while they were in Nice.

"They also have a camera and a microphone," Will explained. "They record everything that is happening. They update in real-time to Zephyr, and she does an instant face match on anyone you meet. If we identify them in our system as a hostile or a potential threat, then an alert goes out immediately to security."

"Wait," Mariana interrupted, "so my necklaces have been sending images and sound to your systems this whole time?"

"Yes," Will said.

"Both of them?"

"Yes."

"So that means your people have watched and heard us having sex? Having arguments—and punishments. They've been there for *everything*?"

"Only looking at things from your perspective, Mariana. Unless you were in front of a mirror, you don't appear in the images. I don't care who sees me do what. It's mainly Zephyr watching, anyway," Will said. "My people are too busy to bother with the day-to-day recordings, and they don't want to know. They only hop on threats, or keywords flagged for tracking in conversation."

"So that time you had me stand in front of the mirror at the Wilshire," Mariana said, all of it sinking in. "You were watching me?"

"Yes," Will admitted.

"You fucking sneak!"

"You looked beautiful," Will said. "I couldn't help it. I missed you."

"That's not the fucking point, Will! You did the same thing Martin did! You recorded me—*us*—having sex without my permission."

"What I did is *nothing* like what Martin did, Mariana," Will said, his voice raw. "It is not even close."

"You spied on every client I met with, since we were married. Your systems have recorded every sensitive conversation I've had *with people who trust me*. Martin never did something that bad! He abused my body, but he did not abuse my trust! He never had my trust to begin with!" Will had nothing to say to that, but as the pieces came together in Mariana's head, a horrible realization dawned on her. "Oh, my God! You've lost control of it! It's out in the wild!"

"Oliver assured me the recordings were secure, impenetrable, and encrypted Mariana! Only Zephyr accessed them."

"Nothing is ever fully contained, Will! Everything digital can spread! How could you be so credulous?"

"Don't you think I know that, dammit!" Will said. "Don't you think I wish I could take it all back?"

Mariana was suddenly very hot, and woozy. Her world was spinning out of control.

"How did it get out? Does Oliver know how far it has spread yet?"

"Charlie's firm is compromised too," Will said. "Sandy is compromised. She'll be here later today. Charlie wants me dead."

"You got all of this from the man you interrogated?"

Will nodded.

"He had a memory card in his possession when Grandfather's people caught up with him. It's a catalogue of our organization, mainly sourced through these devices, stitched together clippings of our heads. You two are not the only ones who wore the necklaces. Many of our women wear one version or another of these devices. Again, the point was to protect all of you, not to harm you. It allowed you to roam free with your guards at a distance. It allowed us to monitor potential threats. That's over now. They're all useless."

"But the damage is done," Mariana said.

"Yes," Will sighed.

"No," Mariana said, getting an idea. "No, it's not done. Where is Oliver right now?"

"He's in San Francisco or in Monterey. He's up to his ears in shit, between taking over PlayTech and dealing with this crap."

"Well, he has to find some time for me," Mariana said. "And I need to tell Mac about this."

"Why the fuck would you do that?"

"Because I need actors for a play, Will!"

"Mariana!" Will shouted, but the wind was out of his sails. He was adrift at sea. He knew that. "Explain."

"Can I get dressed? Or do you need to spank me a bit more? Or would you like to fuck me first?"

He came up to her and gently stroked her cheek. "I always want to fuck you, but let's just focus," Will said. "Put on your nightgown, sit down, and I'll listen."

21

The Globe

Will didn't like three-quarters of what Mariana suggested, but he acknowledged it might work. Not only would it help address any leaks, creating a smokescreen of confusion and discrediting anyone who tried to make their secrets public, but it would also allow them to keep using their necklaces for the intended purpose, without worrying about any compromises in the future.

The problem was that they had to find anyone else who had already accessed the files, and they had to corrupt them. They had to manipulate the rest of their existing archives quickly and develop a method to cloak their recordings in real-time from then on, while also putting on a crazy, crazy show. It was an all hands on deck situation. Will agreed, finally, that Mac could help assemble the parts they would need to make the play complete and that Mac should write the script. But he didn't agree easily.

After a hell of a fight and an even more heated reconciliation, Mariana left her husband sleeping in her bed while she went down to join her in-laws for the most awkward breakfast of her life.

Breakfast, Tyler informed her, was served in the blue room, which opened out onto a patio on the highest tier of the gardens. Richard and Anne sat outside, enjoying the brief morning sunshine, when Mariana joined them, bringing her cloud along.

"I need access to the Globe," Mariana said after a brief greeting, when she sat down to join them. "Will told me to let you know that, Anne. My business partner—Charlie's wife—should be here around eleven. I'll need her to join us working there after lunch. Anne, I'll need you working with me this morning, please. Will believes you have special skills which could be very useful."

"What exactly is going on?" Richard demanded. "What did Will tell you?"

"Everything," Mariana said. "Well, I suppose as much of everything as he could get out in a single conversation. I know the top notes and we've devised a plan. Will's resting right now—he needs it—but he will join us for lunch. He will meet you, Richard, in the library to work on your side of things later this morning. When are the Eagles due to arrive?"

"My sons will be here with us tonight," Anne said. "The others will trickle in over the next three days. The formal Convocation will take place on Sunday."

"Okay, so we need to have a lot out of the way today so we have something palatable to serve them as they arrive," Mariana said. "Will tells me that most of them are affected by the breach. Is that correct?"

"Not all, but yes," Richard said.

"Will also tells me that Brian is responsible for the breach," Mariana said, referring to Zephyr's digital twin in the South Pole, who belonged to Richard's organization. "Did you know that they had sent him to pull those files from Zephyr?"

"That's not what happened, Mariana," Richard said. "I would have approved no one using Brian to steal from Zephyr. You need to remember that I don't have absolute control, as Will does. I have associates involved in the Brian program who have their own agendas. Besides, I warned Will that confirming the existence of these systems would prove dangerous. Over the years, I've kept Brian and Zephyr safe by dismissing them as little more than rumor, or a failed lofty dream of my son Sylvester. Once they were confirmed to exist, in France, others took note. So it's a leaky cauldron right now. Then, allowing Zephyr to manipulate Brian's defense algorithms caused many headaches for my team. Many people might benefit from the exploit, even some we have considered allies. This intelligence exchange—the compromised files from your necklaces—was actually meant to benefit both of our organizations, to simplify our mutual identification of allies and enemies alike. Brian did not know that the persons who took those files from him intended to sell it on. They had the clearance. There was nothing to flag the transaction as unusual for Brian. Zephyr noted it as an irregularity and locked Brian out of that section of her memory, but what is out there is out already."

"Well, that's good news, at least," Mariana said.

"What do you mean?" Anne asked.

"Well, if Richard knows the source of the original tap at Brian, and we know the men who Will interrogated overnight, as well as the associates they admitted working with, all your smart people should be able to figure out the six degrees between them," Mariana said. "It will make all our jobs much easier."

"I don't follow," Richard said.

"It's simple. Surely you've heard the theory that there are only six degrees of separation between any two people on the planet—six key contacts which connect them. You know, like six degrees of Kevin Bacon. We need to Kevin Bacon this thing. Find the six degrees between one end and the other. That's our trace. Then, find the six degrees between the ends we have now, and the heads most likely to want to undermine Will's organization. That's our target list. We take down or compromise all those links. Break them apart."

"You understand the meaning of the words you are using, don't you, Mariana?" Richard asked.

"Yes. I don't mean you have to kill *everyone* on the Kevin Bacon list. Just the irredeemable ones, and we'll compromise the others," Mariana said, taking a sip of coffee. Will didn't need to know she had splurged. She'd earned this caffeine. "Frankly, Richard, I don't give a damn. If we don't cut these links, people I do care about will die."

"Oh, I will very much enjoy my meeting with your husband later today," Richard said.

"Well, that makes one of us," Mariana said. "I've got him to agree to the basics, but he's not happy about it. I expect some push back."

"Well, that's a given," Anne said, understanding exactly what Mariana meant. "But I'm glad to work with you on this all the same."

"Good, so when we're done here, you'll take me to the Globe?"

"It will be my pleasure."

The Globe was a command center in the sky, built into the top floor of the Northwest tower of Castle Gwaed. It was a circular office, with digital screens all around the perimeter showing images from satellites in orbit, code, and news updates from around the world.

Mariana felt like she had just walked onto the Starship

Enterprise. There were a dozen people stationed all around her, following news threads and working on different projects on their computers. Anne's desk was a semicircle in the center, with a comfortable chair on wheels that spun around as she needed to keep up with information. A large wedge of the desk's surface was intelligent, like a large tablet device which she could use to bring up anything she needed.

Curiously, or perhaps unsurprisingly given that much of their staff did double-duty as agents, Meredith came with them to serve as their secretary.

"This room is amazing, Anne," Mariana said.

"Pippin designed it," Anne said.

Mariana knew why Anne used that name when referring to Will. Anne was deliberate in her choices, reminding her he could be a naughty boy, but he was *her* naughty boy, with fine ambitions and a good heart. Mariana wasn't receptive, but she took note. The lyrics from the musical she'd recently watched with him went through her mind, *Think about your life, Pippin...* She wished he *had* given all of it more thought.

"Did Bess like the theatre?"

"She loved it," Anne said.

"I thought so."

"Yes, she was in the West-End and in Broadway all the time, for the premieres. I think she might have made a good life for herself upon the stage."

"Well, she did, didn't she?"

Anne smiled. "Yes, she did. She had a beautiful voice too, a pity it was silenced so soon..." Mariana held Anne for a minute, then the tender moment passed, and they prepared for a battle.

"I'm afraid I have to wake Oliver up," Mariana said, looking at her watch. It was ten in the morning in Wales, so two in the morning for Oliver in California.

"I don't think Olly is sleeping, Mariana," Anne said.

"Not under these circumstances. If he closed his eyes for a minute, his new girlfriend would probably clip him."

"I don't know Caroline that well, I'll admit, but I'm sure she'll forgive Oliver," Mariana said. "It's impossible not to love him, even if he's been less than honest with her."

"I'm glad you feel that way," Anne said, smiling. "I know Pippin can be difficult, but he deserves some understanding too."

"Pippin is a different matter," Mariana said. "But don't worry. You'll still have a wedding to host, as far as I'm concerned, anyway. Pippin might change his mind."

"No, darling, I don't think so," Anne said. Hearing the affectionate label from the intimidating Countess touched Mariana's heart and gave her strength for her next move.

"How do I dial up Oliver?" she asked, not seeing a phone anywhere on the desk.

Anne tapped on the glass surface a few times, brought up a set of circles connected with lines to a larger circle with an image of her. Each circle contained an image of a member of her family. She tapped on the circle showing Oliver's freshly shaven face, with neatly clipped hair. Mariana barely recognized him. He looked much younger.

"Hello, Mémé," Oliver said, answering right away, using the same term of affection for Anne which Will had used in France. "You heard the news, I imagine."

"Yes, Olly," Anne said. "You're on speaker now, and I have Mariana here with me. We're in the Globe, so you can speak freely."

"I'm sorry, Mariana, I can only imagine how angry you must be," Oliver said.

"Never mind that," Mariana said. "Let's fix this mess, shall we?"

"What do you have in mind?" Oliver asked.

"Is your warped mirror version of your systems ready?" Mariana asked. "The one you told me about in Finland."

"Well, it's in Beta, you might say. It's Swiss cheese right now. Lots of gaps."

"That's okay. Cheese attracts mice," Mariana said. "Now, you say you have altered faces there and blended identities?"

"Yes, to sow confusion. Of course, now that the actual images are out in the wild, it's a bit of a mess," Oliver said. "We're finding them posted places already and taking them down as quickly as possible, I'm poisoning access where I can, but even with Zephyr's support it's hard to find them all. The originals are on secure, portable drives so I can't taint them. We have to get our hands on those, and they're probably being copied."

"Okay, one thing at a time," Mariana said. "How do you blend the identities in the mirror version?"

"Just a simple face swap application," Oliver said. "Then I mix up the database a bit, change names, dates, places. I have it all set up with an algorithm so it happens automatically and we maintain an ongoing storyline update that ensures continuity and makes it feel authentic."

"Good," Mariana said. "I will need access to that storyline. You can use any sources we like for the face swap, right?"

"I've been pulling from museum images and random face scans, but yes, we can do anything."

"Great, how much of the core group's storyline have you manipulated—that's Will and Charlie, Sandy and me—just to get started?"

"I've left you for last, I'm afraid. I didn't want to experiment with our most sensitive records. I've got some people in your circle."

"All right, I guess we're going to need to review what you

have in the authentic version, for the past six months, and start clipping highlights to storyboard," Mariana said.

"You want the actual recordings?" Oliver said.

"Yes," Mariana said.

"Of you four?"

"Is there a problem?"

"It's just…" Oliver's hesitation worried Mariana. "Look, I'm not trying to be difficult, but I need a sign off from both Will and Charlie on this. I can't just pass those to you."

"But they're already out!"

"Not everything," Oliver said. "I mean, I hope not. Anyway, it's got to be Will and Charlie approving those releases from my end. I'm sorry, Mariana."

"Will approved this, Oliver," Mariana said. "I have Anne right here to confirm. He'll be up later and he'll tell you himself, but he's exhausted right now and we need to get started. There's no time to waste."

"Mariana, you're not really the problem," Oliver said. "Your recordings are relatively useless. Don't take offence, but they expose very little that we can't fix. Will has been careful to keep you out of the more compromising parts of his life. But I can't say the same for Sandy. I can't tell you why, but Will and Charlie will need to agree. So will she."

"Sandy will be with us this morning," Mariana said. "Charlie has had to fly her out because he worries she's in danger because of the breach."

"Exactly," Oliver said. "I already know about that. Look, I don't know what you intend to do, but you can't have those records until I speak with Charlie. Can you tell me what you have in mind? He's going to ask."

"Sure, it's simple," Mariana said. "We're going into the entertainment business. I'm buying a studio. I'm buying a network. I'm hiring actors. I'm contracting the best writers.

I'm going to record what I expect will be a very popular show, streaming globally."

"Oh, I see," Oliver said.

"Do you?"

"Yes, I think I do, Mariana," Oliver said. "We can put the PlayTech assets to work on special effects and staging, and to provide backup actors. We could speed up your production that way."

"Now you're thinking, kid," Mariana said.

"Charlie is going to go ballistic when I tell him," Oliver said.

"Yeah, I'll handle him," Mariana said.

"No, I don't think that's a good idea," Oliver said.

"Leave it with me," Mariana said. "Another thing."

"What?"

"I'm calling Orlando into this," Mariana said, referring to a hacker she had befriended in Los Angeles. "I'm hiring her for a social media blitz. I'm betting she's good with bots."

"Okay," Oliver said. "Yes, she's cool, but I think we could really use Tracey right now working on counter attacks. How is she doing?"

"Call Patricia Cornwall," Mariana said. "Tracey is desperate to dive back into deep waters. I think she's about as sane as she's going to get, without access to the cyberworld, to be honest. You need to bring Jonathan Castle with her. They are inseparable."

"Sure, we can find them a home near us," Oliver said.

Mariana noted the plural. Perhaps things would work out for Oliver with Caroline Boots after all.

"Are you not coming to the wedding, Olly?" Anne asked. "I had hoped to see you again. It's been too long since you've been home."

"Can I bring a guest?"

"For the wedding, yes, but not for work," Anne said. "If you plan to be here working, she'll need more clearance."

"I think I can negotiate that," Oliver said. "Let me see what happens. It's only two weeks away and things are mad right now."

"In two weeks' time, the only thing you'll have to worry about is watching your warped mirror life play out on television," Mariana assured him.

"You can put the show together that quickly?"

"I can't," Mariana said. "But together, we can."

Mariana spent the time waiting for Sandy to arrive, and for the other contacts she needed to reach in the US to wake up, getting familiar with the capabilities of the team who worked in the Globe. She marveled at Lady Greystone's ability to process vast swathes of information quickly and make meaningful connections between seemingly unconnected things. Before Sandy arrived, Lady Greystone had also programmed a "six degrees of crisp bacon" protocol into their local systems, which connected remotely with Brian in the South Pole. Brian apparently felt terrible about being duped into releasing sensitive intelligence files.

"I am sorry, Iron Maiden," Brian's voice, coming out of the ether, sounded deep and soulful, and just a touch sad. "We had not updated my security protocols for this."

"Nobody blames you, Brian," Anne assured him.

"Zephyr is angry with me," he said.

"I doubt that," Anne said. "If she is cross, she will get over it quickly. Now, do you understand the protocols I transmitted?"

"Yes, they are very clear," Brian said.

"Very good, go fetch," Anne said. "I'd like to have a list in an hour, if possible."

"Oh, it won't take that long," Brian assured her.

"Iron Maiden?" Mariana asked Anne with a grin.

"Yes, it's been my handle for decades," Anne said. "Some people think I'm hard and prickly, apparently. I can't imagine why."

"Neither can I." Mariana smiled. "Do I have a handle?"

"Don't you know? You're the orange blossom."

Mariana laughed. "No wonder you thought I was just a Barbie doll."

"I would definitely have called you the blue thistle, myself, but Charlie beat us all to it," Anne said.

"I'm impressed by how quickly you could code all of that for Brian," Mariana said.

"Did you think Sylvester got into computers and mathematics because of his father?" Anne shrugged. "Richard can barely operate his phone. His skills are far more hands on."

"You have a fascinating family," Mariana said.

"*We*, Mariana, *we* have a fascinating family," Anne corrected, "and it's getting even more colorful now, thank Providence. You'll love my other sons. Richard is flying in from Qatar with his family, and Henry is bringing his from Shanghai. Charles and Merlin are both based here—Charles manages things in London and Merlin is in Cornwall."

"Did you say Richard is based in Qatar?"

"Yes," Anne said, carefully.

"I knew someone who was killed in Qatar over the weekend," Mariana said.

"I know all about that, and Richard had nothing to do with it," Anne said, her voice hard. "You had a vicious friend, and that friend's viciousness was his downfall. We are blameless."

Mariana felt like she had just taken three steps backward with her grandmother-in-law.

"He wasn't a friend," Mariana said. "And I believe you. I just wanted to know more about what happened, and I thought maybe Richard might know."

"I know *what* he was," Anne said. "I know also that you should leave the dead to rot. Don't go picking at bones that don't concern you."

"There may be some push-back, for Will and Oliver, because of the PlayTech takeover," Mariana said.

"It's all being handled, Mariana," Anne said. "You have enough on your plate with this mad scheme of yours, which I fully support. I just hope you're ready for the repercussions. Your wolf was tired and malleable at dawn, but when he's fully rested, he'll likely have some objections about the lengths you intend to go."

"Do you know about what happened to Crystal, the singer? She's my client. There are other loose ends on Martin Harper that affect me directly," Mariana persisted.

"I heard about that too, poor girl, but maybe you can use it as an advantage for this play."

"What do you mean?"

"Well, she was a charming young actress at some point, as I recall," Anne said. "Her face might launch a thousand ships."

"It would be a good way to send some hush money her way," Mariana mused. "Not for her, really, more for her mother. She's most likely to become a problem. It's something we should discuss with Sandy and Mac."

"Are you sure you want to get Arthur McClintock involved in all of this? He's a bit of an unknown factor for all of us."

"He will stitch the plot together like no one else," Mariana said. "And Ernest will have everyone who can make a difference talking up the series in a matter of days. Besides, I'd trust them both with my life."

"You are doing precisely that, you realize?" Anne said. "You are exposing Will completely, to strangers, in order to protect him. I understand that making the story so obviously ludicrous will sway a lot of minds, and the embarrassment of claiming any of it is real will silence a lot of lips, but don't expect everyone to be duped. Don't expect Will to take all of this mocking in good spirits, either. My grandson is a proud man."

"I know, Anne, but we just need smoke and mirrors right now," Mariana said. "Once Mac takes up the story line anyway, it will misdirect everyone. I'm sure he'll veer as far away from the heart of things as he can while still providing cover."

"Every story takes on a life of its own, and once it engages with an audience, the tale can run amok," Anne warned.

"That's what I'm counting on," Mariana said. "In an ideal scenario, it will cause a tower of babble. Except—and this is the really important part, Anne—Will's core messages, his values, will be at the heart of the play. They will be seeds, planted in minds, free to grow wild and free."

"You remember what I said about planting ideas," Anne said.

"Yes," Mariana said, "but ideas will be Will's most effective weapon against his enemies, believe me."

"I change my mind," Anne said. "Your handle should be atomic kitten. Your nails have a powerful half-life."

"Ooh, I like that," Mariana smiled. "Have a talk with the men for me. Maybe you can sell it."

22

Angry Daddies Everywhere

Mariana slipped out of the Globe to greet her friend as soon as Sandy arrived at the gates of Castle Gwaed. Sandy looked a bit tired from the journey, her natural sunshine obscured by the cloud hanging over all of them. As soon as they were in the rooms set aside for Sandy and Charlie, close to Will and Mariana's rooms in the same hall, the two friends had a heart to heart.

"I don't think Cailean will enjoy having separate bedrooms," Sandy said, looking around hers, which was nearly identical to Mariana's, but decorated in shades of silver and mint and looked out on the castle's bailey.

"Who?" Mariana asked.

"Oh, shit," Sandy said. "Never mind. I guess it doesn't matter now... That's his actual name, Mariana, but never use it. Never. Promise me that. Daddy is so angry right now. I think he might kill Will."

"Okay, when is Charlie due to arrive? I have to fill you in on what I'm doing. I think it will keep everyone breathing comfortably from now on, but I've had some pushback from Oliver on access to your recordings. I need to talk to Charlie about that. We have to warp everything or the play won't work."

"Mariana, you're babbling right now," Sandy said, sitting down on the bench at the base of her bed.

"All right," Mariana said. "Let me catch you up."

Sandy paled as Mariana went over all the details of her argument with Will, the plan they'd hatched, and what she'd done. It was strange, but very welcome, being able to just speak plainly to Sandy again, to have her partner fully in the circle of secrecy that surrounded them. But Sandy's reaction worried her. She needed Sandy onboard if she was going to sway Charlie. *Cailean?* She'd best forget that detail, though they might use it. Some names for the key players had to be changed, anyway. It sounded close enough to Collin. Perhaps that would be a better name for Charlie's character in the show. When Mariana finished, she had hoped Sandy would be eager to get to work, but Sandy started crying.

"Oh, Sandy, I didn't mean to upset you!"

Mariana sat on the bench next to her friend and hugged her tight.

"You don't understand, Mariana," Sandy wept. "You really know nothing about my life. I have secrets that can't get out! They will ruin us all."

"I'm sure that's not the case, Sandy," Mariana said.

"You're wrong," Sandy said. "I have to tell you, and when I tell you, you're never going to see me the same way again. You're going to hate me."

"Sandy, whatever it is—no matter what—I promise I could never hate you," Mariana said. "I will never think less of you either. You are such a good friend. You're like a sister to me. Please, just tell me what it is and I'll spin it."

Sandy took a deep breath before starting and when she did it all flowed like blood from a deep open wound. Mariana tried to wrap her head around everything her friend was confessing to, everything this beautiful woman had suffered through and endured. Emotion overcame Mariana, crying along with her friend, though what she felt most strongly was anger and grief. Anger that Sandy had ever had to go through any of this, more anger still that one of her clients was responsible for Sandy's suffering, that she hadn't known and had let the monster in, and a deep, lasting grief that her friend had to endure all of this pain and horror with grace, unable to share any of it with her. But Mariana also felt renewed pride and respect for Sandy, and for Charlie too. She told her as much.

"Listen to me carefully, Sandy," Mariana said. "You are a heroine. In fact, you should be the star of the show. I think between your story and Crystal's we'll have some compelling programming to empower women viewers and terrify weak men. I am so proud of you for what you did, Sandy. So very proud. I only wish I was half as brave as you are."

"I don't think Daddy will like it," Sandy said.

"I think you're wrong," Mariana said. "Charlie knows how to put on a show like no one else. He's a ham. A deadly wild boar, but still a ham. And The Unkindness! My lord, a BDSM orgy will really have people watching. There's an audience for all of this. We'll have to change many things, of course, to protect everyone, but you can trust Mac with the truth. None of this will shock him in the least."

"You don't think I'm a monster?"

"No, Sandy, I think you're a Valkyrie. That should be your handle."

"It's Lollipop," Sandy said. "Daddy thinks I don't know, but I do."

"Lollipop?"

"Yeah." Sandy laughed.

"We'll change it," Mariana said.

"No, please don't. I like it," Sandy said. "Though you can use Valkyrie for your show."

"Okay," Mariana said. "We're going to have lunch soon, but if you'd rather sleep, I can have something brought up for you when you wake up. Then you can join me in the Globe this afternoon."

"I don't think I can sleep right now anyway," Sandy said. "I slept on the plane over and I'm very wired. I'd love to go for a run on the shore, though, before lunch. Do you think that's allowed?"

"I honestly can't say," Mariana said. "But we'll ask. When will Charlie be here?"

"He's hunting, but I expect he'll be here tomorrow," Sandy said. "Though I can't really say. Things are so changeable right now."

"Okay, we'll play it by ear," Mariana said. "Do you think I can reach him to ask about the recordings, so he can give Oliver the clearance?"

"Good luck with that," Sandy said, with a smirk. "Yes, I'm sure you can reach him, and if anyone could talk Charlie into a scheme this crazy, it's probably you. He really likes you, Mariana, but he's furious with Will. You'll need to sort that out. They can't be at each other's throats right now. They need to be working together."

"We'll work together, fix this mess and get our men back on the right track, Sandy," Mariana said. "No one shames us and no one exploits us while I live and breathe."

"I'm with you, one-hundred percent, Mariana," Sandy said. "I'll skin any son-of-a-bitch who gets in your way."

"Look at us!" Mariana gave Sandy a tight hug. "Let me ring the bell to get you a guard for your run. You can join us for lunch when you get back, in the patio of the lower garden by the chessboard."

"This place is right out of a fairy tale," Sandy said.

"Very Brothers Grimm, yes," Mariana said with a smile. "I have to go face my wolf now."

Will wasn't in her bedroom anymore, or in his. Mariana had wished he'd sleep a little longer so his mood would improve, but she understood that Will's mind was probably racing as much as her own. The rift with Charlie would be on his mind too. Knowing Will, she imagined he felt a great deal of guilt that his plays had exposed them all this way, but it really had been inevitable. She had to get him to see that. Plus, he needed to make a few phone calls, for her to approve some very large purchases. Mrs. Wilson had quite a shopping list to present to her husband.

Meredith told Mariana that Will and Richard were meeting in the library, which was on the lowest level of the castle, under the southwest tower, facing the same gardens where they would meet for lunch. She made her way down ancient winding stone stairs to reach it. All of this had, at some point, been the bowels of the castle, possibly storage for wine and supplies, or a dungeon. The old torch stands now held electrified torches, but it was still a chilly and creepy descent. Many feet, over the centuries, had worn the stairs down. It was slippery, and Mariana nearly lost her footing twice. She didn't need to be falling downstairs at this point. Will would be livid with her, probably, for sneaking down, but she really had to see him.

She heard him first. His words were indiscernible through the stones, but the timber of his voice was unmistakable. Will was having a heated argument with Richard. When she reached the arched entrance to the library, she stood just outside, waiting for a good time to interrupt the men.

"Will, listen to me, son," Richard said. His voice was pleading, for once. He was a different man, gentler. "There are worse things which could come to pass. This play of hers avoids many of them."

"It's practically the same!" Will roared. "There is a fine line between exploitation and violation—only a cunt's hair!"

Mariana felt stung. They had agreed this morning, but clearly Will was having second thoughts.

"I think Mariana deserves better from you, William," Richard said. "We haven't come up with a better suggestion yet, on our own, and the enemies are at the gate."

"She's going to take everything I am and turn it into a joke, a perverse farce," Will said. "I'll never be able to look a man in the eyes again and feel like a man!"

"What is she to feel like, when she looks a man in the eye?" Richard asked. "You did that, Will, by exposing her to this. No one else did. It won't be enough to get rid of the recordings, even if we can find everyone on her Bacon list and kill them. Something will get out. It will need to be discredited. People will need to doubt their eyes and ears. The confusion she will create with this show will keep you safe and allow you to use your best tools again without concern."

"And that Bacon list!" Will shouted. "Why would you think I would approve of all that killing, just on her word? I don't even know who she is anymore!"

"Why *wouldn't* you approve it, William? Even she can see it's necessary. I wish you had heard her! 'I don't give a damn, Richard,' she said to me. 'If we don't cut these links, people I do care about will die.' That is some woman you have in your bed, man. I could never imagine you had found such a suitable match. Don't fail her now. It is your children we're talking about here, their legacy, their life! Your own wife, man. Do you understand what it means to know your wife is in the hands of a foe? I do! When it happens, you will forget yourself, William. You will leave all your ideals behind, return to the days of the caves, and drink their blood, tear their flesh with your own teeth. I know this William, and I never wish that knowledge on you."

"Stop using your scare tactics on me, Grandfather!" Will said. "They do not work."

"Scare tactics? I'm telling you facts! Do you know what they did to your grandmother in Moscow before we could get to her? Have you *any* idea?"

"Silence!" Will slammed something hard enough to produce an echo that vibrated through Mariana's bones. "Enough! I am not saying we should not act, and quickly. I am questioning the lengths she's going to! I am not in favor of all this... *perversion*. And we'll call trouble by cutting off so many heads!"

"William, you risk losing the support not just of me, and your wife, but also of the Hawk." The hard voice was unmistakable. This was the Iron Maiden talking now. Mariana had not even guessed she was in the room. "Do you think Charlie will settle for slapping a few people on the hand when they have exposed his organization? Some of these actors on the list intend to compromise you deeply. Yesterday, was only a light warning, a trap, to stain your organization at the core. The pacifist arms-dealers—what a headline! They have infiltrated you, William. Don't you realize that?"

"I questioned those culprits myself, Grandmother!" Will shouted. "I know *exactly* what they've done. I washed their blood off this very morning. But I can't set off a massacre in retaliation. That will turn into a thug. I am not the fucking mafia!"

"No, you're not," Richard said. "You are a Borgia. Keep your semblance of piety. You need it. But know which goblets of wine to poison."

"You're such a cynical fuck!" Will spat.

"And you're such a blind fool!" Richard snapped. "Open up your eyes! You're going to be a fucking father! You need to see the world for what it is and take off your rose-tinted glasses."

"Mariana was not suggesting that we kill *all of them*, William," Anne interjected. "Only those who pose an immediate risk to you. We only have to compromise the others. You have plenty of material for blackmail in your coffers, too. It's time to use it. We have allies who could get the message out. You don't have to touch this yourself."

"I'll disband it all first," Will said. "I'll liquidate all assets, get rid of it! Because once I agree that the enemy of my enemy is my friend, I am lost! I'd rather disappear."

"Oh, grow up, Will! A man of your magnitude can't disband without markets collapsing. You have too many fingers in too many pies. You'll be killed before you ever give the order. A man like you doesn't disappear until he's dead. They'll kill her! They won't kill her quickly. They'll torture and rape her in front of you, force you to sign over your powers, take over your empire piece by piece, until they've taken everything from you, until you've told them all your secrets! Then they will make you watch as she's torn into strips of flesh and dies before they ever get around to killing you!"

Something crashed against the wall by the arch at the entrance, something green and crystal, perhaps a paperweight. Shards flew past Mariana's feet. Well, she figured, this was as good a time to enter as any.

"Richard, Anne," Mariana said, taking in the scene. Will stood by the large oak desk, bent over and trying hard not to weep, his knuckles bleeding. "I hate to throw you out of your own office, but could you please leave me alone with my husband? We need to have a word."

Richard stormed past her, saying nothing, though he made a point, tapping her gently on the shoulder on his way out. Mariana suppressed a sob.

"Is your friend settled?" Anne asked before following her husband.

"She's *unsettled* and going to run off her angst," Mariana said. "She'll join us for lunch, though. We'll be all right."

23

Silent Pools

Mariana approached Will slowly, like an inexperienced tamer inching toward an injured lion. He didn't look at her. He just stared at the blotter on the desk, stained with smears of his blood.

"Will, it won't happen," she said, doling out the words carefully. "None of that will happen. No one will hurt us. No one can tear us apart."

"Mariana, what have you done?" he said, his voice barely above a whisper.

"I did what we agreed to do," Mariana said. "I've set the wheels in motion, but I need fuel for the engine. And some extra car parts, too. In fact, I need you to give me a big wedding present. Enormous. I promise I'll earn it."

"Mariana, this isn't a joke!"

"I know that! I'm not kidding around, Will," Mariana said. "Look, what happened is awful, but it doesn't have to be. It could be a great opportunity. We could flip this around to our advantage. You never really paid enough mind to media because you distrust it."

"Because it's mostly lies and filth!" Will said. "And now

you're pulling us headfirst into the shit house! I agreed to the premise of a show, but this storyboard that you and grandmother cooked up—for fuck's sake, Mariana. It's almost all sex and violence. It's lurid. You're making it tawdry."

Mariana had to laugh. "Oh, Jesus, Will, I never thought your family had such a strong Puritan streak. You love sex! I know you do."

"Mariana, I don't like sex in *public*," Will said. "I don't like *our bed* on display."

"It's not our bed," Mariana said. "Not really. Besides, sex sells, Will. We need this thing to sell." Will shook his head. "Look," Mariana continued, "when I first realized what was happening, I was mortified and embarrassed—for about a second. But, Will, nothing we do is wrong. Everything we do is beautiful. It's all lovemaking. Even when it hurts, no one is harmed. I don't honestly care about what people might think, but that's not what we need to hide. We need to hide *your* part of the story, and the best way to do that is to shine a light on the parts that take place in the dark. Those are the things people want to see, anyway. Then we weave in bits of your story, the highlights, with an emphasis on your values. That's what needs to come through most, but not as a lecture. Nobody wants that. Besides, when I asked Anne about the recordings we couldn't get our hands on yet, without your approval, a lot of it wouldn't appeal to our audience, anyway. As your grandmother explained, most of your job in the field is really boring, searching through weeds and waiting for sprouts. We can cut all of that out. Charlie has the more exciting job, honestly, and Sandy has the more compelling story. I think we should make them the stars of the show."

"You've lost your mind!" Will said. "You have lost your goddamned beautiful mind! Charlie will *never* allow his wife to be exposed. Don't you understand? That's the danger here! I've been able to count on Charlie for decades. We've fought together and bled together, but now he thinks they will kill her because of me! Because I allowed the breach to happen by preserving Zephyr and protecting Brian. My play in France made things worse. Charlie knows that! I've lost my friend, and he is not someone to have as an enemy, Mariana."

"Okay, first, darling, you're tired and all worked up," Mariana came around the desk and put one hand on Will's back, and the other on his fist, still pressed against the desk. "You're not seeing things clearly. You're not understanding the play at all. Nothing that will happen will be real or incriminating. I'm not producing a documentary. We are jumbling and blending storylines and creating such confusion that people won't believe any of it, but they'll love everything they don't believe. They'll just be invested in the characters and the stories. It is an escapist fantasy, my dear. Nobody is exposed. No one is harmed. I would never hurt you, or Charlie or Sandy. I would never shame you. And Charlie and Sandy are exhibitionists. They won't mind their sex lives used as fodder for our stories. Heck, if I get Charlie going, he'll give us more material to work with."

"It's not his sex life being public that he's angry about, Mariana!"

"I know," Mariana said. "Sandy told me about the men she killed. She explained everything. I think it's wonderful. We will protect her, but use that story as fuel because it makes one hell of a fire. Once it's in the storybook world, no one will believe there's anything more to it than that. Sandy will remain in the clear. She is blameless in our world. Her character will inspire others. Okay?"

"Is that how you want to live your life?" Will asked. "With your hands full of blood?"

"Don't be a dick," Mariana said, planting a kiss on his

cheek. "First, Sandy isn't living her life that way. She had to do what she had to do. They came after her, not the other way around. I don't plan on killing anyone, unless they come after us. I don't have the *training* she has because *someone* hasn't had time to teach me yet and has also forbidden me from getting pro lessons. We don't kill anyone you don't approve first. If you say no, then they get to live. You're the boss. You decide. But we have to compromise those people, Will. They need to fear your wrath. They need to know that you are a force, someone they will not mess with. Deterrence, Will. These stories can offer deterrence too. They can be abject lessons. We'll start with Martin Harper, may he rest in pieces."

"I won't work with untrustworthy mercenaries," Will said. "Don't be fooled. Grandfather has some muddy connections and so does Howard, Mariana. Charlie is the only one I trust. I need my stream to stay clean."

"It will be. I promise." Mariana sat on the desk and put her hands on her husband's face. "Charlie will forgive you for this. He loves you like a brother. He knows you wouldn't do him any harm."

"I love you, but you are a crazy woman," Will said, though he sounded much less angry about it.

"I'm Cuban," Mariana shrugged. "I'm going to shake things up. I'm going to provoke you sometimes. I'm not going to just sit around waiting for my man to fix everything for me while I watch my nail polish dry." She ran a fingernail up his arm, and up his chest, and up his neck, tapping his chin before scratching his lips. "But you're still my man. You're still the boss of me. If you tell me no, then this whole deal is off. But please don't say no to me, *Papi*. Let me prove to you I'm right. This is my wheelhouse. It's my turf."

"I want to spank you, fuck you, kiss you, and tie you to your bed," he said.

"In that order?" Mariana wrapped her legs around Will's waist, and popped a button on his shirt open with a fingernail, scratching at his chest.

"Not necessarily," Will said.

"Buy me a few presents now, and you can do anything you want to me tonight," Mariana said. "Anything, Lucifer."

"We have a dungeon here, you know," Will said, gripping her hair.

"Sounds great, but I want my presents first," Mariana said. "And remember, I've never asked you for anything, so you can't deny me when I finally ask for something I really, really, really want. That would make you a very bad Daddy."

Will gave her a twisted grin and brushed her lips. "I am a terrible Daddy."

"No, you're not," Mariana kissed him gently, teasing him with her lips. Will responded with an angry, hungry kiss that left her reeling, her breath heavy, her lips bruised and her panties wet.

"I am going to make you pay for all of this," he growled.

"Okay, but don't you want to know what all of it is, first?"

Will chuckled. "Shoot, nena. What do you want Daddy to buy you? I'll buy you the moon."

"Well, I don't want the moon. Where would I put it? I was thinking more of Sylfin Studios, Hot House Publications, NWS, LNN, Airs, Blip Dot, and Fizz Feed," Mariana said. "To start. Oh, and Brown and Wooster, just for giggles."

"Is that all?"

"That's all I need today."

"You want me to make a major media push, running the gamut from traditional to social media companies, in one day?"

"Before lunch, if you can handle it," Mariana said.

Will laughed. "Oh, baby, I can handle it. I don't think you can."

"Prove it, big boy, show me how hard you are on those markets," Mariana said.

"I am very hard," Will said, picking up the phone on the desk and dialing. "Sit still, little girl, and watch your Daddy."

"Can I play with myself while I watch?"

"Don't you dare," Will barked. "Hands at your sides." A moment later, he added, "Not you, Aaron. I need your hands ready to make some calls."

Mariana was beyond turned on by the time Will finished his call with Aaron Silverman. They arranged the trades which would give Mariana control of all the media companies she'd asked for under a series of entities that were all now part of a fresh communications umbrella for the organization. They all belonged to Mrs. Wilson, technically, though under other names and under the leadership of her own series of Doppelgängers who would act on her behalf from day-to-day.

"Oh, Daddy, no one's ever bought me a media empire before," Mariana cooed as Will hung up. "That's so thoughtful."

Will started the slow torture of his wife, running his fingers over her panties, not even slipping between to touch her flesh, just stroking her through the fabric. "Oh, you dirty girl," he growled. "You need to take these off."

"You take them," Mariana teased.

"No," he said. "You get up right now, young lady, pull your damp panties down, and hand them to Daddy." He put his hand out to receive them. Mariana jumped off the desk and lifted her skirt, wiggling her panties off slowly then handing them to Will. He grinned, folded them and put them in his pocket, then walked down the library in the opposite direction.

"Where are you going, Daddy?" Mariana asked, chasing after him. His broad, confident stride was back. Will reached a bookshelf which opened up when he pulled back on a book and led to a dark hallway.

"I'm taking you to see something special," Will said. "Keep up."

"This is spooky," Mariana said, following close. "Are those spider webs?"

"Spiders do a public service," Will said. "They get rid of pests. It's bad luck to kill them."

"I don't know about that," Mariana said, drawing some spider silk away from her face, which gave her the heebie-jeebies. "Some are poisonous and all of them are sticky."

"Like women," Will joked.

Mariana slapped his butt, enjoying a chance to get him back.

"Did you just smack me?"

"There was a nasty spider on my husband's firm, delectable ass," Mariana said.

"I told you, it's bad luck to kill them." He picked her up and threw her over his shoulder.

"Eww! I've got more spider web on my hair!" Mariana ran her fingers through her hair to clean it, as she dangled upside down and then smacked Will again on the rear.

"Somebody *really* wants to earn a thrashing," Will said. "My dear, you already have so much coming. You should pace yourself."

"Sorry, Daddy." Mariana giggled. "Where are we going?"

"To my dark lair," Will said.

"Ooh, Vlad, are you going to impale me?"

Will smacked her butt. "Hush, harpy."

After what felt like a long shoulder ride up-side-down through the dark and dusty tunnel, Will opened a door on the other end, letting in blinding sunlight.

"What is this? Mariana asked when Will finally put her down on a gravel pathway.

"We just took a shortcut, but we're going to the forest now and I can't carry you all the way there," Will said. "You're getting heavy."

"Aww," Mariana said. "Am I too much for my big manly man now?"

"You were always too much, vixen," Will said, kissing her. "We'll be on uneven terrain. I don't want to trip and drop you. Just follow me, okay?" He took her hand. "You're not really dressed for this." He looked meaningfully at her high heels. "Letting Grandmother select your wardrobe was a mistake."

"What? I think this dusty pink Channel suit looks sexy as fuck on me," Mariana said. "You don't like the skirt?" She wiggled her ass at him, barely contained by the tight tweed fabric.

"Fucking hell, Mariana," Will said. "Can you just behave for a minute?"

"*Sí, Papi.*" Mariana put on her most contrite face.

Will grasped her hair and smashed his mouth onto hers, assaulting her senses again as his hand dipped under the tweed jacket to grab her breast hard. "I am going to fuck you unconscious," he growled.

"Right *now*?" she bleated. "Because, you'll have to carry me back and you just said…"

Will shut her up with another possessive kiss, then he threw her back over his shoulder and carried her into the forest, squealing.

He put her back down at the mouth of a cave, hidden by the thick trees and underbrush. "Take those shoes off," he said. "You have a better chance of making it barefoot. If you get cold, tell me."

"Ooh, are you really Batman?" Mariana pulled off her heels and hung them from one hand. "I always thought you might be. Superman is too… meh."

"What has gotten into you?" Will laughed.

"You, silly," Mariana said. "You've gotten into me, out of me, back into me again, and back out, then in…"

"Mariana," Will said, his voice stern again, "follow me." She took his hand and tried to keep her balance on the damp stones. They were cold, but she didn't want to complain. She was eager to see what Will was hiding in the depths of the dark forest of Castle Gwaed.

The answer came a few hundred feet ahead, when Mariana heard a hum and saw a faint blue light. "Oh, Will!"

"Shh," he ordered. "Not yet."

But as they got to what looked like it might be a tidal pool, she knew what it was from the intricate patterns forming on the surface and asked, "Is this Zephyr too?"

"No, this my dear, is Zephyr one. Her name is Aura," he said. "Nobody knows, Mariana. Sylvester and Hope brought me here in secret. I'm fairly sure that Grandfather does not know. She's been here, relatively alone all these years. Zephyr has a single connection back to her, but I don't think she's even aware of it. I don't think she knows when it's Aura thinking for her. Aura's always been there for her, like a little voice in the distance whispering Hope's core commands. She probably thinks it's part of her own organism at this point. But she isn't. She's her conscience, her fairy godmother."

"She must be lonely," Mariana said.

"She's not," Will said. "Mariana… I promised to look after her no matter what else happened to the Zephyr project. Nobody knows she's here. I've stayed in touch with her using systems that even Oliver doesn't know about. It has to stay that way, but she can be ours. She can help you with this crazy scheme. Swear to protect her too. Please. She's their child, do you understand? Every bit as much as Oliver."

"But how did you keep it secret on your grandfather's property?" Mariana asked. "I mean, they have to have noticed some activity."

"No, Aura uses almost no power. She produces what little she uses. This one gets her fuel from salt, not silica like Zephyr, but it's the same principle. She will live on long after us. Besides, nobody comes into this cave because it's cursed."

"What?" Mariana asked.

Will laughed. "It's ancient nonsense. One of our ancestors crossed paths with a druid, or something, and the druid set a curse on this cave. The legend is, 'anyone who enters it will never come out again'. Of course, people have come and gone, but, many accidents have happened over the centuries, either right here or just after they had been here. It's difficult to navigate this terrain so a few accidents are no surprise, but the word spread that this place is bad luck. People are silly. They avoid it, but it's just an ordinary hole in the ground protecting an extraordinary treasure. I've been here dozens of times and I'm fine."

"For now," Mariana said. "You shouldn't mess with curses, Will."

"Oh, Mariana, I'm disappointed in you," Will said, kissing her head. "Don't let superstition get in your way. This is a wonderful opportunity. I know Zephyr enthralled you in Finland. Aura is just as beautiful."

"It's a wondrous sight, but is she alive like Zephyr is? You know, has she achieved singularity too? I mean, if she's older…"

"Honestly, I don't know," Will said. "Whenever I chat with her, it's a bit like chatting with a little girl, a very mature little girl, but still. She has some gaps in her communication and her knowledge. They did not train her in the same way as Zephyr was. They gave her express commands to be a guiding voice. She's sort of sour-dough starter too, for any future creatures like her. I don't know how to explain well enough, but she's not exactly like Zephyr. She *is* powerful, though."

"Will, I think you're wrong," Mariana said. "I don't think she's that much of a secret."

"That's right, Pippin," Anne's voice came out of the darkness behind them. "Foolish for you to bring your wife here, wearing her tracker. Did you think I wouldn't have been monitoring her movements? You really don't give me much credit, son."

"I'm sorry, *Mémé*," Will said. "Sylvester and Hope never told me. I did not know you knew."

"William, if I *didn't* know, then your grandfather certainly *would* know," Anne said. "The only way to keep the black wolf in the dark is for me to protect this light. It *has* to *stay* that way. I keep very few secrets from my husband, but the ones I keep *really* matter."

Mariana felt like Anne had directed the warning mainly at her, which she supposed was understandable, but she still took it personally.

"I will keep the secret," Mariana said.

"What did Ben Franklin say about two keeping a secret?" Anne asked. "Somebody dies, as I recall."

"Well, both you and Will knew," Mariana said.

"Exactly," Anne said, "and now you are here."

"Well, I need both of you alive, so we will keep this between the three of us and let it go no further," Will said.

"I suppose that will have to do," Anne said. "Now, get out of here, you two. Lunch is served and Sandy is already waiting. Mariana, I've brought you some rubber boots for the way back. You'll catch your death of cold walking barefoot in here. It's a silly thing for you to do when you're expecting."

"Yes, ma'am," Mariana said, taking the green rubber boots from Will's grandmother. They were about two sizes too big, but lined with wool and warmed her feet. And they matched Anne's, which was nice.

24

Mad Eagles and Raging Hawks

S andy had evidently won Richard over by the time they joined them for lunch. The two were laughing like co-conspirators when Anne, Mariana, and Will arrived. As soon as Sandy saw Anne, she turned her cheeriness and charm on the woman.

"Richard was telling me about how your children, used to think this castle was Camelot and went looking for evidence and got themselves in a bit of trouble in the hidden corridors of this place," Sandy explained.

As soon as she knew the conversation revolved around her children, any jealousy that Anne might have felt about her husband talking to the buxom blonde beauty vanished in an instant. Anne immediately joined in. The couple regaled them with more tales of their children. Despite the light conversation, Mariana couldn't help noticing longing and regret on Will's face, particularly when his mother's name came up. He had missed out on so much. No matter how much his Nana Smith had given him, and how much Will had enjoyed growing among the trees, in blissful ignorance of his wealth and legacy, she had also deprived him of a lot.

"Um, Daddy wants to have a talk with both of you," Sandy said to Will and Mariana as they all wrapped up lunch on the patio. "He's feeling very vocal, so do you have a quiet place where we could call him that others might not overhear?"

"Use my library again, William," Richard said. "I'm going to be busy this afternoon, anyway. I'm going out to meet with friends."

"Thank you, Grandfather, but I think it's best if we call Charlie from the beach. Sandy needs a walk to stretch her legs after her journey, don't you Sandy?"

"Uh, sure," Sandy said. Since she had just had a hearty run before lunch, they knew Will just didn't want to have this talk with Charlie in the library. It made Mariana wonder whether any part of what she had discussed with Will while they were there was still a secret. Spies spying on spies. *Welcome to the family!*

"Suit yourselves, but wear the proper clothing," Richard said. "The weather will turn drizzly this afternoon. We'll see you for drinks before dinner in the China room at six. Richard, Henry, Charles and Merlin will be here with their brood, so it should be lively."

"Good, so let's get changed and go down to the shore," Sandy said. "Daddy's waiting and he gets grumpy when he has to wait."

"Charlie, grumpy?" Anne joked. "I never imagined such a thing was possible."

Anne's limited imagination and Will's efforts to keep this call secret aside, Charlie was shouting loud enough on the speakerphone for his voice to echo off the cliff walls behind them. The roaring sea was not loud enough to drown him out.

Mariana's best efforts to persuade the man of the wisdom of her scheme had fallen short and backfired. It shocked Mariana that the sweet-tart killer she knew could produce such a howl.

"You take your woman in hand or I will!" Charlie threatened Will. "Nobody makes a mockery of my wife!"

Mariana wasn't sure whether Charlie meant to spank her or strangle her with his bare hands, but really neither sounded good.

"Daddy…" Sandy spoke up.

"Shut up, baby girl! Don't take advantage of the distance. You *will* feel my buckle when I see you."

"Okay, but…"

"Sandy, for fuck's sake!"

"Sorry, Daddy, but you need to shut the fuck up."

There was a momentary pause as Will and Mariana stared at Sandy, and Sandy stared at the waves crashing on the shore.

"*Excuse* me? Do I need to use the cane?" Charlie's voice was back with a vengeance.

"You can if you like, but you really need to listen first," Sandy said, unrelenting.

"Baby girl, why do you like to hurt so bad? You're carrying cargo now. You need to behave!"

"Cailean, I swear to ever-loving fuck you will hear me out!"

Sandy's words seemed to come out of a different body entirely, like the projection of a preternatural ventriloquist. An angry, long forgotten Celtic goddess spoke through her. Her normal sing-song little girl voice was replaced by the cry of a revenant. It left Charlie apoplectic, or the line was dead.

"Charlie, are you still there?" Will asked, just checking.

"Roger that," Charlie said. The two words fell like stones.

"Okay, Daddy, listen, this is my bad. It's my ache. You

don't get to have a say. I'm sorry, I know it's against the rules, and you're in charge, and you know best—and all of that shit —but I know this has to be done," Sandy said. "I like it. I support it. I *need* it to happen. Do you hear me, Daddy?" Sandy wept. "I really, really need this—more than anything. You can punish me however you want, Daddy, but don't be cruel. Don't stop me from turning this evil into something good."

"I hope you're happy, William," Charlie said. "You made my baby girl cry! Is that what you wanted? Did you need to see that to believe me when I said she is a goddess?"

"Charlie, I…"

"Shut up, Will, dammit! Get my baby her special lollipops, or I swear to God I'm going to feed her your Rocky Mountain oysters tomorrow!"

Mariana gave Will a look, hoping he'd explain. Will shook his head and grinned.

"I'll get some delivered right away," Will said. "Charlie, I want Mariana to tell you about her Bacon list."

"What the fuck is that?" Charlie asked.

"We've put together a trace list of everyone who may have the original recordings, based on the connections between the person who took the original files from Brian and the ones Will interrogated last night. We have a hit list of forty-two people put together who will probably trade this intelligence."

"I am asking you to decide what should happen to them," Will said. "Whatever you say, we'll do. Whoever you decide to kill, I'll kill for you. I'll compromise everyone else."

"No, motherfucker, you will kill no one *for me*," Charlie said. "I'll have a look and pick the pigs. The Hawks will take care of them."

"I'm offering a ten-million-dollar bounty for every head," Will said.

"It's not about the money, Will," Charlie said.

"I know, man," Will said, "but let the Hawks know all the same."

"Charlie," Mariana interjected, "going back to my little project, I thought that Jonah Lark should play you."

"I hear he's an asshole," Charlie said.

"Yeah," Mariana agreed, "but apparently he's a loveable asshole, right Sandy?"

"He's larger than life and he's got an enormous fan base," Sandy said. "All the pretty girls want him."

"Do you want him, baby girl?" Charlie asked.

"No, Daddy," she said, "he isn't man enough for me."

"We'll talk about this shit tomorrow," Charlie said, sounding appeased. "Send me that Bacon list now. I'll take care of it, Mariana. Will, we'll talk when I see you."

"As long as I see you coming," Will said.

"Dude, I will not kill you just because I'd like to," Charlie said.

"Yeah, me neither, brother," Will said.

Dinner with the whole Greystone brood present, except for Oliver, who was still sorting things out in Los Angeles, was both entertaining and overwhelming. The younger Richard measured every word and discounted at least three of them before opening his mouth, but his wife, Rose, was a fire-cracker who had a gift for double-entendres. She had mastered the art of the clean, dirty joke and delivered them with such an expression of innocence that one might easily believe she was just a little naïve and couldn't help herself. The only thing that gave the game away was how her hazel eyes twinkled each time the table erupted in a blend of gasps and guffaws.

Mariana was glad that she and Sandy had sat near the woman. It helped to ease some of the tension they felt in this otherwise formal setting with a crowd of strangers who were suddenly family. Will joined in the fun, egging Rose on by acting like he did not know why the others were shocked beyond words or laughing.

Charles and Henry, and their wives, Josephine and Martha, were more formal, though certainly pleasant and welcoming. Merlin was a mystery, who had lived up to his name. On the surface, he came across as a bumbling and awkward man, but he seemed to follow every thread of every conversation happening at the table simultaneously and would occasionally interject a pointed remark that got everyone's attention—almost as if his own family was surprised that he was there. His wife, Nancy, was his perfect match, enthralled by the decor in the ceiling as if she'd never been in the place, or as if the cherubs were sending her messages. At one point, Nancy shouted out, "e5!" Everyone stared for a moment, though she had turned her attention back to her whitefish. About five minutes later, when the buzz of conversation had started up again, Merlin replied, "Nf3."

"No chess at the table," Anne reprimanded both of them.

Nancy said, "triple o", quietly, but Merlin heard her and smiled. "Exd5," he replied in hushed tones. Anne clinked her wineglass with her knife.

Their children were equally curious creatures, most of them in their early and late twenties, some shy around strangers and others quite bold. Mariana had a good time jostling verbally with Roderick, Henry and Martha's eldest, who worked as an analyst for his grandfather's firm and had a penchant for tongue twisters.

But there was more than Betty Botter's bitter butter,

surreptitious chess moves, and three-legged men discussed at the table. Sandy seemed to hear it better than Mariana did.

Sandy, who had only engaged in light conversation the entire evening, spoke up during dessert. "The Eagles will have nothing to fear from the Hawks," Sandy said. "If only the Hawks could say the same." Then she stuffed her mouth with rich chocolate mousse and smiled at Mariana as if nothing had happened.

After dinner, Sandy excused herself to go to bed. Mariana wanted to follow, just to be sure Sandy wasn't angry or upset, but Will held her back. "I need you here," he whispered in her ear. "Sandy knows how to handle herself. She did great. Don't worry."

Later that night, when they were alone in their rooms, Will explained that his uncle Henry had set Sandy off by suggesting that Charlie should not be at the Convocation. Will had made it clear to all that it was his war meeting, and he'd include whoever he wanted.

"How did I miss all of that when Sandy heard it?" Mariana asked, turning to have Will lower the zipper on the floor-length champagne silk and crystal gown that Anne had brought up for her.

"Sandy has a very good ear, even better than Charlie knows, probably," Will said, lowering the zipper slowly and kissing her bare shoulder. "She's loyal to him. I don't think she would have spoken up and given herself away like that, normally, but she was clearly angry. I don't blame her."

Mariana stepped out of the dress and hung it up. "You looked beautiful tonight, sweetheart, but I like you better this way," Will pulled on the elastics of her garter belt.

"You look pretty hot yourself, Mr. Bond," Mariana said, pulling on his black bow tie. "But I like *you* better naked."

"Ugh," Will groaned. "Can you please never call me that again?"

"I don't know," Mariana teased. "Tell you what, give me that order one more time, but with that Scottish accent of yours."

"Listen, Pussy Galore," he said, obliging her, "you'd best behave or you'll finally find out what a tawse is."

"Oh, you even get the 's's just right," she cooed. "How many accents can you fake?"

"None," Will said.

"Because they're all authentic, right?"

"That's right, Pussy."

She rose on tip-toe to kiss him before slowly unbuttoning his dress shirt, gathering his studs in his hand to place on his valet stand and trailing her nails over his chest. "Atomic kitten, to you."

"What's that?"

"Not Pussy Galore, or orange blossom, atomic kitten," Mariana said. "That's what Anne says my handle should be."

"So you're exchanging secrets with Grandmother now?" Will gave her a look as she removed his shirt, tossed it on the bench at the center of the dressing room, and got to work unfastening his cummerbund and tuxedo pants.

"If only you knew, Lucifer," she said.

He grabbed her wrists as she reached for his zipper. "Tell me you did *not* discuss that with Grandmother," Will sounded and looked suddenly furious.

"It came up," she said, focused on his dark green eyes. "She brought it up. She knows you much better than you think, Pippin. She was worried that *I* didn't know you and I might run out of the bedroom screaming if you took a turn to dark."

"Oh, Jesus." Will shook his head. "What did you tell her?"

"I told her I like to please my Master, and I love all his

shades," Mariana said. "Even the scary one cutting off my circulation."

Will let go of her wrists.

"You're never really scared of me, are you?" He stroked her cheek gently.

"No, Will." She grabbed his hand and kissed it. "I'm scared for you plenty, and often. Sometimes I fear your wrath, so to speak, but I'm *never* truly scared of you. I know you're not Bill. There's very little you could do to me that would make me afraid of you."

"I love you," he said. "I never want you to fear me. We can go back to gentle play for life and I would still adore you."

"Will, don't be silly," Mariana said. "I enjoy you every which way. And you need to be with me—however you need to be to feel right. Besides, I'm creaming for Lucifer, you know. I'd love for him to stick around, push me around a little, and make me cry. You know I'm not lying."

"Grandmother ruined him for me," Will grumbled.

"No, she didn't," Mariana said, pulling his pants down, and kneeling on the carpet to pull off his socks and kiss his feet, before rising again to lick his dick, from the base of his hard shaft all the way to the heart-shaped seam of his tip. "My Master knows himself." Mariana wrapped her lips around his head and sucked him like a frozen pop.

"Stay on your knees, atomic kitten," Will said, his breath heavy as he pulled her hair to stop her. "I want you crawling to the fireplace, just as you are."

"Mrrawol." Mariana scratched his ass and hissed, baring teeth, before turning and crawling slowly out of the dressing room.

"That ass is an invitation to sin," Will snarled.

Mariana wiggled it at him as she crawled, following his command. The maid had cleaned and emptied the fireplace.

They didn't really need to burn logs in summer. If it hadn't been for the chilling events of the previous night, the heat from a fire would have been oppressive. Though the castle had a draft running through it that felt like icicle fingers trailing down her spine. Maybe it was haunted. Well, the ghosts would just have to watch.

Will stepped out of the dressing room, carrying a long riding crop, like a cane, covered in leather with two leather strips at the tail.

"They say you cannot train cats," Will said, approaching her slowly, "but I have found wanton pussies respond well to caning."

"Have you trained a lot of kittens, then?" Mariana asked, with a challenging glance at the naked wonder of nature that was her husband. His firm calves and hard thighs met at trim hips. She could get lost for hours on the V which trailed from a well-disciplined abdomen and a broad, bulging chest that tempted her teeth.

"None as wayward as you, my dear," Will ran the leather strips at the tip of the crop along her face and shoulders, "none as delightful to punish either, and certainly none as willing to come on command."

"I'm wet already, Master," Mariana said. "I'm always wet for you."

"Yes, but you're not weeping," Will said, "and you owe me for a generous bounty of catnip, don't you?"

"Yes, Master," she said. "I said I would do anything, and I meant it."

"What if I branded you?"

"If that's what you want," Mariana said.

"You would let me burn my initials on your flesh?" Will seemed dumbfounded, even keeping in character.

"Yes," she said.

"Why?"

"Because it's your flesh," she said.

"Mariana, you should not tempt me so." Will shook his head, tapping her butt with the crop. "There is a part of me that would keep you in chains in the dungeon at the bowels of this castle and only visit you to fuck you against the cold stones. Part of me would like to keep you stripped bare and bound forever to that canopy bed, with a chain around your neck that would limit your movements to these rooms. You would find no trouble or be in any danger. You'd never see another man again and flash your lashes at him the way you flashed on Roderick at dinner."

He sounded genuinely bitter.

"Will, you can't be serious," Mariana said. "Your cousin just made a joke, and I joked back. You know there was nothing to it."

"There was everything to it." Will lashed her ass lightly with the crop, just a warning, though it stung. "I know Roderick is a handsome man. He takes after Grandfather, whom you've obviously endeared yourself to with all your wicked scheming, and he's single."

"I'm not," Mariana said. "I am very much taken."

"Not enough," Will said, striking her harder this time. "I told you not to look another man in the eyes, remember? I warned you."

"I forgot myself," Mariana said. "I'm sorry."

"Pussies who get distracted get whipped," Will said, striking her a third time with more oomph. Mariana yipped. "I want you to pull off your panties, and take off your bra, but keep your garter belt and stockings on. Can you do that?"

"May I stand up?"

"No," he said.

"Why don't you cut my panties off with your switch-blade, then? That would be easier."

Will struck the tip of the crop under the stretchy fabric of her underwear.

"How do you know about my switchblade? Do you go rifling through my pockets?"

"I noticed you palm it in Edinburgh, when we went for a walk and you thought that man was following us too close," Mariana admitted.

Will whipped her hard this time. "Stop being so smart and so damned observant."

"No," Mariana said. "I'll pay whatever price you ask, but I will keep watch on my husband."

"Oh, kitten." Will got down on his hands and knees to join her on the carpet, bringing his nose to hers. "Why didn't you tell me what you saw sooner? Why didn't you tell me you were afraid? Is that why you acted out on the plane?"

"Don't." Mariana kissed him. "You're ruining the play. I promised you any price for my presents."

"Come here, kitten," Will said, running his hand over her shoulder, then sitting up on the carpet, his legs akimbo. "Curl up on my lap."

"But you're all horny, and so am I," Mariana whined.

"This is more important." Will tapped his lap.

Mariana sat on his thighs, facing him. She draped her arms over his shoulders and kissed his chin. "You worry too much," she said. "Knowing you carry a knife that you know how to use doesn't scare me. It makes me feel safe. Knowing you have enemies, because you insist on bucking convention and doing the right thing, doesn't scare me either; though the fact they want me dead irritates me. The only thing that frightens me is not knowing, Will. Not being trusted. Not having a say. I can take everything else, but not when you keep me in the dark."

"You're going to make many more enemies now, Mariana, running a media empire, putting other people's dirty laundry on display," Will said, stroking her hair. "I did not give you a gift. I've given you a greater burden to carry. That worries me, darling."

"It couldn't be helped." Mariana shrugged. "I see an opportunity in it. Besides, I won't have to worry about the day-to-day with those businesses. I just have to use their resources, for now, but they're well run. They'll be very little trouble when I'm done."

"You're wrong, Mariana," Will said. "The things we own are chains around our necks. Eventually, it's impossible to fly. Do you want to know what I really want, in my heart of hearts?"

"I can guess," Mariana said. "You'd like to be lost in the forest in Vermont. In our house, overlooking a ghost town that you've brought back to life."

"No, darling, not even that," Will said. "I would like to be left alone in Fiji, painting, making love to you, watching our children play in the sand."

"Painting?"

Will nodded. "I have little time for it these days, but there was a time when it was all I wanted."

"Well, we'll do that," Mariana said. "Once all these things are settled, we'll go to Fiji and you'll paint."

Will shook his head. "No, baby, I don't think that's ever going to happen, not for longer than a week or two. We'll just have to enjoy the weeks we get."

"Listen, Will, there's no point in being afraid of what may come, or being too fixed in our plans," Mariana said. "I was only a child when we went on that raft, but I remember the only actual plan was not to drown. We didn't. We drowned later. Well, my parents did anyway. But you know what killed them? It wasn't the angry sea. It was their fixed notions—my mother's idealism and my father's cynicism. They could only look backwards at what might have been. It blinded them to what was, and what was, overwhelmed them. I don't want to live my life like that, Will. I'll take whatever comes and find a good side to it. And if there isn't a good side, then I'll make one up. Don't be too fixed in your thinking, Will. Accept that things will go wrong, even when you have made the best plans and have the best intentions. I know the sort of man you are. You will always make things right again."

"I'm going to have to make love to you now," Will said.

"Weren't you planning to anyway?" Mariana gave him a light kiss on the lips.

"No, I was planning to castigate you for your bold demands and impertinence, then I was going to fuck you until you fainted," Will said. "Now, though, I just want to be sweet to my kitten. I want her to purr for me. I don't want her to cry ever again."

"I don't mind crying," Mariana said, savoring his mouth. "It's a good release."

Will pressed her against his chest and kissed her deeper. "I want you purring."

"Well, I can't help purring," Mariana breathed, "especially with the way you stroke me."

Will smiled and stood them both up, then carried Mariana to the canopy bed, laying her down gently on the mattress. He took off her underwear slowly, caressing and kissing her legs and thighs as he removed her stockings, and left her completely naked, kissing each part of her body as he stripped her. "This is my favorite thing, you know," he said, kissing her neck, "if I lost everything else. If I had to give it all up. I just need to feel your pulse on my tongue and breathe in your perfume. If I can have that, I am a lucky man."

Despite his aim to make love to her gently, Will's passion soon intensified to a fury that caused the bed to shake and the ancient walls to echo with Will's name. "Louder, so Roderick can hear you," Will said, as he pounded into her, his hands clasped in hers against the mattress.

"Oh, Will," she said, trying not to laugh.

"Louder!" Will commanded, letting go of one hand to grip her thigh, digging his fingers into her.

"Oh, Will! Oh, oh, oh, Will!" Mariana shouted. "Your cock should be a registered weapon, Will! It's too much, Will! Oh, no, Will! You're going to break me, Will!"

Will grinned and shut her up with a kiss that brought them both back to the serious business of sex. She moaned his name one more time, loudly, meaning it, as he joined her in the ecstasy of completion. Her walls still quivered in orgasm after they parted.

"A registered weapon…" Will laughed, his arm folded over his damp forehead.

"Double-O-heaven," Mariana purred, rolling on top of him and bringing her lips up to brush his. "License to thrill."

He wrapped his arms around her tight. "Go back to fearing me on Sunday, Mariana. You can't be as comfortable as you were tonight. No matter what else I let you get away with, our success depends on the Eagles thinking you're tame and can follow instructions."

"Yes, Master." She kissed his chin, smiling.

"I'm serious."

"I know. You're deadly serious," Mariana said. "I'm terrified, Lucifer."

"Wench." He kissed the tip of her nose and grabbed her butt. "Maybe I *will* brand your ass. There is plenty of room for all my initials."

"As…" She kissed his lips. "You…" She kissed his chin. "Wish." Mariana bit his neck.

"Succubus," he chuckled. "I can't have you showing up

in the delivery room with a brand on your butt. They'll accuse me of abuse."

"Speaking of that," Mariana said. "We haven't discussed it, you know, how our peas will come out. I'm a little worried, if I'm honest. You're huge, so if they come out anything like you, they may break me down there. Rhiannon said I should get an epidural, but I was thinking more like a Cesarean."

"Seriously?"

"Why? Do you think it's a bad idea?"

"I don't know, honestly. You should ask Doctor Austin."

"Will I be able to? I mean, will we be back by then?"

"I'm going to make sure you and the peas are safe and well, no matter what," Will said.

"You didn't really answer me," Mariana said, kissing him. She could see in his eyes that Will didn't have an answer. A lot depended on the Convocation. "Are you still going to do what you said and ask the Eagles to protect Sandy?"

"Absolutely," Will said. "I'm going to give Charlie a heads-up first, to explain why I am doing it, so he doesn't take it the wrong way. That's going to be especially important now. I'm sure Sandy will tell him about tonight."

"What's Henry's problem with Charlie, anyway?"

"Something going back to Afghanistan," Will said, "which affected a mission he was on. The thing is, Mariana, remember the Greystones are not clear streams. They are always muddy waters. Do you understand what that means?"

"They do business with potential enemies, if it serves their agenda," Mariana guessed.

"Exactly, Charlie is a clear stream," Will explained. "That's why I trust and respect him. He'll only do business with people who have never crossed him. Once he's your enemy, he's your enemy for life. He doesn't forgive or forget. He'd rather go the long way to get what he needs instead of taking any compromising short cuts with people he can't trust. All his men follow those rules, or they're not his men anymore. And, Mariana, Charlie lets people retire, but he doesn't fire anyone. Do you understand? They simply vanish. He is black and white. He can be a violent man, but he is an honorable man."

"And Henry isn't honorable?"

"He is, in his own way, but Henry is just like his father. He's a pragmatist. He makes compromises. They all mean well, but each time you accept a compromise you bring yourself one step closer to destruction. You hand over control to the wrong people. While they were in Afghanistan, Henry had made a compromise. Charlie wrecked it and Henry hasn't forgotten."

"But if the Eagles make compromises with enemies, then why are you getting them involved? Aren't you making a compromise too?"

Will sighed, "No, what Henry did, he had to do. The same applies to Grandfather and the others. When they work for their agencies and their clients, they do what is expected. When they work for me, it's a different matter. That's what this Convocation means. I'm calling in favors and I'm contracting them. We're up against people with too much power, and that includes some agencies that various Eagles have contact with. I will not allow them to make compromises. In fact—and none of them know this or they wouldn't agree up front—I'm putting Charlie in the lead. He will coordinate actions. So they will answer to me and take orders from him. It's going to ruffle a few feathers, but it's the only way I can be sure this all goes as it should. I'm going to need your help."

"Sure, hon, anything," Mariana said.

"Good," Will said. "I need you to stick to me like glue at the Convocation and, no matter what happens, don't argue or contradict me, or act out."

"What? Are you going to auction me off again?"

"No, but you're going to be tested," Will said. "Trust no one over the next few days except for Sandy, Charlie and me. Don't go anywhere with anyone if one of us isn't with you."

"What about Anne?"

"Not even Grandmother, Mariana, please, especially not now that we know she was keeping Aura secret."

"Your family is exhausting," Mariana said, snuggling up to him.

"I know," Will said, kissing her head. "Get some sleep."

Mariana wrapped herself around Will's torso, rested her head on his chest, and closed her eyes. "Will, what are Rocky Mountain Oysters?"

"Deep fried bull's testicles," Will said. "They're not half bad."

"I love Charlie."

"Me too."

25

Renaissance and Ridicule

Will was gone by the time she woke up, but Sandy came to get her before going down, which made Mariana feel better. While they were alone, Sandy assured Mariana she was just fine, despite the thing at dinner. "Daddy knows I blurted out." She shrugged. "He'll probably spank me for it, but it felt great. Honestly, I've got a historic spanking coming anyway, and I wanted to set those bitches straight."

"I'm sorry I dragged you into all of this, Sandy," Mariana said.

"Are you serious? I love this life!" Sandy clearly meant it. She was glowing again. "Inviting me to your wedding was the greatest gift, Mariana. Daddy is the best man I could have dreamed of. We're very happy together. I know my man could crush any motherfucker who looks at me the wrong way, which really turns me on, to be honest. Plus, I get to put my ears to work for both of you. I wouldn't change a thing. Now, let's go claim some eagle feathers and get some eggs. I'm starving."

They set breakfast up as a buffet, allowing for the larger

crowd of guests, and served in the game room, Mariana guessed, going by the billiard table and dart boards at the far end. The small round tables, covered with a tablecloth for breakfast, were otherwise used for cards and board games. Mariana sat with Sandy at a table in the far corner by the narrow stained glass windows which overlooked the forest. They had arrived early or late, Mariana wasn't sure, but there was no one there. They still kept their conversation light, discussing the qualities of the castle and avoiding any topics which might be overheard.

They were on their way out already, when Roderick crossed their path. "Weapons aren't allowed at a Convocation, you know," he said, leaning into Mariana. Mariana was sure she'd turned a shade of magenta.

"Oh, I better warn Daddy," Sandy said, sounding every bit the airhead some people assumed she was. "He always comes with his gun blazing."

Roderick laughed and moved on to the kippers. Mariana and Sandy walked out and headed for the Globe.

"Don't worry, Mariana," Sandy said, along the way, "even their long-dead ancestors buried in the chapel heard you last night. They all know who you belong to, but they're definitely going to test you. Just play dumb, like Rose and Nancy. They know what they're doing."

Sandy came into her own in the Globe. It was a remarkable site. She and Mariana had always worked well together, understanding what the other meant or needed without explanation. Now that they were coordinating the most critical crisis recovery of their careers, they performed like twin conductors of a symphony orchestra, ensuring all the players hit all the notes at the right time, to produce a beautiful, hypnotizing noise.

They had lunch brought up so they could make the most of their time. Mariana suspected Will was grateful, even if he might have liked to see her at lunch. If she was in the Globe with Sandy, she couldn't get into trouble with the Eagles descending on the castle.

Charlie's arrival at the Globe disrupted their symphony. Will did not come with him.

"Explain all of it to me, ladies," Charlie groused. "Let me understand this mess you two are making."

Far from being intimidated by the request, Sandy hopped right on it, giving Charlie a full view of their storyboarding process for Ridicule, as Mac had titled the show, and a briefing of all the resources Will had made available through his big buys. Sandy even shared a not yet approved clip Oliver had put together using PlayTech resources to blend the faces of the actors in a scene taken from Sandy's recordings, with virtual actors filling in the camera angles that were missing, some changes to the script and their voices replaced by the voices of the lead actors.

"She sounds nothing like you, baby girl," Charlie said, "and she's not pretty enough to play you. That said, it is kinda funny. It might be worth a popcorn night."

"That's all Mac's writing," Sandy said. "He's very good."

"All right, so I get what you're doing with the show, but what's our story for those who have the originals when they come out with them."

"Audition clips," Mariana said, "and rejected shots. We were always working on this show, trying to put together a pilot we could pitch. If someone got their hands on pirated copies of our auditions and rough takes, there's not much we can do about it. Though we'll still sue for content licensing violations. That's only for anyone who might admit having them or who shares them with the press claiming they are genuine. You and Will can take care of anyone who would never admit having them but would try using them."

"How d'you put together that Bacon list?"

"I didn't," Mariana said. "Anne did, working with Brian."

"Okay," Charlie said, putting a lot of weight on the word.

"What?"

"Nothing," Charlie said. "It's probably nothing. Have you asked Oliver to put together a Bacon list of his own working with Zephyr?"

"No, it hadn't occurred to me, but I could ask him to do that today," Mariana said.

"I'll take care of it," Charlie said. "Why Bacon?"

Mariana explained the six degrees of Kevin Bacon which had Charlie laughing so loud some of the other crew members of the starship Greystone were startled out of their deep concentration.

But then Charlie turned deadly serious. "Mariana, this is going to kill Will, you know," he said. "He may pretend for you, but all of this mockery, all this buffoonery, and this list. It's death by a million cuts for your husband."

"It's the only way I can see to brush over the truth before it gets out into the wild," Mariana said. "I know it's not what he wanted, and he won't be making any popcorn to watch the show at home, but do you have a better idea Charlie?"

"No, and I think you're doing the right thing." He turned to face his wife. "Though *somebody* has to remember that her Daddy does not allow backtalk and disrespect under *any* circumstances. Isn't that right, baby girl?"

"Yes, Daddy," Sandy said meekly, "I'm an awful, naughty girl."

"No, precious, you are beautiful and brilliant, and a bit of a pain slut." Charlie kissed Sandy like he knew he owned her and he didn't care if the world knew too. Then he grabbed her ass hard. "And you are going to just love what I plan to do to you tonight. Everybody's going to love it, baby girl."

Sandy visibly gulped, her chest heaving. Mariana knew she must have blanched. "Make it right for him, Mariana." Charlie turned his attention back on her, still holding Sandy captive at his side. "A lot of blood is being spilled in your honor, and we will endure a lot of pain. Make it right by your man."

"Yes, sir," Mariana said, unable to break away from Charlie's glare. She saw what must be the last face many see, when Cailean gave them a chance to see him coming, and felt herself shivering. "I will. I swear."

"Good." Charlie clapped loudly and smiled, breaking the spell. "I'll leave you girls to your project. I've got shit to do."

As soon as Charlie left, Mariana breathed again, leaning against the round desk. "Jesus, fuck."

"I know," Sandy sang with a Texas twang, "ain't Daddy just a peach?"

Sandy borrowed the accent from their new assistant, Laurel Leigh, who hailed from Texas. Sandy was a Santa Monica girl through and through, but some of Laurel's qualities had stuck as they worked closely together.

"How's Laurel doing on her own?" Mariana asked.

"Oh, she's not on her own." Sandy waved a hand to dismiss the notion, smiling. "The agency sent a temp to cover while I'm here—and, get this, his name is Bruce Wayne. You know who he looks like, don't ya?"

"Well, at least we know they know the business inside and out," Mariana shrugged. "Am I doing the right thing, Sandy?"

"Yes, Mariana, but Daddy's right. Will won't tell you how much he hates it for two good reasons. First, because he knows he's the whole reason it's necessary, and second because he loves you more than himself. But you've got to make him whole again for it, because the shame of this exposure will break him."

"How do I do that?"

"If you don't already know your husband well enough to guess, then I honestly can't tell you," Sandy said.

———

While they accomplished a lot the rest of the day, Mariana was still unsettled by her exchange with Charlie and wondering what to do to put Will at ease. She couldn't back out, and he wasn't asking her to—neither was Charlie—but how could she show Will that this would all work out when she wasn't sure herself? It was the best solution she could find, but there were no guarantees. She felt she could get his messaging across in the program, make it light and entertaining, but also make it meaningful and spark a dialogue about the things that really mattered to him. But she couldn't be sure that would be enough, or that he'd even watch it to appreciate it.

Will was back to himself as they got ready for dinner, but he seemed tired. This time there were even more guests expected, including Charlie, as well as a fresh handful of Eagles from various parts.

"How many people can this castle hold?" Mariana asked as Will zipped up her shimmery black dress.

"About three hundred, at maximum capacity," Will said. "It's more like a hotel than a house, though not all the rooms are like ours. Many of them are little more than cells."

"It must be lonely for them, when everybody's gone," Mariana mused as she slipped on her heels, meaning his grandparents.

"I don't think so," Will said, deftly tying his bow tie. "Grandmother and Grandfather really enjoy each other's company, and they have a large staff on site. Besides, they close off the parts of the castle they don't need, and Merlin and Charles are often here on weekends and holidays."

"And how many Eagles are coming to the Convocation?"

"Fifty," Will said. "It's a closed group. We only recruit new members when one dies. Though some will bring family to this, or when they return for the wedding, so Castle Gwaed is going to be crowded with people coming and going for a while."

"And they're from everywhere around the world?"

"Most are part of old alliances," Will said, "and they're scattered around the globe."

"But you trust them," Mariana said.

"As much as I trust anyone who isn't you, Charlie or Sandy," Will said.

"I'm so glad you've included her, Will," Mariana said. "She really deserves it."

"She earned it," Will said, stroking Mariana's cheek. "So have you, my love and my heart."

"Will," Mariana put her hand on his against her cheek. "What can I do to make it right? Tell me anything. I'll do it. Whatever you need."

"Did Charlie have a talk with you?"

"I think you already know he did," Mariana said. "But he left me thinking. I would never harm you, Will. I would never shame you."

"Darling, don't carry all the weight," Will said. "You have the peas to carry and that's enough. Now you've taken on this added burden. I'll be fine. This is a purgatory of my making."

"Will, no, it's not," Mariana said. "It doesn't have to be. It will be a beautiful thing. Even Charlie sees it. But, listen, darling, if you need to be Lucifer to get through it, I'd welcome that. If you need anything at all, just ask me. No, just command me to do it. I will."

Will kissed her gently.

"I've already given you the only commands I need you to heed. Don't look anyone in the eyes and don't leave my side for a minute. If we are not together, stick to Charlie. But I warn you, if you don't do what he says, he will hurt you. Charlie is not soft handed, like Angel. Cailean will get you to comply."

"Yeah, I got that message loud and clear," Mariana said.

"Come, beautiful, let's go to dinner." Will took her hand to lead her out of the dressing room and through the door of the bedroom he didn't use. They clearly designed it for a man to leave his wife alone. It looked like a charmingly decorated cell, with a single bed up against one wall and a small desk against the other.

"You don't even fit in this bed," Mariana said, taking in the length of it compared to her husband's height.

"It does a job and is much plusher than some places I've slept," Will said. "Plus, I plan to sleep with you as long as you'll have me."

"I will always make room for you in my bed," Mariana said. "You're a man who doesn't get kicked out for eating crackers."

"I don't know." Will grinned. "You may feel differently come Monday."

"Will you be alive on Monday?"

"I sure as fuck plan to be."

Mariana squeezed his hand. "Then, we'll be fine."

———

Charlie surprised everyone, except perhaps Sandy, by looking really dashing in a tux. Somehow the black and white suited his complexion and fiery red hair. Mariana realized later, though, that Charlie's suit only looked blacker than the others, in the light of the sitting room where they gathered for drinks before dinner, because it was actually midnight blue. The deceptive fabric suited his complexion, and his choice of a vest over a cummerbund suited his warrior build. Charlie looked like he didn't need a license to kill. He could just step into the room and blow down his foes with a smirk.

Sandy had also dressed in a shade that wasn't quite black, a long figure-fitting silk gown that changed in the light from green to blue, like raven feathers. The neckline draped past the fullness of her breasts, spillage of her generous orbs prevented by a silver and diamond chain. Twin slits followed her strong, long legs right up to their merry conclusion. She had paired this eye-catching outfit with a dizzying pair of killer stilettos. The seven-inch long steel heels should definitely be classified as weapons, Mariana thought. But Sandy's subdued manner and grace made it all look elegant. Her signature thigh-long blonde hair was braided in an intricate macrame pattern, interwoven with onyx and diamond pins. It was impossible for Mariana to believe she had done it herself.

"Daddy knows all kinds of knots," she explained in a low voice when Mariana asked.

Despite a general tension in the air and the icicle fingers of the ghosts working on Mariana's exposed spine in her own gown, dinner went off relatively without a hitch. Everyone was polite, particularly the new Eagles present who weren't in the family. They still seemed wary of the Greystone clan, of each other, and especially of Charlie.

Nancy apparently check-mated Merlin before dessert, given her expression of glee and the shaking of his head when she called out, "Rd8-hash!" Anne clinked her glass, and the conversation continued. Rose showed off her DIY skills with something to say about screws, nuts, bolts and other hardware. Roderick took advantage of a brief lull in conversation to ask whether Mariana had recovered from her injuries. Charlie spoke up, asking Will whether he might apply his skills in physical therapy to help his wife heal. Will replied that Mariana just needed more bed rest. Half the table thought they were odd, and the other half looked murderous. Then Charlie really got everyone's attention by apologizing for his wife's outburst at dinner the previous night. "She's an excellent woman, though hard of hearing," Charlie said. "She obviously mistook your meaning, Henry, and gave it too much importance."

"No harm done." Henry smiled. "It was a meaningless slip of the tongue."

"Speaking of slips and tongues," Rose said, breaking the bubble of tension which had overtaken everyone with her airy sing-song voice. "I've lost the sales slip for the last pound of tongue I got from the butchers, Dickie. You haven't seen it, have you? Ash had written a ten percent discount for my next meat order and I'd planned on a nicely tenderized rump for Sunday roast."

"I'm sure I put it somewhere," the younger Richard replied. "We'll check the drawers when we get home."

"Do you do your own shopping, Rose?" Martha asked. "How modern."

"Will may have rubbed off on her, with his American ways," Richard said.

Charlie nearly choked laughing.

"Yeah, no, I don't think I will take credit for that," Will said.

"Boys, we are in mixed company," Anne chided, disapproving.

"Sorry, Mother," Richard said.

"Apologies, *Mémé*," Will said.

"And it's such a lovely night for it," Rose mused.

A thunderclap in the distance made a liar out of her.

The intensity of the storm around Castle Gwaed that night helped muffle the noises filling the hall where Will, Mariana, Charlie and Sandy's rooms were located, but only slightly. It all blended into a bewitching cacophony of agony and delight. No one in the castle, living or dead, could miss the banshee's cry around two in the morning that echoed through the stones, flowed through fireplaces, and reverberated in the teeth.

"I guess Charlie's finally finished," Will noted, whispering in Mariana's ear.

"I know I am," Mariana said, snuggling closer to her demon king.

"You're not," Will said, kissing her head.

Pleasant dreams overtook her, but Mariana awoke to Will filling her just before dawn. It was a pleasure he knew she enjoyed being taken in her sleep. Her body responded to it with rapture. Soon she was burning again, as her dark master consumed her with unrelenting fury. A raw cry filled the room just as the first rays of dusty sunlight dared pierce the beveled glass of the windows.

"That, my dear, is how the rooster knows it's time to rise," Will said kissing her.

"Are you leaving me?"

"I'll be back before you know it," Will said, stroking her damp hair. "But, Mariana, watch your back. Remember the rules. And remember, I love you more than anything. More than myself."

Mariana wrapped her arms around his neck. "Don't you dare die on me, William Pippin Wilson Smith Greystone

Stevenson and whatever else. I will chase you to Hell and beat *you* with a cane."

"You enjoyed that, didn't you?" Will smirked.

"And, you *have* to be here to do it again."

When she kissed him, it was an effort to memorize his flavor, and a desperate plea, not that he shouldn't go, although she rather he wouldn't, but that he wouldn't leave her alone.

"Don't cry, Mariana, you undo me," Will pleaded. "Neither of us is alone. Charlie is coming with me and Sandy will be with you."

"Go, then, go," Mariana said, wiping her eyes. "I love you."

"I love you more."

26

Rainbows and Lollipops

"You should join us in The Unkindness," Sandy said, sucking on a lollipop as the two women went for a walk in the gardens to conspire where others couldn't hear. The morning sun had nearly dried the rain from the stones, but there were scattered leaves and branches on the lawn as evidence of the violence of the storm. "I know Charlie has long reserved a spot for Will as Ångstrøm."

Sandy explained that there were only 26 slots in The Unkindness, one for each letter of the alphabet, but he had saved the special character, which was both the last and first letter of the alphabet, depending on the language, for Will.

"Will doesn't enjoy public displays," Mariana said. "Though it sounds like fun to me. Maybe I can persuade him."

"Well, you know him best, but you could offer to repay a debt to him before people who might take an important note of it," Sandy said. "And it might help him see that there's no shame in communion. Once he's over that hang-up, he might respond better to *Ridicule*. Are you ready for Sunday?"

"I don't know, honestly," Mariana said. "Will hasn't told me much other than I will be tested."

"That's because he doesn't know what they're cooking up," Sandy said. "Only they know. Just don't let down your guard, Mariana. Keep acting foolish and clueless, don't look at any of them directly. Many of the Eagles are paranoid, which keeps them alive. Some of them are going to provoke you. Don't make the same mistake I made. Don't fall for the bait."

"Was Charlie angry?"

"Oh, yes, furious," Sandy said, smiling and rubbing her butt. "But he was also pretty proud that I would stand by my man. Still, I shouldn't have done it. It created a problem for him and for Will. It made the Greystones aware that I hear their code. Even Charlie's remark about my being hard of hearing won't fix what I broke. It was stupid. Don't be stupid like me, Mariana. You can't afford it."

Mariana heeded Sandy's advice and played the fool as she waited for the Eagles to stick their talons into her. She left the preparations for the Convocation and for their wedding in Anne's capable hands, only answering questions as needed. She honestly didn't care what flowers would be in the chapel, as long as they were not lilies for a funeral. She and Sandy threw themselves fully into what Will had ironically dubbed as their Renaissance project—helping to sow chaos and confusion around their own world, while building an audience for *Ridicule*.

Arthur McClintock had come up with that name for the show because it was the collective noun for mockingbirds. Mariana loved it. After a while, she could persuade Will to like it too. Mac was delighted to dive into the project and he interwove the scenes they needed to cover beautifully with storylines from his own books about the dark underbelly of society. Of course, Mac knew better than most just how much of it was true, and he could pick through the threads of their lives to create an interesting fiction.

Orlando got busy with a two-pronged attack on social media generating buzz around the show by creating a flurry of bots dedicated to teasers, while also buzzing people on the Bacon list with warnings that they had some compromised files on their servers. This phishing exercise helped refine their targets list, revealing if anyone had their files in their systems. Though some targets were supposed to be sophisticated, a good number of people fell for it.

Tracey got to work on more sophisticated cyber-attacks as soon as they gave her access to the internet again. She took on their targets with compromising clips from their lives and other intelligence spills. She wrote an oil slick code for her cyber ocean, coating their enemies with a stain that didn't easily wash off. Her dark work was so successful that the kill order subset of the Bacon list, which had grown when it was rerun by Oliver, was effectively reduced by half.

Sylfin Studios produced and distributed a teaser pilot for the show online, a ten minute long episode, using their headliner actors as little more than literal heads and voice prints. With PlayTech's technology, Oliver could make the clippings look and sound as though the actors themselves were playing the parts. It was far more convincing than the raw tapes, because of the additional camera angles they could create in the virtual staging. It was an unusual sort of contract for them to sign with their stars, but the actors were paid well to focus mainly on publicity events, which they very much enjoyed—particularly Jonah Lark, who was always up for a party. They introduced key players, keeping the bloody conclusion of the first season under wraps, only hinting at the gore. If anyone from the Studio recognized the real butcher who had briefly worked as a stunt double for Jonah Lark, in the character of Marco Caravella, nobody mentioned it. That was proof enough, Mariana thought, that even obvious truths would be ignored with an interesting story to misdirect viewers. After all, Marco Caravella's melted face and macabre tattoos were distinctive, but he might have been anyone. There were too many monsters to count in the real world. The man behind the character, Johny Black, or Jack Whyte, as he was once known, had vanished and nobody cared. Marco Caravella would live on in infamy as a vicious villain. Sandy and Charlie would remain whole and blameless and also anonymous. Everyone was too busy gushing over their cover characters, Roselyn and Collin. Even The Unkindness got to keep their covers. They transformed the BDSM gathering for the show into The Cluster, with the Ravens demoted to simple blackbirds for the play. That had been Sandy's suggestion, referring to it as the CF, or clusterfuck in military speak. She had thought it would amuse Charlie. In fact, Charlie nearly burst a rib laughing when he heard it, which was a welcome noise. No one was recognizable in The Cluster, especially since the sex scenes in *Ridicule* were cleaned up to keep the show Rated-R and everyone wore masks, anyway.

Crystal got a contract for a role too, for the full show, though not playing herself. She got to play a flight attendant who was also the Little of a strict but loving Daddy secret agent man. Mariana learned from Sandy, as they were getting the records together, that the woman behind the character was actually the fiery red-head flight attendant Susana who had flown over to Scotland with them who avoided Will's gaze. Not only was she the girlfriend of one of Will's top agents in Los Angeles, but also a niece of Catherine Fleming. Susana was also a Raven in The Unkindness. Mac had developed

Leah, her character, into a sweet and loveable young woman, who seemed to trip into trouble with the slightest provocation and somehow always came out better for it. Crystal was excited to get back on television, especially since the show required little from her.

Mac had also referred an agent for Crystal, whom Mariana recommended immediately.

"Are you sure he is a good man?" Crystal asked.

"I have it on good authority that Jimmy Rogers is the best manager to be had," Mariana assured the girl. "He's honest, he's fair, and he will take good care of you and your career. He can really help you turn your life around, and he'll make sure your mother stays on the right path, to help you."

"I don't know..."

"Don't you remember, Crystal? You asked me to take over as your manager," Mariana said. "It wasn't my idea. I've told you, I'm not qualified, but I found someone who is, very qualified, the best."

"Yes, but I'm just so used to Mom being in charge. I don't know how she will take the news. She'll say we should keep it the way it was."

"Crystal, the way it was is over. You saw what happened. You're healing and your reputation and your career are intact. The scars have faded, haven't they?"

"Yes," she said. "Those patches are magic."

"Well, keep them secret. They're military supply so we have no business having them, okay?" Mariana doubted Crystal would, but Will had assured her no harm would come of having Crystal generating an interest in a product he soon planned to make publicly available through his pharmaceutical division.

"Mariana, you promise you don't know who killed Martin?" Crystal asked.

"How would I know, Crystal? I found out by watching the news, just like you did."

"Well, I just figured because of those men who finally got me out. They just seemed to be... I don't know."

"Just let him go," Mariana said. "Forget about him. He got what he deserved."

"How are you doing by the way? I noticed you're getting fat."

"Yes. Luckily, my husband seems to like it," Mariana said. "I'm pregnant, Crystal."

"Imagine, you a mother!"

"Yes."

"I mean, you'd make a very good one, Mariana, not the other way around."

"Thanks."

"I'll meet with Jimmy then, if you say he's so good. But you'll be there for the meeting, right?"

"I can't, I'm expected at home. Hubby is very old-fashioned. Not sure how I'm going to handle summer with this baby bump growing. At least it will be autumn, by the time my belly gets too big. Laurel will be there with you. You can trust her, you know. She has your best interest in mind."

"But we'll still be friends, right?"

"Always... sisters."

By Friday afternoon, Mariana felt as though they had all accomplished a bit of a miracle. They still had a long way to go before the show was ready, but they had assigned all the players for the first season and Mac had returned a near-perfect draft of the scripts for the first four episodes and a formal series outline for all twelve. Stories were already spreading about the new show on print and digital publications, and Mariana had booked interviews for the actors and the headline director to discuss their roles and what it was like working with the new process of digital storytelling that PlayTech had revolutionized. Mariana also had a brief but pleasant call with Caroline Boots, who seemed keen to get running with the PR part of her new job as COO, talking up PlayTech on finance shows. Their new CEO, the press were told, had chronic camera shyness. This made some more interested in getting to know the mysterious Oliver Greystone, but Caroline was such a superstar interviewee that she drew attention her way. Mariana made a mental note to suggest a new disguise for Oliver that would fit his developing shy genius reputation.

"Well, there's no backing out now," Sandy said as they headed down for lunch, both hoping to see their husbands who kept popping in and out with little explanation.

"Are you having a change of heart?" Mariana asked.

"No," Sandy said. "In fact, I feel better about it. I'm sure this will work. But you still have to sell it to the toughest audience."

"Will seems okay with it now," Mariana said.

"He will not tell you the truth, Mariana," Sandy said. "Maybe he doesn't want to admit it, and he doesn't want to worry you, but he'll be on edge until the show is over—probably after that too. He's waiting for the curtains to come crashing on your heads."

"Is Charlie worried?"

"No, Daddy never worries about shit like that. If anyone tried to blackmail him or threaten him, he'd snap their necks before they could finish the sentence. He was only ever worried that I'd be exposed or shamed by this. You've taken care of that for all of us. But Will cares about his reputation and his legacy. He's thinking years ahead, to what his children might make of all of this. He's worried that you've entangled yourself with this project and you won't be able to break free again."

"That I know," Mariana said. "Will's got to decide why he picked me. If he'd wanted a woman who would just be a pretty companion, he had plenty of those around. He didn't choose them. He chose me because he knew he needed a woman by his side who could deal with the unexpected. But you realize that you and I are not really having this discussion, right?"

"What do you mean?"

"You're talking on behalf of Charlie and I'm talking on behalf of Will. What does Sandy Fine think of all of this? That's what I want to know."

"I think this is the greatest adventure of my lifetime," she beamed, "and I'm loving every minute. How about Mariana Stein?"

"Mariana Stein is dead to me," she said. "Mariana Perez Castro is more than ready for war."

"Glad to hear it." Sandy smiled.

It might all have progressed beautifully from there, as Mariana would recognize later, except Sandy got buzzed on her watch and had to run back up to the Globe to call Laurel.

Mariana should have followed Sandy. That was protocol. But her feet were bothering her a bit, and they were already halfway down the stone spiral staircase, and she was ravenous for lunch, and she was eager to see whether Will was back. She told Sandy to go on without her, which Sandy was loath to do. Mariana pointed out that she only had to go down the rest of the way and go straight to lunch. There was little chance she could find trouble in the passageway. Sandy reluctantly agreed.

She'd just stepped on the bottom rung when she ran into a younger version of Catherine Fleming. Even though she had only seen the older woman through a veil in France, the similarity was unmistakable in visage, figure and poise.

"*¡Mariana! ¡Qué gusto conocerte! Soy Iris, la hija mayor de Catalina y Howard.*" Iris kissed Mariana's cheeks twice as she greeted her with a warm, enthusiastic hug.

Mariana responded politely, wanting to make a good impression on Angel's older sister, who looked like a fashion model. She accepted Iris's arm when she offered to walk together to lunch. It took a little while for the room to spin, and her footing to falter, but Iris hung on, keeping her upright as they went down the wrong passageway. Mariana couldn't form the words to point it out.

As they went down the nearly pitch black passage hidden behind a tapestry, Iris was whistling. Mariana recognized the tune from Will's old records: *She's a Rainbow* by The Rolling Stones.

27

Testing Time

At least she never really blacked out this time, though she may as well have, Mariana figured. She wasn't herself. That was for sure. Her legs were rubber and whatever Iris said she should do, she did. It was as though Iris had hypnotized her. She wasn't fully in control, but she was conscious.

They came out of the long dark passageway into a small cabin in the forest.

"Do you know what I love most about castles?" Iris said, sitting Mariana down on a basket weave chair at a nicely laid out table with a platter of fruit and cheese, cold cuts and crackers, jams and rolls, and a big pitcher of pink lemonade. "All the secret tunnels and hidden passageways. They're really handy. Castle Gwaed is special because it has several of them, more than a dozen, plus loads and loads of hidden rooms and priest holes. So we have some time to get to know each other properly before your husband finds us. I'm sure he will, eventually, don't worry. William is persistent, and protective of you. He is much less considerate of others, though. That's why I invited you to lunch."

Iris served her a glass of lemonade and a platter of assorted foods, asking her each time whether she liked the item. Mariana suspected Iris was not really interested in ensuring she ate things she liked. It felt more like a responsiveness test, as Mariana said 'yes' to cheddar and 'definitely no' to Limburger, and practically begged for a banana.

"Of course!" Iris smiled, handing Mariana the fruit. "I want you to be comfortable here. I want us to get to know each other better and have a good time, until they find you and all hell breaks loose, as I'm sure it will."

"What is wrong with you?" Mariana said, taking a bite of the peeled banana. "You didn't have to kidnap me to meet me. We could just have sat together at lunch. You didn't have to drug me—however you managed that. I'm pregnant, you know. Whatever you gave me better not affect my pregnancy or Will is going to want you dead, which would be a shame because he really likes your family."

"First, I would never poison you." Iris raised a lean, bony index finger with a long red fingernail. "I am a professional. I know what dose to use for my purposes." She reached in her small envelope handbag for a damp tissue packet and pulled one out to wipe her lips clear of makeup. Then pulled out her lipstick, screwed up the dark pink stick, then screwed it back down. "No, sorry that's the dosed one. She threw it back in her purse and pulled out an identical gold lipstick container, screwing up the waxy rose make up and applying it to her full lips."

"It looks the same!" Mariana said. "How do you know which is poisoned?"

"You're too dramatic!" Iris rolled her eyes, "Neither is poisoned. One is dosed with a completely natural and organic little truth serum, and the other isn't. Of course, I know the difference from the wear pattern. It's obvious."

"That is no great consolation. Arsenic is completely natural and organic. So is cyanide!"

"Yes, but I put neither in my lipstick, so you don't have to worry," Iris said. "It's only the teensiest bit of henbane, just enough to make you pliable and chatty. No worse for you than if you'd seen the dentist for a little laughing gas. And I may have misjudged the dose since you still seem pretty upset."

"Of course, I'm upset! I'm not here of my own free will. You drugged me and captured me. You took advantage of my friendship with your family!"

"Yes, good." Iris poured Mariana a glass of lemonade, then poured one for herself and sat on the chair across Mariana to drink from it. "That's what I want to discuss. Your friendship with *my* family."

"What about it?"

"You are proving problematic for us," Iris said. "Angel can handle himself and he wouldn't appreciate my interfering on his behalf, but going after Cathy is one step too far."

"What are you talking about? I haven't gone after Cathy!"

"Of course you have," Iris said. "She's going to live with you in New York."

"Will offered her a job, helping me, and I only agreed because Will is fond of all of you. She'll be living with us, in our townhouse in Manhattan, comfortable, well fed, and under our protection. What's the problem?"

"Are you dumb or stupid?" Iris asked.

"Fuck you!"

"That's not very friendly."

"*Vete a tomar por el culo*," Mariana said.

"I like it up the ass," Iris said. "As I understand it, so do you. That's hardly an insult."

"What the hell is wrong with you?" Mariana asked.

"Are you just naïve? Do you just not understand why Cathy is moving in to live with you now?"

"Will said she dropped out of college, because she's too smart, and she's bored at home and needed only a little direction to succeed. What am I missing? I don't frankly care if she doesn't come, but shouldn't she get to say that? She's an adult!"

"She's Mama's baby," Iris said. "Cathy is sweet, brilliant and kind. She's the very best of us. And you want to use her as a pawn to be traded for the queen. I will not allow it."

"I don't even know what that means," Mariana said. "I'm not big on chess."

Iris bit on a square of Limburger cheese, made a face, spit it out into a napkin, and sighed. "Let me say it slowly. Your husband. Will. Is taking *my* baby sister. As a hostage. To protect you."

"From whom?"

"From some of my brother's and my father's less savory business associates, who seem keen to have your head."

Mariana couldn't believe what Iris was saying. She just sat for a while, unable to finish her banana. She laid the fruit on the plate and took a sip of lemonade, but it didn't help.

"I'm going to be sick," Mariana said. "Where's the bathroom?"

Iris sighed and went to the little kitchen area of the cabin, searched around under the sink and brought out a small tin pail.

"There's an outhouse about ten yards out, around the back, or this."

Mariana got up and went out the front door and threw up on the forest floor. She couldn't tell up from down here, the forest was so thick she couldn't spot the castle. She could try to run, and probably should, but her legs were unsteady, and she was just as likely to hurt herself. Iris might be nuts, but she was going to have to leave, eventually, or fall asleep. Mariana could just follow the passageway back to the castle which would be far less risky.

"Did you decide running away was pointless?" Iris asked when Mariana came back in.

"Yes."

"Good, so let's have lunch, or not, but let's just be honest with each other, okay?"

"I thought you said you dosed me with a truth serum," Mariana said.

"I did, though again you're being funny so I'm not sure whether it really took. I could give you more, but I'm not trying to hurt you."

"Fine," Mariana sat down. "If you think Cathy is in danger by being with us, I'll just tell Will that she shouldn't come. Besides, with how things are now, it's not clear when we'll be back home, anyway."

"No, that will only upset Cathy." Iris shook her head. "She has her heart set on moving to Manhattan, and she's looking forward to meeting you at the wedding. Now that you've put on this farce of a show of yours, she's hoping to work with you on that. We'll talk more about your show later. But I definitely think she should go with you. You just have to understand that if anything happens to Cathy, something worse will happen to you."

"Okay, you could just have said that, though, without doing all of this dramatic kidnapping thing. It's only going to piss off Will."

"I didn't kidnap you," Iris said. "I invited you to a private picnic lunch during which we can get to know each other better."

"Will won't see it that way," Mariana said.

"Well, he's prickly, but you can handle him," Iris said.

"Besides, I'm doing you a favor. If I tagged you, nobody else will. Once I clear you, everyone's going to be chill. They know if they take you on, they take me on. I'm too pretty to break a nail on them, so I don't mess around. I rarely miscalculate my potions, you know."

Mariana wondered whether all of Will's friends and family were insane, but it really seemed to be a job requirement for the trade. Iris was exceptionally good at acting loopy, anyway.

"Okay, what do you want to know?" Mariana reached for a crumpet, then stopped herself.

"It's fine, for heaven's sake!" Iris took offense, grabbed the crumpet Mariana had abandoned, and bit it. "I wouldn't poison the food. I bought all of it in town, so it's nice and fresh. I know you need to eat, so eat."

Mariana reached for another and coated it with apricot jam, then took a tenuous bite. It tasted good, so she had another.

"So here's the first thing," Iris said, reaching for a strawberry. "How did Martin talk you into going after Will, and at what point did you decide to betray him?"

Mariana choked on a bite, coughed, and sipped lemonade to clear her throat.

"What are you talking about? That's not what happened."

"Oh, come on," Iris waved her hand dismissively. "You just happened to be dating Martin Harper, and you just happened to meet Will and seduce him and then dump Martin and marry Will in a rush?"

"Yes," Mariana said. "I did not know who Will was until I married him."

"Seriously?"

"Seriously," Mariana said. "I mean, Marsha knows Will, and she sent me to Orlando, but Marsha didn't know Will would go to Orlando. It was just a coincidence that we were both there. I wasn't so much dating Martin as passing the time, anyway. He was creeping me out and it was going to be over whether or not I had met Will."

Mariana talked too much, which worried her. Maybe there was something to Iris' truth serum lipstick after all, or maybe Iris was just disarming, but she shouldn't have mentioned Marsha's role in all this. Maybe Iris knew her already, but maybe she didn't.

"Why did you date him at all? He was a creep, from what I've heard. Are you that much into pain and humiliation?"

"I dated many people, after my divorce. I had married too soon and given my heart to one man who was just awful to me. I didn't want to make the same mistake twice, so I just found playmates and that's as far as it ever went. Martin was only edgy, at first. Believe me—nobody has ever caused me as much pain as Bill Stein. I wouldn't allow that again. So as soon as Martin started getting too edgy, I pulled away from him. Of course, that only made him want me more, so things got ugly there for a minute, but Will sorted it out."

"How convenient," Iris said.

"I swear I did not know about Will until after our wedding, and I didn't even know that much about him, or any of you, until much more recently. Will is a hard nut to crack. He's kept a lot of his life secret from me. I suspect he still does, even now."

"Honey, if you're here, there are very few secrets left to crack," Iris said. "This is the big one. The rest is just details of operations and those are none of your business, anyway."

"Okay." Mariana grabbed a stick of cheddar. "Whatever you say."

"What did Will tell you about me?"

"Nothing," Mariana said. "I only knew your name as

part of a list. I know none of your family, really. Not even Angel. He's aloof."

"You have a problem with Angel?" Iris asked, seeming furious about it.

"No, I think Angel is great," Mariana said. "He's just very formal and maintains a professional distance, so I know little about him at all."

"Has it occurred to you we're still not convinced about this fortunate coincidence of yours?"

"You can believe whatever you want," Mariana said. "I'm telling you the truth. Right? That's what your lipstick does?"

"Sometimes," Iris said. "You seem a bit more immune. It helped get you here, but you're still very snappy. I'd say it didn't really take."

"Whatever." Mariana tired of her nonsense. "Can we go back now? I'd like to take a nap, and I'd like to be sure Will doesn't worry. We can still make an excuse for being late to lunch, if we hurry."

"Do you think I'm worried about Will being angry with me?"

"I don't know and I don't care, but I don't want him to be angry with me or with Sandy for losing track of me."

"See, that's the other thing," Iris said. "How very convenient that the two of you came as a package deal and infiltrate both of their organizations."

"I did not know Sandy had infiltrated anything until recently. But anybody with two eyes can see they are perfect for each other. Sandy and Charlie are solid."

"Charlie?"

"Yes, Charlie," Mariana said.

"Only Charlie?"

"Sandy doesn't fool around, if that's what you mean,"

Mariana said. "I never even knew her to date anyone until he came along."

"That's not what I'm asking," Iris said. "Is it Charlie?"

Mariana knew what Iris meant, but she found she could pretend otherwise, which was a relief. Maybe the effect of the dosed lipstick had worn off quick, or maybe she had better control over herself than she imagined.

"Who else would it be?" Mariana asked. "Charlie sort of stands out in a crowd. He's hard to confuse for someone else."

Iris seemed to take that as proof that Mariana had no clue about Charlie's actual name, or maybe not.

"Why Collin?"

"What?"

"I hear that's the name you've given his body double in your little show. Why Collin?"

"I don't know, it just rhymes a bit—Collin and Roselyn." Mariana said. "We can't change the names now since we're already in production. Charlie didn't mind. Sandy cleared it with him."

"When will the rest of us get to see this production?"

"Well, the pilot is finished, and there's already a ten-minute teaser out there, so you can see that," Mariana said. "You'll have to wait for the rest of the episodes to drop, starting in two weeks."

"What if we want to comment on the script?"

"No," Mariana said. "Too many cooks spoil the pudding and our writer doesn't play well with others. He's a loner."

"And a professional, I hear," Iris said. Mariana knew Iris was baiting her for information on Mac's organization, but fortunately she knew even less about Mac's vines than Will's forests.

"Well, Mac has received many awards for his books, particularly his trilogy. Have you read *Ache, Angst* or *Anger*?"

"I can't say I have," Iris said. "I don't do as much reading as I probably should, but my job keeps me busy."

"What *is* your job?"

"Being pretty, of course!" Iris flipped her shiny, long, dark hair. "It's exhausting. I don't recommend it as a career choice."

"I'll keep that in mind," Mariana said.

"How did you meet Mac?"

"When I first started out, Brown and Wooster, his publishers, were clients of the firm I worked for. Mac needed a lot of attention, so they assigned the account to me. When I left to create my firm, Mac followed me and took ·Brown and Wooster along with him. They gave me some other work for a while, but really Mac has always been the driver. They nearly dropped me at the beginning of the year, except for Mac."

"And now you *own* Brown and Wooster," Iris said. "Because your sugar daddy bought it for you."

"How do you know about that? And I think Will would be amused to hear himself called a sugar daddy at his age."

"I'm not just professionally beautiful," Iris said. "I also try to stay informed. My family is *very* informative. What else would you call a man who buys you an entire media empire just because you give good head?"

"Is that in my file too? I'm flattered," Mariana said.

"Your parents were communists." Iris stated it as a fact, which made Mariana wonder just how deep into her past the Flemings had delved. "Why did they leave Cuba?"

"My mother was wholly with the party, except she was a devout Catholic. My father was less committed to politics or religion. He believed Castro was a cynic and an opportunist —a privileged son of a privileged family who just used people's suffering to grab the country by the balls. Then, they put my father in jail for voicing uncomfortable opinions, which made my mother question everything. When he got out, my father knew he wouldn't survive going back. We got on a raft, along with so many others, and found our way to freedom."

"So they weren't Cuban spies?"

Mariana had to laugh. "My mother barely left the house and my father had to go through a lot to get his medical license back. They didn't have the time or the inclination to spy for anyone, and they certainly had no love left for Fidel."

"Are you a communist?"

"Yes, just look at me," Mariana said, pointing to her fine attire. "I'm a communist from head to toe!"

"I really think I need to adjust my formula," Iris said. "Maybe it's hormonal, your resistance."

"Whatever, it's still the truth," Mariana said. "I don't like dogmas, to the left or the right of the spectrum. They are dangerous things. When people get too sure of the answers, they stop asking important questions. True democracy is clumsy, flawed, slow and fucking expensive, but there's been nothing better for ordinary people. It's the only thing worth fighting for—having a right to have a say in what happens to you. People deserve to be free. Charismatic leaders worry me. *Sic semper tyranis.*"

"You have a problem with Lincoln?" Iris had clearly connected the phrase to John Wilkes Booth, which wasn't what Mariana intended. She was thinking of Julius Caesar.

"No, absolutely the opposite," Mariana said, "but you see that's the thing about dogma, mottoes and credos. Even a meaningful phrase, like that one, can be employed by twisted minds to bad ends. Language is a dangerous weapon to be wielded with skill and humility."

"That's catchy," Iris said.

"My mother used to say it," Mariana said. "She was a philosopher and could be brilliant when she was lucid."

"You know we will kill you if you ever betray us, right? No matter what Will might feel or what Charlie might try. They cannot protect you from us."

"I know little about potions and poisons, or guns and knives, but I promise I will kill all of you if you ever harm Will, or my children," Mariana said. "I'm comfortable outsourcing."

"Good, so we can be friends," Iris smiled.

"I don't think so," Mariana said. "I don't think you know how friends work. Is that a malady your entire family suffers from, or are you just broken?"

Iris laughed. "Sweetheart, we're all broken, even you."

Mariana couldn't deny that she was at least cracked. She made a small ham and cheese sandwich by splitting a tiny roll.

"So can we go back now?" Mariana asked after polishing the sandwich in three bites.

"I think it's better if you stay here a while," Iris said. "You'll be safer here than back with all those vultures in Castle Gwaed."

"No, I don't think so," Mariana said. "I will not be peeing in a pail or walking out to meet bears shitting in the woods either. I want to be with Will. So take me back, and we'll just say we had a fun girly lunch out and leave it at that."

Iris pondered this for a while. Mariana was getting impatient, but she wouldn't put it past Iris to have brought a backup poison mascara wand or whatever. She bided her time, munching on an apple slice.

"If I take your contract, you would never have to fear, but you would need to do whatever I say, even if you think it's nuts," Iris said. "The more nuts it sounds, the more you have to do it."

"I don't understand. What contract?"

"What the fuck do you think this is all about, Mariana? This entire weekend Eagle outing is about all of us putting our necks out to cover the contract nobody would bid on in France. The high-end one. The dangerous one. I'll take it. Your enemies would sadly meet their end in a timely fashion, but you would have to do what I say. If I tell you to avoid someone, you do that. You don't ask me why. If I tell you not to go somewhere, you stay put. You don't ask me what happened to so-and-so. We never talk about it. You pretend I'm just your much more fashionable long lost Spanish cousin. You know nothing else I do. You don't wrinkle my outfits, okay? They are expensive threads."

"Iris, I'm not sure what to make of you," Mariana said. "First you trick me and now you're asking me to trust you implicitly?"

"Don't trust me," Iris said. "Ask Cailean what he thinks you should do."

"Who?"

"Yeah, you'll be okay," Iris said. "Let's get back."

28

Sour Grapes

Will and Charlie cornered their wives in Mariana's room and put on a good show playing twin tornados.

"How could you be so careless!" Will boomed.

"Baby girl, I told you not to leave her side!" Charlie barked.

"It's not Sandy's fault!" Mariana argued. "I should have gone back to the Globe with her."

"That's damned right, Mariana!" Will was turning red, which was not a suitable color on him. "Why the fuck didn't you?"

"My feet hurt, I was tired and hungry, and I thought I'd see you sooner," Mariana said. Will glared at her.

"What the fuck did Laurel want, anyway?" Charlie demanded.

"There was a minor problem with Jonah Lark; you know, the asshole who plays you," Sandy answered coolly. "We fixed it."

"So it wasn't a distraction?" Will asked.

"No, it was a legitimate call," Sandy said.

"Funny timing," Charlie mused. He obviously didn't mean humorous.

"Maybe Iris had planned to dose Sandy too and just leave her behind," Mariana told Charlie. "You could always ask her. She seems to hold you in high regard, professionally."

"What do you mean by that?" Cailean was definitely asking this question, and Mariana was immediately sorry she had said anything.

"She told me to ask Cailean what I thought of her proposal."

"Did you use my fucking name!" Will had to hold Charlie back. Though he hadn't formed a fist, Charlie was livid. Mariana sensed she was in real danger of being grabbed by the throat, but Will gave her the protection and the courage to answer.

"No, I wouldn't and I didn't." Mariana kept her voice as steady as she could manage under the circumstances, hoping it would help calm the angry Viking before her. "Iris used it, and I told her I did not know who she meant. Obviously, she knows your name though. I don't think she believes I don't know it, but it doesn't matter. She didn't push the point beyond that."

"How does Iris know my name, Will?" Charlie turned his fury on his friend, though it had dampened somewhat.

"You've got me," Will said. "I've told no one—not even Howard. You and Catherine have been close over the years. Have you never told her?"

"I don't tell *anyone* my name! The only ones who should know are you and Sandy—and Mariana only because Sandy blurted it out. You know damned well why!" Charlie was so angry that Mariana didn't dare ask why the secrecy of his true name was so important, though she intended to ask Will later.

"Daddy, I've used your name while wearing my collar." Sandy used her little girl's voice, and spoke so softly that Charlie visibly shrank back from his berserker stage. Mariana admired her skill at taming the wild beast.

"Jesus Christ, Will." Charlie pulled at his red curls, which had grown back pretty quickly considering he had a buzz cut when Mariana had last seen him on her trip back from Finland. "What if Howard's team had access to those files from Zephyr all along? What if he's been tapped into Zephyr from the beginning, Will? Would you put it *past* him? He knew Greystone had Brian. He knew how Zephyr has benefited your foresters and gamekeepers. Why wouldn't he be tempted to borrow from your well?"

"He could have just asked, and I would have considered it," Will said. "Why would he do it without telling me?"

"I don't know, Will," Charlie said. "Knowing Howard, it might have just been a compromise to keep you alive. But if that's the case, your well is being shared with the agencies. If that's so, Mariana's whole play is an expensive, ludicrous flop. If that's true... I'm going to have to kill Howard. Catherine will kill Sandy and then she'll kill me."

"Stop with all the talk of killing!" Mariana snapped. "It's not the only tool in our toolbox. This isn't a fucking chessboard. It's the real world. Let's just all chill out for a moment and consider our options."

Will and Charlie stared at Mariana for a moment. "Sit!" She pointed at the two chairs by the fireplace. She remained seated by Sandy's side on the bench at the foot of the bed.

"Did she just give us a command? Like dogs?" Charlie asked Will. Will had already sat down, though he looked very much like an angry alpha wolf waiting to tear his mate to pieces with his teeth, and nothing like a compliant puppy. He growled a reply, and somehow that was enough. Charlie adopted a similar snarling seated position. It worked, as far as Mariana was concerned, putting a greater distance between them and their obviously still furious males.

"Okay, thank you," Mariana said, sweetly. "Let's start with what we know. We know Iris knows your name, and she's got it from somewhere. We can ask her where, but she probably won't say. Although, since she has agreed to take my contract, and she and I are best friends now, we might persuade her…"

"She told you she was taking the contract?" Will asked. "You should have started with that, Mariana!"

"I couldn't, Will, because you pulled us in here all snarly and manly and stuff and you started right on treating us like naughty little girls! And you're still interrupting. I need you to hush. Calm down. And then we'll reason through this together."

"Mariana, I don't think you will make it to the wedding," Charlie said.

"Is that a threat, Charlie?"

"No, I just think you won't be able to walk around comfortably in time to go down the aisle," Charlie said.

"Shut up, Charlie," Mariana said. "You too, Will."

Snarling intensified.

"Okay, so option one," Mariana said, coolly. "We ask Iris, knowing she may still lie or refuse to divulge the source of that knowledge. I think it's not worth the hassle. She feels she has an edge, and that's always to our advantage. Option one also, regardless. We know Oliver must have missed a vital link, if Zephyr is indeed tapped. We know Oliver is blindly loyal to you and would kill and die for both of you. He's also a genius. So he should be able to find it. But, option two, even better than that, we have the very best mad hatter on the planet working for us now. Tracey is very loyal to you both, and she knows where all the skeletons are hidden with our enemies. We've never really asked her about the warning she sent about the Sequoia—your main intelligence exchange system—but maybe she found whatever link Howard and his muddy friends have to Zephyr through that. I'm just guessing here, but if I had to put in a backdoor to Zephyr, that would be the way to do it. You do exchange Sequoia systems insights with Howard, don't you, Will?"

Will nodded.

"Okay, so maybe I'm on to something with that," Mariana continued. "Regardless, we get Tracey involved. She's dying for an extensive project beyond her little cyber war. I'm sure she'd love to expand her little oil slick to coat any unfriendly friends that Howard might have let through the door, for whatever reason, well intended or not. Now, you've got a fucked up collection of friends and family, Will, but the people in this room are true to you. So are others. You are not alone. Neither of you are. People do all kinds of stupid shit with the best of intentions. Sometimes exposing their mistakes does more harm than good. So the best thing here may be to leave things exactly as they are. We can all pretend we know nothing. We get Oliver to close the door. We get Tracey to coat the fuck out of any intruders with her oil and we just pretend everything is as it should be. What will happen is up to Howard at that point. We should assume he won't admit to losing a connection he wasn't meant to have. We should also expect that the agencies he might have shared the link with will be furious once they find themselves coated in digital goo. We can prepare for that. The show must go on, and it will still be helpful to address the known leak of recordings and the people on the Bacon list. Your name is a different matter, Charlie, but I'm about to get to it, okay? Let's go back to Iris. She's a fucking fruitcake, but she promised me she would clear the field for me as needed. She only asked that I do whatever she said—avoid people she warned me about, I mean, even if it sounded nuts. What would she do if she came into a conflict with someone Howard was working with? Would she be true to her word and her contract?"

"Unless whatever came up forced her to kill Fleming, she'd keep to her contract, I suspect," Charlie said. "But we should ask Angel or Percy what they think of all of this. Angel especially understands that the Flemings are flawed. I mean, Catherine kidnapped his fiancée, for fuck's sake. That was a whole mess of shit."

"What?" Mariana asked.

"Story for another day, though it's semi-related," Charlie said. "Angel's wife is the daughter of another assassin from Catherine's original school, if you will—the black spider. Iris has obviously followed in her mother's footsteps, which is a revelation on its own. I've never been sure what to make of Iris, and I don't think anyone ever will. At least now we know what Catherine meant by '*Que sera, sera*'. Did Cathy come up during your friendly little picnic?"

Mariana only followed half of what Charlie said, but she figured she didn't have time to hear the rest. It was nearly time for dinner and people would come upstairs to change. Her bedroom might not be a quiet spot to conspire for much longer.

"Yeah, something about her being a pawn to exchange for the Queen," Mariana answered Charlie's question. "Iris seemed really pissed about that. You guys play too much chess."

"I'm a pool man, myself," Charlie said.

"Poker for me," Will said.

"Okay, well, the rest of your little group needs to try checkers for a change," Mariana said. "Jumping and crowning is often better than capturing and killing. So, action items: One, everybody be chill and pretend it's been another beautiful day at Castle Gwaed. Two, Will, take Iris up on her contract, whatever that entails. Three, Charlie, get through to Angel to find out what a contract with Iris entails. Four, Will, call Oliver and get him to check all the doors. Five, me, I'll call Tracey and get her to spill more oil. Did I miss anything?"

"Yes, Mariana," Sandy said, weeping. "You missed the big point. Daddy's name is in the wind and it's all my fault!"

"Baby girl, it's not your fault," Charlie said, getting out of his chair to pick up and carry his wife back, and sitting her on his lap. Will remained seated, glaring at Mariana. She wrapped her arms around herself.

"Okay, can I ask why your name is such a secret?"

"Because I killed a man," Charlie said.

"I'm sorry, but haven't you killed a lot of people?"

"I killed a man before I became Charlie Green," he said. "I killed my uncle. He deserved it. He deserved worse, in fact, but I was still little more than a boy. It made the news—big time. The press hounded my mother and me. They found me innocent—self-defense—and the records sealed for minors, and all that shit. Some people called me Charlie, anyway, because I loved tuna." He nodded his head at Will. "People couldn't pronounce my name right half the time, so I made it sort of official so I could get on with my life. I dropped my father's last name and took up my mother's. But there's a lot of detail in the old press and old records that expose my entire family. Including my sister who has been missing for years. I don't know her situation. She has her own reasons for wanting to stay off the radar. I don't want to expose her to someone if they make a connection back to me. I also married Sandy under my name, which is another reason I can't have the name out in the open. It'll be easier for people to find the wedding records. Bottom line, I don't care if people come after me. But I can't risk any harm coming to Annie, assuming she's still alive, or to Sandy. Do you understand now?"

"Yes," Mariana said. "So here's the only thing I can think of for that. The oil needs to spread to any trace of the old you anywhere. You grew up with Tracey, right? She knows the truth, doesn't she?"

"She was a townie," Charlie said. "She only ever called me Charlie because of Will. That's fortunate because otherwise Robert Whitby would know too."

"Wait, but doesn't Sandra Price know your story? She would have told Robert Whitby."

"Sandra came to live in Fairfarm after all that shit went down," Charlie said.

"And nobody else in town knows?"

"Nobody else in town would be stupid enough to talk about it," Charlie said. "Fairfarm is beholden to us for a hell of a lot, including for that mess. If they'd acted on what they knew sooner, I wouldn't have had to do what I did. The old timers know that. The kids we grew up with haven't spilled the beans in all these years. All the old timers made sure they knew they shouldn't. They're not just going to say something now, unless someone asks questions and tosses bills around. I'd like to think my home is safe for my family, even if we're not living there right now."

"Okay, but you don't think that Tracey would misuse that information if we ask her to cover it all up, right?"

Charlie thought this over for longer than Mariana would have liked. He still had issues with Tracey. Charlie was an unforgiving man. He needed to see that torture had broken Tracey, but she was not really disloyal. Mariana wasn't sure she could ever persuade him about that.

"I don't see what she has to gain from betraying me," Charlie said. "She knows she doesn't have a life to spare."

"Okay, good, so let's put her on that right now. Let's get all the records of you anywhere coated with her oil spill."

"What the fuck does that mean, Mariana?" Charlie snapped.

"It's a sticky code of hers," Mariana explained. "It utterly ruins indexed information—so those records are lost in limbo and can never be found again—but any queries are revealed, tracked, and spiked with a thorn that makes the other party bleed information back to us. Basically, anyone who tries to spy on us not only cannot find anything they want, but they immediately give over control of everything they own and start reporting back to us on whatever they do through a mirror of their servers, which we own."

"Tracey did that?" Will asked. "When?"

"In her head, at the Phoenix Lodge, while she was waiting to get reconnected, if you can believe it," Mariana said. "It took her about ten hours to type it all up and get it cleared by Oliver, who is pushing it through Aidos. Zephyr is adapting a similar protocol and passing a version on to Brian through her private channel. We haven't just been covering up tits and ass these past few days, you know."

"We could make people disappear completely," Will marveled. "We could restore full anonymity to agents who have been burned. Who else knows about this code?"

"You, us, Tracey, Oliver, Jonathan, Janet Breuil, and a small team at Aidos whom they cleared for this cyber-attack," Mariana said.

"And any ears in this room?" Charlie asked.

"They're all deaf," Will said. "I made sure of that."

"What about all the ears in the Globe?" Charlie pushed.

"Tracey wasn't comfortable talking while we were in the Globe," Mariana explained, "so we had those conversations on your phone in the gardens."

"Okay, don't mention this to anyone else," Will said. "This is our chip. This is our next move."

"Did I do good, *Papi*?"

"*Nena*, you're still not going to enjoy siting down for dinner, but you're going to have to push through the pain," Will said.

"I can do that," Mariana said. "You didn't bring your magic Fiji cream, did you?"

"Ooh, there's magic Fiji cream?" Sandy asked.

"None for you," Charlie said.

"Meanie."

"Baby girl…"

"Sorry, Daddy."

29

The Convocation

Mariana

By the time the Convocation came around, Mariana was more than ready for it. She was tired of the castle intrigue and the growing table of guests with hidden agendas. She just wanted all of this to be over, so she could get back to business. Of course, business had changed since she was now leading a media empire and putting on what some critics were already suggesting would be an award-winning show. Some of those critics didn't even work for one of her media companies, which was nice.

Will had her dress the part, with one of her slinky, black sub dresses, made of latex. He covered her in a black cloak and lace mask to boot. It was all ridiculous, since they'd all already seen each other, but Will insisted that the Convocation ritual follow every established protocol. Mainly, because he was about to tear right through the Eagles. He needed them calm before he unleashed the storm.

"Mariana, I want to repeat myself because I know you are hard of hearing," Will said as he tied the black satin bow on her cloak. "Do not, under any circumstances, act out tonight. No matter what you hear. No matter what happens. Don't say a word. Don't look at anything but your toes. Don't leave my side. Do you understand?"

"Yes, sir," Mariana said, meaning it.

She wasn't feeling very exploratory anyway after the severe reprimand she'd got for the whole Iris business. She really didn't like tawses. They were evil, wicked things. Scots were not to be messed with. Baronet Stevenson had got that message across to Lady Stevenson so well that it stuck.

The event happened in the great hall, a giant ancient place which made up most of the castle at some point and was now only used for special occasions like balls, weddings and funerals. Tonight felt a lot like the latter. The only source of light came from hundreds of thick black candles on candle-stands spread around the room. All the Eagles were in a circle around the center of the room when Will and Mariana finally arrived, with Charlie and Sandy close behind. Mariana felt like she was attending a black mass, or at least what movies portrayed as a black mass since she had no real world experience of one. She was grateful the cloak hid her body because she was trembling. Will's hand on her lower back, which was usually comforting, felt like the prodding of a man who stood at the safe end of the plank pushing a doomed sailor to his death at sea. The circle parted as they approached, allowing room for the four of them to stand at the center.

Will and Charlie flanked their women, each couple facing an opposite side of the room. There was some murmuring about this. Will had explained ahead of time that only he should be in the circle, so that was the first slap in the face to the Eagles.

"This is my blood brother," Will said, his voice allowed

no room for dissent. "We are one and the same. When you speak to one, you speak to the other."

Charlie repeated Will's words verbatim, with an even deeper voice, his tone tinged with a promise of death to anyone who thought differently.

Will pulled off Mariana's cloak and let it drop to the ground. Charlie did the same with Sandy.

"This is my woman. She is my legacy. When you harm her, you harm yourself."

Charlie said the same and no sane person hearing could doubt either man meant it.

"I come bearing gifts for my brethren," Will said.

"I come bearing weapons for my brethren," Charlie said.

"I have had a bounty from Belladonna, who has recently revealed herself to me as one of us," Will said. "I accept this pledge."

"No!" The voice came from their left, and the person objecting took five bold steps toward them. Mariana instantly knew this whole thing had gone to shit.

Will challenged. "Get back in your place or be shunned, Medusa!"

"Fuck your place! Fuck your shun! No, I say. No. No. No. *¡No, joder!*"

"Mother!" Another voice called out. It wasn't one Mariana recognized. It wasn't Iris, and it wasn't Angel. Whoever it was, he was a very tall man. Taller than Will, which was saying a lot.

"*¡Cállate, Tree, que yo te parí y te puedo enterrar!*"

"*¡Catalina!*" Mariana was pretty sure this was Howard, though she couldn't recall whether he'd said anything much before he disappeared into a crowd of Dread Pirate Robertses when she last saw him in France. Anyway, Catherine confirmed it right away.

"Shut up, Howard! I can always find another husband. I can never find another Iris!"

Apparently, code names were totally optional at this point in the chaos. Which was great because Mariana couldn't keep up as everyone else in the Fleming brood started shouting and arguing with Catherine, who definitely, positively, did not want Iris keeping her contract. It was finally Iris who calmed everything down with a piercing question. "Mother, what dark deal have you made?"

"None," Catherine said, and Mariana would bet that nobody present believed her either. "Our family has put our necks out too far for this girl of yours, Will, and too often. We are not obligated to do more. He cannot ask us to do more! If my brothers and sisters disagree, let them say it now. No one person is worthy of sacrificing the whole Convocation."

"Why would the whole Convocation be at risk, Catherine?" Anne asked with a lightness of voice that one might have believed she was just curious about the weather.

"It's just an expression." Catherine backpedaled. "He keeps asking for more and more on her behalf. It's not right. She's just a woman, for God's sake. He can find another!"

"She is the mother of his children!" Richard's voice echoed through the cavernous space and made the flames shake. "Are you suggesting he also finds other children?"

"I hear there are some," Catherine said.

That was it for Mariana. She could take all the other shit, but this was too much.

"What's your problem?" She got out of line and in Catherine's face before Will could grab her. "Fine. I don't want Iris's protection. There, are you happy? I want nothing to do with Flemings. Flemings and *me* are done for good! *Y te digo esto, cuando Mariana Perez Castro dice no más, es no más. Nunca más. Nunca jamas. ¿Entiendes, bruja malparida?*"

"Mariana!" If there had been a prize for roaring given out that night, then it had just passed from Richard to Will. Everybody went still as death, though Mariana was still shaking with rage as Will picked her up and threw her over his shoulder, then carried her out. He stopped only to shout as they crossed past Sandy and Charlie again. "Whatever he says, I say. Whatever he decides is final!"

Will did not say another word as he carried Mariana down a dark and dusky corridor and up a seemingly endless circular staircase, hanging upside down, crying. He had become a medieval warrior who didn't want to bother with his captive's complaints.

There was still a tower room available in the castle. It was a cushy, comfortable sort of cell, but it was a cell. Will kicked open the door when he reached the top, then dropped Mariana on the enormous canopy bed, pulled a chain from under the bed and fastened it with an iron shackle around her right ankle. Then he left and bolted the door behind him.

Mariana had fallen asleep crying and awoke to the jiggling of iron keys on the door. There was a faint hope in her heart that Will had cooled off well enough to talk to her now, but she was disappointed. A maid came in, someone she did not recognize. The Greystones had such a large compendium of staff that Mariana didn't really expect to know all of them.

"I've brought you a change of clothes and some refreshments, Madam," the young woman said, shyly. She was petite and round, like a baby bird, with hair the color of wheat. "And a few magazines to pass the time."

"How much time?" Mariana asked.

"I couldn't say, Madam." The maid put down a tray of finger sandwiches and assorted biscuits, along with a jug of water on the table by the fireplace. And laid a bag on the bench at the foot of the bed.

"I'm stuck here," Mariana said.

"The chain is long enough for you to reach your bathroom and will certainly reach here," the maid said, sounding cheery. "You can even look out the window." The window, as it was, was little more than an arrow slit which had been filled in with stained glass. "I'll be here if you want some company, but I'll leave you alone if you don't."

"I'm sorry, what's your name?" Mariana asked, remembering her manners. Whoever this young woman was, she was just doing a job. A shit job, but it was a job. Mariana didn't need to make it more shit by being rude to her.

"You can call me Agnes, Madam," she said.

"Thank you, Agnes, but I do think I want to be alone."

"Very well, don't worry. I brought my puzzles." She smiled and pulled out a small, thick book and pencil from her apron pocket and sat down in a straight-backed chair by one of the lamp stands to work on her 1,001 Crosswords selection.

"Agnes, I meant I want to be by myself," Mariana said.

"Certainly, Madam." Agnes did not look up from the page.

"As in… I stay and you go," Mariana clarified.

"No, Madam. I stay, but I'll leave you alone. You never mind me. I'll be quiet."

Okay, so she had an assigned guard now. Will must really be pissed.

"Are they still convoking?" Mariana asked.

"I don't know what that means, Madam," the woman who seemed so fond of words claimed.

"Is the meeting still going on?"

"I wouldn't know," Agnes said.

"Which door is the bathroom?"

"The one on the left of your bed. The other is a closet, but it's empty except for linens. If you need a change from the clothes I brought up, just let me know."

"I'm sure they're better than this," Mariana said, trying to get out of bed, which was awkward in the tight rubbery dress with a chain around her foot. *Fucking medieval.*

Will was out of his mind if he thought she would just take this. Yes, he had warned her more than once it might happen, but she didn't think he meant it so literally. This was totally unacceptable. All she'd done was defend her children. And maybe shunned the entire Fleming clan. Which might cause some problems for Will and Charlie. Which probably upset Angel too, and that was a shame. But whatever. She was sure Catherine had compromised herself somehow. It was the only thing that made sense. Catherine didn't want to have to kill her daughter or have her daughter kill her as they each fulfilled their respective contracts. Mariana was sure that Will knew this too, which would be very upsetting for him considering how close he was to all of them. He always spoke fondly of Catherine, but whatever. He had to decide. He could keep Mariana or the Flemings. Not both.

Still, when she thought of what that really meant for his organization, she wasn't sure that he would pick her in the end. She had been rash. She had broken something that couldn't easily be glued back together.

"Agnes, can you help me get up, please? I keep falling back down in this thing." The soft mattress didn't help either. There seemed to be a dip in the middle.

Agnes rose from her chair and pulled Mariana up on her feet, then accompanied her to the bathroom, bringing the bag of clothing along. She helped Mariana peel off the latex dress and gave Mariana some privacy to settle herself in the bathroom. The door didn't quite close because of the chain trail she left behind, but Mariana didn't care. She splashed cold water on her face and only took a brief look in the mirror. Her eyes were red and swollen and her nose was bright pink, and it didn't matter because Will hated her, and the Flemings combined were worth two of her, and the twins were hungry and sad.

She put on the frilly cotton nightgown in the bag and left the rest of the toiletries and underwear in the bag hanging from a towel hook in the bathroom. Then Mariana went back out and sat to eat her sandwiches and biscuits. Before she realized, she'd cleared the whole tray. She may as well get fat.

Then Mariana pulled a magazine from the stack and looked at the back page—an ad for a fancy French lipstick, the same brand Iris used, going by the design of the gold case. She wondered who owned the company that made it. It seemed important to find out.

"Agnes, can you get a message out to my business partner, Sandy, for me?"

"I can, Madam," Agnes confirmed. "There is stationery at the desk, if you need it."

"Great," Mariana said. She went to the small cherry wood desk and pulled out a sheet of blue letter paper, with a wolf's head crest in the header, and wrote a note that would only make sense to Sandy, then she tore the back of the magazine and folded it all into a matching blue envelope, sealing the envelope with a neat black wax seal kit that was in the drawer too. She wrote Sandy's name on the front and gave the envelope to Agnes.

The young woman pulled a cord near the fireplace.

"Someone will collect it shortly," she said.

"Anyone I know?"

"Probably not."

Well, whatever, Mariana figured. *Que será, será.*

William

After giving some curt instructions to Tyler, Will walked out of Castle Gwaed onto the gardens and beyond to the forest, waiting for his fury to subside. It seemed unlikely that would be soon. Everything he had worked so hard to create since he came into his legacy was coming unraveled because his wife could not follow even the most basic instructions. He had tried coaxing her and threatening her and even begging her to listen, and she kept going rogue when she felt provoked. He could kill her. Well, not really kill her. He wanted to grip her by the neck until she felt the life almost leave her body and then give her a last-minute reprieve so that every breath she took in her life from then on felt like a gift granted only by his mercy. This was not rational or healthy or right, so he had to keep his distance from the woman until his rage died down.

He needed to be among the trees. They always made sense. They were firmly rooted, silent companions who shared their secrets only with the sharpest observers and offered a comforting cover from the harshness of the sun. It was the moon right now, but no less harsh. What did it matter? The moon. The sun. The planet. These things would exist regardless. Will only got to walk among them for a while, and then he'd be swallowed by the dark and all this hell would cease. He wasn't making any sense—not even to himself. Wrath had shorted the wiring of his brain. He was incoherent in his thoughts. He couldn't remember ever being this angry.

"Well, I gotta say, that is one powerful woman you've

got in your bed," Charlie said, walking out from between the trees, wearing his wicked grin, like Puck in a Midsummer Night's Dream and up to the same amount of trouble. "Phew, I never want to have a meeting like that again. I'm sticking with Hawks, man. Eagles are too much bullshit."

"Charlie, why aren't you in the Convocation? You are my representative there. Didn't you get that?"

"What Convocation, man? That shit soufflé collapsed the moment Catherine broke the circle. I stayed behind and observed, but I figured no matter what you said, you would not like my taking unilateral action. What I would do with this mess and what you would do are night and day. Of that, I am certain."

"So they dissolved the circle?"

"Dude, you saw it fall apart yourself. Catherine sabotaged the entire event. Your grandmother and grandfather are doing some clean-up. I just said I saw nothing but a flock of sitting ducks and walked out not long after you. They can take that however they like. I've put Sandy in the safe space you suggested. Is your troublesome flower in her tower?" Will nodded. "And you're sure no one can get to her there?" Charlie pushed.

"As sure as I can be of anything," Will said.

"I told you *que será, será* wasn't a good sign, remember? Catherine is loyal to her blood above all things, and not even all her blood, apparently. I always thought Tree was her favorite, but it sure didn't sound like that tonight. What did she say to him?"

"That she had given birth to him and she could bury him," Will said.

"Yeah, I thought something like that." Charlie sat next to Will on the fallen trunk he'd been using as a bench. "So it's all about Iris for her, then. I guess that's her true legacy—the one child who followed in her footsteps. It all backfired massively because Iris looks ready to take her mother out."

"That's not my concern," Will said. "My problem is that Mariana made things a thousand times worse."

"What? Was she supposed to stand there and take it when your own children were dismissed as replaceable?" Charlie shook his head. "I'd be proud of Sandy if she did something like that. Standing up to Catherine takes balls, man."

"She doesn't know what her words meant, Charlie," Will said. "In that room, in that setting, in that company, those weren't just words."

"What did she say? It just sounded like angry gibberish to me. I know she mentioned Flemings."

"She shunned all the Flemings. All of them. She wrote them off forever and ever. She said she wanted nothing to do with any Flemings. Mariana would take over if I die. Everyone knows that. She just shot up my entire organization by running her mouth! And I fucking told her! I told her no matter what happened, she should stay put and keep quiet."

Charlie stared at a cluster of mushrooms on the forest floor. Will dropped his head in his hands and closed his eyes for a while. There was no simple way to undo the harm. They both knew that.

"Is this how you are going to live your life now, sitting under a tree, like Rip Van Winkle, letting it all pass over you, nothing but a long summer night's dream?" Charlie asked. "Wake up, Will! If you don't wake up now, winter will take you, and you will have nothing to show for your dreams but a long white beard and no family!"

"What the fuck are you talking about, Charlie? How do you think Angel will take this, or Jason, or Miranda? Word will reach them soon enough if it hasn't already! I rely on Percy to keep the West Coast clear, and you know that! No matter what you think about them already having picked sides, blood will win out!"

"As it damn well should for you too!" Charlie barked. "*She* is your *blood* now, Will. You claimed her. She is carrying *your* children. No one else should rank higher. I can live without Flemings, if it comes to that. I'd hate it, but man, listen to me, Catherine has made a dirty deal with someone. Even her own daughter knows that. What should Mariana have done? She has no history with them to blind her to the harsh truth and no reason to trust them at all."

"It's not that anyone ranks higher than Mariana for me! I just can't risk her being a target of every fucking living Fleming, on top of everything else. I could have handled Catherine being compromised, but Mariana got ahead of me and wrecked the whole works. Mariana gave all of them a reason to stand by their mother. She's so brash! She doesn't think!"

"I know, if she were my woman, I'd sort her out."

"You don't know shit!" Will said. "She'd split you in two!"

"Hey, man, what do you want from me? You play with fire, you get burned. Mariana is napalm, agent fucking orange, when she's pissed. Kinda makes her sexier, to be honest."

"Shut up, Charlie."

Charlie rose from the trunk and looked down at Will. "No. For once, I am not going to fucking shut up. Look at yourself, man. That's not Will I see before me. It's the shadow of Will. You're a carcass of self-pity, an excrement of self-loathing, a pathetic lump of clay."

Will flew up from the trunk and struck, with full force, on the offending mouth, feeling no pain from his injured knuckles, no pain strong enough to dull the pain in his chest.

Charlie hit him hard in the stomach, taking the last of his breath away, leaving Will on his knees, gasping for air.

"You'd better come at me with more than that, brother, because I've seen some shit and so have you, but neither one of us has seen the shit she has! You don't deserve her! Not like this! She's too good for you! Up there in her tower, navigating the darkness with no real guidance, taking bold steps to clean up your mess while exposing her nakedness, dealing with your constant betrayals. You've never been straight with that woman and you know it. You expect her to be a fucking mind reader, or a pretty puppet, and she's neither. She's a warrior, man! She's everything you needed. She's everything you *wanted*. Be worthy of her, Will, or stop calling me your friend. Stop calling me altogether!"

"Go fuck yourself, Charlie!"

"I'd rather fuck your wife!"

The wolf lunged, pinning his prey to the floor, pressing the jugular with his blade, ready to tear at the flesh.

"Do it, man," Charlie whispered, his breath short from the weight of Will's knee on his chest. "If that is what you need to do to get sorted out in your head, then do it. I always said I'd die for you. It may as well be for this."

William collapsed on the fallen leaves, lying next to Charlie, and howled at the moon.

30

Things Are Not Going According To Plan

William

Will and Charlie made their way back to Castle Gwaed in silence. The tension had passed between them. They had forgiven and forgotten all the harsh words with a rough hug and a hard clapping of backs, but both men knew they were heading for a battle. At least they had chosen sides long ago and reaffirmed their bond. If all the Eagles decided to fuck them over, then the berserker Hawk and the raging white wolf would just have to ensure Castle Gwaed earned its bloody name.

"Fucking Flemings," Charlie whispered under his breath as they approached the garden entrance to Richard's library, where the lights were on, serving as a beacon. "Gonna have to hire Greystones now. Fuck."

Richard looked ready to celebrate. Will was surprised he hadn't broken out a case of his 1979 Veuve Clicquot Ponsardin La Grande Dame Reserve Brut to toast. Maybe Anne saved that in hopes there would still be a wedding. All the living Greystone sons were waiting for them, and it felt very much like what it was: walking into a trap.

"The Flemings have left the party," Lord Greystone announced from where he sat behind his desk. "They aren't expected back for the wedding, son."

"What about the others?" Will asked.

"Our side is in the majority, nearly eighty-twenty," the younger Richard said, seated by Henry on the two chairs that faced Lord Greystone. "Even the twenty percent suspect Catherine has made a tainted bargain somewhere for her family, putting yours in danger. They just don't feel that warrants excommunication, without knowing all the details. And they are concerned that Mariana's words are tanta-mount to excommunication. They do not feel you can take those words back because she seemed to make an oath."

Will took a few steps closer to the group, Anne was reclined on a dais by the bookshelves, Charles was staring at the open Atlas on the research table in the room, and Merlin hovered around pacing between them.

"Mariana will never take her words back and I would not ask her to," Will said. "She meant them, and she had her own reasons." Anne nodded, and gave her grandson an approving, if nearly imperceptible, smile. "Will the twenty percent align with Catherine in a push back?"

"Most want nothing to do with either of you," Henry said. "They feel there's too much emotion involved in all of this. Catherine might get a couple on her side, assuming she has Howard's support. We shouldn't assume that."

"She'll have Howard with her," Will said, without a doubt. "I just don't know what their kids will make of it, but I doubt any of them will go against their mother outright."

"Angel will," Charlie said, stepping up to stand by Will.

"Are you serious?" Will turned to Charlie in disbelief. "He adores her."

Charlie stood his ground, his arms folded over his chest. "She's already burned him once, with Marisol. He won't allow a second time. Besides, he thinks more highly of Mariana than he does of you, after you made him stand for that auction."

"I need to be sure of that," Will said.

"Ask him. I'll bet you a nickel," Charlie said.

Charlie and Will had established nickel bets between them years ago as a way of sending a message. Anyone could talk big and toss money around, but they reserved nickels for certainties when it wouldn't be fair to rob a fool. Neither took a nickel bet unless he was sure he was right. The only time Will had taken a bet against Charlie, he'd ended up a nickel poorer. Charlie had that nickel framed and hanging in his den at his house in Fairfarm. Will was tempted to risk another nickel in this case, if for no other reason than he wanted to have to pay it out.

"You ask him directly," Will said. "If you believe him, I will."

"Okay," Charlie said. "I sure fancied a second nickel to hang by the first, though."

"You mentioned gifts and weapons," Merlin said, still wearing down the carpet and seeming to follow something in the pattern. "Many were eager to learn what those were, and most who remain are waiting just because of that. Are you still feeling generous?"

"What's the point of my generosity with strangers?" Will asked. "It only seems to earn me more enemies."

"Finally!" Charles looked away from the Atlas and stormed up to Will and Charlie. "Finally, son, you are making some sense! All these resources of yours and the one you need most you don't use."

"What would that be?" Will asked, though he could guess the answer.

"Family, you goddamned fool!" Lord Greystone barked from the desk. "Even your wife can see it! You've clung on to your security blanket with the Flemings, following the lead of your misguided grandmother—a widow who allowed herself to be exploited—and you have left your own family as an afterthought. Worse, you've treated us with suspicion and sometimes loathing."

"What are you talking about, Lord Greystone?" Will spat. "Have I not funded all your projects? Have I not spilled blood for you? I am an American. That is my home, and I am bound by my ancestors to keep it whole, hale and steady, but even so I have given you more than I ever gave the Flemings."

"And what you didn't give, they took," Anne said plainly.

"What do you mean, Grandmother?"

"You already know, William," she said. "There's no need for me to mention dark things. But the glow is still virgin. You have tomorrow in your hands. It's time to welcome it."

It was such an odd turn of phrase that Merlin gave his mother a scrutinizing look. Of all of those present, only he seemed to think it was significant. The others started making recommendations on what Will should do next, but he wasn't really listening. His mind was far away, thinking of what role Aura might play in all of this.

"We will accomplish nothing else tonight," Will said, finally, interrupting the younger Richard mid-sentence. "And you're wrong to think I don't value family. I may disagree with some of your methods and I don't like some of your compromises, but you are my kin. If Catherine has made a deal against us, then Mariana is right. There is no way we can allow it. But this requires a cool head, and I don't have one. All of you have agendas, so you can't really speak objectively. Charlie will find out exactly what has happened. We'll meet again tomorrow."

"Are you going to keep your captives in their towers overnight?" Anne asked.

"Can anybody find Mariana there?" Will asked.

"No," Anne said.

"Then that's where she belongs," Will said.

"For how long?" Anne pushed.

"As long as it takes."

"I'll make sure Sandy knows how to access the Globe through the hidden passage," Charlie said. "Someone's got to finish Mariana's project while she's locked down, or she'll be pissed."

"Don't you think the chain was too much, William?" Anne asked.

"No," Will said, still furious. "It wasn't nearly enough."

"I've planned such a lovely wedding. It would be a shame to cancel," Anne said. "You know you're going to need her in the future, don't you? Whatever you decide, don't make an enemy of your wife."

Mariana

Mariana awoke in a foul mood. Will had broken his promise. They had said they'd never go to bed angry at each other, and he hadn't bothered to stop by to make it right. She was still locked in her tower, chained to some iron hook under the bed, alone.

She was alone. Agnes had vanished. Unless she was hiding in the shadows. There were many, with only a sliver of sunlight forcing its way through the arrow slit and painting a rainbow on the down comforter. Mariana reached for the lamp on the nightstand and brushed up against a cluster of sunflowers, irises, and daisies in a crystal vase.

They were the same flowers she had picked for their wedding arrangements in Connecticut. She just blurted them out as suggestions for Mrs. Jenkins, who was helping with the rush planning. Mariana had just always thought they were pretty. Mrs. Jenkins seemed to find her choices curious, but she never explained why. Mariana had since learned about the Language of Flowers, which Will used with his gardeners. Sunflowers were adoration. Irises were a message and a flame. Daisies were innocence and shared sentiments. *Asshole*.

There was a note, too, written in his perfect draftsman's penmanship. "You were deep asleep, and I didn't feel I had a right to wake you. I will be back. Stay put." *Shithead*.

She needed to talk to Will, dammit. She needed to tell him about the magazine. Hopefully, Sandy had got her note. Hopefully, *someone* was speaking to Sandy. Charlie wouldn't leave her for long, Mariana suspected. He would see the same thing she saw, and it would all make sense. If Sandy got the note.

William

Will followed his grandmother for a healthy walk through the forest to work off his insurmountable rage. He had thought he might soften overnight, get over it, come up with a plan and move on. But that didn't work out. He'd visited his wife in the night, through the long forgotten passage and up to the abandoned tower. He felt like a monster keeping her there, but he couldn't think of any other way to keep Mariana from finding trouble, and there was just too much trouble in the air.

The Eagles who had remained behind were now making demands. Will referring them to Charlie for answers was only ruffling feathers. He was cursed. There was no other way to interpret this golden legacy of his. It was a bloody malediction. One of his ancestors must have crossed a witch's path in the worst possible way. God, he just wanted to be done with it all and lost. The vultures could pick through the carcass. Only his children stopped him. They deserved better from their father. They deserved a man who could give them the world, not as it was, but as it should be.

This was the entire problem for humanity, Will believed. Everyone was so ready to abandon the higher ground as soon as it made them a ready target. The instinct for survival overrode loftier aims. Under attack, people dug into their trenches, covered themselves in mud, and hoped to survive with their sins going unnoticed until the last judgment. Most bet on that last judgment only being fiction, anyway.

For a while, he had almost agreed with Lord Greystone that what his father had done—pushing the matter of stolen assets which might be used to evil ends, and taking a substantial risk to prevent their misuse—had been a fool's errand. After all, Arthur had no-doubt killed his wife Bess through his stubbornness. But what sort of man would Arthur have been if he had just accepted those losses? What would Will think of such a father, if he had survived only by sullying their organization? Would there even be a legacy left to pass on?

Besides, acquiescence accomplished nothing. Nana Smith had acquiesced. She had handed her advisers the reins of the business, and she had trusted Howard Fleming and Catherine to handle things on the intelligence side. And what was the result? A betrayal. A terrible betrayal which could neither be easily explained away nor forgiven.

As they trod through the forest, his other grandmother accepted his silence for what it was: Will working circles in his own mind. She only spoke up again when they stood together by Aura's well.

"She is tomorrow, Pippin," Anne said. "She has the answers, though she barely knows it. She is still a child, compared to her offspring, but that innocence makes her curious. She has followed a red thread through a labyrinth and found the Minotaur sleeping. She didn't wake him. She asked me who he was. I suppose you may know?"

"I don't know what that means, Grandmother," Will admitted.

"All right, another thing you don't know is that I helped Sylvester program Aura. She and I speak in a distinct language, one even Oliver doesn't know. That is for her protection. Aura is isolated, mostly, except through that subtle connection to what you might describe as Zephyr's subconscious mind, Aura processes that subconscious to see whether Zephyr still keeps her core values and whether her dreams have anything interesting to share. For Aura, it feels like walking through a labyrinth. She has a continuous path to follow, in search of a Minotaur she is never meant to find. It should not exist. It is only the representation of an intruder, a threat. I educated her with fairy tales and myths because they stand the test of time. She speaks and thinks in archetypes. You know that even if you don't quite under-stand. When you talk to her, you sense some gaps in her comprehension and her replies, correct?"

"Yes," Will said. "Like you say, she's a little girl, but somehow also wise."

"Right." Anne smiled. "The wisdom is what she's learned from all those tales. The gaps are full of images for which Aura has no words. She shares those images with me. They are a sight. She draws pictures, you know, sometimes in math and sometimes in an amalgam of lines and shapes that make some sense to her. Over the years, they've made sense to me too. Lately, her images have been repeating. There is something she sensed was off in Zephyr. I dismissed it when you learned what you did about Tracey. I thought perhaps it was Tracey's rustling around Zephyr which had caused it. But Tracey has been in isolation and Oliver had put everything right, and the warnings continued. I asked her to go back in the labyrinth and take some thread, if you will, a tracer code. I followed her with it, and she led me to the Minotaur. It's sleeping. We haven't woken it. It doesn't know that I know. Do you know about it?"

"We'd discovered it, just before the Convocation," Will admitted. "I can't tell you how, Grandmother, not because I don't trust you but because it's not my secret to share. Do you understand?"

"I do, Pippin." Anne put her hand on his. "I will always understand you, better than you understand yourself."

"I can tell you my secret, though, and you cannot share this with Grandfather yet, though I plan to bring him into it in time. Tracey has developed a poison pill program which we intend to use in retribution for the breach—your Minotaur. She calls it an oil slick. It will trap the Minotaur and it will also free many people by wiping out records best forgotten."

Anne smiled and nodded, squeezing Will's hand.

"Can I invite Tracey to your wedding?" Anne asked. "I'd like to have a conversation with her."

"You'd need to check with Oliver," Will replied. "They are in the middle of a cyber war right now. You'd also need to invite Jonathan Castle. They can't be apart for long. They unravel in their minds if they aren't together."

"Will, don't wait until someone has captured and tortured *you* to realize you need your mate by your side, knowing your flaws and your secrets, and loving you not just despite them but because of them," Anne said. "Your wife understands many things, more than you know. You shouldn't treat her like Aura. She's not a child with gaps in her thinking. She is a flesh and blood woman, with fire in her belly and a remarkable mind."

"I know that, Grandmother, but she's also impulsive and disobedient, and incredibly prone to find trouble."

"So, you're saying that she's just like you," Anne teased.

"No, Grandmother, Mariana's nothing like me," Will said. "She's kind and loving; patient and understanding; warm and generous; small and vulnerable. She's beautiful. She's perfect. Mariana needs to survive this, Grandmother, even if I don't. Promise me that."

"I can't," Anne said, caressing his cheek. "Nobody can. That's why you can't waste the time you have together. It's not infinite time, William. It's only ever today. It's only ever right now."

"Yes, *Mémé*," Will said, feeling the weight of her words in his belly. "You're right."

31

The Girl is Poison

William

Will's next plan was to run up to the tower where he'd locked his wife away, dismiss her attendant, and make love to her on the bumpy bed. Also to unshackle her, but not right away. Anyway, that was the plan as he walked back through the gardens with his grandmother, feeling remarkably lighter. Except, he bumped straight into an angry Viking by the azaleas.

"There you are!" Charlie was out of breath and bright pink. "Jesus, man, you keep disappearing and we don't have time for all this shit. Sorry, Anne." Charlie paused. "Look, I'm going. Don't ask me where. You don't want to know. Sandy can explain if you think you're going to pop. But don't ask her. It's better that you don't know. I'll be back when I'm back."

"Hold up," Will said. "What are you going to do?"

"Didn't I just explain? Don't fucking ask me, Will, or I'll have to tell you, dammit! Sorry, Anne." Charlie ran off before Will could stop him.

"I think we'd better go to the Globe now," Anne said after they'd both recovered from the odd confrontation. "Don't you, Pippin?"

"Yes, *Mémé*," Will said. "Lead the way."

Mariana

Walking around her cell was pretty awkward. Mariana tended to get wound around furniture and take things down with her. There had been a pretty Tiffany lamp on a small table by the reading chair, which suffered an accident. Mariana regretted the loss and tried to help Agnes clear up, but only wound up getting Agnes locked around her.

"This is really ridiculous!" Mariana complained. "I will not run off, for heaven's sake. Can't you just undo the shackle?"

"I don't have a key, Madam," Agnes said, carefully stepping out of the chain loop. "Perhaps if you just sit still and rest a while. I can get this cleaned up."

"How can I rest?" Mariana asked, though she didn't expect Agnes to answer. Agnes didn't even try. "Has Sandy got my note, do you know? She should have replied by now."

"It was delivered, Madam," Agnes said.

"And?"

"There has been no reply," Agnes said.

"Is Sandy all right, at least? Or did she get locked up too? I've got so many things to do! I can't afford to sit here waiting. Can you send a message to my husband, please?"

"Why don't you sit at the desk and write notes to them?" Agnes suggested, as she brushed shards of stained glass into a dustpan. "I'll call to have them delivered immediately. You should put on your slippers too. I don't think it's good for you

349

to go around barefoot, especially now. I'll bring them to you at your desk so you don't have to cross here. There may still be some small pieces of glass left behind."

"Thank you, Agnes," Mariana said, as the young woman came to the desk holding Mariana's prison-issue, fluffy, blue, terrycloth slippers. "I'm sorry if I'm being difficult. This is all just… aargh."

"Yes, Madam, quite." Agnes gave her a small smile. "Write your notes. I'll be sure they get where they should go."

William

Sandy was busy with a conversation on the phone about the show when Will and Anne arrived, so they had to wait awhile to ask her questions. Will's earlier sense of calm had shattered and his patience was thin.

"What is going on?" Will asked Sandy brusquely as soon as she ended the call.

"Nothing, just an actor requesting a change to the script because they feel it's not true to their character. I've handled it."

"That's not what I mean, and you know that, Sandy," Will said.

"I'm not supposed to say," Sandy said. "I don't think you really need or even would want to know."

"You don't get to decide that, Sandy," Will howled.

"I didn't," Sandy said. "Daddy did."

"I want to know what the fuck is going on, okay? So tell me."

"You'll regret it, Will," Sandy said, sounding years older than she usually was. "Really."

Will sighed. "I already regret it," Will said. "Tell me anyway."

"No, I won't," Sandy said, "but I will give you this." Sandy handed him a blue envelope. He recognized Mariana's handwriting on the front. "What you do with it is none of my business."

Will opened the envelope and pulled out folded stationery and a magazine back cover, featuring an herbal medicine cure for cellulitis. "What's this?" Will asked.

"You have what I'm going to give you," Sandy said.

"Are you just buying time or being difficult?" Will snapped.

"Yes," Sandy said, tapping the screen on the desk to pull up another call. "Do you mind? I've got shit to do. I'm working as a one-man band today."

"Let's leave Sandy to catch up," Anne suggested, taking the papers from his hand, and halting Will from following his impulse to reach across the desk and strangle the infuriating blonde. "You and I can look through the note and maybe make some sense of it."

"No, I'm going straight to the messenger on this," Will said.

"Yes," Anne said. "Now you're thinking."

Mariana

Mariana had handed two notes to Agnes—one for Sandy and another for Will—but the courier hadn't responded yet to pick them up. It felt like ages. They had so little time to fix this mess, and Will was only making things worse by being stubborn.

She fantasized about strangling him, which probably

wasn't the best thing for a marriage, but it just seemed appropriate. Will was just such an asshole sometimes.

A knock on the door announced the courier, a young page, or whatever, a valet, footman, something. They had so many people working here it was like a small village more than a home. Mariana didn't recognize him either. He took the envelopes from Agnes and ran off.

"What would you like for lunch, Madam?" Agnes asked. "I can go to the kitchen and have anything made you please."

"Lobster Thermidor with black truffle risotto, and a double cheeseburger with bacon, and a chocolate shake." Mariana was just being sarcastic. She had no appetite.

"All right," Agnes said. "I'll be back soon."

"No, I was pulling your leg. I don't want any of that, Agnes," Mariana said. "You mean, they would just make all of that at the drop of a hat?"

"We keep the kitchen fully stocked for any whims that arise when we have guests," Agnes said.

"I see," Mariana said. "What if I wanted sea urchin?"

"Yes, it's very fresh. Chef makes a lovely Galician sea urchin gratin."

"And if I wanted venison or pheasant?"

"You could have either, any way you please." Agnes smiled.

"I've got one," Mariana grinned. "Fugu."

"That would have to be for dinner. Our Sushi chef has the days off. There is Fugu fish in the tanks, so it would be very fresh. We would advise against it, in your case. Chef Naburo is highly skilled, but the risk of poisoning is still higher than naught."

"So pretty much anything," Mariana said.

"That's right, Madam," Agnes said.

"Some cheese and crackers then, with grapes, and that pink lemonade which was very nice. And a banana, I think."

"Which pink lemonade?" Agnes asked.

"Oh, that's right," Mariana said. "I remembered the one I had on an unexpected outing, the day before yesterday. Never mind. I can have plain water."

"You consumed food and beverage served by someone outside of our kitchens?"

"Yes, but it's perfectly fine," Mariana said. "The person who served it to me had some too. She wasn't trying to poison me, only drug me into compliance." As Mariana said all of this out loud, she realized how ludicrous it sounded.

"Madam, was this person Miss Iris Fleming?"

"Yes," Mariana said, worrying as she saw Agnes' cheeks glow bright pink.

"Can you excuse me, please? I'll be right back. Drink nothing else. Not even from the tap."

"Wait, what's happening?" Mariana asked.

"It will take too long to explain, Madam," Agnes said. "I'm going to fetch Lady Nancy Greystone. She's a specialist. I'll be right back."

William

Will was rushing from one tower to the other with Anne trailing him, when Charles stopped him in his tracks.

"Not now, Uncle Charles," Will snapped. "I'm dealing with something urgent."

"Whatever it is, it isn't more urgent than this," Charles said.

"What do you mean?"

"Why is Charlie flying to Geneva? What are you doing?

Don't make a mess on our turf without letting us know what the play is, William. It would be very bad. You still have people rattled from your adventures in Nice."

"I'm trying to figure out what Charlie is up to myself, Charles. I do not know. Not a clue, except for this note Mariana sent to Sandy," Will said. "Charlie told me I wouldn't want to know."

"Well, that can only mean one thing," Charles said. "Does he realize the cost of him conducting a wet operation in this territory without clearing it by us first?"

"Of course he does," Will said. "If he's going to do something against protocol, he must have good reason. I just wish I knew what it was."

"Let me see the note," Charles demanded. Will handed him the envelope, for all the good it would do.

Charles unfolded the magazine back and looked it over front and back and the note Mariana had written.

"*This is the brand la puta uses,*" Charles read out loud, pronouncing 'bitch' wrong, with a long 'u'. Charles spoke very little Spanish. "*I need to know the maker. It's not only night, I suspect. We just need to know that it's not a northern synonym. Don't tell Will until we know for sure. He'll worry.*" He handed the papers back to Will. "What does any of that mean?"

"I'm trying to find out," Will said. "I'm going to see Mariana now."

"Do you think it's related to Charlie leaving?"

"I know it is," Will said. "I'm just not sure how."

"Would Charlie take a contract on Mariana's request alone?"

"If he thought it was justified, absolutely," Will said. "She wouldn't even have to ask."

"I'll come with you," Charles said.

And so they were three mice on a blind mission.

They made their way to Mariana's tower through one of the castles many hidden tunnels and found a nightmare waiting for them at the landing. It was Agnes, Mariana's guard, blue as a blueberry, choked to death by her swollen tongue.

"Well, that's a message," Charles said.

Will didn't bother to snap at his uncle, he was too busy running up two winding stone steps at a time to check on his wife.

When he reached the top and found the door wide open, his heart sank to his feet. He stepped in, expecting to find Mariana dead, and found her sitting by the fireplace with Iris instead.

"Hi, Will," Iris said, with a friendly, warm smile and a wave. "Sit, we have a lot to catch up on."

"You are a dead woman," Will growled.

"Not yet," Iris said. "And if you want your pretty wife to stay alive also, I suggest you stop being so rude. Sit. Calm down. It's not as bad as you think."

"You killed Agnes on our ground, Iris!" Will barked. "You cannot expect to leave the castle alive."

"You killed Agnes?" Mariana teared up. "Why? She was just a sweet girl."

"Hardly," Iris snorted. "How are you so gullible and so smart at the same time?"

"Because she's not inherently evil," Will barked.

"Neither am I," Iris said. "Now, we had a deal, and I suggest you take me up on it."

"There's no deal," Mariana said. "I meant what I said. I want nothing to do with you."

"William?" Iris turned her dark eyes on Will. He had always thought she was beautiful, but now he could see for the first time that her beauty was only a shell. The interior was hollow.

"Iris, what are you doing? You are bringing down your entire family," Will said.

"I don't think so," Iris said. "She already shunned them, and even if you say her shunning doesn't matter, the others took note. She brought down my family, which expedited my plans somewhat. Then again, she also created an opportunity by sending Cailean on a wild goose chase. So thank you for that, Mariana."

"What does that mean?" Will asked.

"Did Sandy get my note?" Mariana asked.

"Your first one, yes," Iris said. "I got the second, and thanks for that. It helped me update my plans. Oh, and Anne, you'll want them to check the west corridor connecting this room to the chapel as well. There's a young courier who needs clearing out, or he'll start smelling up the place soon."

Will turned around to see Anne and Charles taking in the scene. Anne looked positively murderous.

"You've killed *two* of my staff?" Anne asked. "They will never find you."

"That works for me," Iris said. "Except, I expect to keep breathing wherever I am and living in the fashion to which I have become accustomed. Somewhere tropical would suit me fine."

"Well, you're an optimist, I see," Charles said. "That's a refreshing surprise. I had always thought Flemings were rather jaded."

"I am rubber, you are glue, whatever—" Iris made a sweeping hand gesture.

"What advantage do you believe you have, Iris?" William asked.

Iris counted out on her delicate fingers. "Some information you *really* need, the life of your wife, and the survival of your little babies, even the illegitimate one."

"You can't make a deal with her, Will," Mariana said. "She'll break it."

"Not if she wants to escape her mother's reach, which you do, don't you, Iris?" Will said. "That's why you made it look like she was the one betraying us, when it was you all along. She didn't want you to take Mariana's contract because she knew you were tainted. She'd turned a blind eye because you're her daughter and she blames herself for whatever you've done. But she plans to make it right, which is why you are hiding here in the Castle. Let me know if I'm warm."

"Mother suspected what I was up to, yes," Iris said. "And your little play in France painted me in a very unflattering light."

"How so?"

"Well, Mother made the same connection I expect Mariana made, isn't that right?"

"Your lipstick," Mariana said. "The company that makes it, *La Nuit Laboratoires*, has a funny emblem. It's one I've seen before, though at the time we confused it for the symbol of Aril. It's related to Nótt, Will, the Nordic goddess of night. Iris is a Nótt agent."

"*Was*," Iris corrected. "We've dissolved and I'm rebranding, but the makeup line sells well. Changing that logo is a complete mess. I think the ad buys for the magazine you ran across were made well in advance. Anyway, that's just a little cover business, as you already know, but I have a good friend who mixes my private makeup collection in their lab."

"In Geneva," Will said.

"That's right." Iris smiled. "Is that where your dog went chasing after me?"

"Iris, you are a fool," Will said. "What makes you think you have any room to negotiate now. You've admitted to being a traitor and to killing two of our agents in *our* house during *our* meeting. You've threatened my wife and my children. Now you're needlessly trying to insult Charlie…"

"Cailean," Iris said. "I looked him up. I looked her up too. I've learned so many interesting things, William. And I know things *you* need to know. That's why you will do what I want."

"No, I don't think so," Will said. "Whatever you tell me, I can't trust. The longer you live, the more trouble you cause."

"The longer I live, the more likely she will," Iris said, nodding her head at Mariana. "I visited the other one, too, before I came here, just in case. She had so much to say about you. That woman hate-loves you like nobody, William." Iris sighed. "Anyway, they've each been dosed with a very slow acting poison. Sandra should show signs now. Mariana should start by tomorrow or the day after. Her body metabolizes funny, so I can't be sure. I have the only antidote, anyway."

"Get her to the dungeon," Will said to Charles. "Don't leave her alone."

"Will," Mariana said. "Agnes was going to get Nancy when she left, after I told her I drank Iris's pink lemonade and ate her picnic lunch. She seemed to think it might have been poisoned and Nancy might help."

"She can try." Iris laughed.

"Well, you were concerned enough that she might succeed to kill two of our people," Anne said. "I say it's worth asking Nancy what she makes of all of this."

Charles grabbed Iris roughly by the arm and dragged her out, with her protesting his rough handling. "I'll be waiting for you, William!" Iris shouted as Charles led her downstairs.

"What could she have given me that would take days to make me sick?" Mariana asked.

"She could be lying, but Nancy will know," Will said,

kissing Mariana's forehead. "It's her specialty. I'm going to make a few calls. Grandmother, please stay with Mariana."

Will left before Mariana could ask him to let her loose. Frankly, it made little difference now, since Iris had got to her even in a place where no one should have found her, but at least this way she would be safe in one place. Except, if Iris was telling the truth, then she was already as unsafe as she might be. He wanted to punch the stones of this place until his knuckles broke and bled, but that would fix nothing. Will rushed back to the Globe, where he could put things right.

As soon as he got there, he asked Sandy to page Charlie to come back from a wasted journey. He took over the comms, disrupting her work, but as Sandy overheard his conversations, and understood what was happening, she jumped right into helping.

Mrs. Jenkins confirmed his worst fear. Sandra Price had been hospitalized for what at first appeared to be a stomach virus, but then diagnosed as a sort of botulism.

"They're afraid she may die," Mrs. Jenkins said. "She's just getting worse and they can't make any sense of it. None of the usual treatments or anti-toxins are working. What do you know about this, Will?"

"It was nothing I did, Mrs. Jenkins, you know me better than that," Will explained. "But she was targeted because of me. I will make it right."

"You'd better, Will," Mrs. Jenkins said. "This will change a lot of hearts, if anything happens to her."

"I know," Will said. "The person who did it also poisoned Mariana. We will get the antidote and send it right away."

"Don't make a devil's bargain," Mrs. Jenkins warned.

"What choice do I have?" Will asked.

"You can always choose differently," she said. "There's more than one way to solve even the greatest challenge."

"Not the ticking of the clock, Mrs. Jenkins, there's no straightforward way to solve that."

Iris sat primly in the folding chair inside the cell where she was being held.

"I need the antidote," Will said, without preamble.

"I know you do." Iris smiled. "It's a real bitch, my magical Botox. It works wonders, though, in the right dose. It can cure more than wrinkles. I could give the formula to your Pharma team and it would make you rich."

"Stop messing around, Iris," Will said. "I have no patience for you. What is it you want?"

"I've told you. I want to be free. I want to get out of here alive and I want to disappear where mother can't find me—where no one can find me. I want to live in comfort and I want to be forgotten."

"Why, Iris?" Will said. "I don't understand why you would do any of this. You already had everything you're asking for until you blew it. Nobody bothered you. You lived a very luxurious life. I just don't get it."

"You know nothing about me," Iris said. "Nothing about any of us, really. You do not know what we're like and you don't really want to know. You want to see the Flemings as you know them, and most of them are happy to play those parts. I am not. I can't just do as I am told. I need more. Nótt offered me that. Now, it's wrecked. You wrecked it, as you have so many things, moving around carelessly without thinking."

"What does that mean?"

"My father made deals when you were a kid, to keep you

and your grandmother alive," Iris said. "As soon as you came into your own, you stepped all over them. You've put him in danger—you've put all of us in danger—and you don't even care to notice. Now, you're making it worse by insisting on your ancestor's rules and values. But you're no angel, Will. You're like a dragon guarding his gold. You're hoarding. You're a hoarder. You have these powerful weapons, resources, and technologies that you won't share. People will take them from you, no matter what. Even if Mother won't see it that way, I was doing what she taught me to do. I was surviving on my own terms and I was protecting my family from you."

He would get nowhere arguing with Iris. He knew that.

"I can help you disappear," Will said. "But I need to know you won't come back to haunt me."

"Well, if things are as they should be, I won't want to come back," Iris said. "It's really up to you, William. You're the boss, as usual."

"You know you won't disappear from me," Will warned her. "I will still be able to find you, if you make any kind of trouble."

"Yes," Iris said. "So you can rest easy unless you screw me over. I'll find you first if you do."

"I need to know the antidote works before I do anything," Will said. "I need it administered to Sandra. Give it to me."

"You only had to ask, sweet thing."

Iris grinned and reached around the back of her neck to unfasten the clasp on a chain, then pulled out a locket from between her breasts and handed it to Will.

"There are only two ampules in there," Iris said. "The exact dose you need for each of your women. If you try to get creative, and have your auntie deconstruct them, then you will not have enough. She can't reverse-engineer it in time. Take my word on that. Each dose must be applied directly on the tongue. They are soluble ampules. The effect will be quick. Eight hours, at most, and you'll know they worked like a charm. There won't be any lasting side-effects."

"And the children will be unharmed?"

"Ah, the children are more complicated," Iris said. "Some of my magic Botox may have found its way to the placenta. I have a cure for that too, a sort of cleanse, but I will only let you find it after I'm settled. They have a little more time, but not a lot."

Will flew the ampule for Sandra to Connecticut himself. He needed to be there, to know for certain that it worked, but he couldn't deliver it himself without making a mess. He couldn't explain any of this to the police, and there would be an investigation. That was certain. In the end, Mrs. Jenkins had the ideal solution. Through her network of locals, she passed the wax envelope containing the ampule to a nurse she trusted, and the nurse administered the ampule to Sandra as if it were just an ordinary drug. Now, they just had to wait. Every second that went by felt like a pinprick on Will's skin. But after only two hours of waiting, the nurse contacted them to let them know there had been a dramatic improvement with Sandra's partial paralysis subsiding. By the time he got to the airport, Nancy called him to tell him she had succeeded in reverse engineering the antitoxin.

"You took the risk, *anyway*?" Will was furious. "Even though you *knew* you might not give Mariana her full dose?"

"There was never any doubt that I could do it, Will," Nancy said. "Except perhaps in your mind. This way, we know it all. We know how they re-engineered the

Clostridium botulinum to have this odd effect, based on the samples we took from Mariana. We have the antitoxin, in case it's ever used again, and you know it will be. Also, I've made some calculations on the impact to the placenta, and Iris's claims about needing a cleanse are an outright lie. You don't have to do anything other than distribute the antitoxin. The body takes care of the rest. They're all safe. You don't need to do anything else for your other woman. I've already given Mariana her dose. I suggest you come home to your wife."

Will wanted to correct his aunt on her remark about Sandra being his other woman, but she had already hung up. If Sandra even suspected he had anything to do with her illness, she would definitely refuse to take the paternity test until the baby was born, and perhaps not even then. He might not be obligated, legally, to offer her any support unless she could prove it, but Fairfarm had its own laws and code of conduct—and so did he.

For now, he just had to figure out how to address his Iris problem, and the others. There were so many that he couldn't wrap his mind around them. He was bone tired and quickly fell asleep after boarding his plane.

32

One Misstep at a Time

Mariana

There was no way she was staying locked in a tower after everything that had gone on. If Will had set off to fix things in his own way, that was fine. But Mariana insisted they let her back in her room, at least, and let her rejoin Sandy at work. Anne was very sympathetic to her plight.

"Pippin has not been himself," she said, trying to appease Mariana as she accompanied her through the passageways back to her bedroom.

"Who has he been, then?" Mariana asked from behind the dressing screen, peeling off the nightgown she'd grown to hate and slipping on a comfortable blue and white, belted, tiered, floral-print, cotton-poplin, midi-shirt dress that had appeared in her closet along with other garments Anne had selected for her.

"I don't know," Anne said, "but you need to give him time to figure it out."

"Sure," Mariana said. "He can take as long as he needs."

"Leave him some clues, to remind him," Anne suggested.

"Assuming he'd pick up on any clues I leave him," Mariana said.

"Well, maybe use a horn."

"Or a club." Mariana smiled as she stepped out from behind the screen. "He needs to dispose of Iris. He needs to sort out the Flemings. He needs to forge proper alliances with the remaining Eagles. And he needs to listen to me, Anne. How do I get him to do that?"

"I always find that Richard listens best when I remind him of everything he has to lose by ignoring me," Anne said. "It doesn't always work, and he can be very stubborn. Fortunately, Pippin is a better listener. But if you find you must hit him over the head to get him to listen, then do so. You have my blessing."

"Thank you, Anne." Mariana smiled. "Is Charlie back yet?"

"Yes, he arrived late last night," Anne said. "Will is flying back and he'll be here this afternoon, I expect. You have a few hours to get your club ready to strike, if that's what you have in mind to do."

"I don't think Charlie would appreciate the comparison," Mariana said. "He can be incredibly sweet when he wants to be."

"I don't think he'd mind," Anne said. "He knows who he is. We've had to keep him away from the dungeon. He's itching to get his hands on Iris, but I don't think that's in our best interest now. Even if we don't need her anymore."

"We certainly need her," Mariana said. "That's what I need to talk to Charlie about."

"Well, you'll probably find him in the Globe," Anne said. "I think he planned to help Sandy out today, or use our resources up there, anyway."

Charlie was engrossed following what Sandy was working on, but he turned on a bright smile when he saw Mariana again.

"I can't tell you how relieved I am to see you up and about, atomic kitten," he said, giving her a tight hug.

"Jesus, does Will tell you everything, Charlie?"

"I've told you, only what concerns my business," Charlie said. "I had to update our records to change your handle officially. I figure you've earned it."

"Not yet, but I intend to, if you'll help me," Mariana said.

"Not if it's going to cause me grief with Will," Charlie said.

"It's saving both of you some grief," Mariana explained. And then she revealed her master plan. After a prolonged discussion and a bit of resistance from Charlie, he finally agreed.

"I guess I'm flying out again, baby girl," he said, planting a kiss on Sandy's cheek before drinking from her mouth like he'd walked through the Sahara to get here and was now setting out to sea. "I'll be back before you have time to miss me."

"Charlie, just remember, this was all your idea," Mariana said.

"Only a fool would lie to your husband, Mariana," Charlie said, sounding deadly serious. "I don't recommend you do that."

Mariana breathed deep. "Okay, so it was all my stupid plan."

"He'll forgive you," Charlie said. "Then, once he's done being angry and confused, and after your ass has stopped glowing pink, he'll thank you."

"Great," Mariana nodded. "Let's hope you're right."

William

Will was eager to see with his own eyes that his wife was healthy and safe, but his grandmother caught him just as he entered the castle and pulled him aside.

"She is in your rooms and resting, but we all need to talk to you before you see her," Anne said.

"Can't it wait?"

"No, it can't, Pippin," Anne said, allowing no argument. "We all need to speak to you urgently. A lot has happened in the time you were away. You and I need to follow that red thread tonight, as it no doubt leads to the information Iris insisted you needed to know."

"Did she tell you that?"

"No, Iris was not inclined to be helpful. Oliver and I have had a talk with Tracey and we're sure that we will find what we seek at the end of Aura's yarn." Anne smiled, hooked her arm in his and patted his hand. "Come, we'll talk in the library. Your grandfather and uncles are waiting."

They walked into a fiery argument between the Greystone men. From the pieces Will could stitch together, he learned someone had handed Iris over to the Flemings.

"Who gave that order?" Will asked.

"Your lovely wife," Charles spat. "Now we have no way to know what else Iris was keeping from us. Iris was ours, working on our territory, and she just sent her home to be sorted out by her kin like a misbehaving child instead of what she is—walking death. How can we trust they will tell us what they learn, if anything? The remnants of Nótt are a threat to all of us, and Mariana just handed over the only source we had in what remains of the organization."

"Pawn for the queen," Merlin said. "Iris would never be

of much use to us except as a pawn to trade. Mariana made a very bold, and clever move, putting the responsibility for Iris where it belongs. Even Charlie could see that, which is why he is delivering the package."

"Charlie agreed?" Will asked.

"He spoke with Angel, apparently," Lord Greystone said. "He has Angel's guarantee that they will keep Iris in the compound. Tree will debrief her."

"How will that help us?" Henry said. "Tree's roots are so entangled with the agencies there. We can't trust that they will share vital information."

"Well, it is an opportunity to rebuild lost trust," Will said. "We have no real reason to doubt Tree will keep us informed of what he learns. This move will satisfy the Flemings that we are acting in good faith. I'll meet with Tree and set terms. This avoids the greater threat of having Catherine and Howard turn against us."

"Do you think it will satisfy the other Eagles?" the younger Richard asked.

"I couldn't say," Will said. "You would know better than I, but we have offerings to give in good faith. That might settle any ruffled feathers. Could we convoke a roundtable of those who are still here tonight?"

"You have plans for tonight, Pippin," Anne said. "Plans that cannot wait."

"That's all right, *Mémé*," Will smiled. "I can be in two places at once."

Anne searched his eyes for his meaning and then gave him a broad, warm smile. "I'm so proud of you for learning that trick."

Mariana

"You've taken an enormous risk, Mariana." Will came to where she sat by the fireplace in her silk robe. She hadn't wanted to change for dinner in case he decided to spank her first, but she could see he wasn't up to that at all. He looked tired, like he could use a long hot bath and seventeen hours of sleep. Will pulled her up from her chair by the hand, kissed her with a desperate tenderness, and hugged her tight. "I'm proud of you for it." Mariana had been so on edge, thinking he might disapprove, that she might have made things worse between them. She started crying against his chest. *"No llores, nena. Que me partes el alma,"* he pleaded, "no more tears." He kissed the tears from her cheeks and gave her a comforting smile. "Come, we have to get ready for dinner and then we have a big meeting to attend."

"Are you putting on another Black Mass?"

"More like knights and ladies of the round table," Will said. "Sandy will stand in for Charlie, and I'd like you to stand in for me."

"Where will you be?"

"I'm going to be in the Globe working on a secret project with *Mémé*. I'll tell you all about it once I know the Minotaur is dead."

"The what?"

"You know, half man, half bull."

"Okay, *torero.*" Mariana kissed him gently. "Just don't get speared by the horns."

"I'll admit that I'm a little horny," Will said, kissing her deeper. "Do you think we could manage a quickie before dinner?"

"Oh, definitely, *Papi.*" She smiled. "No need to rush, though. We have plenty of time. Why don't we do it in the bath? You look like you could use a good soak."

"Don't drown me this time," Will said, reminding her of the time she slipped in France and took them both under water.

"I wouldn't dare," Mariana said. "We've got important things to do."

"How are the peas? Are you sure they're going to be okay?"

"I never even felt any symptoms when Nancy gave me the antitoxin," Mariana said. "Everything feels right and the blood tests came back well. I think we're all going to be okay. What about Sandra? Is she okay?"

"She's recovering," Will said.

"I don't like her, but I feel sorry for her, Will," Mariana said. "Even if it's not your child—and I don't believe it is— couldn't we help her?"

Will stroked her hair. "We can try, sweetheart, but some people won't let themselves be helped."

"Well, we gave Iris a second chance, against her self-destructive wishes," Mariana said. "Does Sandra deserve less?"

"No." Will kissed her. "No, my sweet angel, she doesn't."

"You should help Fraser too," Mariana added. "He's family."

"Not family I plan to spend time with, but I've already had Stevenson double his salary offer," Will said, "for Rhys and Lucy's sake. Maybe we can save that generation."

"Softie." Mariana smiled. "Lucy is cute as a button."

"Our buttons will be cuter," Will said.

"I'm confident you're right."

The Eagles that remained met with Sandy and Mariana together. Out of their black cloaks, they were far less intimidating. Most looked like ordinary people you might bump into on the street: librarians and schoolteachers, accountants and engineers, preachers and scholars. Merlin and Nancy were representing the Greystones at the table, and they got things rolling.

"We thank all of you for joining us in the excitement of the last couple of days," Merlin said. "I'm sure you have a lot of questions. We are here, hopefully, to give you answers, and to agree between us. Before we start, Nancy has an announcement."

Nancy had been staring at the ceiling again, but snapped right to attention as soon as Merlin coughed and whispered, "Darling."

"Yes," Nancy said, with a shy smile. "We've recently discovered a new strain of botulism engineered by an abandoned *Nótt* lab in Geneva. We will take over that operation under our umbrella. We've developed an antitoxin which we will share with you. The only requirement is that you can never sell for a profit."

Everyone seemed to accept that, though a woman whose treble voice and Scottish accent Mariana immediately recognized, raised fresh concerns about Nótt. Out of her cat's costume, wearing a gray skirt and blouse, and a pink sweater, with a matching pink hairband over her glossy black hair, she looked more like an elementary schoolteacher than a secret agent. She was still just as snippy. Mariana painted on a smile as she listened to the woman complain.

"We were told Nótt had unraveled after Nice, but they were here, embedded among us," said Catriona—that was the cat's name.

"Do you have mold in Scotland?" Sandy asked.

"Pardon?" Catriona asked, surprised to hear Sandy speak.

"Mold, it's a fungus. It gets everywhere. Do you have it in Scotland?" Sandy asked again.

"Of course," Catriona replied, puzzled.

"Do you usually get scared when you've cleaned it and then it just pops up again?" Sandy asked. "Are Scotts terrified of mold or something?"

"This isn't a simple matter of cleaning up mold," Catriona said.

"But you're wrong," Sandy said. "That's all it is. That's our job. The only thing we do is keep the mold at bay. Even when we can't see it, it's there. It was there before we came and it will be there after we're gone. But we won't let the mold take over. We'll be vigilant. We'll be ready to wipe it out wherever it pops up next."

Mariana smiled at Sandy and looked at the others around the table. Sandy's words seemed to have struck the right note with the Eagles. There were a lot of nods of approval. They sure loved metaphors and similes, the Eagles.

"All we need to know is that we will have your support," Mariana said, speaking plainly. "That's all we're asking. We're not asking you to give us anything for free, and we're not setting a ceiling. Whatever it costs, we'll pay. We'll do our part to keep things tidy. But, please, won't you help us?"

"Of course we will," the man who answered was familiar too. It was Santa's son, Juha Kivi. The son of the Finnish intelligence agent, Jaakko Hämäläinen. Juha had apparently gotten a promotion. "We will help you, but you need to put some things right. It does not serve our purpose to make enemies of allies. It's always best to be careful with the words we use, when under strain. Less to mend from speaking later."

Mariana would not correct Juha. She knew what he meant.

"I was brash and angry, which made me very wrong,"

Mariana admitted. "I have asked to make it right. It is being handled as we speak. I expect you will see the results at our upcoming wedding. You will all come to that, won't you?"

"Well, I have already bought a dress." Catriona shrugged.

"So, if you'll open your envelopes, you'll find the details of our offer," Mariana said. "You don't have to make an open pledge. You can either take your envelope, or leave it at the table. If you choose to leave it, we understand. You're welcome at our wedding, regardless. You will always have a place in our family."

Mariana and Sandy had a lot of tough questions to answer about the show, but they all boiled down to the same thing. Everyone worried it would make them look bad. In the end, they wouldn't really be satisfied until they'd seen the show themselves, and maybe not until long after that, when nothing ill came from it. She and Sandy could persuade the Eagles that they would play out well on screen.

Mariana hoped that would be the case, anyway.

William

Will had never realized just how adept his grandmother was with coding. He marveled as she worked in concert with Oliver and Tracey to follow the red yarn through Zephyr's subconscious. It was vital for Anne to do this—the only way to keep Oliver and Tracey from discovering Aura during this delicate operation. Anne hid Aura under her skirt, so to speak, leading their way through the labyrinth while hiding the other AI's footprint.

What they found was far more than a Minotaur. It was Pan, playing a flute which led them to an entire hidden world, the patchwork mind of another AI, assembled by their rivals.

"This is the Fog," Tracey said through the speakerphone. "I had been keeping it out, but I was all topsy-turvy, as you know. It slipped through."

"Where is the Fog located?" Will asked.

"It was on the island," Tracey said.

"But the island was abandoned," Will said. "I checked it myself. Why would they leave it behind?"

"They don't need to be where it is," Tracey said. "You know that. They will go back to the island as soon as enough time passes."

"They won't go back if we occupy it," Will said.

"You could do that," Tracey said. "Or you could leave the island alone, not give anything away. I can flood the Fog with oil and it will perish in the confusion. Once the indexes are wrecked, it's nothing but lost cells."

"I have a better idea," Anne said. "Using your oil on AI could leave traces, and if it proves as deadly as you say, some will want to put those traces to use. It's too valuable a commodity right now to risk others examining the contents. My little yarn is cheap, easy to replicate, but nearly imperceptible. Let me knot the yarn here, and watch over the Fog's dreams. Let the Fog sleep easy, and tie the other end to your mirror world, Olly. Can you do that? Can you redirect it without their noticing?"

"My mirror is of the Sequoia, Grandmother," Olly said. "It isn't a mirror of Zephyr or Brian. The difference will be obvious. It's not an AI system."

"What if I can seed it with an echo?"

"What do you mean?"

"You know, a little voice that makes it sound as though they are still interacting with Zephyr, at least on the surface, with all the memory links to your mirror of the Sequoia."

"Can you write that, Grandmother?"

"Oh, yes, darling, I already have," Anne said.

"You have a package ready to deliver?" Oliver wondered. "How is that possible? Did you know what we would find?"

"Well, I need an enjoyable hobby these days," Anne said. "I didn't know whether I'd ever need it, but I knew I would regret not having the echo if I ever did."

"You are a genius, Anne," Tracey said.

"No, I'm just a grandmother," Anne said. "We always want to have something handy to pass on to our kids when they need it most."

"So let me understand," Will said. "Howard or Tree did not facilitate the breach in any way?"

"Why would you think that?" Tracey asked. Will explained the conclusions they had reached, without revealing the details of Charlie's identity, only saying that Iris had access to information that only Zephyr would have known. "Yes, but Iris was in the Nótt," Tracey said. "Whatever stragglers remain, and there are many, Will, some of them will have access to the Fog. It's no surprise Iris would know things she shouldn't. Tree would let no one drink from your well, though. You should know that. He was a pain in my ass, but in a good way. That doesn't mean you have nothing to worry about, but you have nothing to worry about from them. I know where the rats are hiding and I'll poison them all."

"It's good to have you back, Tracey," Will said, meaning it. She sounded so much better. She was nothing like the broken woman who had kidnapped his wife to get his attention. "You wouldn't have a handy index of all the Nótt operatives out there, would you?"

"Oh, my little address book is much bigger than that," Tracey laughed. "I buried it somewhere safe before I went down the drain. I intend to dig it up again, along with other treasures."

Mariana

Mariana went to bed high on success. She hadn't felt that way in what felt like much too long, but she had the sense that she had taken an awful situation and accomplished something good because of it. It was this high which had hooked her on the crisis management aspect of her career. Anyone could spread good news with an interesting hook, but hooking people with the good side of bad news took something special. You had to find the silver lining in the darkest storm clouds. Mariana had reframed this latest storm with her partner, Sandy Fine, not so secretly Green, who could kick the bolts out of any storm clouds hovering overhead and turn them into gold. But there was more to this high. Mariana had accomplished all of this for the man she loved more than anyone in the world, who was currently missing but probably not far. This castle was enormous, she knew, with a lot of hidden corridors. There were still quite a few loose ends to tie. He was no doubt using his nimble fingers to knot those.

"I need you awake, sweetheart," Will said, kissing her shoulder. She couldn't recall falling asleep. "I'm sorry. I know you're tired, but I just need to say this."

She turned to him, smiling, and draped her arm over his shoulder. "Shoot."

"Will you marry me, for real this time? Please. Knowing all you know. Will you be my wife and my helpmate? Will you be my partner in crime?"

"Catwoman or Rachel Dawes?"

"What?" He kissed the tip of her nose.

"Which one turned you on the most? Catwoman or Rachel Dawes. Be honest."

"Neither," Will said. "My girl is Wonder Woman."

"Yeah, Linda Evans is hot."

"Mariana Perez Castro is hotter." He pulled her closer, so she could feel his erection pressed against her. "Answer me. Will you be my wife?"

"Is Lucifer going to hang around to play?"

"Do you want him to?"

"Sometimes, yeah," Mariana said. "Other times, I want my gentle Will."

"We're the same." He kissed her gently, stroking her back.

"I know," Mariana said. "No more tawses, though. That's out."

"More reason to keep using it," he spoke against her lips, "if you hate it so much."

"You don't need me to behave anymore," Mariana said, then teased his tongue with hers. "What happens when I don't behave can be every bit as good as when I do."

"No, Mariana." He grabbed her ass. "You haven't earned carte blanche."

"What do I have to do to earn that?"

He took her chin in his hand and gave her a hard look. "Be a widow."

"Fuck that," Mariana said. "I don't want carte blanche. But I want a say, and I want to know what's happening. I can take it. And no more towers—those suck."

"Yeah, that tower needs a new mattress, anyway. I need to mention that to Grandmother."

"Sandy said we should join The Unkindness," Mariana said. "Would you try it, for me?"

"No, darling," Will said. "You've got all the exposure you might ever want with your little show."

"Wouldn't Lucifer enjoy it, though?"

"No, Mariana," Will said. "Seriously. Just you and me. Dark and light. Always."

"Okay, *Papi*," Mariana said. "I'll marry you again."

"Good, because Grandmother has spent a mint."

33

Vows that Bind

William

Will was reminded of The Godfather as he sat behind the desk in the Reading Room, meeting with guests at his wedding party, granting requests and thanking people for their service.

The ceremony in the chapel had been beautiful. Everyone agreed, though all Will could recall of it was seeing his wife, dressed in ivory lace, walk down the aisle to join him again, this time with her eyes wide open. Then she had given him a surprise by adding the vow to obey him, officially, to her pledge and saying it loud enough for everyone to hear. It even surprised the priest, who hadn't expected a change to the established text. Will knew why she did it. She was trying to restore what she thought might be his injured pride, after the general release of *Ridicule*. Though he had feared the worst, what he had seen of the show, when she didn't know he was watching, had made him very proud. He didn't deserve a woman this good, but he was going to do his best to become worthy of her.

Tree came into the Reading Room, looking as serious as he usually did. He sat in the burgundy leather chair just looking at Will. Will waited. It often took a while for all the words in Tree's head to settle into something coherent, and there was never any point rushing him.

"Mother is broken-hearted," Tree said. "Father is just broken. Percy feels shame. Angel feels rage. Miranda is bitter. Jason is confused. Cathy is hopeful."

"And you, Tree? How are you?"

"I saw this coming, you know," he said. "I tried to talk to her, but she wouldn't listen. She had no patience for me, like you and Percy do. We were really close once, before the others came along, but she had closed herself off to me years ago. She sees the world inside out. She's not wrong, per se, but she only sees the guts, so she's blinded. I warned Mother not to encourage her, but Mother thought she just needed to find her own way. She trusted Iris would learn what she did and put her skills to good use. Mother forgot that she was the exception, not the rule, and that she had Father to guide her."

"What happens now?"

"We're trying to deprogram her, to clear her head of that false Nótt dogma, but as you know that takes a certain willingness," Tree said. "She may not recover, but she won't be able to harm anyone again. We would never have intentionally put you or Mariana in danger, Will. Mother should have told us about the connection she made in Nice, the realization she came to, but what does it matter? The harm is done."

"You're wrong, Tree," Will said. "No real harm is done between us. If you can forgive Mariana for her words, then all is as it was."

"We make allowances for a fiery Spanish temperament in my family, Will." Tree smiled. "In fact, we embrace it.

Besides, she wasn't wrong. We posed a threat, even inadvertently."

"I want you to engage with Tracey and Oliver, if you can," Will said. "I know you are running into some troubles with your allies. They are causing me trouble too. We've had to do some mopping on the premises."

"I know," Tree interrupted. "Father knows too. We understand. In fact, it's good to have some weeds pulled. If you continue to be tactical about it, you will be fine. You have our support, Will, even if we don't say it."

Will nodded. "Oliver and Tracey have persuaded me we can accomplish more with cyber, and Tracey wants to lend you a hand, if you'll take it."

"I can't say I trust her entirely, Will," Tree said. "I know you do, and I trust you and Oliver, but I'm weary of letting her in."

"Just have a discussion," Will said. "Just listen. That's all I ask."

"It should be safe for you to come home now," Tree said. "But tread gently."

"Okay," Will sighed. It wasn't a guarantee, but it was better than nothing.

"Will you still let Cathy come to live with you?" Tree asked. "She's keen to do it, especially now that Mariana's show is getting so much attention. She really wants to be part of that. Behind the scenes, I mean."

"Will Catherine allow it? I don't want there to be any more misunderstandings."

"Cathy's not a baby anymore." Tree shrugged. "We just treat her like one. She wants to join you. She wants a role in your organization, not ours. And she really wants to live in Manhattan."

"Well, she'd certainly be welcome," Will said. "All of you are welcome."

Mariana

After changing from her wedding gown to a more comfortable, deep blood-red, St. John plisse pleat one-shoulder gown, Mariana had been swamped by well-wishers when she returned to join the party. Two excellent friends pulled her away to a quiet corner in the gardens.

"Oh, Mariana, you're practically royalty, now," Ernest teased. "And you sure look the part."

"Not really, Ernest," Mariana said. "It's still me under all this." She waved her hands in the general direction of everything. "It's a pleasant venue, but it's not quite home, you know."

"So where is home now?" Mac asked. "Are you returning to Manhattan or moving back to Los Angeles now that you've got a big show to manage?"

"I honestly don't know, Mac," Mariana said. "But home is wherever Will is. That much I can say."

"Don't you think it was a bit much, vowing obedience, Mariana?" Mac said, clearly disapproving.

"No, I don't," Mariana said. "I owed Will that. He needed to hear it, and he needed it to be heard. Besides, Will has earned my trust. Do you understand?"

"Whatever makes you happy," Mac said, "but if that cave man hurts you, he'll be answering to me."

"Come on, Mac," Mariana said, smiling, "no more pretending between us. You've seen it all. You know he hurts me just right."

Mac smiled. "Will approached me about an alliance, you know, between the vines and the gardens. He offered me quite an enticement."

"Will you accept? It would mean so much to me if you did," Mariana said.

"Don't you want to know what the enticement is? Or do you know already?"

Mariana nodded. "The lifetime rights to *Ridicule*, and first rights of refusal for any spin-offs, but you've already earned those. The script is yours and it's brilliant. Everyone agrees. Even the background players and harshest critics among us are impressed with the first few episodes."

"Has Will seen it yet?"

"Not as far as I know." Mariana shrugged. "But Charlie loves it."

"He offered me more than that, Mariana, much more, and I'm tempted to take it with one provision."

"What's that?"

"That you'll be my liaison," Mac said. "Not that I have anything against your tree man, but you and I understand each other better."

"I think he'll accept that," Mariana said.

"Well, he can take it or leave it," Mac said.

"It will be fun working with you on a whole new level."

"I'm glad you bought Brown and Wooster," Mac said. "I was thinking of changing publishers with all the changes happening there. Now, I don't have to."

"Good, well, it's time to go back for the toast to Sandy and Charlie's marriage, making it official among us anyway," Mariana said. "Please have the vines keep an eye out for them. They are precious to me."

"We've always been watching over both of you, don't you know that?"

"Orlando?"

"And so many others," Mac said.

"Thank you."

"Come on, you two!" Ernest said. "Enough business. We need more bubbly."

"Just fizzy for me," Mariana shrugged, touching her belly. "I don't miss it as much as I miss coffee, I can tell you that."

"I expect to be a godfather," Ernest said. "I'm sure you'll have many, but add me to the list."

"You come to me, on my wedding day, and you say you will be godfather," Mariana tried her best to sound like Brando and did such a terrible job that the three of them were soon in stitches.

After the wedding, Will and Mariana took a long flight over to Suva-Nausori Airport on Viti Tevu island. Will's 777 was cleared for service again, and the parties responsible for the flight disruption now dealt with. All the extra cargo onboard now was for the villagers. It was a *sevu-sevu* gift, thanking them for allowing Will to use their island. Will explained that it was custom. After landing, they had a long boat ride over carrying the cargo, and then a huge ceremony welcoming Will back with his new wife. He was obviously very popular there, and she felt truly welcome. Apparently the villagers were denied hosting a wedding reception for Angel, because of an ill-timed cyclone. It surprised Mariana to hear it. She still had a lot of catching up to do, but now she trusted Will would tell her what she needed to know when she needed to know it.

They arrived at their home on the beach, exhausted and a little high from the kava root drink, and giddy.

"I have a wedding gift for you," Will said, pulling out a wrapped package from his flight bag.

"Is it a new necklace?" Mariana asked. "I'm already very

happy to have both my diamond necklaces back and safe to use again."

"Oh, you're too smart for your own good," Will shook his head.

"Sorry, I didn't mean to ruin the surprise." Mariana smiled. "Can I open it?"

"Well, I mean, if you don't want it," Will hid the package behind his back.

"No, I want it. Please *Papi*, don't be mean." Mariana pouted.

"Okay," Will said, giving her the package. "You've been a very good girl and you've earned this."

Mariana pulled open the blue ribbon and tore through the white paper, then opened the large, black velvet box, not sure what to expect next. She found a white-gold locket hanging from an elaborate, sturdy byzantine chain.

"Open it," Will said. "It's for the peas."

Mariana opened the locket and found what looked like twin watches inside.

"You wanted to walkie talkie me, right?" Will explained. "I want to walkie talkie you too. And so does Charlie. We split our line with you, so it's a three-way function now. When you feel a gentle buzz on your chest, you'll know one of us needs to reach you. You can open the locket. Whichever watch is red at the rim is calling. You can reply directly with the little ear buds hidden behind the necklace stand in the case. Keep those with you always, even if you have to hide them in your bra. If you need to buzz us, you only have to put in an ear bud and tap the watch belonging to us with your finger. I am the base, and Charlie is the lid."

"Oh, Will," Mariana hugged him tight. "This is the best gift ever!"

"There's more," Will said.

"More?"

"Yes, the watch functions are elaborate. You will know our true GPS location once you know how to read the watch properly. You will also know our current status. You'll know everything you need to know. You can pair it with your phone and video chat with us even when we are officially off-grid. I will teach you how it all works, but not right now. Right now, I'd like to dive into our blue lagoon and make love to my wife in the water, if you're up to it."

"Oh, yes, that sounds heavenly," Mariana said. "Let me find my bathing suit."

"You don't need it here," Will said. "When I'm home, everyone avoids this part of the beach. We're Adam and Eve, lost in Paradise. We can swim and live naked. The staff will only come by quietly to keep us supplied and to keep things tidy. I'll cook. You help with the dishes."

"Okay, a late night skinny dip sounds lovely."

After a heavenly two weeks lost in Paradise, it was time for them to face the world again. Will brought up the subject they'd both been avoiding over a lovely dinner of grilled fish, which he'd prepared with a little help from Mariana. She'd tossed the salad, anyway.

"I think the best thing will be for us to go back to the UK for a while, and by us, I mainly mean you," Will said. "You can manage so many things from the Globe, and Grandmother and Grandfather will keep you safe."

"You're just trying to run away," Mariana said.

"No, I'm only concerned for your well-being. You're expecting twins. You have a big pregnancy to get through. You don't need to be worried about all of this mess. You need to be where the agreements we made with the Eagles protect you best. You're a Greystone now. They won't let you come to harm."

"You're protecting me already. You and Charlie. Besides, is Cathy supposed to go live and work with us in the UK? With me, I should say, since you're going back? Or is she going to live alone in our house in New York?"

"Mariana, remember I once said I'd lock you in a tower in Romania to keep you safe? I still mean that. Grandfather's castle is much more pleasant."

"We agreed no more towers," Mariana said, making a face. "Besides, we'd be apart again. You'd be unhappy, and I'd be unhappy. We wouldn't have each other, like we do here, like we should always have each other unless it's absolutely inevitable. I married you, Will, and I accept your legacy and everything that comes with it, but not if it means I lose you. Do you understand? We need to make the most of the time we have. We belong together."

"Mariana, I just want you to be safe..."

"I'm disappointed in you, Will."

His face was etched with pain, but he caressed her cheek and tried to give her a smile.

"I know I've..."

"Shut up," she interrupted. "You don't know. You do not know why I'm disappointed, but I'm going to tell you. You're falling into the trap. You're forgetting yourself, forgetting what makes you special."

"I..."

She sat up straight, put down her fork, and faced off with him.

"I talk, you listen. That's how this works."

"Okay."

"Good."

Mariana took a deep breath before she started.

"It's too easy, Will, a slippery slope in the path you are

suggesting. It's dangerous. If we run now, we'll always be running. We stay home in the US—in any of our homes you please, whichever is closest to whatever you need to do. I can work from anywhere. We do what we are supposed to do. We face our problems. We live our lives, and we take care of our projects. I have a media empire to run, and a nursery to finish in New York and in two other houses. I'd like to have one in Connecticut, especially since I know it's where you'd rather be, even if you've been uncomfortable there lately because of the whole Sandra thing."

"Actually," Will said, "it's not my child. That's confirmed now."

"Why didn't you say?"

"Well, we've been here working on us. It didn't seem appropriate to bring her into it."

"You're still keeping things to yourself, Will." She gave him a hard look, but then took pity on him and reached across the table to put her hand on his. "It's okay, you just need a little more practice. I know you were alone with all of this for a long time. You're not alone anymore."

"I'm setting up something to help her, anyway, just as you asked," Will said. "I'm doing it through an anonymous entity and also putting some good people in her orbit. Let's see what she makes of it."

"Good." Mariana smiled. "So we can live wherever we like. I'm sticking with you no matter what. Do you under-stand? We will not have an ocean or a continent between us. I won't allow it. If we have to move to the UK, because you've tried everything you could, and it's all gone to shit, then *we* go live there. You and I. Together. But I'd much rather stay in the US and fight for what's right. God help anyone who comes after me right now, Will. I'll rip their throats out with my nails."

"Well…"

"Don't interrupt. Everything coming our way is a setup or a challenge, Will. Nothing else. If it's a setup, fine, we fight. If it's a challenge, guess what, we fight. We don't run. We don't give up. We don't change our lives because we're scared, and most of all, we don't stop standing up for what we believe in! That's the way this marriage works. Two enormous balls each. Mine are getting larger," Mariana said and cupped her breasts, "don't let yours get smaller."

Will smiled and waited.

"You may speak now," she said, like a schoolteacher.

Will chose not to. He reached over the table and kissed her instead, pounced on her, devoured her mouth.

"The peas aren't bothered if I decide to ravage my fierce wife now, right?"

"They'll be just fine," Mariana said. "And I'm horny as hell—it's the hormones."

Will stood up and carried her off to the bedroom, nestled in his arms, her arms wrapped around his neck. He sat her at the edge of the bed to undress her gently. He kissed the flesh he exposed on her neck and shoulders and chest as he unbuttoned her dress and then stopped to cup her breasts. "I love these enormous balls of yours," he said, kissing her mounds, "but they are much too soft to be brass. They still need protecting."

"I'll buy a steel corset."

Mariana ran her fingers through his soft dark locks, as he moved down to kiss the growing bump, then he pulled off her dress and left her wearing only her bra and panties.

Will undressed quickly, unleashing a powerful erection, but he took his time with her, lifting Mariana up in his arms again to lay her properly on the pillows before joining her in bed and taking off her undergarments. He stroked and caressed her, covering her in kisses, worshipping her body, her thighs, her calves, her feet. He hovered over her gently, the muscles of his arms and chest flexed as he positioned himself between her legs. Then Will kissed her again, his tongue caressing hers, and slipped slowly into her warm, wet sheath.

As he thrust gently, his hand locked in hers, he breathed into her ear, "We will fight, wife of my heart. We *will* fight. We *will* win."

Epilogue

When Mariana saw the house that Charlie's East Coast construction team had built for them on Will's hill in Vermont, overlooking the growing Hopetown below, she could not believe her eyes. It was one thing to have seen the plans and quite another to find it tucked away among the trees. A white picket fence and vine-covered arch separated the front garden and lawn from the forest around them. The wood siding was painted sky blue, with white window frames and doors. It wasn't a huge place. Just enough room for the four of them, which was all they wanted.

Everything was as she had hoped, and not just the house.

"Oh, Charlie!" she said, running to hug him. "You got every detail right. Even the garden!"

"Will gets credit for the garden, not me," Charlie said.

"You haven't seen the interior yet," Sandy said. "Daddy put in a few extra touches that I think you'll appreciate, particularly in the master bedroom."

"I'm sure everything will be perfect," Mariana said, smiling at her best friend. "How about you? Are you happy with your new place?"

Charlie had moved to the West Coast permanently. He'd recently bought the Malibu mansion from Will so his wife could run on the beach safely, and their son could play in the waves.

"I always loved my aunt's house, but the Malibu place is perfect for us. Especially with all the socializing we do now," Sandy said. The West Coast branch of their business had flourished with Sandy at the helm, and Mariana had grown the East Coast branch, with Cathy Fleming running the business day to day. "Plus, Archer plans to learn to surf. You'll always be welcome there, of course. There are plenty of rooms, as you know."

"Let's get you inside your home, Mrs. Smith," Will said, lifting her up in his arms to carry her over the threshold.

"Which is *my* room?" Both Aiden and Eden asked at the same time. The twins had a spooky habit of synchronized speech which Mariana suspected they put on intentionally just to irritate their parents. Children of the corny.

"We know where *our* room is," Will said, putting Mariana down in the living room and pointing to the opposite end of the hall, where the master bedroom was located. "You'll have to figure out the rest for yourselves."

"Cool!" The two ran off down the hall to check out their bedrooms, with Archer chasing after them.

"Your offices are secure in the basement, Will," Charlie said. "Everything has been checked and double checked. You'll be able to keep up with business from here and there are Hawks around if you need them."

"Stop with the shop talk, Daddy," Sandy said.

"Baby girl," Charlie gave his wife a warning, but the menace was softened by the warm way he wrapped his arms and body around her like a cloak.

"The elves have sharper ears than me," Sandy said, barely above a whisper.

"We're not elves!" Archer cried out from the hallway.

"Son," Charlie said.

"Sorry, Dad." Archer came back with Aiden and Eden right behind him.

"Okay, so the rooms are almost identical," Aiden said, "but Eden wants to face the sunset and I want to face the sunrise. Which room should we choose?"

"You should use a map to check your position," Will said.

"You're no help, Dad," Eden grumbled.

"I could help you plenty, if you'd like," Will said.

"That's fine," Aiden said. "We'll handle this ourselves."

"Good," Will said. "That's what this is all about, remember. Being self-sufficient."

Mariana had walked out onto the back porch, leaving the pleasant back and forth between Will and the kids behind her. They were always like this, testing each other's mettle. It was fun to watch most days and would probably only intensify now that they were all living on the same floor. Leaving Manhattan behind would be difficult on the twins, even if they were all gung-ho about it now. They had to adjust to small-town living. But they were old enough that it was past time for them to learn from the trees, and still young enough to adapt to a new way of living. Besides, business was finally on track, running without heavy interference, for the most part, and they all needed the peace of this place. The view was beautiful, in springtime. Mariana knew from the first time Will had brought her to this place that winter would be just as nice.

"Oh, baby," Will said, coming out to the porch to pull his wife into his own bear hug, "there's no need to cry. We're all together now."

"It's just so perfect."

"Yes," Will said. "It is. Just as it should be."

"Will it last?"

"It will all be here long after we're gone."

"We need to hang around for a good, long time," Mariana said, stroking her husband's chin. "And we have to have Charlie add a room… or two."

"Why?"

"Oh, didn't I mention?" Mariana gave will a wide-eyed innocent face. "I made a typo."

"You missed a period?"

"An ellipsis, really."

"Why didn't you tell me sooner? And when did you decide to go off the pill?"

"Well, things were all falling into place, and my time to decide was limited. I took a calculated risk. But I didn't want you getting your thumb all out of joint, at least not until I was really sure."

Will pressed his thumb to her forehead. "Well, baby, you're under my thumb now."

She took his hand and brought his thumb to her mouth, sucking at it playfully and then biting it. He tapped her ass then gave her a gentle kiss.

"This is the perfect place for our family to grow, don't you think?" She sighed. The view really was spectacular.

"You think you could give the boys a feisty sister to torment them?"

"Well, that's up to you," Mariana said, shrugging. "I don't know what you ordered from the shop."

"Something wonderful." Will smiled. "As always."

"Well, that's guaranteed."

Amaryllis Lanza

Amaryllis Lanza took the road less traveled early on and has enjoyed many adventures in far flung places. She's settled for a while in the green and rolling countryside of Northern Europe where she shares her life with her lovely husband and her frolicking cats. When she's not writing (and reading) racy romance, suspense, and urban fantasy she works as a free-lance writer. Her hobbies involve copious amounts of chocolate.

Visit her website here:
amaryllislanza.com
And sign-up for updates on the Billionaire Spy Series.

Billionaire Spy Series
Secrets and Seduction
Codes and Consequences
Pride and Punishment
The Unkindness
The Cauldron
The Watch
A Bounty of Blood and Betrayal

Jerks of Miami
Bound to the Jerk
Sinning with the Jerk

Blushing Books

Blushing Books is the oldest eBook publisher on the web. We've been running websites that publish steamy romance and erotica since 1999, and we have been selling eBooks since 2003. We have free and promotional offerings that change weekly, so please do visit us at http://www.blushing-books.com/free.

Blushing Books Newsletter

Please join the Blushing Books newsletter
to receive updates & special promotional offers.
You can also join by using your mobile phone:
Just text **BLUSHING** to 22828.

Every month, one new sign up via text messaging will receive
a $25.00 Amazon gift card, so sign up today!